Praise for the novels of
SUSAN R. MATTHEWS

AN EXCHANGE OF HOSTAGES

"An unflinching look at the physical and emotional
consequences of anguish . . . an intelligently written
book full of unexpected moments of beauty."
Sherwood Smith, author of *Crown Duel*

PRISONER OF CONSCIENCE

"Andrej is a compelling character . . . [The universe of
Jurisdiction] makes a powerful background for these
tales of heroic torment—and leaves room for
interesting exploration in future volumes."
Locus

Other Avon Books by
Susan R. Matthews

AN EXCHANGE OF HOSTAGES
PRISONER OF CONSCIENCE

HOUR OF
JUDGMENT

susan r. matthews

AVON · EOS

AVON BOOKS, INC.
1350 Avenue of the Americas
New York, New York 10019

Copyright © 1999 by Susan R. Matthews
Inside cover author photograph by Geoff Manasse
Visit our website at **http://www.AvonBooks.com/Eos**
Visit Susan Matthews's website at
http://www.sff.net/people/Susan.Scribens/
Library of Congress Catalog Card Number: 98-93290
ISBN: 0-380-80314-3

First Avon Eos Printing: January 1999

AVON EOS TRADEMARK REG. U.S. PAT. OFF. AND IN OTHER COUNTRIES, MARCA REGISTRADA, HECHO EN U.S.A.

Printed in the U.S.A.

WCD 10 9 8 7 6 5 4 3 2

This book is dedicated with love to my mother (than whom I could not have chosen a better, had it been mine to choose) because Two has always been her favorite character in the story. My mother's children have always been her favorite characters in their lives, and between her and my daddy they raised all six of us with astounding tolerance and grace.

Acknowledgment

I would like to gratefully acknowledge a "random act of kindness" committed by a gentleman on a plane last October who, when we arrived at SeaTac Airport, chased me half the length of the concourse to bring me my manuscript book, which I'd been writing in during the flight and had left on the seat. There were forty pages of manuscript that I hadn't typed up in that book, and if it hadn't been for him I would have lost it all. Thank you again, sir, and may your tribe increase.

◇ One

It was early evening in Port Burkhayden. The air currents that blew toward the bay in the morning hours had stilled and reversed themselves, and the breeze grew colder by the day; but it was warm on the back steps still, sheltered from the wind by the bulk of the great house behind them.

"All right, then," the gardener said, his tone light and challenging. Almost Sylphe wanted to call it affectionate; but that wouldn't be proper, not with the distance between them. Skelern Hanner was a good gardener. But that was all he was.

Plucking a bit of black-twigged greenery out of the little pile that lay between them on the steps, Hanner continued to quiz. "You're solid on the sdotz, one and all. Sdotz are good for color, but delicate tones need background, don't they now?"

It was Hanner's game to tease her, when all she'd ever done was ask him questions about his gardening. He didn't take her seriously. Why should he? Because she had been to school, and he had not—but there was no question that he knew much more about his garden than she did.

"Markept-branch?" she guessed, eagerly, frowning at the twig of evergreen Hanner held out to her. "Or—no, it's markept-branch. Surely. Oh, tell, Skelern."

He laughed at her eagerness, and Sylphe blushed, wishing the breeze would turn and carry the prickling heat of her own gaucherie away from her face. She hated to see herself blush. She blushed in splotches, obvious and awkward, and it always

1

made her blush when Skelern laughed. She wasn't certain why. She only suspected that it had to do with the suddenness of the sight of his white teeth, when the rest of him was ruddy-brown with sun or sweat.

"Perfect marks, little maistress, markept-branch it is, and from the far reaches. From Perkipsie, in fact, come across the Senterif vector to Burkhayden before the Bench came down upon us."

If she was right, why had he laughed? He teased her too often. It was unkind of him. She didn't know why she tolerated his impudence; and yet she'd had nobody else to talk to, not these six months gone past. Standard.

"The Danzilar fleet is only four weeks out, they say." The Senterif vector, somewhere past Burkhayden's pale new moon this time of year. Sylyphe frowned into the darkening sky, wondering where to place the spacelane's terminus. "There will be an end to the Bench, Skelern, in a sense at least. That will be good, won't it?"

The Danzilar fleet was what had brought her mother here six months ago, to position Iaccary Cordage and Textile among the industries eager to enter into partnership with prince Paval I'shenko Danzilar to exploit his newly indentured world. The Bench had been sending Nurail into exile here for longer than that; but Skelern Hanner himself was a native, bred and born in Burkhayden.

And bitter about what had become of Nurail under Jurisdiction, for all that he did not seem to blame her for it. Not personally. "Sold is sold, sweet Sylyphe. I wasn't born cattle. And I had a mother and a father, once."

It was hard to blame him. He had suffered loss and privation under Jurisdiction. It had all been for the preservation of the Judicial order, she was sure of that; though it was hard to understand what threat a gardener could have posed the Bench.

"All the same." She didn't like to argue with him, especially when she felt he might have good cause to feel resentful. But she wished he wouldn't sulk. There was nothing either of them could do about it, after all. "The first step toward citizenship, Skelern. They're odd people, from what I've heard, but practical.''

Well, perhaps that was a little overgenerous of her. Dolgorukij were practical, yes. But more than that, Dolgorukij were ferocious competitors, notorious for milking any commercial exchange for everything it might be worth. Not people one would chose as one's employer, if one had the choice; and it would only depress Skelern to remind him that he had none.

Why had she tried to say anything?

Sylyphe hugged her knees to her bosom and frowned at the back of the garden, disgusted at herself.

Hanner spent some moments picking out pieces of grass and fern with a great show of concentration on his dark sharp-chinned face. ''The Danzilar fleet. Well. There'll be parties, little maistress, you'll want for a corsage.''

The suggestion startled her into turning her head, meeting his black eyes over the posy he offered. It was a perfect little bouquet, wrapped in a leaf and pinned into a tidy bundle with a thorn. Beautiful. Sylyphe took the delicate favor with confused delight, admiring it in the failing light as Hanner spoke on.

''And with the fleet. An escort ship, the *Ragnarok*, have you heard of the Jurisdiction Fleet Ship *Ragnarok*, Sylyphe? It's a man with the blood of Nurail souls on his hands that carries the surgery there, him from the Domitt Prison. Black Andrej.''

Sylyphe frowned.

The Domitt Prison . . . it had been years ago, five years; she'd been much younger. The Judicial briefings had mesmerized her mother, and Sylyphe hadn't ever quite understood what the fuss had been about; and still—

''Andrej Koscuisko, do you mean, Skelern?'' And still she could recall one image among many, one image that sprang up readily before her mind's eye. A slim young officer, blond, and wearing the black of a Ship's Prime officer—the Ship's Inquisitor, Jurisdiction Fleet Ship *Scylla*. Andrej Koscuisko. *I have cried Failure of Writ against the administration of the*

Domitt Prison, and I will hazard my life against the justice of my plea.

"The same." Skelern was looking at her with rather an odd expression on his face. She blushed once more, without knowing quite why. "And there's more than several here in Burkhayden in these days to remember him from Rudistal, but he's got nothing to fear from us. Not after the Domitt. Unlike young Skelern, now—"

Tumbling the pile of flowers into her lap with one swift gesture Hanner rose to his feet, talking as he went. "—who's much to fear from my respected maistress your lady mither, if I don't get the turves trimmed up in the tea-garden before the morning comes. I'm off."

And in a bit of a hurry all of a sudden, as well. What was on his mind? Sylyphe gathered the cuttings into a loose bunch, careful to keep her posy from being crushed. "Black" Andrej Koscuisko. It had a wicked sort of resonance to it.

The Court had awarded him execution of the sentences passed down at the conclusion of the hearings; he had killed men, and at the Tenth Level of the Question. Taken vengeance for the Bench against the criminals judged responsible for the Domitt Prison. There was a measure of attractiveness to the idea of such a man—an indistinct figure of glittering menace, irresistible with the demonic allure of all of one's darkest nightmares . . . an Inquisitor. Torturer. Executioner.

Perhaps she would meet him at a party, since there were to be so many when the Fleet arrived at last. She would be presented, he would bow; she would return the courtesy with calm—self-possessed—fearless maturity, and he would check himself and look more closely at her, struck by her unusual poise, her womanly grace. . . .

The sun was going down. The breeze from the hills behind Port Burkhayden worried at the leaf-laden branches of the trees at the back of the garden, and the summer's growth of climbing-rose canes bowed anxiously down before the wind's whisper of ice as if in supplication. Sylyphe tucked her armful of cuttings under her arm and stood up, putting her idle fantasies away from her with a mixture of regret and childish guilt.

Enough was enough.

She went into the house to set the cuttings in a vase, to wait for her mother to come and arrange them.

Captain Griers Verigson Lowden—tall and thin, big bones, brown mustache—strolled down the halls towards the senior mess area with all deliberate speed, fuming. The news from the Bench was not at all satisfactory: no Inquisitor to be assigned, not any time soon. No Inquisitor was even identified for assignment yet, since the latest class at Fleet Orientation Station Medical wasn't scheduled to begin for several weeks yet. If he'd convinced Koscuisko to commit to an additional term of service . . . but he hadn't; and the Bench meant him to suffer the lack accordingly.

Nor was he so naive as to believe that the two Bench intelligence specialists who were visiting from the Danzilar fleet had no ulterior motives. He knew all about Koscuisko's appeals to the Bench. He had connections, and paid well for information pertinent to his survival and prosperity. Koscuisko had been trying to get the *Ragnarok* declassified for Writ for years now: to no effect.

What would Koscuisko do, Lowden wondered, if Koscuisko ever realized that the money that thwarted his purpose at every turn, the money that did such a good job of protecting Captain Lowden against the best of Koscuisko's arguments, the secret influence that baffled Koscuisko time and again was funded directly out of Koscuisko's own handiwork?

Copies of the Record, copies of interrogation cubes, were the property of the Bench, and were to be strictly controlled and accounted for at all times.

That only made them more valuable.

And whether or not torture at Koscuisko's level of expertise was functionally restricted to the Protocols—there being no law to interfere with religious practice under Jurisdiction, should religion demand frightful contrition rituals—there was no question but that Koscuisko was a genuine artist in his field. Captain Lowden had never seen anything quite like Andrej Koscuisko in Inquiry. The man was phenomenal. His tapes had proved phenomenally lucrative in turn, over the years.

Now Koscuisko was leaving, and that would be an end to new material. And though Lowden knew he could live quite comfortably off his banked proceeds, he couldn't help but resent the fact that Andrej Koscuisko was to leave him alone on the *Ragnarok* with not so much as a replacement Inquisitor to remember him by.

Sour as his mood was, Lowden almost looked forward to staff meeting. There were good odds that he'd find an outlet for his irritation before the eight was up; and in that hope Captain Lowden went into the room.

They were waiting for him, of course. His senior officers were already rising to their feet as the lowest-ranking officer in the room—Jennet ap Rhiannon, newly assigned—called the formal alert.

"Stand to attention for the Captain, Lowden, commanding."

Command and Ship's Primes, Jurisdiction Fleet Ship *Ragnarok*. Here were Ralph Mendez, the *Ragnarok*'s First Officer, to whom the bulk of the daily tasks involving the operation of a ship of war—or even an experimental ship on its proving-cruise—devolved, by Lowden's own benign neglect and implicit order.

The Ship's Engineer, Serge of Wheatfields, the overtall Chigan responsible for moving the ship from place to place and keeping the cyclers up.

Ship's Intelligence, the Desmodontae known as Two, one of the few non-hominids with senior Fleet rank under Jurisdiction; two strangers with her, male and female, wearing unmarked uniforms of the peculiar shade of charcoal gray that identified them as Bench intelligence specialists.

His Lieutenants, and finally his Ship's Inquisitor, Andrej Ulexeievitch Koscuisko, the youngest of his senior officers and by far the most valuable—as well as most high-maintenance.

"Well, let's be started," Lowden suggested, pausing on his way into the room to draw a flask of vellme. Plenty of shredded ciraby on top. "You've all got work to do. I don't want to keep you from your tasks. First Officer, report."

Mendez was a tall, long, green-eyed sort of Santone, his face tanned and deeply lined from youth spent under the dry glare of the Gohander desert sun. "Ship's Mast and staffing, Captain. Ship's Mast. Violation of critical safety protocol cried by Ship's Engineer against technician second class Hixson. Adjudication of penalty recommended at three and thirty. Your endorsement, your Excellency."

Passing the record cube across the table, Mendez recited the Charges drily, sounding bored. Lowden turned the cube in his fingers for a moment or two. Should he press Mendez on this? It would be perceived as merely petty, to squeeze Koscuisko for an extra ration of punishment so close to Koscuisko's departure date. Koscuisko would enjoy it, but he would hate enjoying it. No. Too obvious. Lowden coded his counterseal on the record cube and tossed it back without comment.

Nor did Mendez insult him by looking surprised. Mendez knew better. His First Officer had been part of the *Ragnarok*'s original proving crew, a good First Officer, a competent officer, but one who had stood on principle one too many times for there to be any real chance of a Command in his future. "Very good, Captain. Staffing, a new requirement just in, Chief Warrant Officer Brachi Stildyne has been offered a First Officer's berth on the JFS *Sceppan*."

Had he indeed? Lowden glanced quickly at his Ship's Surgeon out of the corner of his eye. The four-year association between Andrej Koscuisko and his Chief of Security had been marked by conflict, misunderstanding, even a species of power struggle—great fun, all in all. If Koscuisko were not leaving he might be glad to replace Stildyne or he might be reluctant to face the breaking-in of a new Chief of Security. But Koscuisko was leaving. Koscuisko didn't care. Or Mendez had tipped Koscuisko off; or both.

What a bore.

"Well, congratulations are in order for Stildyne. Please pass them on to him from me. He's done good work for us." *And we're sure that Koscuisko has no cause to complain of him*, Lowden wanted to add, but restrained himself. Once again the provocation would be too obvious. "Very well. Serge? No? Two, then."

Desmodontae were newly integrated under Jurisdiction, an intelligent species of night-gliding mammals that subsisted on the protein-rich blood of a species of cattle they nurtured for that purpose. Very short compared to most hominids, Two stood in chairs rather than sitting in them; as far as Lowden had ever been able to tell she couldn't sit at all, in the conventional sense.

Standing in her chair now, Two dipped her velvety black head sharply in token of having heard and commenced to respond, clashing the sharp white teeth in her delicate black muzzle in his direction rapidly, her pink-and-black tongue flickering back and forth in a disconcertingly random manner.

In a moment her translator began to process. By that time Two had finished speaking; and rested her primary wing-joint with its little clawed three-fingered hand against the table's surface, waiting patiently for the translator to catch up.

"I have here some guests for us, to tell us all the gossip, what it is. Bench intelligence specialists Ivers and Vogel, and this means I do not need to give my report after all, because you are distracted by their information. Yes? Of course yes. I admire this cunning, in myself."

Lowden never decided how much of the personality in Two's language was actually hers, and how much an artifact of her translator. They had to have a translator; whether or not Two was capable of speaking Standard—and there was no particular reason why she should not be, when other nonhominid species had learned to manage—few of them were capable of hearing her, since her voice's natural range dropped down into the upper limits of audible tones Standard only occasionally.

"Specialist Vogel, then," Lowden suggested. "We've been expecting you?" He had no clue as to which was which, Vogel and Ivers. The woman—black eyes, black hair, a little shorter than her partner—betrayed no sign of Iversness or Vogelicity, any more than the man looked Iversish or Vogellic. Two's descriptive statements frequently lacked precision, in translation. Lowden had decided years ago that she planned it that way.

"Transfer of preliminary defense locks to your shuttle." Of the two of them at the end of the table it was the man who spoke. Middling tall, middling bald, with a voice that gave neither cause for offense nor any other information—younger than his hairline, Lowden guessed. So he was Vogel. "For transport ahead of the Danzilar fleet, to be ready when prince Paval I'shenko arrives. You're sending?"

Bench intelligence specialists didn't observe rank, didn't conform to the norms of military titles or respectful address. They didn't have to. They were Bench-level operatives chartered on an individual basis by the Bench itself and accountable not to any given Judge, but only to the Jurisdiction's Bench in formal convocation.

"My First Lieutenant. G'herm Wyrlann." Who fortunately had the good sense to rise to his feet and salute when his name was called. Whatever unspecified rank a Bench intelligence specialist might hold it was good odds Vogel outranked a mere Command Branch First Lieutenant. "The shuttle's loaded and waiting for immediate dispatch, Specialist, ready bay five down three over? Serge? Yes."

They needed to get Wyrlann to Burkhayden as soon as possible. It was to be Wyrlann's formal responsibility to complete the final inventory that would be incorporated into the formal contract between Danzilar and the Bench. "If you'd care to accompany Lieutenant Wyrlann, Specialist."

Bench Indentured World, Burkhayden, Meghilder space. Danzilar to be planetary governor, and responsible to the Bench for tax revenues; to be left to himself to exploit Burkhayden as he saw fit as long as the cash continued to flow. Lowden wished Danzilar luck with his enterprise. There was nothing left worth taking off Burkhayden that the Bench hadn't taken—and nobody there but Nurail, resettled from the dregs and scrapings of the Nurail worlds in the bloody aftermath of the promulgation of the Political Stabilization Acts.

Vogel bowed and cocked an eyebrow at Wyrlann, who took his cue and started for the door. Just as they reached the doorway Lowden remembered the advice he had meant to give; important advice, in light of Wyrlann's history on ground detach.

"Lieutenant. Let's be prudent this time around. There are still Bench resources at Burkhayden." *And you don't want to go breaking anything while Fleet still has to pay for it.* Lowden hoped and trusted that the point would be taken, even implicit as it was. Wyrlann had a heavy hand at times. He had to learn prudence in the timing of his little exercises of authority.

Wyrlann didn't like being reminded.

But there was nothing he could do but accept the rebuke and go.

Once the door closed again Lowden turned his attention to the remaining Bench specialist, who by process of elimination could only be Jils Ivers. "And your role in this convoy would be . . . ?"

Convoy was perhaps not the right word. There were eights of ships in the Danzilar fleet, and its flagship—prince Paval I'shenko's *Lady Gechutrian*—displaced space at twice the volume of a mere cruiserkiller in the *Ragnarok*'s class. One Fleet ship in escort was a mere token, its ceremonial nature emphasized by the fact that the *Ragnarok* was not a chartered warship but an experimental test bed sized and shaped like one.

"In this instance to pay my respects to your Chief Medical Officer." Ivers' voice was level and uninflected. Unrevealing. Unimpressed. "And to present the First Secretary's compliments. You may recall having cleared the interview, Captain?"

Well. Perhaps. If he thought about it. He'd wondered at the time why Chilleau Judiciary bothered to send an envoy to Koscuisko. They could hardly hope to succeed where Lowden himself had failed, and persuade Koscuisko to renew his term.

Koscuisko himself had half-turned in his place to frown at Ivers skeptically, ignoring for once the unwisdom of turning one's back on Serge of Wheatfields if one was Ship's Inquisitor. Wheatfields only glared down at the back of Koscuisko's bared neck in turn. Maybe Wheatfields was mellowing. Maybe not.

"I, er, may have neglected to forward the appointment through to Andrej's scheduler, now that you mention it." His turn to come under that mirror-silver glare of Koscuisko's, but Koscuisko was too well trained to let any real displeasure show. Koscuisko was autocrat, surgeon and Inquisitor. But Captain Lowden was his master, and Koscuisko knew it. "Sorry, Andrej. Recent excitement and all, I suppose. Do you have time for Specialist Ivers this shift? Now, for instance."

Koscuisko hadn't had a prisoner in Secured Medical for upwards of two weeks. All Koscuisko had on his scheduler was running his Infirmary. Koscuisko could make time. Koscuisko would.

"Of course, Captain." Koscuisko's clear tenor matched Ivers's own tone for inscrutability. Being irritated about it would get Koscuisko precisely nowhere. It only amused Captain Lowden to see how easily Koscuisko could be annoyed. "If you like, Specialist. My office?"

Koscuisko almost didn't even pretend to wait for an answer, rising as he spoke. "If the Captain will excuse us, of course."

Lowden nodded in reply to Koscuisko's perfunctory bow, secretly delighted. He had not thought to have this much amusement at staff. He was going to genuinely miss Koscuisko when Koscuisko was gone. "Quite so. Good-greeting, Specialist Ivers. Andrej, ward report, my office, second and six."

Could he get rid of the rest of his staff in time to have Two open a channel into Koscuisko's office?

Or should he rather let this staff play out, and pump Koscuisko for the details afterward?

He hadn't heard anything from his Lieutenants. And he was supposed to be paying attention.

"Lieutenant Brem. There's an inventory shortage on the

Wolnadi line, I understand, and you were to have a report for me this morning.''

Resigning himself to an indulgence postponed, Lowden set his concentration on analyzing cargo loads, and put Andrej Koscuisko to the back of his mind for later.

If he thought about it, Andrej believed he might remember this woman. She was shorter than he was, and many women weren't, since he himself was to the short side of the Jurisdiction Standard. Chilleau Judiciary had sent two Bench specialists to the Domitt Prison at port Rudistal, these five years past; they'd arrived in time to assist the inquiry into the Administration's crimes, but Andrej had never managed to convince himself that they hadn't been originally dispatched to cover things up.

"So, then, Specialist. You travel with my cousin Danzilar's fleet to Burkhayden.''

Strolling through the corridors of great *Ragnarok*, on the way to Infirmary and his office. There was no sense in being gratuitously unpleasant. He was going home, after all. He was to be free from all this within a very few weeks' time. He could afford to let bygones be bygones, just this once. Justice had been done at the Domitt Prison at last, whether with the help of or despite these Bench specialists. He should be at least polite.

"Audit authority, your Excellency. One last check on inventory before everything goes to Danzilar. Your cousin? Don't tell me, sir, Dolgorukij aristocratic genealogies make my head hurt.''

As a matter of fact they did his, as well. "It is either third cousin four times removed or fourth cousin three times removed. I do not know which. It is safest to call them all cousin and forget about it.''

He was to go home because eight years had passed since he had sworn his oath to Fleet, and eight years was all Fleet and his father could demand of him. Well, Fleet would have kept him on, because there were not enough Ship's Inquisitors to go around; but eight years had been agreed upon and eight years had been suffered and eight years were passed.

He was never going to be able to forget them.

"The Danzilar prince sends his regards, sir. And said something about cortac brandy. An armful, I think he said."

Had Shiki brought liquor? Well, of course Shiki had. "A crook of liquor, Specialist, four bottles, three under one's arm and one in one's fist. Very promising of Shiki. It is through here; sit down, do you take rhyti?"

Hearing himself engaged for an interview with a Bench specialist had not been a very welcome piece of news, just now. But his office was his own territory. He felt more comfortable just stepping across the threshold, and more inclined to be hospitable accordingly.

"Thank you, your Excellency, no. With respect, sir, I'll come straight out with what I have to say."

He did remember her from the Domitt Prison. Surely he was being paranoid to blame either Ivers or Vogel for crimes that Chilleau Judiciary should have noted and prevented long before his own arrival. Bench specialists were not partisan players. They would have done the same as he, had they found themselves in the same position. Surely.

"Excuse me that I draw a flask, then; I am thirsty. Out with what, yes, I listen."

Once he'd had a moment or two to think about it he didn't even feel she'd changed. That hint of a frown was something that Andrej could remember having found rather fetching, before, for no particular reason.

"Very well." She waited for him to join her in the conference zone of his office, watching him set his flask of rhyti down on the low table between them with an air of concentrating on her thought. "Your Excellency. The term of your initial tour of duty is due to expire very shortly. It is understood that you have not been very satisfied with your placement here on *Ragnarok*, in recent years."

No, he had been critically dissatisfied with his tour of duty on the *Ragnarok* from the moment he'd first set foot to decking. Andrej settled back in the slatwood chair, templing his fingers in front of him, suspicious. What did she mean, his "initial" tour of duty?

"Captain Lowden is not fit to direct my Writ, or any other. So I have pled. I am sure the documentation has been made available for your review."

Captain Lowden was not a support to the rule of Law. It was precisely abuses of power of the sort that Captain Lowden indulged so shamelessly that gave subversion its ever-increasing numbers of champions under Jurisdiction. The Bench had heard his cry against the Domitt Prison; why did the Bench not hear his complaint against his Captain?

But Andrej knew the answer to that question already. It was Fleet and the Bench, this time. "You have not come all this way to give me a going-away present related to this issue, Specialist Ivers?"

Not likely. He was a Bench officer, to the extent that he held the Writ. He was also a Fleet officer under Captain Lowden's authority. Fleet resisted the Bench on principle, regardless of the merits of the case.

Ivers smiled politely, but her smile ended well short of her eyes. "To the extent of assuring his Excellency that no Inquisitor has been identified for immediate assignment, yes." She sat carefully at the edge of her seat, and her back was as straight as an abbess's. "His Excellency has declined to renew his term with Fleet and the Bench."

Indeed he had. And it was in the poorest possible taste to have even expected otherwise. There was a shortage of Ship's Inquisitors? Very well. There should properly be a shortage of Ship's Inquisitors. There should properly be no Ship's Inquisitors at all, especially under Lowden's direction; but Andrej wasn't going to say as much out loud. There were limits.

"Fleet does nothing to protect the bond-involuntaries, Specialist. Tell me that they are all to be reassigned and I will be well satisfied. What is your point?" Because after all they both already knew that he'd refused the offer of a second term. And if she had no news but for the denial of yet another appeal against Griers Verigson Lowden she need not have wasted time and effort telling him how carefully the Bench had considered the merits of his plea.

"The Bench cannot afford the loss of critical skills, your Excellency. The Free Government grows more persuasive daily. Sabotage takes the lives of increasing numbers of loyal citizens, and the Bench must have the weapons it needs to fight the battle against this—one could hardly dignify the Free Government by the name of 'enemy.' "

Ivers's hatred and contempt was clear in her words, regardless of how calm and level her voice was. Andrej could empathize to an extent: terrorism was terrorism, and never to be condoned. It was just that the Bench itself also practiced terrorism, and against its own, against the self-same loyal citizens it claimed to be protecting. Torture was terrorism. Andrej set his hands to the armrests and straightened his spine, decisively.

"Then the Bench must criticize its moral self, Specialist Ivers. Fearlessly." When would the Bench realize that the practice of institutionalized torture as an instrument of statecraft and the maintenance of civil order had just the opposite effect from that intended? "It is by the health and contentment of the body politic that one is to evaluate the rectitude of the State."

Skating perhaps a little close to politically questionable discourse, but nothing actionable. Ivers seemed annoyed.

"Resources must be carefully husbanded in unsettled times, your Excellency. As you may be aware the Bench can exercise the power of annexation of critical resources. According to the provisions of the Political Stabilization Acts the Writ to Inquire is a Bench-critical resource."

Now of a sudden the flooring fell away from underneath his chair, and Andrej knew he dared not so much as glance into the bottomless chasm that gaped open at his feet or else he would fall in. He gripped the armrests of his chair desperately. He could feel the suction of the moiling vortex of black Hell: He had to hang on.

"Annex critical. Resources. Name of all Saints, Specialist, what are you saying?" It had been eight years, eight years, eight years, he was done with this, he had fulfilled his term, he was free to go—

"His Excellency declines to continue service in Fleet. That is understandable in light of his Excellency's stated convictions and dissatisfaction with his post. The Bench cannot afford to lose your skills, sir." She could not see the abyss that yawned hugely between them. She could not have spoken so calmly had she done. "First Secretary Verlaine offers you pride of place at Chilleau Judiciary, command of the sector's medical resources and all the rights and emoluments accruing thereunto. The need is too great, your Excellency. The Bench must make difficult decisions for the greater good of all under the rule of Law."

Chilleau Judiciary.

No.

Andrej swallowed hard, focusing on the talkalert on the far wall to anchor himself in the world. He had to control himself. He could not panic. There was no reason to panic. She could not mean what she seemed to be saying. It was intolerable.

"Specialist, no one could wish me to this work a single day the longer, Judicial Order or no. Not even for my sins should it be wished on me, and you must know that they are many, and grievous."

Her expression was pained, almost irritated. Andrej didn't care. The rule of Law was no excuse for torture. He had to press what advantage he had, while he could still feel that he had the advantage—

"Say therefore to First Secretary Verlaine that I would rather sell myself to a Chigan brothel and suckle at fish than have anything to do with Chilleau Judiciary. Or the Protocols. Not one day the longer, Specialist Ivers. It has been *eight years*."

Irritation had shaded over into stubbornness in her face, somehow. Andrej wasn't quite sure how that had happened.

"You've earned a rest, sir. No one dreams of disputing that. You have three eighths of a years' worth of accumulated leave, and I have the privilege of bringing word from the prince your father"—reaching into her overtunic, as Andrej stared in horror —"with a personal message. Your Excellency."

Holding out a heavy square of folded paper she waited. Andrej was afraid of that message, suddenly. He didn't want to disgrace himself by showing his fear in front of the Bench specialist. It was an effort, but he forced himself to reach out his hand in turn to receive the note, his hand almost absolutely steady. There was his name on the note, in script so black against the clotted fabric of the writing-cloth that it was almost red. And bled as Andrej stared at it, the blood draining from the letter to stain his hand and overflow his fist down to the floor.

Son Andrej.
It will be good to see you again, child. We are glad of the First Secretary's charitable gesture, in letting the past forget itself. Come home and kneel for your mother's blessing before you go to Chilleau Judiciary.

His father's hand, his father's voice, more loving than it had been these past eight years, and as much as Andrej ached for his father's blessing he could not force himself to accept that he would have to pay so high a price to purchase it.

"I cannot go." He whispered it half to himself, half to the room, transfixed with horror. "Oh, it is too much. I cannot be made to go, Specialist Ivers, surely. And my family. I owe duty there that I have much neglected."

Ivers sat unmoving in her chair, straight-backed, formal. Unyielding. "And the First Secretary understands, sir. There need be no impediment to a long and well-earned duty leave to see to personal business. The facilities at Chilleau Judiciary will be awaiting your arrival upon the conclusion of your leave. I'm sorry, sir—"

She hesitated, but she said it anyway. What, did she see the roiling pit at last, and hear the tortured screams of damned souls in horrific torment? "I'm sorry, your Excellency. Secretary Verlaine has communicated with your family, and has taken great pains to explain the value of your technical qualifications to your father. How much Chilleau Judiciary needs your skills. And it is a Bench prerogative to annex, sir.''

He had known that he could not escape his dead, he had known it all along. He almost didn't want to escape them— they had a natural right to be revenged. That was right. It was proper. It was decent and moral. But he had been certain that there would be no more of them once eight years were finally over, finished, done.

The enormity of this disaster left him without the capacity for coherent thought.

''It is intolerable to suggest that I should be punished in this manner. I have done my duty and upheld my Writ, and if the Bench has not heard me to disenfranchise Captain Lowden of my Bonds nor has the Bench any complaint to make of my performance—''

Except. Except, that he had cried to Heaven at the Domitt Prison, and been heard. And Chilleau Judiciary had held the responsibility for the Domitt Prison. Was it for the pride of Secretary Verlaine that this carefully planned torture had been prepared for him?

''Indeed no such thing is contemplated, your Excellency.'' It seemed that he had genuinely startled her; Ivers spoke slowly, as if putting her thoughts together with care. ''The First Secretary holds no grudge of whatever sort associated with the unpleasantness at the Domitt Prison.''

He could not sit here for a moment longer.

This horror was too huge and terrible for him.

''Very well, Specialist Ivers.'' Reaching for his rhyti flask he drained it in one half-convulsive draught, letting the sharpness of the heat in his throat pull his energies into one solid and protective core within him. ''You have come to me, and told me. I am not to be permitted to go home to my child.''

Why had he ever imagined anything different? He could not go home. How could a man so much as look on his child, with such a stain on him? ''Very well, I have of this understanding, and you have delivered your message.''

Rising to his feet, Andrej reached out his hand to help Ivers up, politely. There was a peculiar ring of chafed skin around her wrist beneath her sleeve, showing for a brief moment as she moved. Chafed from cold? Or had she recently been in manacles?

"Now it remains only for you to explain how it is that I am to get around it. I do not believe that I can go to Chilleau Judiciary and live, Specialist Ivers. I have only this long survived because the longer it was, the nearer to the end it became."

Was that grammatical? Did it make any sense?

Did it matter?

Andrej hardly knew what he was saying. It surprised him to realize that he was trembling; but whether it was fury or horror or a combination of the two Andrej could not begin to guess. "Tell me the way out of this, Specialist Ivers, or I am lost."

"I'm sorry, sir," Ivers repeated. She sounded as though she was surprised at the evident sincerity in her own voice. "In my professional opinion the First Secretary has covered all vectors of approach. I have no advice for you except to enjoy the perks, because as far as I can see you're to be genuinely stuck with the duty whether you enjoy the perks or not."

Polite of her, to gloss over that issue of enjoyment so delicately. She was a Bench intelligence specialist. She probably knew as much as his own gentlemen about what Andrej enjoyed, and how, and when. Or where. And yet her reference was utterly innocent: Oh, yes, very delicately done indeed.

"Good-greeting, then, Specialist Ivers. You will excuse me. I must to someone go speak, to understand the meaning of what you have just told me."

Nodding gravely in acceptance of her dismissal, Ivers gave him the bow without another word. Just as well. Too much had been said already. Andrej accepted Ivers's salute in turn with a nod of his head, and she left the room with swift silent dispatch.

He was alone, and the enormity of the disaster that had just overtaken him weighted him down until he could hardly so much as breathe. A sleep-shirt made of lead. An atmosphere of viscous fluid of some sort, that sat in a man's lungs and gave no air, but could not be coughed loose.

He could not stand here in his office. He would choke.

Possessed with dread and driven by horror Andrej fled the room for the one place on board of all *Ragnarok* where hope could be found—if there was any hope, any hope for him at all.

It was a quiet morning, all in all, now that Lowden's staff meeting was out of the way. Convoy duty was not very challenging; things were quiet in Section. Ralph Mendez was treating himself to a little inconsequential talk with Ship's Intelligence when Koscuisko—as blue in the face as a man near-dead of cold—staggered through the open door into Two's office, palming the secure on his way past with so much force that Mendez half-expected he'd put a dent in it.

"I cannot endure it," Koscuisko said. "I will not be asked to tolerate. Your pardon, First Officer, Two, you will tell me, if there is to be no way out of this?"

Straightening in his seat, Mendez waved Koscuisko's apology off, interested. He didn't usually see Koscuisko so exercised in spirit. Angry, yes, and from time to time in an ugly sort of state of savage amusement—when Lowden was working him particularly hard.

This didn't look like angry, or frustrated, or hostile, or—otherwise distracted. This looked like somebody's mother was due to be sold to the tinkers for a drab, and no seven-hundred-thousand tinkers Mendez could imagine could possibly begin to afford the mother of the prince inheritor to the Koscuisko familial corporation. Not even if they pooled all their resources.

Two rearranged herself in a rustling of wings from her anchor-perch in the ceiling, and her translator sounded—its calm precise Standard diction at odds with the peculiar idiom of Two's speech. "To you I will certainly tell, Andrej, but a hint would be much appreciated, what 'this' is it?" No telling whether she could catch Koscuisko's state of mind or not. As difficult as it was to decipher Two's expression when she was

on the ground, it was next to impossible when she was at her
ease hanging upside down in her office.

Koscuisko paced the floor between them, gesturing with his
small white hands raised beside his face as if what he really
wanted to do was tear his own head off. "This woman that
Verlaine has sent, Two, she claims that I can be requisitioned
to the Bench, if my father permits. And I cannot trust my
father to understand, so you must tell me."

What Koscuisko's father had to do with things Mendez had
never quite understood. He'd loved his father too, as far as it
went—which didn't go anything like as far as it seemed to
go with Koscuisko. No accounting for culture.

Two reached a wing out casually to the far wall to code up
a display on her speakers. Mendez knew she couldn't actually
see that far; it only made the unerring precision with which
she found her target all the more unnerving—that, and the
fact that her wings spanned the entire room when she
stretched them.

"Well. There is a plot in motion, Andrej. I have not discussed it with our Captain because he is cross enough about
the issue of your replacement."

Didn't that call for a question? Ralph wondered. If she had
known of plots in motion—

"Two, if there were things of which I needed to be ap-
prised—I cannot understand, why was I not warned. Surely
you could not have thought of it as of no interest—"

Koscuisko was still pacing, visibly tense with unexpressed
conflict. But at least the level of the body language had toned
down a bit.

"I am uncommonly clever, Andrej, it is true, but I cannot
see more than three days into tomorrow," Two scolded. "And
it is not established that the draft would be approved. So Specialist Ivers has been just a little forward, if she told you that
it was done."

Finally Koscuisko stopped, and sat. Threw himself into a
seat, pushing the fine fringe of blond hair up from off his
forehead with one hand as he did so. Mendez was just as glad

that the cup of konghu that he had on the side-table was half-empty, the way it shook.

"She did not say that it was done." Koscuisko needed a haircut; Koscuisko usually did. Nothing to do with actual length, and everything to do with straying from its place. "She said that it would be accomplished, if Verlaine had anything to say about it. Is there nothing to be done, except be damned?"

"It is metaphorical, this 'damned'?" Two demanded. Not unreasonably. "If you are not pleased to be desired you are certainly in a bad place, Andrej."

Mendez felt it was high time he found out exactly what was going on between his officers. Between Two and Koscuisko, that was to say. Nothing went on between Koscuisko and Wheatfields except for bad language, and the occasional physical assault.

"Somebody fill in the First Officer?"

"The maddening thing is that it was not even anything that I did, in the beginning at least," Koscuisko replied. As if he was explaining. "There was a student in orientation with me. She puffed me up to her Patron out of spite, and Fleet gave me the choice to wait for him to requisition me or leave for *Scylla* before the Term was ended."

Which in turn had meant that Koscuisko had had to perform his final exercise, his benchmark Tenth Level Command Termination exercise, when he was already on active duty. Mendez had heard about Koscuisko's Tenth Level even before Koscuisko had been posted to the *Ragnarok*. He'd wondered what kind of psychopathic maniac Koscuisko was at the time; but now that he knew Koscuisko a little better—after four years of breathing the same air—he was regretfully aware of the fact that the question was a little more complicated than that. "You went to *Scylla*, he took it personally, and that business with the Domitt didn't sweeten him on you?"

Koscuisko shuddered. "I cannot go back to the Domitt, First Officer, I swear it. Not in one lifetime. And to submit to the First Secretary would mean the same, even if the name of the place itself were to be different."

No need to ask whether Koscuisko had believed the testimony presented to the Bench about poor decisions made by subordinates, errors concealed from the audit branch, abuses not sanctioned.

"But Verlaine's set up to draft his Writ." Now that he felt he understood the background maybe Two's information would benefit both of them. She cocked her head at one corner of her room, listening to the speaker—he assumed, since he couldn't hear a damned thing. Then she nodded, which always gave him the chuckles, when she was upside down.

"It is confirmed, yes. Very much does Verlaine want Andrej Koscuisko. He has spent many favors which I am not at liberty to divulge, many of them irreplaceable. Once our Andrej leaves this ship—there are several months of accumulated leave, you could go and visit my children, the cave is large. It would perhaps be possible for you to become lost."

The humor did not appear to penetrate far enough to touch Koscuisko in the state of mind that he was in. "If I could have known. It might have been better to have gone to the Bench in the first place. I did not understand that such a place was even possible, as the Domitt Prison."

"So tell me, Two, if Andrej is too depressed to ask." Moral support. "Is there a way out of Verlaine's draft?"

It was of only abstract interest to him, of course. Koscuisko wasn't a bad sort as a Chief Medical Officer, once one got past his personal quirks in the Secured Medical area. But Mendez wasn't sure he really cared one way or the other.

"It is a problem for Andrej. No one can decide it for him." Two had learned to shrug as an old woman, she had told him, and he was to treat her accomplishment with the respect due to the aged instead of asking her if she needed her back scratched between the shoulderblades. "If the Combine protested there would be difficulty, and perhaps Verlaine would not be able to accomplish his goal. But the Combine has received many benefits from Chilleau Judiciary. Especially recently."

"My father wrote to me, after the trials." Koscuisko's sudden interruption startled Mendez, since Koscuisko had seemed well sunk in silent gloom a moment ago. "He said that I had done well, that he was proud. That I should also behave with more humility, in future, because when all was said and sung a man should have respect for authority, and it did not present a pleasingly filial appearance for me to have appealed to the First Judge in so public a manner."

Mendez winced. If Koscuisko's people could say something like that to him, after those trials, then they simply didn't live in the same world as that in which the Domitt Prison had existed, and that was all there was to it.

Respect for authority, yes.

Complicity of silence in atrocities of that nature—well, no. Nai.

Never.

"Well, there." Two let so long a pause develop that Mendez wondered if her translator had failed; but no. She seemed to be expecting a response of some sort, her beautiful brilliant little black eyes fixed on Koscuisko's face. Koscuisko made a gesture with his hands of either helplessness or confusion, and that seemed to clue Two in that she hadn't made her point.

"You are clever, Andrej, you can see. There are four things that you can do, and one of them is to go to work for the very influential First Secretary—who wants you very badly—of the woman who will quite possibly be First Judge someday. You could make your practice in the border worlds, but there are people out there who might recognize you, and you are not much qualified for such a life of crime."

So Two didn't think that voluntary self-imposed exile was a viable option. "Of course you could also go to your home, and—what is the phrase—slide on the ice into fruit-butter, because your life has no more astringent seedlings. Is this the Standard? I am not sure I translate the idiom correctly."

For himself Mendez was almost certain that she hadn't, but her meaning was clear enough. Still, she'd said four things, and Koscuisko was waiting.

"Or there is only one other thing. I must come down to you for this so as to gauge my effect. It will be one moment."

Walking across the ceiling like an impossibly large stalking insect, shifting her weight easily between her strong little feet and the steely three-fingered hands at the first joint of her great leathery wings. Reaching the ground with a final hop from her ladder on the wall. Crawling up onto the surface of the table beneath her anchor-perch, sweeping it clear of its litter of bits of document-cubes and the stray container of fruit that had been dropped onto it from the ceiling with a gesture of one wing as she settled herself once more.

"Because it will be a joke, and it is good to share humor with others, it helps one to remember not to harvest from them. The joke is about the shortage of replacements for our Andrej. It is a thin joke, because the shortage is very short."

"No." Koscuisko stared at her, his face full of blank horror and disbelief. Two stretched out her wings and put her tertiary flanges over Koscuisko's shoulders where he sat; a curiously tender gesture, a Desmodontae embrace, of sorts.

"It is of course not funny, as a joke, but such is the way of things. And it could be that there would be a transfer away from here, since you would volunteer, and you would be more useful on an active-duty craft."

Mendez decided that he didn't want to look at Koscuisko, just at present. Inspecting his manicure instead, he found the point that Two was making all too obvious, even if written in a scant thumbnail's space.

Koscuisko had put Fleet between himself and Secretary Verlaine, at the beginning.

Fleet had loaned him out only grudgingly over the years, because a good battle surgeon was almost as hard to find as people who could live with themselves as Inquisitors, if what Koscuisko's life had come down to could be called living.

And now, just at the point when Koscuisko had thought that he was clear, just at the moment when Koscuisko had believed he could get away—Verlaine blocked his path.

And only Fleet could stand between Andrej Koscuisko and First Secretary Verlaine.

"What must I do?" The voice sounded more than half-strangled, but it was not Two's voice, so it had to be Koscuisko. "First Officer?"

"You'll be obliged to write a statement explaining why you changed your mind about renewing." He still didn't want to look at the man, because his sympathies were engaged. That annoyed him. Koscuisko was smarter than he was, richer than he was, better educated, even better dressed, within the constraints of uniform.

Koscuisko was also put to it more brutally than any bond-involuntary by this turn. Well, more brutally than any bond-involuntary on the *Ragnarok* since Koscuisko's arrival, at any rate, Koscuisko being a little odd about his people.

Stildyne was going to need to know about this.

"Oh, holy Mother."

Now that he had to look—now that the naked despair in Koscuisko's strangled voice demanded attention—he couldn't see, because Two had Koscuisko covered over with her wings, sheltered within a matte-black cocoon of rustling skin.

"I will never get away from here."

A pause, and Koscuisko's voice strengthened, leveled out. "Thank you, First Officer. I would . . . rather . . . even whore for Captain Lowden than for the man who should have known about the Domitt Prison."

Stildyne needed to know because Stildyne wasn't going to want to leave the *Ragnarok* with Koscuisko still on it. Stildyne needed to know because Koscuisko was clearly in desperate need of moral support, and Mendez was not in a position to provide it. Koscuisko was closer to his Security than anyone else on board of *Ragnarok*.

Though whether or not Stildyne himself had ever been admitted to that intimacy was something that Koscuisko and Stildyne were apparently still negotiating, and none of Mendez's business either way.

"I'll send Stildyne with the documentation, Andrej. Soonest. Two, send a stop order on the termination payments, tell Fleet Medical we're processing a variance in lieu of replacement."

Koscuisko would get a significant increase in pay for renewing his term. It probably wasn't a good time to mention that. As if an increase in pay meant anything to a man like Koscuisko, who had once offered the Bench to buy his bond-involuntaries out—all nine of them, two hundred and fifty thousand Standard each.

Too bad, Mendez told himself, with fleeting regret.

Too bad he couldn't just arrange to have the signing bonus and the longevity increase credited against his own pay records, as long as Koscuisko was not paying attention.

Unfolding her wings slowly, Two kept one delicate little claw on Koscuisko's shoulder, either following him as he stood up or steadying him. Mendez couldn't tell which.

"I will go back to my place, then, and wait."

He'd best be started himself, and call for Stildyne.

He was almost certain that Captain Lowden would be too surprised to even gloat.

Garol Vogel pushed his duty cap up off of his forehead irritably, rubbing the little tuft of hair that was all that remained to cover the dome of his balding head. "One more seal on the deadbox, and Burkhayden will be out of our hands. That Lieutenant's got a dirty reputation."

Their quarters on the *Lady Gechutrian* were ornate and luxurious in proportion with their Bench status. It annoyed him, all the padding and carving. Jils came out of the washroom in her towel-wrap and sat down on one of the heavy wooden chairs to comb out her hair, cocking an eyebrow at him. "That whole ship. The Lieutenant's small game. Problem?"

He had claimed the least padded chair as his from the moment they'd joined the Danzilar fleet. He tilted the chair back against the liquor cabinet, now, trying to ignore the clinking of bottles as he did so. Bottles. Glass, actual breakable silica-based crystal for drinking out of. Wooden furniture. Thick napped carpeting made out of animal hair, hand-loomed by virgins dedicate, for all he knew. These people had too much money for their own good, and they disgusted him deeply, in an abstract sort of way.

"No problem. No new problem." It was an old problem.

She was probably as bored with it as he was. "How'd it go on your end?"

Jils declined to look at him, working on a tangle. "He's unstable. We knew that. But he's not stupid, and Verlaine's got him pretty much locked this time."

"Listen. Jils." That was another problem, though she didn't know the extent of it yet. And he had to be careful. "Are you sure it's all to the good of the Judicial order? Koscuisko, I mean. Uncharacteristically petty of Verlaine."

They'd known each other too long for him to risk an overt deception. They understood each other too well. Intimately, if not sexually so, but as far as Garol was concerned once you'd been stuck with the same person in a burrow on Sillpogie for a week sex could only be a letdown.

Jils didn't answer him immediately, concentrating on her plait. She was still getting used to having to deal with the traditional Arakcheek-style working-braid that she'd selected for propriety's sake. Dolgorukij women of rank wore their hair long, so Jils had gone for a quick forced-patch before she'd reported. The more they looked like Dolgorukij the less notice would be taken of them; and that could be one of the most valuable weapons in the inventory. "Koscuisko's got the juice, Garol, you know it. One of the few Inquisitors in the inventory you can count on when you have to get actual answers, and not trash."

She wasn't answering his question, but he couldn't push it. He was unhappy about what he thought might be happening at Chilleau Judiciary, but he couldn't really explain all of the details without compromising his Brief. If it was a Brief. If the Warrant he carried for the life of Andrej Koscuisko was a true Warrant. Things just didn't add up. Or what they seemed to add up to was not an issue he was willing to face just yet.

"So he's good." An argument would cover any hesitation she might detect in his manner. "He should be rewarded, not punished for it. We should let him go home."

Why would Chilleau Judiciary have issued a Warrant on

Koscuisko's life if the First Secretary was to have what he wanted from the man?

"Personal sacrifices are sometimes required in support of the greater good. You know that." No, Jils wasn't quite convinced, but she'd get stubborn if he pushed her.

"And if you think this has anything to do with the Judicial order instead of Verlaine's pride you're wrong."

This was working to distract her—a bit too well. He was picking a fight, again. Why shouldn't he? Wasn't conflict just a part of that constant honing of wit and interplay that made Bench intelligence specialists so good at what they did? Yeah. Right.

"One way or the other." Jils, being charitable, was ignoring his best attempts to be irritating. "We can't afford to let a resource of that magnitude escape us, Garol."

Resource his ass. But that was the problem, right there. Koscuisko had the potential to be a resource; and Koscuisko was unquestionably the inheriting son of a very influential family within a respectably powerful bloc in Sant-Dasidar Judiciary.

People like Andrej Koscuisko couldn't be quietly assassinated without someone noticing; and there was the Malcontent—the secret service of the Aznir church, the slaves of St. Andrej Malcontent—to consider.

"Crazy people, she means. A man with his surgical qualifications, and all Lowden ever uses him for is taking people apart. There's intelligence out on Lowden. You know it."

She'd finished dressing, now, and threw his exercise uniform at him from across the room. "Crazy is as crazy does. Four years with Captain Lowden, and he's still alive, and that's more than can be said of the last three. Where there's survival there's got to be a species of sanity. Come on."

It was a point, about Lowden. Unfortunately part of the point could as easily be that Koscuisko had opted to survive by forgetting that he'd ever wanted to be a doctor. "You got a mindsifter on it that you haven't told me about?"

"Garol—"

Oh. He'd pushed too hard, then. Finally. He was in for it

now, and only himself to blame. Yes, he knew that he and Jils trained well together, and that was eighty-seven parts of an intel spec's survival in an uncertain world. The Danzilar prince was going to wonder about the bruises, even so.

"Okay. Okay. I'm coming. Don't hurt me. I take back what I said about the mindsifter. You're a good psychotech. You don't need a mindsifter. I'm coming."

Vogel knew how good Jils really was at what she did. His respect for her professional ability was deep and sincere, and she had saved his life—not to speak of what he laughingly referred to as his career—on more than one occasion. So he didn't really want to push her too far on this.

And the last thing he wanted to do to a friend was bring her in on a bad Warrant, if bad it turned out to be.

◇ Two

It got dark early at this time of the year, but the curfew for Nurail hadn't been shifted yet. Hanner had plenty of time to have his payday treat and get back to his garden before the Port Authority would be patrolling. The Port Authority was generally just as willing to beat a Nurail as look at him, and they didn't need to justify their actions as long as there were no bones broken.

Hanner was prudent.

He would be back to his garden in good time.

The Tavart had got a residence-chit for him, and had suffered him to make a modest habitable place in one of the garden's outbuildings so that he could live there without charge to lodgings and save his wage. The Tavart was a good maistress. She always paid full earnings on the contracted day, and there'd been a nice bit of extra this time, too, that had come into his hand with a vague mention of the winter coming on. He had a new coat of the extra. A new coat, a secure lodging, leave to take his prunings and trimmings in and out as he wished: Life was not half bad, just at the present, as long as a man could manage not to mind about Danzilar and the Judicial order.

He had it better than Megh did, for a fact. And here she was, coming through the back way from the service-house into this little hire-kitchen, where even a Nurail could sit and have a bit of meat and not be molested.

Megh.

Taller than he was, shaped very becomingly, and if her lip had got set a little thin over the years of slavery she'd served her eyes were dark and glittering with life and even laughter sometimes yet.

"Hullo, there, cousin Hanner, I was afraid that I'd mistook the day. How do you go?"

She slid into the booth beside him, setting a bottle of ale down between them on the table as she did. Criminal Megh was in the eyes of the Bench, sentenced to thirty years of involuntary servitude for supposed crimes against the Judicial order. But still she was allowed a surplus ration, now that she had passed the first third of her sentence.

Service bond-involuntaries past their first third got a surplus ration of food and drink and more administrative than personal chores assigned. Security bond-involuntaries were issued a more serviceable grade of boots and better fabric for their uniforms.

"I'm a rising young man in the affairs of state, here, Megh, I'll have you know. My maistress has called up a whole field of botanicals, I'm to discover how they thrive in the salt air, see?"

He was not a slave in the same sense as Megh; he wore no implanted governor to monitor his internal states and punish an infraction. He could think treason all he liked, so long as he did none.

He set his little posy to the Megh side of the bottle, keeping his eyes on his plate. It gave her pleasure to have a little bit of flowering straw, and a bloom that was not too unlike a golden ice-flower. Skelern felt it prudent nonetheless to wait until she had had a moment to master the pain that it also brought her before he could evaluate the success of his gift.

"Skelern, I've heard something."

Startled, he looked up at her before time. She sat very still, very quiet, turning the stem of a piece of sheep-fern between her fingers. It had been for a joke, the sheep-fern; it was fodder for the animals, nothing more, but Maistress Tavart had seemed to find it rare and exotic.

"What's the matter, Megh, nothing to grieve you?"

He should have known better than to make such a joke. He was a gardener's son, a gardener. He knew little about the high windy, nor cared to. But Megh had come from the high windy, on her own world. Megh was a herder's daughter.

"Nothing to grieve over, no, cousin. Maybe nothing at all but just the accident of a name." There was a little frown between her honest eyes, an uncertainty between pleasure and fear. "There was a patron, here, these few days past. I served her her meal. And she wanted to ask about the patternweave."

Megh put her hand up to the shawl across her right shoulder, a little uncomfortably. It was a cruelty to make her wear it at all, even if it was no honest weave. They liked to remind people that they could do anything they wanted, *and you'll accept it and be grateful, my girl.*

"But she was polite, Skelern, thoughtful-like. As if she really cared to know. And she kept looking at me as though I reminded her."

She was an exotic in a public house, was Megh. The most part of her job was parrying the constant curious questions of customers eager to be titillated with a bit of genuine Nurail folklore. Skelern opened the bottle, pouring two glasses full without comment. It was Megh expected to keep quiet, and let other people talk. He wasn't about to stop her words in the small space of time that she had in which she could speak at her will. He was a gardener. He knew the value of letting well enough alone.

"She seemed kind enough. I'm not forbidden to say only so much as where and from whom. And so I told. The truth, not this rag of lies I wear, and I'm from Marleborne, you know that, Skelern."

And her father's people had once held a famous war-weave. The Narrow Pass, he thought it had been, though he had always tried hard not to brood upon the matter, keeping his mind on his own garden for prudence's sake. If it hadn't been for the war-weaves and the warlike fury they aroused in Nurail hearts the Bench might not have seen them for a threat, all of those years ago. He might have been a free man, then, and his family yet living in decent comfort here in Burkhayden.

"And she interrupted me, Skelern, startled-like. And your mother's people hold the Ice-Traverse, she said. As if she knew, cousin, but how could she know the weave, and still say my mother's people?"

The faint hint of outraged modesty made him want to smile. "Most improper it is, cousin. Surely she meant no harm."

Picking up her glass Megh stared at the surface of the beer, tilted back as it was, as though to see her reflection in its surface. Skelern realized with a mild concerned shock that she was blushing. "Skelern, you'll grant me your sweet pardon, but I have to say this. My . . . my father's wife . . . my brothers' mother, her people, they—"

Oh. Skelern made a smoothing gesture, fearful that she would say the taboo thing. "So how did she know of the weave in Marleborne, do you think? And yet not know the rest of it?"

"I asked her that, I did." There was the swallowed sob of anguished hope in Megh's quiet voice; it made him want to weep. "I couldn't help it." Nor would he have been able to resist the same impulse if he'd been the one ripped from his native place, with no news ever of his family. "She couldn't think of why she thought of it, and we spoke no further on that reckoning. But she sent word a day or so after that, and it was a Security chit, so they let it through to me still as it left her."

Else everyone would know what Megh had learned. Whatever that was. No Nurail had a right to privacy, not here in Port Burkhayden.

The glass was empty, now, but Megh hadn't set it back down for a refill in friendship and in courtesy. She held the glass to her instead with both hands wrapped fiercely around it at its middle.

"She had met once a Security troop, and had some cause or another to have remembered him. Bond-involuntary, Nurail. And she didn't remember what his slave-name was." Not as if that would have told Megh anything. Other bond-involuntaries took slave-names from the Judiciary where they'd been condemned, and carried the identification of the place that defined their shame until their Day was past. To Nurail alone even that much identity was denied.

"But what she had called to her mind was a trial that she was at, a talking-drug, something. I don't know. Being tested on a Nurail bond-involuntary. It's what she remembered him telling, that his name was Robin, from Marleborne. And that his mother's people held the Ice Traverse."

There was no missing the significance. Skelern chewed on a bit of the meat from his stew-bowl thoughtfully, not wanting to intrude on the intensity of her feeling. She worried at the fringe of the shawl that she wore; after a moment he felt it might be safe to speak to her. "Your brother, then, Maistress Megh. Do you think it could be?"

Megh had thought that problem up one side of the hill and down the next, so much was obvious. "I saw him last taken away by Jurisdiction, and they were merciful to us, cousin, they let us see each other alive and whole before we were to be parted. Wanted to fight, he did, but it was kindness to let me kiss my brother, with the rest of us—all dead—"

"Hush, now," Skelern warned, hastily, alarmed. "Hush, now, Megh, you'll give yourself such a headache, please, be gentle."

She turned her head and wiped her face with his napkin, crumpling it in her hand. "Look you aren't late for curfew, young Skelern," she said, with a certain weight of tears to drape her admonitory tone. "I believe you are the same age that my brother would be, of course not so tall. It is to hope, that's all."

Little enough to hope for, surely. Bond-involuntary Security had thirty years to serve at labor that was both hard and hazardous. And to be forced to put the tortures forward, at the order of an Inquisitor—

"I'll dream on it with you, then, if you'll permit." There were Nurail here in Burkhayden who had come through the camps at Rudistal, and one of the staff at Center House who had survived the Domitt Prison itself. They said that Koscuisko for one had used his Bonds tenderly, with respect. But Skelern knew that it would never have been remarked upon unless that was unusual.

"I'm glad for all the good you care to hope me," Megh said with plain simplicity, kissing him on the cheek as she rose to go. "Come and see me again, cousin, I'll tell you all about our new maisters, and whether they are any different than the old ones were."

He watched her move gracefully to the back of the shop and through, her shoulders straight beneath the mockery of the weave that Jurisdiction put to her to wear, dignity and suffering alike in the gentle movement of her head.

If it were up to him there would be an entire army of brothers for her, if only they could give her comfort.

But it wasn't up to him.

And he had to mind the curfew.

He finished his meal and went out while he still had time to get back to his garden before curfew fell over the Port and prisoned Nurail behind doors.

Skelern Hanner leaned against his grubbing-hoe and rested himself, the cool still air very pleasant next to his bare skin. His shirt hung on a nail outside the shed for the saving of the garment from the sweat; which made things a little awkward, of a sudden, because here was sweet little Sylphe come running across the blueturves to seek him.

He watched her come with embarrassment, with fondness, and with dread. A man would prefer to be decently covered in the presence of a lady, especially when a man knew he was too skinny by half to be judged beautiful. He was fond of Sylphe. She had a good nature. He fervently hoped that she did not want to talk to him about politics.

"Skelern, Skelern, Mother has news for you, there's a job—the Danzilar prince's garden, for his party, there's a Fleet Lieutenant here, and—"

He'd had ample moments of warning, but he hadn't stirred himself, busy watching her come scurrying over the grass. It was a pleasure to watch her, child though she was. She

stopped abruptly and drew back when she saw him, the back
of her hand coming up to cover her little mouth as if she'd
never seen a man without his smock on before, ever.

"Oh, Skelern, this is—surely most improper, please, go
and dress yourself."

He wanted to laugh. But he went to fetch his shirt, instead.
"If my little maistress doesn't think it seemly, I would suggest she not come looking for her mother's gardener come
spring. A man likes to work in his hipwrap when it's hot,
sweet Sylyphe."

She was blushing as deep as a vine-ripened acidplum, and
she did it very prettily, too. Well, perhaps not; her cheeks
were blotched and blighted with embarrassment. It looked
pretty enough to him.

"I shall carry bells. And call out warning. What are you
doing, Skelern?"

She was interested in gardening, that was true. "I'm head-
ing the late starchies. If you don't trim them to the ground
they waste themselves away in the winter light as though it
was spring, and you lose the spring blossom." Bending down
for a clump of leaves, he shook it free of dirt to offer it to
her, half-joking. "Flowers, for the little maistress of the
house?"

"Oh, don't be ridiculous. Imagine, wearing a vegetable."
And yet she tucked the base of the leaf-bundle into her bodice,
and arrayed the green leaves carefully in a symmetrical pattern
upon her bosom. "There, how do I look?"

"As if you were wearing a vegetable. Of course. What were
you calling to me, on your way out? A party for me, is it?"

"Um." She was distracted by her corsage still, making further adjustments. There had been a year when such rubbish
as Sylyphe's corsage would have been his dinner. They'd
eaten less likely things not so very long ago. "Gardeners for
the Danzilar prince's garden, to make ready for his party.
Mother's offered you, but you're to be paid, of course, and
to have a holiday after."

He wasn't quite sure that he liked being "offered," as if
he were a bundle of packaging. Still, the Tavart treated him

well enough to take the sting out of any real resentment on his part. Surely the Tavart had earned the right to lend him out, with pay and bonuses. There was a good deal to be said for the contractual value of a new coat before winter, and a warm dry room safe from the weather for his bed. "Tell me about the party, Sylyphe. Am I to have a day to finish up my starchies, here?" He wasn't going to want to let the tubers go. He needed a day or two yet in the late sun to be ready for the ice that was to come.

She dimpled at him, seeming grateful for a chance to talk about it. "It's to be three weeks yet before the Fleet arrives. The master-gardener says a week's worth of work, but a month's pay is offered, Skelern, say that you aren't cross? I mean—"

She meant that he was prickly with her on the issue of being told where to go and how to go when he got there. "Na, there's good to it, then. Plenty of time to finish up what's needful."

It was a little selfish of him to be so self-absorbed when she was all alone here and aching with the excitement of it all. Once the Danzilar arrived there would be more doing in Port Burkhayden, and probably more company for Sylyphe— company more suited than his to her high place.

"And your Lieutenant, Sylyphe, tell me about him, do." No doubt he'd go back to being "Gardener Hanner" then, if she had time to speak to him at all. It was probably just as well.

He could not bear to think of Sylyphe trying to cope with the life of a Nurail gardener with one small room in a gardener's shed of a wintertime, and that was the sum of the best he could ever hope to offer her.

"G'herm Wyrlann. Fleet First Lieutenant, Jurisdiction Fleet Ship *Ragnarok*." She spoke the uncouth name with careful precision, as if testing the contours of it in her mouth with studious attention. "Command Branch, and he looks very stern. The uniform! And Security, they all move perfectly, Skelern, perfectly, you should just see them."

She'd been with her mother to some public function, no

doubt. As prepared as Sylyphe was to be excited they could have sent a maintenance crew, and Sylyphe would have taken them for splendid.

"The Danzilar in four weeks. Oh, your mother's to be busy." Parties all over town, no doubt. He'd want to see about forcing some of his second flat of ice-blooms; the Tavart liked the ice-blooms, and she made good capital of them as well. The Danzilar wanted to exploit the specifically Nurailian nature of its newly indentured world. Ice-blooms were apparently a useful token of Iaccary Textile and Cordage's commitment to the Danzilar's goals.

And on the tail end of his musing, a random thought, come strolling forward from his mouth before he saw it. "Shan't be having much time to chat with you, Sylyphe."

She bridled at the idea, seeming as surprised as he was to have heard it. "Why, whatever can you suppose that to mean, Skelern?"

There was a silence for a moment, each staring at each, she and he confused alike by why the thought had come and why it had seemed so objectionable. Then Sylyphe recovered herself, to an extent. It was her breeding.

"There will be plenty of time to talk. Later. There's winter gardening, I've read about it, I want to hear all that you can teach me."

But her reassurance, gracious as it was, came too late for either of them. The point had been made, and there was no recalling it. Gardener Hanner it was to be. There was no way it could be otherwise.

"Later, of course." He could only agree, or else give offense. He said it with a certain heaviness of heart all the same. "You'll want to go into the house, before your mother catches you with a tuber in your bosom."

"Oh, Skelern, don't be silly. As if Mother would care."

There was no longer any conviction in her protest.

She removed the now-wilting greens with grave decorous grief, and handed them back to him without meeting his eyes.

*   *   *

Standing in the empty echoing foyer of the Center House, G'herm Wyrlann eyed the overgrown garden through the unwashed panes of the old-fashioned clearwalls with distaste. Captain Lowden's promises aside, he was not enjoying his brief taste of absolute power; there was so little to have power over—so little privilege to abrogate or enjoy.

Fleet's Provisioners had done their job too well, down to the very last. There was precious little left to beguile a man in Port Burkhayden, and there would be no one to carpet these bare dirty floors—to hang the high walls with insulating fabric as a barrier to the damp falling dark—to stock the kitchen with anything more than survival rations; not until Danzilar came.

"Oh, yes, very well done indeed," he snarled, at no one in particular. He'd been all over the port inside of the past few hours—what there was left of the port. "Nothing left in the armory, nothing. Nothing left in Administrative Quarters. Nothing left here, and I swear that it would not surprise me if the local Bench itself had been carted off to Stores."

His contact, the Fleet Liaison Officer, merely bowed as if in receipt of a compliment. And Wyrlann hadn't meant it as a compliment. The local Fleet Liaison had gone disgustingly native, from what Wyrlann could gather. He'd received the mildest of the comments Wyrlann had felt called upon to make about Nurail, about Meghilder, about Port Burkhayden itself in particular with a blank stare of disapproval that Wyrlann hadn't cared for, not at all.

No doubt the Fleet Liaison was already on Danzilar's payroll behind Fleet's back. The Danzilar's local majordomo certainly seemed comfortable enough with him; and the Danzilar's majordomo was Nurail, probably Free Government. There was no getting away from Nurail at Burkhayden. The place was filthy with them.

Nor had the welcoming party been so much as properly coached in the expected expressions of respect and gratitude; it had instead been apparently assembled more or less by accident, through mere word of mouth.

Four weeks until the *Ragnarok* arrived, and he was stuck

here until then. If he'd realized that it was going to be like this, he would have suggested Lowden send ap Rhiannon instead of him. It would have been a good experience for the creche-bred junior officer to be isolated in the middle of a derelict port for four weeks with only a suspicious—and suspiciously reserved—Fleet Liaison Officer for company.

Wyrlann sighed. The sun was going down, and if the draft was any indication the wind was picking up as well. "I've seen all I need to see of this, for now. Which isn't saying much." He had no intention of spending the night here, with the heating systems all turned off and no liquor to be had.

He hadn't any doubt that the majordomo's personal quarters were comfortable and luxurious enough, but Artigen was just the sort of icicle-up-his-ass administrative officer to take exception to any suggestions on Wyrlann's part that they go find out. "There's a service house here, isn't there? Or have you had that shipped out as well?"

Now the majordomo answered, and he hadn't been spoken to. Wyrlann wondered that Danzilar's people would put a Nurail in a position of such influence and authority. On the other hand it was Danzilar's lookout if the Nurail robbed him blind. "There is indeed, Fleet Lieutenant. It's part of the contracted package, still in place for the Danzilar prince's use."

Which probably meant that it wasn't very profitable, which in turn probably meant that it wasn't much of a service house. As if anything different could be expected in this stinking Nurail port full of stinking Nurail. Still, as a Command Branch officer he didn't have to pay at service centers.

He could have anything he wanted for the asking. And for now what he really wanted was a little entertainment. The service house would be adequately heated, if nothing else. "Well, let's go, then."

"Yes, Lieutenant." Artigen, once more; Wyrlann was glad to see that at least the Nurail hadn't forgotten his place to the extent of presuming himself to be included. "Your Security as well? Of course."

Captain Lowden would expect him to evaluate what amenities remained in Port Burkhayden.

Good subordinate officers were quick to anticipate and execute the wishes of their senior officers.

She'd told young Hanner that she would tell him all about
their new maisters. That she had. So Megh examined this
Ragnarok's First Lieutenant covertly as she set his meal to
table, mindful of the necessity to keep the inner elbow-point
of her patterned shawl out of the food.

Not a sound. Not a single clink or bell-like ting or muffled
thud; she knew the trick of it, setting the place without a
single stray bit of noise to distract the officer. Tallish. Stout-
ish, but like it was all muscle and bone, no hint of any easy
living, any fat. Mouth that seemed always in a sneer, even
drinking his liquor, which should make a man at least stop
frowning if it didn't make him smile.

She glanced over at the officer one too many times and met
his cold sarcastic gaze, which quite unnerved her. Startled,
she let the silence stretch too far for a graceful recovery, and
the realization unbalanced her even more. She bent her head
to stare at the napery still in her hands, thinking hard and fast.

"The Lieutenant is but half a day in Burkhayden, yet?"
she asked with studied timidity in her voice, falling back into
the exaggerated Nurail lilt expected of her for camouflage.
"How does the officer take to our salt sea, and our proud new
skystarport?"

Burkhayden had been a seaport, once, but the marsh had
gotten too far into the bay, and the Jurisdiction had not cared
to dredge for navigability when higher tolls could be taken in
other channels.

"Can't say that I like it at all." The voice was harsh,
amused. She knew that voice; it meant that she'd become a
target, once again. That was what she was here for, of course,
her primary function; one wretched Nurail slave to mock at,
so that the Jurisdiction could forget the menace that it had
once felt from the war-weaves.

"Well, it's a poor mean place, compared to what the officer—"

He interrupted her without the slightest hint of discomfort.

"You're Nurail, aren't you? I know the accent."

Of course the Lieutenant knew the accent. It was the Juris-diction Standard accent for a Nurail slave, one she had learned early on. The fact that it had nothing to do with any honest Nurail lilt that she had ever heard was just another part of the point that they were making about Nurail.

"I wonder that you caught it, sir, it takes a keen ear—"

Interrupting again, with obvious relish this time, the Lieu-tenant—Megh realized—was enjoying the fact that he was being rude. That he could be as rude as he liked with impu-nity. "Don't try any of that whore-pap on me. I know better. That's not a Nurail pattern, either, so what *was* your weave? Tell me about it."

Yes, the old question, the old chore. Swallowing a sigh of resignation Megh lifted the shawl down from her right shoul-der, and began to count the callings that defined her life.

"Seven tones in a Nurail scale, and four half-tones to each. This color of green's the chord called Dogwood Blossom. These notes together in this set, these chords, it's the defining phrase for the tune of Dancing Meggins, which has been a treaty-record tune once of a time. So this space of threads gives you the Nurail Conventions at Berrine, before the Po-litical Stabilization Acts, and here—"

He'd risen from the cradle-chair he had been resting in and come to stand near her. The house's best room it was, separate bath, no sound from the outside, bed big enough for five to sport in. She'd spent her time in a room like this, but not recently. She was beginning to show too much of her history, and was only bidden to smaller, more utilitarian rooms when she was bidden to provide sexual services at all.

"I thought I told you. I already know that's not a Nurail weave."

She couldn't decide on his tone of voice, whether gentle or threatening. She did know that it made her uncomfortable.

"With the officer's permission, it's the only weave the Bench will have me speak of—"

"Not good enough." Draining his glass, he sat down on the table so forcefully that the cutlery jumped. "I told your

proprietor that I wanted amusement. I don't need to hear the
damn fake weave, I want to hear your weave. The one you
used to have. Before you got what's coming to any insurrectionary, you filthy little traitor."

And she wasn't an insurrectionary except by default, and
she wasn't any kind of a traitor, not to her weave and kind.
The weave she wore was the only one she was allowed to tell
over in public. It was the only one that people were permitted
to demand of her.

"Begging the officer's pardon, but it is my weave, it has
been so for going on ten years . . ."

Eyes respectfully lowered, she didn't see the hand coming
across her face, and the shock almost as much as the blow
itself made her stagger back half-collapsing to the ground.

"*Your* weave." Crouching over her, now, and the smell of
his breath was heavy with malice and liquor. "Tell your other
customers whatever damn lies you please. But to me you tell
the truth, understand?"

Well, it seemed clear enough. But she could not speak of
her weave even to please a difficult patron, even if it might
save her a beating. Her father's people had held the Narrow
Pass. She was strictly prohibited to rehearse it, and her governor made sure she would not do the forbidden thing.

"The Fleet Lieutenant surely understands better than anyone else. The weave, it's proscribed, I may not—"

This time she saw the blow coming, but she couldn't avoid
it even so. Back against the heavy base of the sideboard she
went, and fetched her head sharply up against it.

"I've had just about enough of this. Do you have any idea
who I am?"

Oh, yes. She knew exactly who he was. He was a bully
who beat up women, but there wasn't much she could do
about that. Influential patrons were left more or less to do as
they pleased, as long as the house got its money.

Still, his musical entertainment would be coming, she could
get away from him when the musicians came. And the estab-
lishment husbanded its livestock responsibly. They would not
let her suffer too much pain after an undeserved beating.

"His Excellency is the First Lieutenant of the *Ragnarok*, Command Branch—"

He dragged her away from the sideboard and hit her yet again, keeping a good grip on her arm so that she couldn't put any distance between them. "Wrong. Dear me. The little whore thinks I'm an Excellency. Is that what you think, little whore? Do you think that I'm an Excellency?"

He wouldn't stop hitting her face, and her thoughts rattled against each other into incoherence with each blow. The inside of her cheek was cut against her teeth. It was difficult to speak distinctly.

"The officer is Command Branch, surely."

"But not an Excellency. Maybe it's Koscuisko you have in mind. He spent a lot of time getting to know you Nurail, remember? At the Domitt Prison?"

She kept on trying to get away. She knew he hadn't cleared this with the housemaster, and she couldn't help but try to escape pain. She tried, but his grip was like iron, and it only seemed to make him angrier.

"Everyone knows about Black Andrej. And the Domitt Prison." Keeping her voice low on instinct, Megh kept testing for the right approach to appease him, to get him to stop for long enough for her to get away. Once she could get away she would be safe, the house staff would surely intervene to protect her. She couldn't be beaten for not singing her weave, even had her governor permitted it. It was a killing offense to sing any weave, let alone a war-weave like the Narrow Pass.

"Oh, well, perhaps you're disappointed, then. You'd sing the weave for him, soon enough, but not for me, is that it?"

He shook her and let her go, but she couldn't get to the door, because her legs came out from underneath her as soon as he released her upper arm. And he was still talking. It was important to pay attention to what he was saying; she had to find a way to placate him.

"I'll tell you something, though. I've seen him work. There's really nothing very complicated to it. Anything he can do, I can do, and better."

It was his boot this time, and not a fist at all. A boot sudden and brutal put to her stomach, making her cry out loud of it. And yet another boot, to take the wind out of her belly, so that she rolled her arms around her middle and curled onto her side, trying to find her breath.

"There's his tapes, you know? I watch them sometimes, with the Captain. And if Koscuisko was here I know just what he'd do. Here, we'll pretend I'm your precious 'Black Andrej,' shall we? And when we're done you can sing me your weave like an obedient little slut. Whether you want to or not."

Stooping down to her on the floor he grabbed her wrist, and pulled her flat at length on the carpet. She tried to smooth her breathing out, to be ready for the next blow. It helped sometimes to try to guess the course of a beating, to concentrate on whatever one could use to create an illusion of control.

"And if Koscuisko were here he'd probably start with . . . well. He'd use the butt end of his driver to fuck you wide open, he does amazing things with that whip. Haven't got a whip. This'll do, though, just as well. I'm sure."

He seemed minded to rape her with his boots, never minding the other ugly things he said. There didn't seem to be anywhere that she could get to, to hide from him. He drove her across the carpet to the far wall with his blows; and when she could flee no further he stuffed her shawl deep down into her throat and raped her horribly with the wine-flask. She thought it was the wine-flask, he'd had a wine flask, but whatever it was forced her belly up into her throat with agony.

"Damn thing's broken, well, if you think I'm going into your stinking cunt after that, you can just think again. Not to disappoint you, I know how much you crave it."

Where were the musicians? Hadn't it been an hour, two hours, half a day since she had come up here to set the table, and she still left here all alone at the mercy of this monster's brutal whims?

"Of course in the end the simple things are best. Traditional. You Nurail like tradition? You'll like this."

She was choking on her own screams, trying to breathe. And she could not stop screaming even so.

The Port Authority had come and gone, the emergency aid team had left with the injured woman, and the word went out into the silent whispering streets of Port Burkhayden.

The Ragnarok's *First Lieutenant, in the service house.*

There were menials on night shifts, ready to provide hot food to comfort the patrols coming in off the streets for their warming-periods, and the message followed each mobile vendor from station to station as the night deepened.

One of the women, making his meal ready. He tried to make her sing her father's weave.

The city's communications nets were old and poorly maintained, and now that the Jurisdiction had pulled its resources out there were chronic problems with lapses in the net. Strictly licensed Nurail maintenance crews were on call to respond at any hour of the day or night. There was a steady stream of emergency restore orders, and the news was left at nexus after nexus as the hours wore on.

Support staff, not a bed-partner, only setting the table out. Beat her with his fists, put his boots to her. Cut her with broken glass, you can guess where, because nobody wants to have to say.

During the coldest hour, the oldest hour, the least respected of the city's servants rose up out of their meager beds to see that all was waiting, nothing wanting, when the city's maisters rose. Fuel for furnaces, water-heaters brought up in time for them as had the luxury of showers, baths. Fresh sweet milk from outside the port's boundaries, the morning's fresh-picked flowers for the fastmeal table. A bite to eat for the Nurail that lived in lodgings, that had to be up and doing before the kitchen would be open to provide for them: and the sorry tale came whispering to Skelern Hanner as he stood in the darkness of his gardener's shed and washed his hands and face in icy water, getting dressed.

The woman Megh, the Nurail, at the service house. Raped by the First Lieutenant, and with a flask, a piece of broken furniture, nobody knows what else. Taken off to charity ward, but there's no healer there for such wounds as she's taken. She may be dead already.

Skelern stood in the dark silence of his shed, half-dressed, his face still dripping with the cold water of his early morning wash, frantic phrases rushing through his mind. Megh, poor Megh, he had to go and see her.

He couldn't hope to go see her, not on his own, they wouldn't let him in.

He could wake Sylyphe, that he could, she was pitiful if misguided, she could take him to the hospital.

He could not possibly involve Sylyphe.

She was young and privileged. She did not understand the cruel truths in life, and the cruel truth was that a Command Branch officer in any civil port could do such crimes without reproach. Without reprisals.

If he even told Sylyphe she might make a scene in public, and her mother could be compromised by implication. He owed the Tavart for too many favors to want to see her compromised, nor her daughter permitted to make a fool of herself in public. He couldn't see Sylyphe.

He could ask permission to ask the Tavart, but the Tavart was out of town on business, and by the time he could make his request—the day after tomorrow, sometime, and he'd need a chit from her, too, to give him authorization from his employer to go where he'd no business being otherwise—poor Megh could be dead by then, if she wasn't already.

But he was Nurail as well as Megh was, and she would not thank him for courting a beating by risking it on his own just to see her corpse. Nurail, and a slave, and if the Port Authority did not have the legal right to use his body at its pleasure as the *Ragnarok*'s First Lieutenant had done Megh's there was no lack of reasonable pretexts to torture a Nurail gardener for stepping outside of his place, for involving himself uninvited in the affairs of his betters. And no one watching to see that the punishment was restricted to the Jurisdiction Standard, either.

He washed his face again, to rinse the tears away. He would

have to wait. The Tavart would grant him leave to go, he was sure of that.

And maybe Megh would not be dead before he could come to grieve for her in hospital.

◇ Three

Lights were dimmed and room was quiet, but Garol woke with immediate certainty that he'd heard something. He kept his breathing slow and regular, his eyes still shut, listening hard. There was only Jils in the room with him, Jils in the bed beside him as companionable as a sister. It wasn't Jils who'd awakened him, then; not unless it had been her signal.

Garol opened his eyes and sat up in the dim hush, cautiously, and the tone came at the outer door, the door at the end of the room outside the bedroom. Someone in the corridor.

Jils was awake now too, and he could trust Jils's judgment better than his own. She hadn't signaled danger: not yet. Very well. They'd see.

Pushing his feet into the slewsocks that Dohan Dolgorukij wore for bedslippers, Garol belted his heavy blue brocaded bedrobe—a present from the Danzilar prince—around his waist as he made for the door. The signal was tuned to its lowest intensity, but it was persistent.

He keyed the admit and opened the door, and found himself face to face with the Danzilar prince Paval I'shenko himself, standing in the corridor with a household technical officer and some Security behind him. Bowing, Garol wondered; the Danzilar prince had never come to him in quarters, and had never interrupted his sleep-shift, either.

Danzilar himself seemed to have just gotten up, if the butter-yellow jacket he had on over his thin white silk bedsuit

50

and the tousled condition of his nondescript brown hair was any indication.

"Do not waken the lady, I beg it of you," Danzilar said, softly. "No woman should have to hear of such a thing. There is a problem, Garol Aphon, and I believe that I must insist on an immediate response."

Jils was listening in the other room, Garol knew. She would pretend she was still asleep, then.

"At your disposal, your Excellency, of course. At any time." The "Excellency" had been a little distracting to Vogel, because the same title that translated for the respectful language due a Dolgorukij aristocrat applied to Fleet superior officers in Standard as well. Andrej Koscuisko was an Excellency twice over, even as the Danzilar prince was. And neither the Danzilar prince nor Jils Ivers knew what Garol held in his keeping for Andrej Koscuisko. "Is there a place where we can go to talk?"

Danzilar nodded grimly. "Come, and we will discuss. We can use a side room, here—"

Not far from his quarters, and servants already standing by with service tables. As far as Garol had been able to tell, fresh beverage and hot bread was next to godliness for Danzilar's Dolgorukij. Jils would probably remind him that people whose body temperature ran high usually did need to eat a little more frequently to keep themselves going.

"Here is the master of communications, who has brought me this. You will oblige me by reading it for yourself, Garol Aphon. We have had it done into Standard, and I am unwilling to go into the details."

The Danzilar prince habitually called him by two of his names in the formal Dolgorukij manner. Garol had a hard time really resenting it, even though he had never liked his second name. The Danzilar prince looked so young. But looks were deceiving; the Danzilar prince was forty-seven years' old, Standard. Older than Garol himself was.

Garol took the report slate that the watch-master offered him and sat down.

From Burkhayden, not too surprisingly. A protest against

damage to property specifically included in the terms of the Contract, more or less predictable. Except that the property was a woman, not a public building or a farm utility vehicle. The whole issue of bond-involuntaries had always given Garol a raging case of the toe-cramps. And the report was brutally precise on the important issue of exactly what was meant in this case by the "damage."

There didn't seem to be anything for him to say. Garol passed the report slate back to the officer.

"Yes, your Excellency?"

"There is nothing to be done about the vandal, I know that." Danzilar had seated himself in a well-padded chair as Garol read; now he smoothed the broad band at his wrap-jacket's hem carefully over his crossed knees, frowning. He meant Wyrlann, Garol guessed.

Danzilar was right.

There wasn't anything that anyone could do about Wyrlann, except what Garol had been sent to do about Koscuisko. And he had yet to exercise his authority to revise a Bench warrant, regardless of the provocation. He wasn't about to start with a warrant he could not even decide was legitimate.

Danzilar was still talking. "But the staff of a service house is not of small importance, because comfort must be had. And the contract has been signed."

What was Danzilar getting at? "His Excellency will of course be compensated, once the review board has validated loss of function." It didn't make sense for Danzilar to be as upset about this as he seemed to be. The price of any sixteen bond-involuntaries could be easily lost in even the smallest detail of the contract's fiscal stipulations. Yet Danzilar was not only visibly upset, he seemed not far from actually furious, rising to his feet with a ferocious if controlled gesture of rejection.

"I do not want her price, Garol Aphon. I want her worth, as I have been promised in the contract. Her symbolic function at this point is of paramount importance. She belongs to me, Garol Aphon, and I demand her rights."

Of which she had none, whoever she was. Apart from the

obvious, of course. "I'm afraid I don't quite understand, your Excellency."

"Aah, it is the middle of the night. I am only—very angry."

Why?

It was perhaps not inappropriate to indulge oneself in a certain degree of moral outrage, under the circumstances. But Danzilar was not a child, no matter how much like a twenty-five-year-old he looked to Garol. The Dolgorukij had defined atrocity, at least as far as the Sarvaw were concerned; and Danzilar's second cousin thrice removed—or fourth cousin five times distant, or whatever the hell the relation was—was the self-same Andrej Koscuisko who held a Writ which authorized him to practice very much the same sorts of things that Wyrlann appeared to have done to the poor whore at his will and good pleasure, in support of the Judicial order.

So it couldn't be that Danzilar had simply never run into this sort of thing before.

What was going on in Danzilar's mind?

Garol kept silent, and after a moment Danzilar continued. "To do this thing so casually, it shows a lack of respect. For me as well as for the holy Mother. I cannot afford to discard this woman as a piece of spoiled goods. What kind of treatment would any other expect from me, if I did that? These people are to be my people, Garol Aphon. I am responsible for their well-being."

Well, it was true that Dolgorukij were peculiar in that respect. As with Danzilar's cousin Koscuisko, again; and nobody touched Koscuisko's Security, not after what Koscuisko had done to the people he had decided to consider responsible for the death of that bond-involuntary Emandisan of his at Port Rudistal.

"No disrespect is intended, your Excellency. I'm simply not sure what you want me to do about it."

Danzilar glanced at the report slate in the watch-captain's hands with what seemed to be a shudder of horror, or of barely suppressed disgust. "Four pieces of glass, it says, Garol Aphon. And the wounds as long as my hand is broad.

There is no surgeon in Burkhayden to address such injuries effectively. My medical administrator says that we will not have a trauma surgeon on site before it cannot but be too late for this poor woman."

Garol started to shrug in involuntary perplexity; but smoothed his shrug out, thinking quickly. He was beginning to think that he knew what the Danzilar had in mind.

"You want Fleet to send a trauma team to Burkhayden. Possibly when Jils and I leave." They were scheduled to depart inside of ten eights, and a ship of the *Ragnarok*'s size carried modular units for just such requirements—although they were usually used to bring newly repossessed or liberated facilities on line.

If there was a hospital building still standing in Burkhayden the *Ragnarok* could furnish a surgery and a surgeon, up and running in—how long? Garol did some calculations, concentrating hard. The report was already ten eights old. They had a day and a half or more in transit time, ahead of them; maybe if they left a few hours early—

"I want Fleet to send the best surgeon at its disposal here and now. The Chief Medical Officer's personal involvement would send the strongest possible signal to my people in Burkhayden. That is what I wish you to have done."

"Koscuisko?"

The name escaped Garol in an involuntary yelp of disbelief. Send Koscuisko to minister to a woman raped? Send the single most notorious painmaster in the entire inventory to tend to a woman brutalized by his own ship's First Lieutenant?

Koscuisko.

It made a certain amount of sense, once he thought about it.

"There are two things that the most uneducated of rabble knows about my cousin Drusha," Danzilar replied, with utter seriousness. It took Garol a moment to make sense of the name: Drusha, from the intimate form of Andrej. "No, perhaps three things. First, there is of course the obvious. Second, that he is the Chief Medical Officer on board the *Ragnarok*. And finally, that there are none better at what he does, irrespective of the capacity in which one invokes his expertise. Is it not so?"

Well, maybe not really. Once the first point had been raised and controverted the rest faded a bit in significance. Still, Koscuisko was recognized as a senior officer by token of the Inquisitorial function that he performed, if nothing else. Koscuisko's symbolic subordination to a Service bond-involuntary was probably a pretty damn solid way for Danzilar to make his point, if that was what Danzilar was after.

"I'll send an emergency override, your Excellency." It was within his authority to demand that Lowden comply with any measures he deemed necessary to complete the transfer of function. Garol decided that he might very well enjoy making a point of that. "The ship's Chief Medical Officer to travel to Burkhayden with me, and to treat the traumatic injuries this woman has sustained to the maximum extent of his professional ability. Shall I report to his Excellency when the requirement has been communicated to Captain Lowden?"

"Four pieces of glass, Garol Aphon." Danzilar stared at the closed door, clearly distracted. "Please, yes, let me know. This must be addressed, and it cannot be done too soon, you understand."

Maybe there was some cultural peculiarity that made Wyrlann's particular crime especially horrible to Danzilar.

Or maybe Danzilar was simply a decent sort at heart, with decent instincts.

"I understand. If you'll excuse me, your Excellency, I'll go to communications right away."

Nodding, Danzilar put his hand out to Garol's shoulder, walking with him toward the door and talking with evident intent to lighten the atmosphere somewhat. "Yes, thank you, Garol Aphon. Excuse me to my cousin that I do not greet him before you leave, beg for me his forgiveness. And remind him. There is to be a party. There will be dancing."

The more Garol thought about it the better he liked the idea of Captain Lowden forced to make good the senseless damage his First Lieutenant had done.

*   *   *

Captain Lowden usually enjoyed disciplinary events on a number of levels, but today was different.

Today his secret knowledge of the joke he planned to play on Koscuisko distracted him to such an extent that he almost wished Koscuisko would just get it over with, and Koscuisko wasn't off his game, no, nor was the guilty technician unresponsive to the impact of Koscuisko's whip. Koscuisko's performance was, as always, a thing of abstract beauty; as great passion and great control were always beautiful, perfect in form and in execution.

Discipline administered as adjudicated, Technician Hixson, if Lowden remembered correctly. Three-and-thirty. Hixson, bound by the wrists to the wall, two Security troops standing facing the room on either side at several pace's remove so as to be out of danger of any stray blow.

Ship's Engineer, the aggrieved party, present as much to keep an eye on Koscuisko as to provide witness that the penalty had been administered and the grievance satisfied. Jennet ap Rhiannon, counting the strokes, because Lowden felt it was important to involve junior lieutenants in the full range of their duties as Command Branch officers.

The room was crowded. All the better. Koscuisko would swallow down questions he might otherwise ask, to spare listening ears the unpleasantness; and that would help the joke forward.

"Twenty-six, twenty-six, twenty-seven," the Lieutenant counted, her voice flat and free from any inflection that might betray any emotion she felt. Did creche-bred have emotions? Lowden wondered. Neither Fleet nor the Bench had much use for emotions, so why would creche-bred have been issued any? Apart from the Standard, of course.

Whether it was her dispassionate demeanor or something else that Lowden hadn't noticed, Koscuisko apparently objected to the Lieutenant. Or to something she had done. "Twenty-eight, Lieutenant, the count is twenty-eight. Twenty-nine. Thirty."

Yes, right, now that Lowden thought about it she'd counted

twenty-six two times over, just now. Lowden had thought the stroke a hair on the light side himself, but there were good reasons not to challenge Koscuisko on it.

For one thing Lowden was serenely convinced that Koscuisko wouldn't dare actually muddle his count with his Captain in the room. It was the officer's mess, not Secured Medical, so there were no record tapes to review to determine a true count. But Koscuisko was too well trained.

"With respect, sir, the Standard calls for—"

The Standard called for blood to be let on every stroke or the stroke repeated. Koscuisko knew that. Koscuisko was the Judicial officer on board. It wasn't very appropriate for the Lieutenant to challenge him on his count.

"Thirty-one, thirty-two, thirty-three," Koscuisko called firmly, ignoring the Lieutenant. "Three-and-thirty. Gentlemen. Release the technician. Wheatfields, your man."

ap Rhiannon stifled well; yes, Koscuisko had interrupted, but Koscuisko was the senior officer. Lowden rose from his observation post and stepped down from the Captain's Bar to examine the evidence and decide the issue for himself.

Koscuisko had handed the whip off to one of his Security already, and was drinking a flask of rhyti in his shirtsleeves. Discipline was warm work. Koscuisko always took his overblouse off. It had only been three-and-thirty, though. Apart from his loosened collar and rolled-back cuffs Koscuisko seemed unaffected by the exertion: He wasn't even breathing hard.

There were medical people standing by to take Hixson to Infirmary, because though Koscuisko had called Wheatfields to take custody of Hixson—as per standard operating procedure—in reality Hixson was to go to Medical to have the welts on his naked back salved. The orderlies and Security stood away for Captain Lowden's approach, of course.

Lowden counted the welts, one ear to the conversation taking place behind him. Koscuisko was apparently in a mood.

"Lieutenant. While I appreciate your concern for the letter of the Law I must say that your behavior surprises me."

Koscuisko had every reason to be in a mood. He'd had that

fateful interview with Jils Ivers days ago, and Ivers had accomplished miracles. Lowden was in her debt without being in the least actually obligated to her, which was the best of both.

Koscuisko had been drinking ever since, almost as heavily as though he'd had an assignment in Secured Medical. If Koscuisko hadn't been Dolgorukij—Lowden thought to himself, walking his fingers from welt to welt, counting as Hixson trembled—Koscuisko's body would never have been able to support the demands he made of it.

"I apologize, your Excellency." ap Rhiannon meant no such thing. It was the approved formula, no more than that. "It was an error on my part. I felt his Excellency would think less of me if I failed to note the . . . what seemed to me to have been a mis-stroke."

Thirty, thirty-one, thirty-two bloodied tracks, and one mere bruise, purple and weeping clear fluid. Well. Either Koscuisko had missed or the final stroke was laid too exactly over an earlier one to be called out as such. Koscuisko could have missed. But if Koscuisko had dared to try a cheat in his Captain's presence—and Lowden really didn't think it had been deliberate—the joke he was going to play would be entirely adequate punishment.

And junior officers should not controvert with their superiors on principle.

"Three-and-thirty," Lowden said firmly, turning away from Hixson with a gesture for the medical people to come forward. "I call it good. Lieutenant. I shouldn't have to remind you that Koscuisko's count is the true count here. If he says three-and-thirty the only person on board this ship who can say differently is me."

Koscuisko bowed in formal appreciation of this endorsement, but he didn't look surprised or relieved. It had been as Lowden had thought. If Koscuisko had made a mistake it had been a genuine mistake, one of which he was genuinely unaware.

Koscuisko could be excused a mistake, just this once. The

joke Lowden had in mind would be that much more effective if it was unlooked for.

ap Rhiannon could only swallow the rebuke. He'd left her no room to cry an honest error. "Of course, Captain. My apologies, your Excellency, no disrespect was intended. It was a failure of good judgment on my part."

Not that Koscuisko cared. "It is forgotten, Lieutenant," Koscuisko assured her, fastening his cuffs before he allowed his Security to help him into his overblouse. Unlike portions of the uniform that were visible from the outside there was no Jurisdiction Standard for underblouses; some classes of hominid—the particularly hairy ones—weren't even required to wear an underblouse in uniform.

The underblouses that Koscuisko wore had a short little collar that stood straight up from its seam, and very full sleeves, a good deal of fabric gathered into the yoke of it, and fastened with ties slightly to the left of center. Lowden had often wondered what it would look like with blood soaking through it from the other side. "Captain?"

Nobody could leave the room until Lowden as ranking officer had, with the exception of the medical team and their patient. Lowden had no intention of depriving himself of an audience for this.

"Andrej, something's come up. It's difficult." Something had come up during the early eights of first-shift, as a matter of fact. He'd been asleep. But Bench intelligence specialists were allowed global override on privacy channels, any time, any place. "I'm really sorry to have to do this to you. There's been a draft on services, your services. At Burkhayden."

And there *was* a draft on Koscuisko's services, too—Vogel had made that quite clear. Andrej Koscuisko—no other—and the surgical unit. And immediately. Two eights into third shift, actually, and only an eight left to second shift now—Koscuisko would have no time to think twice about it. Perfect.

Koscuisko looked pale, but then Koscuisko had looked pale from early on. He wasn't well. He drank.

"Services, your Excellency." Koscuisko's tone of voice made it quite clear that he thought he knew precisely what

Lowden had meant in selecting that word. "Forgive me for asking, but can it not wait? We will at Burkhayden arrive soon enough."

Quite so. For himself Captain Lowden tried to give Koscuisko adequate anticipation time; it sharpened Koscuisko's appetite and improved Koscuisko's performance. Koscuisko was a resource of very significant value . . . not only to the rule of Law, but to Lowden himself, personally, intimately. Monetarily.

"I regret, Andrej. But Vogel was very insistent. Nothing will do for him but that you travel to Burkhayden immediately to support his requirement."

And now he was to have Koscuisko for another period of time—who knew how long? He had connections. Chilleau Judiciary was going to be in no mood to endorse any request for reassignment; quite the contrary, he could rely on Chilleau Judiciary to come up with good reasons why Koscuisko could not be spared from *Ragnarok*, even though Standard procedure was to rotate every four years. *Ragnarok* had demonstrated its ability to make full use of Koscuisko in his Judicial function. It was Koscuisko's experience on the *Ragnarok* that had finally convinced Koscuisko to renew his Term. Yes.

"According to his Excellency's good pleasure." Koscuisko knew better than to press it any further. "Name the time and the place, if you will, sir."

And what would Koscuisko not do, to protect his assigned troops from sanctions?

Could it be that Lowden was to find a way to have his wish, and watch the blood flow from fresh livid weals on Koscuisko's own smooth-skinned and aristocratic back?

"Docking bay downforward three, and at third and two. First Officer is sending one of your senior Security as acting Chief, I understand. The documentation surrounding Chief Stildyne's refusal of that promotion to First Officer on JFS *Sceppan* isn't complete, and he has to answer to the evaluation board for it. Reasons for declining, and so forth."

Koscuisko hadn't heard about that, either. The pupils of Koscuisko's eyes had shrunk to small angry smoldering coals surrounded by ice. Oh, it was very gratifying, very gratifying indeed.

The only person who wasn't getting the joke was ap Rhiannon, too new to have heard all about Stildyne's personal predilections, and how he had used to treat the Bonds, and how that had changed with Koscuisko's arrival. And why, And why, and why, and why, and why. She'd get an earful soon enough. Lowden knew he could rely upon his other officers to see to that.

"Very good, sir. Downforward three. Captain."

He'd done everything he'd wanted; his joke was set, primed, and ready.

"And we'll see you in a week or two. Thank you, gentles, well done all 'round."

It was only a matter of time before his joke went off in Garol Vogel's face; and that would serve Vogel right, for shaking a senior Fleet officer out of bed in the middle of his sleep for no better reason than that Wyrlann had beaten some Nurail whore.

Again.

Jils Ivers watched the *Ragnarok*'s loaders position the surgical unit beneath the courier ship's waiting cargo area, soothed as she always was to see a task done quickly and done well. The Security that was to travel with them to Burkhayden stood waiting for their officer near the passenger loading ramp; Jils thought she could put names to some of them, after all these years of watching Koscuisko for Verlaine.

The tall Nurail would logically be Robert St. Clare, whose lapse had almost ruined Koscuisko for them before he'd even reported to his first duty. Godsalt, whose precise role in the riots at Arnulf had yet to be determined, whether or not there had been Evidence enough to convict him—and impose his Bond.

One man she didn't recognize, but since he was Pitere to look at him, he was probably Garrity.

And the smiling man with the light brown curls might be Hirsel, who had escaped a full Eighth Level inquiry so narrowly in his previous command. They hadn't been able to prove enough to pursue the offense on such a terminal level. But they had sent him to the *Ragnarok*, right enough, and before Koscuisko had come that had been almost as bad where bond-involuntaries were concerned.

Brachi Stildyne she knew: there was no mistaking that wreckage of a face. Stildyne had come from mean streets, and his face showed his history; one eyebrow off center and lined through with scar tissue, one cheekbone noticeably higher than the other, and his nose had been broken so many times it hardly even mattered any more.

Stildyne was talking to the big black Scaltskarmell who would logically be Pyotr Micmac, or Micmac Pyotr, whichever; but that made six in total. There were one too many. Not only that, but there was an officer's duty-case with the Security that Jils thought she recognized—and found out of place.

What would Koscuisko be wanting a field interrogations kit for?

"Garol, give me an eye or two here."

"Um." Garol had been in a bit of a mood since early this morning, and she wasn't exactly sure what the matter was, because it seemed to run deeper than any combination of perfectly reasonable explanations for Garol's being on the brood. "Whatcha got, Jils?"

She pointed. "What does that look like, to you?"

There was a pharmacy tech down there now, and a little genial frisking seemed to be taking place between St. Clare and the woman with her issue-pouch while the senior troops' backs were obligingly turned. "Looks like a date to me, Jils, has it been that long? Really?"

"No, you idiot. The box on the deck." The tech was leaving, but St. Clare had the issue-pouch. Garol crunched in closer to the view-port, frowning.

"What the . . . ? Stinking three-days-rotten ftah." Well, it wasn't just her suspicious nature, then. "What does he want to travel with that thing for? Jils, I'm not having it on board this ship."

The surgical unit contained the surgical machine, the sterile unit, supplies to address gross trauma and delicate microsurgery alike. That box down on the decking with Koscuisko's Security contained other things, the things that a Chief Medical Officer might need if he was being sent to the field for another reason entirely—field interrogation. Instruments of field-expedient Inquiry, Confirmation, and Execution.

"Listen, Garol." Jils had an uneasy feeling that she just might have guessed at what was going on. Lowden was a master manipulator. She'd known that about Koscuisko's superior officer for years. "You didn't talk to Koscuisko, did you? Just to the Captain?"

"Damn it, Jils, I'm not having it, we're not on a search-and-mutilate, not this time—"

Overreacting a bit. Garol didn't usually get emotional about the Judicial function, and it was a little funny to see him bouncing around so far outside of his normal operating mode of depressed disgust. "So we don't know what Lowden told Koscuisko." And it was just the sort of thing that would appeal to Lowden's sense of humor, too.

Garol had his eyes fixed on the scene outside. Trying to identify what it was that he found so fascinating, Jils followed his line of sight and discovered Andrej Koscuisko just entering the loading bay from the far end.

"Well, I'm going to find out."

Garol was halfway across the room before she could say anything, but his intent was screamingly obvious. Jils hurried to follow him. She wanted to know how Koscuisko was holding up after what she'd told him about his new post with Verlaine.

And she had a good notion that Koscuisko wasn't about to chat with her over a friendly game of relki, not even if it was to take a month and a half to get to Port Burkhayden rather than a day and a half or so.

Security might have heard Garol coming, or they might just have been quick to respond to Garol's surely unexpected entrance. They were at attention one way or the other; Jils didn't think Stildyne had seen Koscuisko yet, he was still talking with Pyotr. Garol was just intercepting Koscuisko when she caught up with him, well short of Koscuisko's waiting people.

"Your Excellency." The formal address always sounded disconcertingly casual coming from Garol. Koscuisko had stopped where he stood, looking past them to where his Security detachment waited for him. "I'm Vogel, your Excellency, Bench intelligence specialist second sub seven Garol Vogel. We've met once before, but only briefly. His Excellency may not remember. We'll be traveling together to Burkhayden, sir."

Koscuisko looked at Garol with suspicion and hostility evident in his pale eyes. He didn't look well. "The Captain has told me that you require my professional services. Specialist Ivers."

Acknowledging his nod in her direction with a careful salute, Jils realized just how good Lowden really was. Garol did in fact have a job for Koscuisko that required Koscuisko's "professional services," and Lowden need only have said that much and no more to create the absolutely opposite impression of what was to be asked of him in Koscuisko's mind.

"Well, actually, it's the Danzilar prince who insisted upon his Excellency in person. Because the woman was very badly treated, and Paval I'shenko feels very strongly that the best surgeon Lowden's got should be the one to put her right."

Nor was there anything explicit in Garol's statement to make his question too obvious or his suspicion too clear. It was just the kind of thing that anybody could have said, offering further information about a mission that had—of course—been fully explained to Koscuisko already up front. Lowden had done no such thing: Jils knew it from Koscuisko's face.

"Mister Stildyne." Koscuisko's Chief of Security had joined them, posted behind Garol and Jils and waiting for Koscuisko's word. "I shall have a word for you, Chief, in a moment. Specialist Vogel. Be very careful what you say. Captain Lowden has given me to understand that I am needed for an interrogation, and I can only take your meaning as to the contrary."

"There may have been a bit of confusion on Lowden's part, sir. But Wyrlann isn't denying it, and the Bench doesn't Inquire into cases like this anyway, since the woman's just a service bond-involuntary." Carefully, carefully. Garol put his words simply and succinctly, as respectful of rank as Garol could be when nobody had given him any reason yet why he should not. "His Excellency is needed to perform reconstructive and restorative surgery. Nothing more."

Koscuisko grimaced suddenly in ferocious pain and turned his head to one side, down and away, the white of his underblouse gleaming unexpectedly between his neck and the dark of his duty blouse. Garol took a half-step closer with his hands held quiet at his sides. "Are you all right, sir?"

Stildyne stepped forward three paces, as though he would have got between them if he could have managed it. "Give us a few eighths, Specialist," Stildyne suggested, the deference due Garol's unspecified rank as evident as Stildyne's determination to be rid of the two of them. "His Excellency will be along presently."

Retreating a full step, Garol bowed politely to the silent figure of Andrej Koscuisko. "Take your time," Garol agreed. "The sooner we leave the sooner we get there, though." There was nothing more either of them could possibly say. She and Garol returned to the courier ship, leaving Koscuisko to sort things out with Stildyne. Garol was swearing under his breath; she could guess at what he was probably saying to himself, because of long experience of Garol's moods.

Needs a wire, he does. Needs a full energy charge, about gut-level. Needs the Sisprayan plague. Yeah. Needs a bullet.

So was he talking about Lowden, or Koscuisko? Lowden for deliberately creating the certainty of an abhorrent duty in Koscuisko's mind when quite the opposite was in fact intended? Or Koscuisko himself, since Garol's stated opinion was that there wasn't anything to choose between the two of them?

"Hey." She didn't need him in this mood, especially not at the beginning of a trip. "So it's all right, now, okay? Come on."

Safely inside the ship, now, Garol turned toward her suddenly and put his fist to the wall the way he did when he was so unhappy that only inflicting gratuitous physical pain on himself could make him feel any better. It was a problem that Garol had; they'd been living with it for years. "All right nothing, Jils, you've got to know better than that. You saw the look on that sorry jack's face—it's not all right at all. What a cheap trick, jerking on a man's chain like that—"

This was almost funny. "That's good, coming from you, Garol. Just the day before yesterday, was it, that Koscuisko was a deeply disturbed sicko who wasn't worth the consideration you'd give the average asswipe? Remember?"

Being reminded of his own excesses always drove him wild. Garol rolled his eyes in utter exasperation. "He's a man, and any man deserves a little basic decency. You saw his face, Jils, come on, you saw it, the same as I did."

"Yeah, right, sure, and he's probably kind to children and small animals, too. As if that means squat. I don't believe you." He was letting things get a little out of control, if anybody asked her. Which they hadn't. "Ready to promote him to human being just because Lowden didn't give him all the facts?"

"There's more to it than that." He was calmer now, but stubborn still. "I don't like the way that Stildyne tiptoes around him. Something's going on that no one's telling us, and that could be dangerous, Jils, when it's somebody like Koscuisko that we're talking about."

Whatever it was that had upset him so deeply he wasn't able to quite put his finger on it. At least not yet, or he'd tell her. "We've got company, Garol. Go start the shutdowns. I'll make nice with our guests for you."

Garol stomped off ungraciously toward the control room, and Jils sighed to herself, arranging her face even as she did so.

Even Koscuisko—hostile and resentful as he was bound to be—was company to be preferred to Garol, when Garol was in a mood.

*   *   *

This was not good. Stildyne knew how much pleasure Captain Lowden took in setting up his little pranks; before Koscuisko's arrival and subsequent agreement with the Captain had put an end to it, many of Lowden's best gags had resulted in assessment of two-and-twenty on up for whichever bond-involuntary happened to be closest at time of occurrence.

"Your Excellency, I'm—"

Sorry, Stildyne started to say. *Sorry you had to stay. Sorry I'm not going with you to Port Burkhayden, but we both know that Pyotr would be Chief of Security if he weren't under Bond. I'm not sure he doesn't outrank me even with his Bond. You'll be fine with Pyotr.*

Unfortunately Koscuisko wasn't having any of it. Stildyne wondered, just that fraction of a moment too late, what other humorous trap Captain Lowden might have set recently.

"Tell me then that this nonsense of refusing *Sceppan* is also a lie." Koscuisko challenged him directly, his voice flat and cold and wickedly cutting. "And I will say no more about it. I am waiting to hear, Mister Stildyne."

Koscuisko wouldn't hear what he was waiting to hear. Because that much was true. Why hadn't he said anything to Koscuisko before?/Koscuisko had been drunk, that was why. Koscuisko had had problems of his own.

"Very well. If you want to hear more lies." It wasn't going to be pleasant any way he looked at it. Maybe it would be just as well to get it done and over with here and now. Koscuisko was leaving for Port Burkhayden; Stildyne wouldn't see him for more than a week. That could give Koscuisko time to accept the idea and become reconciled to it. One way or the other Stildyne wasn't about to back down.

"You are offered the post of First Officer. It is the culmination of your career," Koscuisko noted; quite calmly, really. "And you know as well as I do that such slots are created only by attrition or new commission, and there are precious few new commissions in these troubled times. How long will it be before there is another chance for you?"

So far, so good. "If his Excellency wishes to state that he finds my performance unacceptable, then do so to my face.

Because otherwise I'm not going. I have responsibilities here.''

That concept was still as new and alien to him as when he had first realized that he was going to refuse *Sceppan*, and why. Responsibilities. He, himself, Brachi Stildyne, every man for himself and the devil take the hindmost. Koscuisko was at fault. Koscuisko was at fault for so much.

''Stildyne, we have to go, I do not have time to dance with you. You must know how things are. You do not imagine they will change. Why will you not go to *Sceppan*?''

Yes, he knew how things were. On *Sceppan* he would have respect, responsibilities, the safety of a crew and the effectiveness of its fighting troops as his to nurture and protect. On *Ragnarok* he had—what?

''I knew that I was going to decline the promotion when First Officer put it in front of me, your Excellency. And that was before anything changed your plans.'' On *Ragnarok* he had nothing but grief. No perks left to being Chief Warrant Officer over bond-involuntary Security when Koscuisko disapproved so strongly of anyone taking advantage of sexual access to them.

No particular degree of rapport with Koscuisko himself, who was not inclined to admire other men and who emphatically resented being openly admired himself. Nothing. ''You were going home. There would be nobody to look after God-salt and the others.''

Nothing but grief and worry. Koscuisko had tricked him over the years, somehow. Lured him into feeling responsible for the Bonds, while he wasn't looking. Into wanting to do what he could do to protect them from Lowden's sense of humor for no other reason than that they were not permitted to protect themselves.

''For the gentlemen you have made this decision?'' He'd caught Koscuisko off guard, startled him. That was funny. Andrej Koscuisko, caught off guard. ''Mister Stildyne. I am astonished at you. I had thought—''

He knew what Koscuisko had thought.

Am I never to be forgiven for having once desired you?

Stildyne knew better than to say the words, though.

Koscuisko turned the phrase away, and continued.

"And yet they will not be unshielded here now, because I have the bargain arranged with Captain Lowden. Therefore you need not turn away from the opportunity."

"Yes, right, and you can do it all yourself. You've done it all yourself these years past, haven't you?" A man could get exasperated. "Sorry, sir, it's not negotiable. If you want to get rid of me you'll have to bring a complaint before First Officer. Why don't you load the courier, sir, and leave me to do my job."

He wasn't staying just because he liked short lithe intransigent blonds. If he liked Dolgorukij he knew where he could buy them, at least for a few hours, even if they did run a little high to market—Dolgorukij men in service houses were relatively uncommon, but not impossible to find. Stildyne had hired his share of them over the course of the past four years. It never seemed to make dealing with Koscuisko any easier: So obviously whatever it was about Koscuisko wasn't just wanting him.

Stildyne wasn't interested in thinking it through more thoroughly than that. He had enough problems.

"As long as we are clear, you and I," Koscuisko said thoughtfully. "Because you are quite right, I am not proof against Captain Lowden, and to the extent to which I have implied that you have not protected these gentlemen beyond my ability to do so I apologize to you, Mister Stildyne, from my heart. I am a very great sinner. It was not my intent to attempt to deny respect to you."

That probably meant something, and he would probably figure it out. Sooner or later. For now he had to get Koscuisko on board the courier and away.

"Don't think twice about it." *And whatever you do don't try to explain anything.* Koscuisko's explanations never seemed to explain. They only made things worse. "You're wanted on courier, sir."

For a moment Stildyne thought that Koscuisko was going to open his mouth, say something. For a moment.

Then Koscuisko apparently decided that it would be not only expedient but appropriate to yield the last word, because he only nodded.

Stildyne stepped aside.

Koscuisko crossed the decking toward the courier and climbed the ramp into its waiting belly, and never once looked back.

That's the way to do it, Stildyne me lad, Stildyne told himself.

Never look back.

You've bought these boots now well and truly, and paid cash money, too.

It's up to you to break them in and wear them.

◇ Four

So this was Port Burkhayden, in Meghilder space.

Andrej chafed the palms of his hands together irritably in the bleak bare prep room of the loosely-to-be-described-as hospital. It was cold, and the light was thin, when it managed to clear the heavy dark clouds that seemed to be blanketing most of this local geographic. Cold made Andrej uncomfortable. He snapped at the thin young man at the doorway without taking thought for the intruder's clothing.

"Yes, what is it now? Has the heating system also been repossessed? What?"

Security appeared from the other room as soon as he spoke, and Andrej could hear other people in the corridor outside. The intruder himself looked much more frightened than apologetic; he could hardly be on staff, Andrej realized, not dressed like that. Unfeeling of him to threaten so, when he knew perfectly well that the news of his identity had reached the hospital well before he had.

"His Excellency's pardon." So purely parochial an accent Andrej hadn't heard in a long time. He had a particular weakness for Nurail all the same, because of Robert, because of the mettle of the victims of the Domitt Prison, because of too many miscellaneous instances to be remembered. "It's a mistake I've made, my maistress gave me leave to see a woman, if the officer will excuse."

Staff Security was outside, behind the young man. His own Security were standing between Andrej and the intruder now,

71

looking very stern indeed. Unfriendly hands reached through the open doorway to pull the young man out into the hall with rough efficiency. Andrej frowned to see it; he could smell a beating in the making.

"We're very sorry, your Excellency. Some sort of a mistake, we'll be sure his Excellency isn't disturbed any further."

And a raised voice, outside, the same accent. "Disturbed, you with the collar on, what do you mean disturbed, he's nothing to do with my Megh—"

It was so easy to lose control of situations like this. Sighing in resignation—not unmixed with amusement—Andrej waved his Security away from him, beckoning to the staff security. "No, there is no problem. Bring to me this person, I will talk to him."

"Well—"

Andrej could all but read the scan in the staff security's mind. First, an embarrassing incursion, unexpected, makes us look bad, we'll just see about that. Second, strong language, shows disrespect—he's earned it for himself, now. Third, on the other hand, he hasn't really done anything so very wrong, and who knows what Uncle Andrej means when he says "talk?"

"And see if you can obtain for me a glass of rhyti, from the kitchen. If you would. My gentlemen and I have not had a chance to take a meal since we made planetfall. Do you think it can be managed?"

Torture seemed incompatible with fastmeal from one end of the Bench to the other. An appeal for physical comforts on his people's behalf frequently had the positive effect of both reassuring host Security and recruiting their sympathies at the same time. It was a natural impulse of the sentient mind, one that Andrej knew and appreciated.

"Of course, sir, right away." Once again it worked for him; and the chill in the air was diminishing, so the facilities staff had got some warmth redirected at last. All to the good. "This person does have clearance for a visit, your Excellency, but his Excellency's best judgment takes precedence, of course."

The young man reappeared at the doorway, escorted almost

benignly by the staff security. Looking confused, as well he might.

"Thank you, shift leader." He had an hour's wait, maybe more, while the surgery was prepared. He was scheduled for pre-op, but he had nothing in particular to do until then; the hospital administration had to be given time to round up all the requisite staff.

The patient document was waiting for him in the reader at the window, but Andrej thought that there was time to see what the matter was with this young man. He had already studied all the information that Vogel had been able to provide. He was fairly secure that he knew what was needed in that area.

"Come and tell me, you, what is your name. What woman did you come to see, and why?"

Speaking as gently, as reassuringly as he could, still Andrej wondered why he bothered. A man with a reputation like his could try all he liked and still be incapable of convincing that there was nothing to fear from him.

"Skelern. Hanner. Your Excellency." Scale-airn. Not an uncommon name, he'd seen it before, if the Standard script spelling of it did not quite describe the sound of it to Andrej's ear. "It's just a woman that I came to see, she lies here somewhere. Not to go in where I'm not wanted, your Excellency."

There was a delicate balance there between the native distrust of all Nurail for authority and the young man's quite sensible awareness of his vulnerability within the unequal power structure of Port Burkhayden. "Of course not, nor was any such thing suggested. Do you work at the service house?"

Oh, the affront, so quickly hidden away out of embarrassment. "No, if it please the officer." And be damned before he would; that was the unspoken part. "A gardener—the Tavart is my maistress. Iaccary Textile and Cordage, it is. I only bring Megh the trimmings, when they're of a sort to remind her. It gives her a little joy to remember the hill country."

"Is she from the hill country? I hadn't thought there were Borderers, at Burkhayden."

Hanner had an honest face, open. Obvious. It showed his

thoughts quite clearly: surprise that Andrej connected hill-stations with Borderers; speedy self-reminder that—as everybody knew—what Black Andrej didn't know about Nurail after the Domitt Prison was not worth knowing.

Andrej had never quite understood why he was "black" Andrej, since he was as blond as any of the fairer run of Nurail—or more so. There was a descriptive element to the word that had nothing to do with hue—black for something that was destructive, something that was powerful.

Nurail had black uncles and other uncles, depending on which had been their mothers' favorite or oldest brother, the one with the most influence over their lives. Andrej had been Uncle Andrej, and he had been Black Andrej, but to the best of his knowledge he'd never been honored with the title of "black uncle," and perhaps that was just as well. For his ego.

"Not from Burkhayden, your Excellency. She's from Marleborne, but she's all alone in the service house—she's the only service Bond imprisoned there. And any Nurail could be my sister, his Excellency knows that."

Or my brother, or my uncle, or my niece. A Nurail proverb of recent coinage, a response to the Bench's determined dispersion of the Nurail nations and the destruction of so many of them.

So Hanner brought Megh flowers, and tried to be a brother to her. "Come back later, Hanner, you don't want to see her now. I'll send a chit to your employer." Especially if he was fond of the woman, he didn't want to see her now.

Hanner frowned and pursed his lips. "Please let me see her, your Excellency, such frightful things I've heard, I'll not be able to get leave again with the Danzilar to be coming. And I'm afraid for her."

Well, it was a reasonable point, and good marks in Hanner's favor as well. Andrej had known enough other reasonable, sensible Nurail who had not quite found the courage within themselves to challenge a torturer on anything. The weather. The brod-toast. Anything. Still—

"She's not to be gaped at for a curiosity. If she had next of kin—but I must insist. You may not see her now. Wait until she is somewhat recovered, and can speak to you.''

On the other hand maybe Hanner wasn't a sensible Nurail at all, merely a stubborn one. The color mounted in his brown face, and his dark eyes flashed with a species of sudden unexpected defiance. ''Then I claim her by the Narrow Pass and by the Ice Traverse, your Excellency. By her father's weave and her mother's weave I claim her. And you'll let me see my sister.''

Andrej could hear the choking sound that St. Clare made behind Andrej's back in shock at this display. He was a little taken aback himself; but not so much as Hanner seemed to be dismayed by his own rash demand, to judge by the way that the color fled his cheeks.

This did change things.

If Hanner knew her family, her father's weave and her mother's weave, then he had a right—in Nurail terms—to be considered as her brother, even if only in a limited sense. He could have made them up, true. But under other circumstances he might be in considerable trouble with the Port Authority for so much as stating them.

And there was a significantly powerful prejudice among Nurail against citing both at once. As if it were equivalent to displaying a sexual act in public, more or less. They could be such prudish people, for all the blunt cheerful explicitness of the language.

''Very well.'' Vogel's report had only discussed the worst of her injuries; there was no particular reason for Andrej to suspect that she was badly marked, as well as injured. Except that when bullies like the *Ragnarok*'s First Lieutenant beat a woman they generally made an horrific mess of her face, and Andrej couldn't help but feel that no brother could easily bear sight of the evidence to what a sister had suffered from such a brute.

It was hard enough when one was not related, and had the benefit of having seen it all before. One never became inured to brutality. If one was lucky. ''Robert, you take Hanner here into the next room for a bit, keep him out of staff security's way. Don't worry, we'll give a shout when fastmeal comes, and if there is fried cold-meal mush you shall sort it out between the two of you.''

He would have a look at the patient's documents, he would have a look at the patient. He would do the best he could for her, poor woman. Poor anonymous woman, poor slave, with only a thin—dirty—and incautious gardener to take her part against the misfortunes and the injustices that had befallen her.

''Come along, then, Hanner, you heard the officer.'' St. Clare's voice was surprisingly harsh from behind him, and Hanner swallowed nervously, but came meekly enough. Good man; Andrej approved. St. Clare had a sister somewhere, Andrej knew. That was why Robert was so painfully sensitive about the abuse that service bond-involuntaries suffered.

Other bond-involuntaries that Andrej had been privileged to know treated service Bonds as members of one family in token of their mutual slavery, calling them all ''cousin.'' Robert's pain was a little more personal and immediate than that. Any given service bond-involuntary could very well be somebody's sister. But somewhere out there was his.

His sister Megh?

No, Andrej told himself, a little embarrassed at his romanticizing. He was imagining things. It was a common name, whether or not he was misremembering something he'd heard from Robert eight years ago and more. But any coincidence of names would only make St. Clare even moodier. Best to get the two of them out of anybody's way until the gardener could be sent safely home.

And then he would see whether a public-funded hospital in a Nurail port could find decent healing work for a Dolgorukij torturer: and keep himself too busy to think about his future, about Captain Lowden, about the Fleet that had created G'herm Wyrlann and would protect him for as long as he held rank.

Center House, Port Burkhayden. The place was swarming with Danzilar's advance party, even at this late hour of the evening. The grand foyer looked very much like a theatrical stage in mid-shift, to Jils Ivers. Garol had been in a state ever since he'd first heard about the Lieutenant's little escapade; and for herself Jils had already decided that Wyrlann deserved everything that Garol was likely to say to him.

The *Ragnarok*'s First Lieutenant had sent his own Security to meet the courier—a gesture possibly calculated to ingratiate himself with them. It hadn't worked, Garol's ingratiation threshold being as high as it was. Now it was time for Wyrlann—waiting for them amid the ladders and the carpet-layers, the glaziers and the technicians—to face that uncomfortable fact.

"Good greeting. Ivers, isn't it? Right. And Vogel. Welcome to Port Burkhayden. Had a nice transit?"

One thing was immediately obvious from Wyrlann's self-satisfied expression, his easy—if somewhat condescending—banter. He didn't think he had anything to apologize for.

"Yeah, well, not too bad. Lieutenant." Garol even in his foulest moods did try to stay away from provoking confrontation. It wasn't out of respect or diffidence, no. He just hated to waste energy. "Have you got the survey forms completed? Let's go, get it out of the way and all that."

Wyrlann coughed, as if embarrassed. "There's been a bit of an unexpected problem. A little local unrest."

She'd just bet there'd been unrest. Garol wasn't taking the hint, though, which meant that Garol was ignoring it, just to be difficult. "To be expected, when a port's in transit. Well, we'll just sign off on the survey, and we can be out of each other's way."

There was a third party involved in the transaction, though he hadn't said anything one way or the other until now: Fleet Liaison Officer Artigen, a well-respected career man, good to have on site in an unsettled environment. "With the Lieutenant's permission. I felt it best to advise the Lieutenant not to complete the survey until the arrival of additional Security, Specialist Vogel. We've had a predictable upswing in anti-Fleet sentiment these last few days."

"Predictable when ranking officers make like eight-to-the-Standard bruisers? That the kind of 'predictable' you mean?"

Garol made no effort to keep his voice down, and there was no mistaking the sentiment among the local workmen. Wyrlann evidently felt the hostility as personally directed, for whatever reason.

"Listen, Vogel, I'll thank you to stick to your agenda, and keep yourself out of things that don't concern you. 'Bench intelligence specialist' is all very well, but I have to tell you, I don't like your attitude."

Jils sighed. If she'd had a marker she could have tossed it. Wyrlann had done it, now.

"And I don't like your face, Lieutenant. Your face, your voice, your behavior, your Captain. You disgust me, you disgust them, and Artigen was right to keep your sorry ass off the street, because you deserve a wire, and the only reason I hope you don't get one soon is that nobody deserves to have to pay for it, transmit received?"

And all of it in a perfectly reasonable tone of voice, not raised, not lowered, no hint of anger or even much emotion. Of course Garol sounded just as if he was merely stating a few facts. Because that was exactly what he was doing, no more, no less.

"Ah, if I could make a suggestion, Specialist Vogel—" Fleet Liaison Officer Artigen offered, tactfully. "The Lieutenant had completed the primary surveys prior to the, ah, controversial event. In light of the fact that it was due to my advice that it's incomplete, I'm sure Captain Lowden will accept your best judgment on the balance."

Wyrlann had been about to make an issue of Garol's lack of professional courtesy, so much was obvious. But Artigen had said the magic word. The magic name, rather; as soon as Artigen mentioned Captain Lowden, Wyrlann paled and shut his mouth, transferring his attention to the new parquetry underfoot. Interesting.

"Yeah, I guess. Anybody going to want to shoot at me? What do we have left to do?"

"Perhaps best if we simply went alone, Specialist Vogel. They don't know who you are, or Specialist Ivers, of course. And I'm expected to make the tour on a regular basis. There's the hospital, the service facility, the Port Authority, the civil holding facility. That sort.''

"Whattaya say, Jils? Take a walk? Fun-filled excursion to all the attractions, beautiful exotic port like Burkhayden? Naked maidens, dancing boys? Damn. It's starting to rain again, isn't it?''

Maybe if he went out in the rain for an hour or two it would take the gain down a couple of notches. Cool things off all around. ''No, I'll just have to stay behind and do the administrative work while you run off to the service house under the transparent pretext of an inspection. Let me know if they've got a bone-bender on staff.''

It was a particular weakness of hers. She got her spine worked by a bone-bender every chance she had, whether or not Garol and the Jurisdiction Standard alike believed it did any good. There was plenty for her to do here, though. She needed to inspect the quarters assigned to them.

She needed to trail in to the house-net, to see what it could tell her about the last few days. She needed to assess the snoopers, and make sure that if there were any left that the Danzilar prince's Security didn't already know about they were hidden well enough that they would never be found.

But as Karol turned to leave with Artigen, Wyrlann raised his voice. ''If you see Koscuisko at the hospital.'' There was a note of nasty gloating there, as if Wyrlann felt he was paying Karol off on exponential margins. ''Tell him there's been a priority transmit—we received it two eights ago. His extension's been approved. But Fleet won't reassign him in the foreseeable future, in light of Captain Lowden's critical requirement for the resource.''

Extension?

Koscuisko, on extension?

Garol was waiting for her cue, but Jils couldn't think of anything to say. Wyrlann turned around and sauntered off, smiling, content that he'd brought bad news and enjoying the impact it made. Jils met Garol's eyes, helpless to respond. What could make Koscuisko desperate enough to extend his contract with the Fleet, even knowing as he must have done that he had no hope of getting clear from Lowden if he did so?

Verlaine.

"Less effort all around if he'd just cut his throat and be done with it." Garol commented, to cover for her confusion, she guessed. "I'll tell him, Jils."

And Garol had to know how hollow the jest really was, the number of times Koscuisko had tried to simply cut his throat and be done with it. Except that he had never quite succeeded; partly because he had been prevented, but also at least partly because he wanted to be free but not to die. Too desperate, in his mind, to be able to accept what he could not change, what he was not permitted to change.

Too clear-eyed and well-grounded to be able to ignore the fact that it was his own actual—permanent—death that he was essaying. Too sane to want to die enough to make it work, not while there was a slim chance or hope of escape, somewhere.

"Thanks, Garol, I'll be doing."

An extension was the only thing that could keep him from Verlaine, though it was so extreme a step that she had honestly not thought of it until now.

It was an irrational impulse on her part, an unreasonable conviction.

But suddenly Jils Ivers knew that if Koscuisko finally succeeded in taking the final escape after this news it would be herself that she would blame.

For murder.

Andrej stood at the inside of a conference-oval in the hospital surgery's prep room, looking around him. "Who have we got, then? Gentles, if you would be so kind, bearing in mind that I'm the hired man from out of town."

It was a short staff, but it would have to do. Half of them were Nurail: That was a plus, if he could rely on them to know how hill-people differed from other folk. Their biggest problem was that it was the middle of the night, well past third-meal. People would be prepared to sleep, not to operate.

And yet the sooner they were started the better chance they had. The woman had been waiting for them too long already. Nobody dared wait a moment longer.

"Orthopedics, your Excellency. Heron Jamoch." One of the weaves was Heron Black-pelt, Andrej remembered. But he had no right to the knowledge. Though he had not taken it by force it had come to him as the last desperate gasp of a dying man, unwilling to let his mother's voice be silenced forever.

"Soft tissue displacement. Sonders Connlin."

Orthopedics had work, but not too much work; soft tissue displacement had the uglier task. "Thank you, Sonders Connlin, you and I have our work cut out for us. Yes?"

"Internal, sir, renal trauma and respiratory malfunction. Aan Jardle. Some experience with smooth muscle tearing, but not enough."

Wyrlann had kicked the woman when she'd been down. In the belly. There was smooth muscle damage, on top of the gross insult to her womb. The sacred cradle. Andrej shook himself just a bit, to try to get centered.

"We are lucky to have any smooth muscle experience at all, Jardle. I'm a beginner in that field, I'm afraid. We haven't heard from everyone yet, though. Who is left?" Probably sensory and micromovement. Or perhaps merely gross trauma.

"Gynecological, as the officer please."

There was more of a surprise there than just the specialty. Andrej hadn't hoped for gynecology; it would make things much easier on them all—well, easier on him, at any rate. But that wasn't the sum of it. The phrase was familiar, but underneath it—what did he think he recognized?

"And your name, sir," Andrej prompted. Gynecology was the oldest person here, quite possibly pushing sixty years Standard to look at him. That meant something. What was it?

"Barit Howe. His Excellency won't remember me. Administrative staff at Fleet Orientation Station Medical, sir. Pending the dawning of the Day."

Reborn.

Barit Howe had been a bond-involuntary, and had lived to

see the Day dawn at last. It was no wonder that Andrej's
subconscious mind had insisted he knew something quite important about that man—

Bowing, Andrej fumbled for words with which to express
the respect due a man who could survive for so long the life
to which the Bonds had been condemned. "A very great
honor, Master Howe. I am in your presence humbled and
silent." Though of course he couldn't afford to be, not liter-
ally. He was senior in rank; he was expected to coordinate
the surgical attack.

"Very good. I have heard your names; and it may be ar-
rogance on my part, but I believe that you already know who
I am. Neurosurgical. Andrej Koscuisko. And a baseline com-
petence in general practice, which we do not for this exercise
particularly need. Shall we to the problem at hand turn attention?"

The woman Megh, Wyrlann's victim. Her injuries had been
stabilized, but the hospital had waited to encourage aggressive
healing for the arrival of someone who knew how to repair
the nerve damage before it scarred over. Four days ago. Not
quite five. It could not wait for very much longer.

"If his Excellency will review the material onscreen,"
Barit Howe suggested. Respectfully: But Howe was a reborn
man. The suggestion was not very far from the mark as an
order. "We had taken the liberty of preparing a proposed
approach. We didn't know we were going to get a surgeon
with your qualifications. We need to fine-tune this a bit."

No, they hadn't expected him. His being here was his
cousin Danzilar's idea, and very sound reasoning on his
cousin's part too, as far as Andrej could tell. "Of course. With
the lower body cavity let us be started."

The sooner they finished review of the problem the sooner
they could be started to work.

And there was a good deal of work to be done here.

Unfortunately the first tasks fell to Andrej.

It was an offense to approach such a woman in the surgical
machine rather than on his knees in reverence. Andrej could

only hope that the holy Mother would forgive the impertinence, because there was no other way in which he could approach the injured bond-involuntary, if he hoped to do her any help instead of further injury.

Secure within the all-embracing environment of the surgical machine, safely insulated from the pitiful reality of her damaged body, Andrej began his calibration exercises, a litany from his childhood uninvited—stubborn—in his distracted mind.

Forgive us, Saint Polaka, that was raped with the fencepost of the impious. That was raped by the company of the impious in violation of all decency. That was raped by the member of a horse at the hands of the impious.

Polaka was a Sarvaw saint, and her litany didn't represent her literal martyrdom—which had actually been a fairly mundane gang-rape if he remembered his religious history correctly.

The litany was more global than just young Saint Polaka, though. Collected into it were all of the atrocities committed against a captive Sarvaw population by its Dolgorukij overlords less than three hundred years ago.

Andrej had learned it in his childhood as part of the observances during the days of contrition, when it was considered to be pious to pretend that one felt guilty for the sins of one's ancestors while continuing to enjoy the fruits of their crimes.

There had been a joke to the litany in the cheerful days of his innocence, an adolescent speculation on what the martyr would look like if represented with all of the purported agents of her glorious death. He had not then believed that such things had been done.

He had not then believed that such things could be done.

He had not then believed that such things were still done, and in the same sweet breathing world that he looked on. He knew better, now, and hoped that the saint would accept this Nurail Megh for her own cherished daughter and grant him grace to salve her wounds in shamed humility.

It was time to begin.

He had no faith. He had so offended the holy Mother over the years that it made no sense to even try to pray any more. Perhaps this once, though, she would listen, because it was not for himself that he petitioned, and there was no under-standing of her mercy to be had. Andrej closed his eyes within the waiting stillness of the surgical machine and stood a sup-plicant in the presence of a deity in whom he no longer quite believed, making his prayer.

Asking for the privilege of being used as the instrument of blessing. Asking for a good exercise without flaw or fault, because there was no room for fault or flaw.

Asking for the holy Mother's blessing on the work of his hands, and that of the rest of the surgical team. Asking for a good recovery, health of body and of spirit, because nothing that they could do to heal her body would avail them if her spirit would not accept contrition on her behalf. Asking for full functionality for the woman's sake, for the sake of the thin young gardener who claimed a brother's right to care what became of her.

Then he put it all out of his mind: Saint Polaka, the sacred cradle, the holy Mother's mysteries, all. He set his mind to the simple certitudes of blood and sinew, nerve and bone, and dissolved himself into the surgical machine to suspend his very existence for as long as she should need for him to be the mind of the machine and do his surgery.

The gray filament wires slipped gently, without injury, be-tween cells around the lidded eye of the unconscious woman, to seek the optic nerve-bundle at the back of her eye and massage a range of sensors there back into alignment.

Andrej forgot his life and went to work.

Robert St. Clare stood for hours in mute misery behind the officer where he sat in the by-room of the operating theater.

It was his sister. It was Megh.

As much as he dreaded the sight of what the Lieutenant had done to her he could not keep himself from straining to see, all of his love and all of his grief focussed hungrily on the pitiful limbs of her, naked and helpless, bruised and bloodied and broken, in the operating theater below. Days and days it had been; they had cleaned her up carefully, but the evidence was still so terrible that he could curse his own eyesight for the keenness of it.

And still he could not bear to turn away. His sister. His Megh. The only one of his family that yet lived, but there was an end to his father's weave, because what the Lieutenant had done to her could not be made right.

Not after three days.

What the Lieutenant had done to her he had done to her father, to her father's mother, to the father of their father's mother, to the whole family lineage of the Narrow Pass. She would be whole, if she could be made so, but she could never bear a child of her body.

What the Lieutenant had done to her . . .

"Your Excellency." The query from the theater sounded, one of the doctors below asking for advice. "Not quite happy with respiration, sir. Can an increased dose of elam be risked at this point?"

Oh, if only she wore the mask, he would not have to look on her. But she could breathe on her own, so her face was uncovered and ghastly in the bright light. The officer shifted.

"How much longer need we maintain her on cynerdahl? Well. It will be safe to increase to nine parts. But let's try not to go ten, if it can be managed."

The officer's subspecialty, in pharmacology. Psychopharmacology, but the basics were the same. Settling back in the hammock-slung seat, Koscuisko chanced to glance up at him; what, had he been too quiet, too still?

"Robert. You are suffering. What is the matter, please?"

He was suffering. Yes. It was true. He could not look at Megh without rage in his heart for the beast that had fouled her. And the beast was an officer, against whom he could rage all he liked in the quiet of his mind but in whose presence he was a slave.

"It's hard to look at." Choking the words out, Robert could only hope Koscuisko understood. And then hoped Koscuisko didn't understand too much. "Sir. With respect. It's something about just the fact that she's Nurail."

And my sister. He wanted to say it, and he could not. He had no claim to Megh while he was still Bonded. He could not say. He could not claim her. He could only make generalizations—

"And no one to avenge her, because after all it's the Lieutenant. Sir. But it cries out for revenge. If it please the officer."

He knew the uneasy prickling at the back of his neck, the tingling tension in his skull as his governor tried to decide if what he was saying violated his orders and whether he should be punished. But he was speaking to Andrej Koscuisko, and in the presence of Andrej Koscuisko he was safe from the governor. Even from that.

Koscuisko was watching him, wary and measuring; but Koscuisko did not send him away. "Talk to me, Robert. Tell me how it is that she should be avenged. And I will tell you how it would be, on Azanry."

Pretending that it was an abstract sort of issue, a discussion initiated to pass the time. For the officer's amusement. Making the words that ached in his heart an obedient answer, nothing treasonous there.

The governor quieted.

"Well. When a man's done a crime, it's for him to make up the loss, in the hill country." Emboldened, he came forward to stand next to the officer, closer to the clearwall. Where he could watch Megh. Where he could see her. "And killing is one thing, but this . . . It's another. A killing can be made right with a child. But how can it be made right if a man has murdered a woman's children, in such a way?"

He wasn't sure he made sense. He knew what he was saying. A killing robbed the weave, and a man could make up for it by making the weave whole with a child of his body. What was more precious to a man than his own childer?

"Robert, you seem to say that if I killed her brother I would make amends by—engaging with her?"

That was it precisely, though to hear the sound of the officer's voice he could not quite believe it. Robert could only nod, eyes fixed in misery on the scene below. His sister. His Megh. Oh, his poor darling, and naked in front of all of these people, with no one to care that she would feel shamed by it . . .

"Practical, really. Sir. If you think on it. You've got to convince her that you're really sorry, first." Children were the wealth of the weave, after all. And that was the bottom of what killing meant, a killing robbed the weave. A weave could be made whole. "But a rape means an injury, if the officer please. And I heard you say. To Doctor Howe, there."

Oh, careful, careful. How could he say it, and not reproach his officer? Koscuisko, who had been a good maister to him, though neither of them had chosen their roles. Koscuisko would understand. Koscuisko would not reproach him. The officer frowned, watching below.

"I admit I am not hopeful." Because of the rape, because of the manner of it. Robert could not think. He could barely breathe. "And still it may come out right. It seems odd to me, Robert, that any crime would be worse than a killing, is it indeed so?"

Oh, it was so. It was so exactly. A killing took one life. This thing took the lives that Megh might have had in her, and showed disrespect for a mother's womb. "In the hill country, your Excellency. Yes. There is no way to make such a crime right."

Except by killing. Except by killing the man who had done it, and killing his children, and killing his women lest they carried life that had sprung from a man who could do such a crime. And even then killing could not make it right. Killing solved nothing. Killing was a waste.

Killing the Lieutenant—

Robert waited long moments for the governor's rebuke to punish the thought, unbidden though it was.

There was no rebuke.

The governor was silent.

Was it because Robert knew he was right?

"Hill-country Nurail," the officer said, in a musing sort of voice. "Robert. I wonder. Do you believe he is in blood her brother? Oh, well, never mind. He'll do as well as any, I suppose. When this is over we to the gardener should go and speak. I have an idea. Because he is a gardener."

Down in the operating theater the orderlies were moving pieces of surgical equipment back toward the wall. One of the physicians was leaving the room, stripping off the sterile layer of her garment as she went. Two of the orderlies came to the side of the operating level, one to each side, and shook a sterile covering over her naked body, covering her at last. Megh, poor Megh. His sister. His own.

The officer spoke on. "And I have also promised that he could see her, once we were finished. Come along then, Robert. Let us go see Hanner home to his garden. And hope for a greenhouse."

Whatever that meant.

He had seen his sister. He had spoken his mind, and to Koscuisko who received it with care and respect. He could do nothing about the Lieutenant.

He wasn't sorry he'd thought it, even so.

It was very early in the morning, scarcely sunrise. Sylphe Tavart stood half-asleep, half in shock at her mother's side in the front business room, staring at the visitors that had come upon them so suddenly. Security, four of them, all of them tall, and green-sleeves—green piping on their sleeves, bond-involuntaries. So straight, so still, so perfect; and with them was their master.

"I must beg to be forgiven for this untimely intrusion." Andrej Koscuisko.

The language was so stiff as to almost be insincere. Coming from any other man, it might have been; but Sylphe could not imagine anything more perfect than the way in which Koscuisko chose his words. And how he spoke them. "I had not marked the time. And it is my fault to have kept your garden-master, may one hope he could be excused his morning's work? Because I have kept him up all night."

Andrej Koscuisko. Slim and elegant in his black uniform,

with the dew glittering in his blond hair. He was so fair it was almost unnatural, and if he was not beautiful he was important—more important than any man she'd ever seen so close up.

Her mother stirred in her seat. "It shall be so, your Excellency, since you wish it. But I hardly think you came all of this way simply to make excuses for my gardener. You'll pardon my saying so."

Skelern looked white in the face as well, but he was in the sun all day and was not so pale as Koscuisko. Skelern looked tired and worn. He'd been to see his friend in hospital, and Sylyphe had wanted to know all about his friend, but hadn't been able to quite puzzle out how to ask without giving the wrong impression.

"You are quite right." Koscuisko smiled a little with his ruddy mouth, tilting his head a bit back on his shoulder. A little to one side. He had a perfect smile. Perfect. "It's because the young man is a gardener, and our patient is Nurail. I hoped to beg some medication from you. And here I have come at too early an hour. I shall go away."

It *was* early. Her mother was in her fastmeal-wrap and Sylyphe had only put a smock on over her nightdress. It was a very decent smock. But she knew that she was in her nightdress. If Skelern should guess she would die of humiliation. And still she could not bear to leave the room.

"No sense in running an errand twice, your Excellency, and an honor to receive you at any time. Can I offer you something to eat? What could there be in my house for medication that isn't in hospital stores?"

Sylyphe could hardly stand still, she was so embarrassed. Her mother. Short and plain, and no cosmetics to disguise the pallor of her cheeks, the thin line of her mouth, the weathering of her face. Thin brown hair tied up in the single most unbecoming knot in known Space. And Andrej Koscuisko, dark and dangerous, with an aura that scintillated with the glamour of his craft. Those Bonds. Bound body and soul to the Inquisitor, to do his bidding at his word or suffer the consequences . . .

"If you will permit, Dame Tavart." The housemaster had come in with the beverage set, but Koscuisko paid no attention. How could her mother be so gauche as to offer an Inquisitor his fastmeal, in the first place? As if he was a salesman or a business partner, and not a senior Judicial officer with custody of a Writ to Inquire?

"There is an ointment in the pharmaceutical inventory that originated amongst the Nurail hill-people as a simple fatty salve infused with jellericia flowers. I have asked Gardener Hanner, and he says there may be jellericia flowers in your hand to grant, but more than that he very properly declines to say."

Why would that be? This was confusing. If Skelern had flowers . . . because they were her mother's flowers, perhaps. And Skelern didn't want them simply taken. That was odd of Skelern, why would he be protective of her mother's property, when he so much resented being made near-property himself? Why would Skelern care?

"I still don't understand. The flowers are yours, of course, with all of my goodwill." Sylyphe thought she knew which flowers, now. They were small and very red. The fragrance was subtle if distinct, and the blooms were difficult to force under artificial light. Skelern had worked very hard on the jellericia flowers. Would Koscuisko appreciate the effort? "If it's in the inventory there must be near-naturals to substitute, surely."

It was Andrej Koscuisko who asked for them. An Inquisitor could not easily be denied. "It's only because the patient is Nurail hill-station, Dame Tavart. Her subconscious mind will recognize the fragrance. It's very difficult to match with near-naturals. That is the particular reason that I ask. She will know the fragrance and be glad of it, and it will speed her healing."

It was true that there were fragrances that continued to deny the perfumer's art. It was a comfort item, then. Sylyphe couldn't help but wonder why a man of Koscuisko's rank should stir himself to such an extent for any patient, let alone a woman from the service house.

Sylyphe's mother nodded one final time, in acceptance or

agreement—Sylyphe couldn't tell which. Rising to her feet, Sylyphe's mother made her decision known.

"What you have requested shall be yours, your Excellency. I can't promise you the use of my gardener to assist you, though. I'm sorry, but his labor has been committed to other tasks. Is there someone at the hospital who can make up this ointment for you?"

Koscuisko didn't answer, not right away. Skelern cleared his throat, and when Koscuisko—raising one eyebrow, and looking as though he was amused at something—looked back over his shoulder toward where Skelern stood in the back of the room, Skelern spoke.

"The Tavart's lady-daughter knows how to handle the blooms, with the Tavart's permission. She could do it as well as I, your Excellency, or maybe better; she's mindful in such matters."

Sylyphe's mother stared. Sylyphe could see the color rise in Skelern's face even from where she stood. She would have blushed herself in sheer vexation to have her intimacy with a mere gardener exposed in so compromising a light before the Inquisitor, except that part of her was glowing with pleasure to hear Skelern's praise.

"If the daughter of the house would be graciously pleased to oblige, then," Koscuisko said, to her, to her directly. "I will be very much obliged to you both. For my patient's sake. And for your courtesy in receiving me at this early hour."

"Hanner will give you instruction, then, Sylyphe," her mother agreed. "And see to it that the kitchen gives him a good hot meal, since he's been up all night. Gardener Hanner, speak to my daughter, and then go rest yourself. You're needed at Center House tomorrow in the morning."

Dismissing her. In front of Andrej Koscuisko, dismissing her, and Hanner with her. But she was to have a job to do that would support the prestige and put forward the agenda of Iaccary Cordage and Textile at least as much as anything Hanner did. It was the first useful thing she'd had to do in a long time.

Andrej Koscuisko bowed to her as she went past him to go

out of the room, bowed to her almost as if she had been a grown woman and not just her mother's daughter. The daughter of the house.

It made up for her smock and her mother's thin brown hair.

Out of the room and down to the kitchens with Hanner in tow, to be sure that he got a good meal; and walking on air, every step of the way.

◇ Five

The power was off again tonight as it had been last night. Port Burkhayden ran on hydroelectric power drawn from the tides in the Worrical Bay several eights to the south; but since the Bench had decided to sell the world to the Danzilar prince no maintenance on the saltwater cylinders and the watergates had been done. The city was subject to brownout and blackout every night: That was what Garol had been told.

It suited Garol's purpose well enough.

The sky was overcast, and the clouds picked up what little light there was and diffused it over the port. It didn't make it easier to see where one was going, but it made it very obvious where one's goal was to be found if one was headed for an area with auxiliary power.

The public-funded. Then the service house.

Garol found his way into the public-funded through an open door at the back of its great silent kitchen. There were orderlies on staff, right enough, nursing a brewer and some trays of hotbreads under makeshift warmers rigged on temporary circuits; Garol went like a shadow or a stray thought, letting a breath of wind catch the half-open door and swing it wide, waiting patiently just beside a sheltering stack of produce-boxes as the orderly swore and cursed and pulled the door more firmly to.

The kitchen was an industrial one, built to serve round-the-clock for a hospital population fully one-half the size of all Burkhayden. The Bench had built up Port Burkhayden for a major commercial center, and relocated a significant population of Nurail to fill out its infrastructure.

It hadn't quite worked.

The Nurail that could find their way out of Port Burkhayden did, fleeing in small craft across the great dead reaches of the Baltrune vector to Gonebeyond space. Some of them made it, and some of them didn't, but it made little difference in Port Burkhayden. The result was the same. The port had never prospered since the Bench had made Meghilder a Bench concern.

So the hospital was larger than would be needed for twice Burkhayden's actual population, and less than the eighth part of its capacity had ever actually been used. The Bench had built the public-funded but lost interest in staffing it once it became clear that the Nurail at Burkhayden were not going to bide quietly and turn to trade. Huge, and stripped now of everything but the most basic equipment, so that the night-kitchen had to use laboratory ovens to warm midnight meals.

The service house was a little less ravaged; a service house had to at least seem well-stocked. But the linen was old, and there was only just enough of it, and nobody had rotated staff for more than a year now. That was hell on morale at a service house. People liked variety.

Garol had reviewed the inventory with the housemaster: all of the standard luxury items, but the Bench had gutted the surveillance systems. The house grid was useless, its coordinator ripped out by some overzealous hand salvaging the chemos from the fire suppression systems, leaving the whole house to rely on the most primitive defenses imaginable.

Firewalls.

Some parts of the system had been recharged, true, but with plain water.

And the fire alarms still worked; or at least Garol had seen no reason why they should not. Maybe it hadn't even been the Bench; maybe it had been some enterprising Nurail, taking advantage of an opportunity. Fire suppression chemos could be sold. They could be used, too, for fuel if need be, to power an escape across the Baltrune vector.

Now Garol strolled quietly through the silent halls of the hospital, using the light from the emergency exits to navigate. Koscuisko's people had set up camp in a ward three corridors removed from what portion of the clinic area was in use—to Lieutenant Wyrlann's clear if unspoken disgust, and Garol's own unspoken amusement. Wyrlann was at Center House under guard, for his own protection. Garol wasn't the least surprised that no one wanted to keep him company.

And Koscuisko, having claimed hospital duty as his excuse for staying well clear of Center House and Lieutenant Wyrlann, had followed through with a will. Garol needed to have a word with Koscuisko about that. But just at present he was curious about arrangements. He held a Bench warrant. It was second nature to find out about arrangements.

Garol didn't know exactly where Koscuisko's sleeping quarters were. He didn't need to search long, as it happened. Someone was on watch. And whoever was on watch had company. The sound of voices told Garol where to look.

"It's only natural to wonder. And I drew the frayed end."

One of the voices was female, coming from within a bay that ran three open doors along the corridor. The voices were at the far end of the bay. Garol had checked into another such bay on his way here; he knew the layout. Cautiously, he angled his body through the door to see what there was to see.

"I'm not the man to cry you shame for it. But look Chief Stildync doesn't catch us gossiping; he's tender about the officer's dignity."

The Nurail troop. Robert St. Clare. There was an inner bay to this ward, and a long hall that paralleled the corridor; St. Clare sat at the doorway to the inner bay. Quite correctly, too. Controlling access.

But Garol wanted in.

"And is it really so simple as that? A man of his nature. One would have thought, surely."

The woman's voice faded as Garol retreated down the hall. The ventilation system on these wards was not quarantined; these had originally been intended for day-clinic areas. Climbing the service stairs to the floor above Garol found the flue-vent, but he didn't break the vapor seal. Retracing his steps he counted paces till he was as close to his goal as he needed to be. Then he looked around.

"—shoulders." There was the intake, and once Garol had got well inside the capacious vent he could hear St. Clare's voice from below. He could even hear that St. Clare was teasing, just a bit. "But it's his lady to take the lap-seat, maistress. That's the way of it when they aren't Dolgorukij women. Elsewise there's fear of doing an injury, whilst a man isn't paying the attention that he naturally ought."

Wedging himself shoulder and hip in the cross-shaft Garol worked his way down to the room behind St. Clare's back, where Andrej Koscuisko's bed was made up. The Security post was through the doorway to Koscuisko's private room, and the door was only half-open. There was no reason for it to be otherwise. It was no failing on Security's part; no one could stop a Bench intelligence specialist from getting to where he wanted to go.

And at the same time Garol had particular reasons for wanting Koscuisko's Security to be alert.

He popped the secure on the ventscreen with a click so subtle that it would not carry across the room, let alone through the door and outside into the hall. As far as he could tell St. Clare had as yet heard nothing; listening to the lady, perhaps. Whoever she was.

"It's ungallant, surely, to make the woman labor at such work. And still if that is all—there's nothing to be feared from him, then?"

Free to move around inside the room, now, Garol found the thing he wanted and flipped the lid. The dose-packet that St. Clare had gotten from the orderly, shortly before they'd finished loading the courier. Garol needed some way to signal to Security to step up their surveillance; and at the same time he was curious.

What doses?

Why?

Why carried separately? Why separately delivered?

It was a standard dose-pouch, the preloads registering system integrity on display. Garol tipped a handful of the styli out of the pouch and held them up in the palm of his hand to be close to his face so that he would be able to read the encodes in the dim light.

Not narcotics; and yet under normal circumstances only narcotics or other Controlled List drugs warranted such special handling.

A hypnotic, yes.

Specific for Dolgorukij.

Hypnotics and stimulants and two doses of an antipsychotic psychoactor—the hypnotic was specific, it said so, and if the other drugs were not uniquely prescribed for an Aznir autocrat the dosage levels clearly pointed at some class of hominid whose weight or metabolism exceeded the average index—

Drugs for a sick man, for a man half-mad with conflict and self-loathing. Garol remembered the scene in the loading bay. Psychoactive drugs for a man who was perhaps insane, if only periodically sociopathic.

Exercising his Bench warrant would be an act of kindness, then. Euthanasia. Putting Koscuisko out of his evident suffering.

If only he could be sure about the source—

Carefully, Garol returned the doses to their pouch, making sure to transpose two doses as he did so. The dust should catch someone's attention. It didn't need to be anything as obvious as leaving the ventilator's grid unsecured. Security would sense a discrepancy, and then they would notice the dust Garol had carried into the room from the ventshaft. Then they would search, and when they searched they would find that the seal of the ventshaft had been broken, and that someone had been looking at the dosepouch.

This part of Garol's mission was accomplished. A quick check of the clinic and a stroll through the shabby halls of the less-than-recently-renovated service house, and he would be ready to go to bed.

To the extent that he'd done what he'd come to do—alert Koscuisko's security to the potential existence of a hitherto unsuspected problem—he was satisfied.

But the more he learned about Andrej Koscuisko the less he was inclined to credit his Bench warrant.

Well past sunset, and the clinic was finally clearing out—not so much because everything that could be done had been done as that it was three eights past curfew and people could no longer safely travel to arrive. Andrej Koscuisko leaned back against the cool edge of an examining table and folded his arms across his duty-smock with a deep sigh of satisfaction and weariness.

He wasn't used to being worked so hard, so long.

He enjoyed it.

And with any luck it would be the same for him tomorrow. It seemed clear that his name and his Judicial function was not, after all, enough to prevent pragmatic Nurail souls from taking advantage of the opportunity that an extra physician on duty represented for obtaining free medical care.

A knock at the door, and through the long high narrow windows of the examining room Andrej could just make out the balding head of Garol Vogel with a Security escort. What was Vogel doing here? The door swung open; well, he'd find out, then. Or he wouldn't. Vogel was a Bench intelligence specialist. There was no telling about his ilk.

"Good-greeting, your Excellency, and the evening finds you?"

Polite. Neutral; Vogel only cared to the extent that any ordinary person would care about the health and welfare of a casual acquaintance. Fine as far as Andrej was concerned.

"Very well, thank you, Specialist. The same for you, I hope, and where is Specialist Ivers this evening?"

Vogel stepped into the room and closed the door, leaving it ajar. So that if Andrej was needed he could be got at, Andrej supposed. Good protocol for hospital receiving areas: Bench intelligence specialists were expected to know what the appropriate behavior was under almost any circumstances. It wasn't a matter of memorizing rites and practices. It was a simple question of common sense, and the intelligence to grasp what was needful.

"Center House, sir. The woman will recover? I heard the technical report but I'm not much good at interpreting it. If you'd summarize for me, your Excellency, I'd appreciate it."

Fair enough. "The short answer is yes. The long answer is that physical therapy will be required, she may or may not become infertile, and I hope before Heaven that the guesses I had to make about the nature and intensity of her sensory response to sexual stimulus are close to correct. I am favorably impressed with Paval I'shenko, in pulling rank the way that he did. Gardener Hanner for one will be sure to defend my cousin henceforward."

Vogel grinned, a gesture which suddenly squared his otherwise somewhat round face. "What I like is that that was only part of his reasoning. The rest of it was good old-fashioned decent moral outrage. There isn't enough of that around, these days."

No indeed. "And speaking of moral outrage. I believe you may wish to reinventory pharmacy stores before the rest of Fleet arrives, Specialist. Someone has broken into stores and made very free with some quite expensive medication, and I am sure that Paval I'shenko would regret having to make an issue of the discrepancy."

Vogel's expression somehow lacked much of an element of surprise. "I'm shocked, your Excellency. Shocked. This person, you wouldn't happen to have an idea of who he was or where I might find him, would you?"

As a matter of fact Andrej was tolerably certain that both he and Vogel knew exactly what was going on. "Quite a good notion, actually. Enough of one to know that regrettably the villain cannot be prosecuted. There is no reason why he should not be identified, however. I hardly know what worse Fleet could do to me than it already has."

Because it was he, himself, Andrej Koscuisko, who had forced the secures and issued the stores. Under the Privilege of the Writ he could not be brought to account for misappropriation of Fleet or Bench stores; nor could any of the subordinate physicians to whom Andrej had released the materials be faulted for simply receiving normal stores in personal ignorance of the exact manner in which release had been authorized.

"Ah," Vogel said, with an odd little gesture of his chin that was supportive and admonitory at once. "Oddly enough that reminds me. News from Fleet, extension approved, no transfer in the foreseeable."

Well. It was only as much as he had expected. There was no sense in noticing the voice in his mind that still raged in protest. He was tired: and Vogel was still talking.

"Hoping the news isn't all bad. Good-night, I'll be on my—oh. Almost forgot."

What kind of trick or trap was this, then?

Andrej waited, deeply suspicious.

"The Danzilar prince. I was to tell you particularly. He apologizes for, let me see, what was it, for not greeting you prior to departure. And promises that there is to be dancing at Center House."

The message was unexpected, and took Andrej by surprise. Dancing?

Had he even thought about dancing, at any time that he could call to mind, over the past eight years?

And Shiki—his cousin Paval I'shenko—and he had been widely acknowledged as quite good dancers, when they'd been younger. Before Andrej had gone off to school. Paval I'shenko had always been on the lookout for opportunities to test himself against Andrej, and see who would clear the floor in triumph this time.

He was doomed.

"I have not danced so much as a miletta since I came to Fleet." And Paval I'shenko would know that. Andrej could trust his cousin to be thinking, every moment. "Still less anything more strenuous. I have only two chances."

One, he had not danced, but he had learned to fight; and perhaps some part of the two skill-sets would prove to be more closely related than he would have thought them.

Or, two, that his cousin the prince Paval I'shenko Danzilar might sprain his ankle, and it would not be an issue.

"Sir?" Vogel was waiting, politely. But Andrej was tired.

If Vogel wanted to know he could just bring his own special Bench intelligence specialist skill-set to bear on the issue. Though—it suddenly occurred to Andrej—if he could enlist Vogel's help, might Vogel not find a way to engineer the spraining of an ankle, to the preservation of the dignity of a Judicial officer?

No.

Perhaps not.

"Earthquake or flood, Specialist Vogel, because nothing less will keep my cousin from his darshan. I am going to bed. You will excuse me. I do not invite you, it is nothing personal."

He needed to get to bed, because he wanted to be able to open the clinic as soon as curfew lifted in the morning, which was about an eight before sunrise. Vogel bowed.

"Of course. Good rest, your Excellency. I'll see you at the party, if not before."

There was no reason to suppose otherwise. Was there? There was something in Vogel's voice, something in Vogel's bow that half-convinced Andrej of the existence of some secret.

Well, if it was a secret, then that was what it would have to remain.

"And you, Specialist. If you would call for my gentlemen on your way out, please."

Alone in the room now Andrej unfastened his smock and bundled it into the laundry-drawer. The laundry-drawer already contained a discarded smock; it made Andrej wonder whether the hospital was in a position to be able to afford to keep a decent linen schedule.

Robert came in with Andrej's overblouse and a load of toweling over one arm. If there were towels, didn't that mean that the laundry was running?

"Thank you, Robert." Andrej didn't need help to get dressed. But accepting help was part of accepting the fact that Robert elected to offer it, since Robert knew that body-service was something Andrej considered strictly optional for bond-involuntaries. "I don't know if I have the energy to wash.

Perhaps I will rather bathe in the morning. Is there of rhyti a flask for me in quarters?''

Holding the door open for Andrej as he went out Robert shook his head, with great determination. ''Na, the officer is mistaken. You want your wash in now, sir. Truly. And quarters are being shifted.''

Years ago when they had all been much younger, Robert St. Clare had suffered through the ordeal of the prisoner-surrogate exercise at Fleet Orientation Station Medical to win a reduction of his Bond. Robert had not failed; but the trial had failed, and over the space of several days Robert had lived in an agony both physical and spiritual awaiting the formal declaration of the sentence of his punishment—which was clearly understood by all as amounting to a sentence of death by slow torture.

During that time, the ferocious stress levels Robert had endured had forced the calibration of his governor to one side in some manner. Robert's governor had never been quite right in all of the time that Andrej had known him since. But as long as it was wrong in the right direction Andrej didn't care.

Now as always Robert spoke to him more freely than any of the other Bonds, quite clearly and distinctly telling him what to do.

Andrej would comply with Robert's instructions, of course. Instruction received was instruction implemented, for bond-involuntaries at least, and since it was that way for bond-involuntaries Andrej saw no reason why he should refuse to grant obedience as he was given obedience.

The obedience he was owed by his Bonds could be said to be a simple question of the fact that the governor forced it, on the face of it. Andrej knew better. The obedience he was granted by his bond-involuntaries was given him as freely as even a man enslaved could choose to make a gift instead of paying a debt.

''Shifted, Robert? What was wrong with quarters, that we should shift?''

They were dark and depressing, true. As vacant and empty

as any abandoned ward. But wasn't one abandoned ward much the same as any other?

Robert sounded serious now—for perhaps so long as three eighths. "Security issue, your Excellency. We think we had a visitor while quarters were empty. The ventilation system can be compromised. Pyotr's shifting for prudence's sake—"

Robert had led him down a long hall that led into a communal showers. Only a portion of the showers were apparently in use: the majority of the walls and floors and drains were bone-dry, with the powdery fragrance of concrete on a humid day.

"—and here's a sauna for you. I've taken the liberty. I'll take your boots, sir."

And rest-dress by implication would be waiting in the warmth of the dry sauna, with clean linen. Capitulating, Andrej sat down on the changing-bench and started to strip. A man was slave to his servants from one end of the Bench to the other, Andrej mused to himself. There was no sense in arguing with people who had gone to such lengths for one's benefit.

How had Robert managed a sauna, with Burkhayden so starved for power?

Perhaps it was just as well if he did not wonder about that.

A sauna was an intrinsic good, after all, and he would enjoy it just as much as if its warmth had not been thieved from sources unknown.

Andrej Koscuisko came into the day-clinic with a flask of rhyti in one hand and a wrap of bread and meatpaste in the other. He was late. He'd been up well past midnight last night, because it was not to be imagined that anyone should be turned away from day-clinic, and some of them had been waiting all day. He'd been up late the night before, for the same reason, and slept past the mark this morning, so that it was already past the lifting of curfew.

And the clinic's waiting-room already full. People were lined up all down the corridor, women with children in arms, children with younger siblings, men with aged parents. Andrej bowed to the waiting room, keenly aware of the lack of respect inadvertently implied by greeting his patients with his fastmeal in both hands.

"Good-greeting, gentles all, I hope that you will forgive my tardiness. But we will turn none of you away, my oath upon it."

The on-site staff were used to this. There were too few of them, and none with the generalist's skills Andrej had gained in eight years as a Ship's Surgeon. None with his peculiar specialty skills, and they had ceded seniority to him almost without his noticing, as glad as these waiting folk to have his help to accomplish their task. He was in charge of day-clinic here and now.

His gentlemen broke away from post behind him as Andrej crossed the room, going to their own stations. They'd been requisitioned early on to help the physician's aides; they had good triage skills. He was going to owe them a holiday when this was over—but not at the service-house. That was unthinkable.

At an off-license house, perhaps, which would mean scavenging in Port Burkhayden for food and drink to make a party. He would see if he could find a skilled provisioner to the task.

There was a signal for him from the records-desk, the keeper on duty coughing into his hand politely as a young woman rose to her feet from a chair near the desk. Quite a young woman, and the look on her face was so appealing—open and vulnerable. Something in her hands, what had she brought him, and why did she gaze at him with so much tense reluctant longing?

"His Excellency asked after this preparation," she said; and Andrej recognized her at last, the little girl from the gardener's house. The daughter of the house, the young lady Tavart, bearing for him a pot of ointment. Of salve. "I hope that this may serve? It's the first time I've tried it, I'm not sure it's quite right but I didn't want to delay any longer."

She held the ointment-pot out to him, her hands shaking almost imperceptibly. Andrej raised his hands in turn to re-

ceive her gift, but his hands were full, and he gestured helplessly, feeling as awkward as if he had been so young as she
was all over again. Had he ever been so young? In his life,
ever?

"Oh, but my apologies, Miss Tavart." He thought she was
a "miss" yet, an unmarried woman in her mother's household. "If you would be so good as to come through. I find
myself at a disadvantage."

Through to the treatment room, where he could disembar-
rass himself of his fastmeal and take the ointment-pot into his
hand, tipping the lid off with a careful twist. The creamy fat
inside was rosy with the pale ghost of the color of jellericia
flowers, and the fragrance—though subtle—was distinct.

It was unusual, so soft, and yet so penetrating—strong
enough for all its delicacy to penetrate the insulted brain of a
beaten woman and carry its message of comfort, its memory
of home, to her dreaming mind. Something to encourage her
to return to the world, if only for the fact of such a perfume.

"It is precisely the thing, Miss Tavart. Is it that I shall call
you 'miss'?"

She blushed, and Andrej wondered if he was being irresponsible. He was flirting. No. He was not. A man had no
business flirting with such a young woman. Let her cleave to
her gardener. They were not suited in station, but neither were
she and Andrej suited in station, and at least her gardener was
of an age. And seemed to be a decent hardworking young
man, while for himself though just at present Andrej was
hardworking he could not in honesty believe that "decent"
could describe him.

"My name is Sylyphe, sir. I've brought these other things,
as well—"

She had a carrying-sack with her, and opened it now, setting it on the level to draw her treasures forth. They were
alone together in the treatment room, though the door was
open. Andrej stood beside her to see what she had brought,
straightening up as he noticed himself leaning rather more
closely than he ought.

"Hanner has been called away, and I don't have his . . . his knowledge. He said to wash the spent blooms in alcohol to take the last of the scent.''

A flask of rose-pale water, but when she unstoppered it a delicious fragrance of jellericia filled the room. It addled him, all of a sudden. The fragrance was as clean and as pure as a maiden's first love; and she was a maiden, clean and pure, who carried within her the awesome divinity of her still-only-potential womanhood. To be the man to dance with her, to lead her across the threshold between childhood and grown age, to be the man to see her first come into the pride and power that was her birthright as a woman—

She passed the vial to him, and their hands touched. Her fingers were cool, as delicate as the spear-shaped leaves that clustered around winter-blooming yellow-trumpets in the snow. She seemed to recoil back from the contact, startled; the same touch grounded Andrej, in some sense, recalled him to the understanding of who and where he was. This was a child that stared at him with such dark lustrous eyes, her blushing mouth half-open. She was perfect, tempting, all points delicious, but she was a child—or at least too young to be a woman to him.

Andrej capped the flask. ''Very well done indeed, Miss Sylphe. And what else is it that you have brought us? I am overwhelmed with this surfeit of bounty.''

Miss Sylphe, yes, that was the way to do it. She dropped her gaze to her carry-pouch, confused, but composing herself with admirable poise. She was to be a formidable woman, when she came into her majority. Was the gardener man enough to partner her?

Why should he wonder about the gardener, when this child of privilege would surely find her match amongst men as privileged as she?

''There was half-a-flat of jellericia coming into bloom already, your Excellency. The flowers lose their fragrance; it was too late to use them for the ointment, but they do still smell a bit, don't they? And they look nice. I thought—''

Call me Andrej, Andrej thought. *You are not angry with me, surely, why should you be so cold as to say ''Excel-*

lency?'' No, you must call me Andrej, all of my friends do.
As if he had any. As if anyone had called him Andrej in the
past eight years. *Call me Andrej, come back later, we can talk
more freely when the day is done and we can be alone together.*

She held out a lush bouquet of jellericia, its dark green
foliage begemmed with tiny crimson flowers. He could see
what she meant, if he looked carefully. The blossoms were a
little worn, in fact, and the fragrance scarce discernable.

"I applaud your instinct, Miss Sylyphe." And he could do
so honestly, without ulterior motives. "This will indeed make
a pleasing decoration. Of those out there it may be there is
more than one, that remembers what these look like."

When she smiled she was all child, and he was safe from
himself. "If the ointment is all right I can have more of it in
three days' time, your Excellency. Hanner showed me what
needs to be done to force the next flat."

Andrej hefted the pot of ointment, now all adult once again.
There was enough here for several days' treatment of the
woman from the service house. "If you could let me have as
much again in so much time, yes, that would do very well.
Thank you, Miss Sylyphe. I am to you indebted, and still now
I must ask that you excuse me to the work of the day."

Now he could take her arm and turn her toward the door,
and cosset her like an uncle his favorite niece. Now he could
be an uncle to her, and not a man of whom her mother would
be right to be suspicious. It was a relief. Because he had been
so tempted.

"Of course, your Excellency. Thank you, sir." And once
he was well settled as an uncle she found her own voice as a
niece. Was it his imagination, or was there a suspicion of
regret in her tone? "And a very good day to you, your Excellency."

"The best of good days," Andrej agreed heartily. He was
not a man. He was the adult male relative of her mother, and
that was something else entirely. "My respects to your lady
mother, Miss Sylyphe, and my very great appreciation for

your hard work. Perhaps I will see you again in three days' time.''

And perhaps he would be very sure to have people with him when he did so. There was only so much a man could be expected to take.

She nodded, blushing, and walked away through the wait-room without more words. Andrej watched her go, trying not to notice what a sweet soft cushion there was to her hips, nor how nicely she carried her back and shoulders.

Well.

''My apologies for the delay, gentles, if I might have the first patient. Please.''

That had been a pleasant start to a man's morning, and by the grace of the Holy Mother he had neither disgraced himself nor soiled the innocence of that woman-child by taking advantage.

Now he had better concentrate on work.

Fleet Captain Lowden stepped across the cracked flooring that paved the threshold to the hospital's wait-room with precision born of distaste. What a depressing place this was, this public-funded; and yet his errant Ship's Surgeon took to even so pathetic a clinic like debris to an intake pump. Drawn in so strongly that a man could almost hear the suction.

''Captain Lowden. A surprise, sir.''

Alerted by the orderlies Koscuisko came out of a treatment room to greet him. Koscuisko's smock was soiled and his face was haggard, but there was amusement in his expression that Lowden could identify—if not appreciate. ''Just in to port, your Excellency?''

Wiping his hands on a bit of sterile toweling. The orderlies were showing Koscuisko's patient out of the treatment room; a young woman, infant in arms. She only glanced in their direction. Her eyes were all on Koscuisko's back when she did.

''Oh, it's been the odd hour, Andrej. We weren't expected for another day or two, yes, I know.''

Or else Danzilar would be all ready for his party, and they

could get that over with and leave. Yes. But also Koscuisko should have been at the landing field to greet his superior officer, and Koscuisko hadn't been. Lowden could excuse that, but he wasn't going to let it pass unremarked upon.

"Were we not." Koscuisko was tired; it took him that extra fraction of an eighth to realize that he was being called to account. And still it was clear to Lowden at least that Koscuisko had genuinely lost track of the time. "I must then beg your pardon, Captain, not to have joined the welcoming party. No disrespect was intended."

Once he did realize, however, Koscuisko accepted the rebuke with grace and dignity, not stooping to insist on tiresome details that would explain and excuse his failure. On the one hand it was appropriate that Koscuisko bend his neck in submission to his superior officer. On the other hand Koscuisko's very humility only emphasized how little Koscuisko cared.

That was all right.

Lowden had never required Koscuisko to care. Merely to obey.

"I've been reviewing the discrepancy lists with the Danzilar prince's people, Andrej, and there seems to be a problem with drugs-stores. And I wonder if that problem has your name on it." He had time. He had four more years to break Koscuisko to his will. Koscuisko was well humbled already. Inside of a few months Koscuisko would be his, body and soul; and all it would take was enough bodies for the torture, and no time in between.

Koscuisko bowed, only barely not grinning. "I felt it my right and due prerogative, Captain. Have I my authority exceeded? Because I the Lieutenant outrank, after all."

And Lieutenant Wyrlann's self-indulgence, also noted in the discrepancies lists, cost the Bench almost as much as what the allowance for the medication Koscuisko had issued over the past few days amounted to. It was an interesting approach. Lowden smiled in acknowledgement of the creativity it displayed.

"I'll take that into consideration, Andrej. Now that we are here I'll expect you to return to your Command, of course."

And stop playing doctor with this roomful of stinking unwashed Nurail. He would provide Koscuisko with other play-
things soon enough.

"Of course, Captain. But. If I may be permitted. I have
these gentlemen been working hard, I owe them—and myself,
with your permission—a holiday. Perhaps I may have your
leave to the service-house to go, before this team which has
been so overburdened is relieved."

Lowden thought about it.

Koscuisko was tired.

Koscuisko had few opportunities to go to service houses,
and Lowden liked it that way, because the less frequently
Koscuisko enjoyed human intimacies in a perfectly bland and
pathetically mundane manner the keener the tension Koscuisko had stored up within him to focus on his work in Secured Medical. But a man could not be kept from women too
strictly; a certain degree of access was required to maintain
Koscuisko's bodily health. Captain Lowden was a firm be-
liever in preventive medicine.

"Very well, Andrej. You'll have to take your kit with you,
of course." Lowden called up one of his Security with a beckoning gesture of his hand. "I'm not sure how it happened,
exactly, but you seem to have left the ship without it."

Koscuisko's field interrogations kit. Had he known Koscuisko would be asking leave to go to the service house he
would have left it under guard at Center House, but that was
academic now. Koscuisko had not gotten the full benefit of
the joke Lowden had set up for him, after all. Vogel had
ruined the punch line. Koscuisko could just hang on to his
field interrogations kit.

Koscuisko grimaced, but bowed. Koscuisko knew perfectly
well that Lowden was his master. "Of course, Captain. Even
as you say. And to report in the morning, then?"

It always gratified Lowden to see how clearly Koscuisko
understood his position. Koscuisko's submissiveness sweet-
ened Lowden's mood now.

"Midmeal, Andrej," he corrected genially, extending Koscuisko's holiday to midday. "I'll see you at table."

Koscuisko could go to the service house, but Koscuisko would brood; and carry the field interrogations kit with him, to serve as a constant, unwelcome, reminder of what his duty was.

There would be some salvage value to his joke after all, and Lowden carried that pleasing knowledge with him as he left the hospital for Center House.

It was cold in the curfew-darkened streets of Port Burk-hayden, a cold that chilled to the bone even in the absence of wind. There was a little rain, but only a little one, so that Andrej could not decide whether it was soft mist or a very low cloud—or the spume from the sea-spray, come up from the marsh to plaster itself greedily against glass and window and leach as much warmth as it could suck from frame and sash.

Captain Lowden doubtless expected them to go to the service house, but what Captain Lowden didn't know wouldn't harm Andrej—at least not tonight. He had not so much as told the Port Authority where he was going, though he had no doubt they could find him if they had to. Stildyne was going to be angry with him about that. He would work it out with Stildyne somehow. In the morning. Later.

The local escort Andrej had recruited at the hospital brought them through black narrow streets to a secret part of town, hidden away behind warehouse walls and traffic diverters, to a dark house standing in the middle of a lot that seemed surprisingly large to Andrej for the middle of the city. Dark house, narrow gate, overgrown path, overgrown garden; and though there was no wind, the trees in the half-wild garden seemed to creak and clatter at him in a manner that Andrej did not find in the least welcoming.

Once inside, though, once through the heavy weathered wooden door cracked reluctantly open only so far as necessary to let them in, once safely within the house it was quite different. Dark, yes, because most of Port Burkhayden was without power yet again tonight, and only a few public utilities—the public-funded hospital, the service house, Center House itself—were on auxiliary power. Dark but welcoming even so, because it was warm inside, friendly with occasional lights powered on reservoir and candles.

Andrej stood bemused in the great foyer while their guide, one of the physician's assistants from the hospital, went forward to complete final arrangements with the management. Candlelight. Candlelight was more practical than not in any service-house, but especially in an off-license house, where the women were by and large of a wider range in age and looks than one might find at the more elite establishments. At an off-license house at least they were all volunteers, or as much volunteer as a man could fantasize any woman to be whom necessity had forced to tender the privilege of her flesh as a commodity for lease.

A girl came out of a side door with a hand-held beam and invited them to follow her with a wordless gesture and a very pretty bow for Andrej himself. She was a pretty little thing all in all, and would be a woman some year doubtless, though she was surely no older than the daughter of the House Tavart—and he was not even going to speculate about that. A man did not have to do with children. No matter how prettily their petals trembled on the border between innocence and experience. No.

They sat all together in a common dining hall and took their meal: Andrej, his Security, their guide, the lady of the house, some girls. Well, some of the house's women. It was a species of pleasure in and of itself to sit in near-darkness and have his supper, while his gentlemen—knowing that it was a holiday, having been strictly instructed that they were on holiday and not on duty—relaxed by degrees, to disport themselves with ladies.

And Pyotr, being black, was very exotic, and liked two at a time, and could give good account of himself as well—at least from report. And Hirsel was generally open to affectionate play from any direction, and the female direction was fully as enticing to him as any other.

Godsalt could usually be prevailed upon to make a woman with dark hair feel appreciated, which was just as well since there were more dark-haired ladies present than otherwise. Garrity was celibate, within the requirements of the community of bond-involuntaries, and would happily sleep alone, which only left all the more for Robert.

Robert liked ladies in more than a casual sense. He really liked women, and from all Andrej had been able to determine women by and large returned his genial if impertinent interest with charitable forbearance—

When Godsalt threw a pinch of bread at his senior fellow Pyotr, and Pyotr in retaliation sent an only half-cleaned fruit-pit into Godsalt's glass of drinking-spirit to splash half of the liquid into Godsalt's plate, Andrej decided it was time he went upstairs.

The lady of the house rose and withdrew at the same time, pausing only to nominate one of the girls to show "the officer" up to his room. It was one of the girls who carried serving-dishes back and forth; she did not mean for Andrej to take his guide to partner—Andrej was secure in that. But it was clearly high time he withdrew and left his gentlemen to their holiday.

He was not going to be the least bit sorry to have a bit of a holiday himself. Even if only a few hours' worth.

Up the stairs, then, and to the wing of the house furthest away from the dining-room. The girl let him in to a large well-warmed room with an actual fire, a wood fire, burning in a grate against the wall; charming, if anachronistic. She wished him the best of his bath, and asked if anything seemed lacking, and made sure he knew how to summon her up should anything be found so; and then while Andrej stood on the threshold of the bathing-room, toying with the concept of asking for her help to scrub his back, trying to determine whether or not he had designs on her—she excused herself, and went away.

Probably just as well, Andrej admitted to himself. And no denying that he took particular pleasure in being left to himself for a little while. On board ship there was always the officer's orderly, always, whoever's turn it was to pull the duty. And whenever he was not on board ship he lived in the middle of a Security squad. A man could hardly so much as urinate in private.

Andrej had been raised in public, in a sense, because he had been raised by body-servants in his father's household. Even as a child Andrej had realized that there was something wonderful about being alone, quite alone, hiding in the closet or riding perversely in an unexpected direction to disappear into the winter forest before anyone could stay him.

But never for long. And never long enough.

It was not decent to hide for long. A person's servants got anxious, and it was not in the least bit thoughtful or respectful to play tricks on them.

Andrej took a good long hot soak in the old-fashioned water tub, concentrating on shutting everything out of his mind except the soothing comfort of the bath and the to-be-anticipated company of a lady. His reenlistment, his ruined hopes of freedom, his despair in facing the future—shutting it all out of his mind. Sylyphe Tavart, with breath so sweet a man all but had to taste that pretty little mouth, so young—and so willing to be charmed with him—

Shutting that out as well. She was a child. A man did not insult the innocence of children, no matter if they thought that they were ripe to be enjoyed. He knew; Sylyphe did not; it was not for him to be the one to teach her. That was all.

When he was washed and dried and belted into the wrap that lay warming on the rod for his use Andrej went out into the bedroom. Someone had come and gone, so quietly—in the manner of servants in such places—that Andrej hadn't noticed; the fire was refreshed, the table laid with snacks and wodac. Also some rhyti. The bed was large, but the mattress was uneven; sitting down at the edge Andrej noticed that a book had been laid open on the bedside table, the bright colors of its illustrations catching his eye. He picked it up, curious.

A fishing-book.

A book of fish-stories.

A fishing-book in the old sense of the term, or in the Dolgorukij sense of the term, a book of natural history, of pictures designed to educate. That was the excuse, at least; to educate—and to beguile, interest, arouse . . .

He was leafing through the fishing-book when the knock came at the door, and the lady of the house came in. Distracted, Andrej did not stand when she crossed the threshold; and gestured toward the book that lay now open in his lap by way of an excuse, apologizing.

"Do you know, I had one of these, or one like it." Well, not exactly like it, of course. One found in a corner of the library where historical curiosities were kept, an antique. Really. Antiquarian interest. Yes. "There is a gallery at Chelatring Side, where we went in the late part of the summers. My cousin Stanoczk to be bribed consented, to let me in, and Marana with me."

There had been endless vigils to keep in penance afterward, when it had all come out. The vigils had done no good. They only gave him time, private time, quiet time, to meditate on the pictures he had seen in the Malcontent's secret gallery at Chelatring Side, and Marana hand in hand with him, exploring. Experimenting.

The lady of the house had poured herself a dainty cup of rhyti, carrying it over to sit down beside him on the bed. She had changed her garments for bed-dress, and her robe was but loosely knotted around her waist.

Well.

He had not quite expected such an honor, and still it could be that he was mistaken to assume that she was to be his partner. She was the house-mistress, and engaged only for her own recreation, or to pay special honor to a patron. It was only that his fish was as beguiled by the pictures as by his passing memories of that afternoon with Marana in the Malcontent's gallery, so long ago.

His fish would disgrace him, if he was not careful.

With luck she would not want to take the book.

"Let me see, young Anders," the house-mistress suggested, reaching up her left hand to pull out a pin from the damp cloud of hair that lay loosely gathered against the nape of her neck. "Which is your favorite, here? I'll show you mine. But you must show me yours, first."

There was no mistaking the implication of that. She was mistress here; no need for delicate language, surely. "This is an outland fishing-book, not a Dolgorukij fishing-book. Else there would be much more of this sort of recreation to examine."

He found the place where the couple who shared their transports for the pleasure of the beholders did so with the lady in her lover's lap. It was not strictly true that there were more like that in a traditional Dolgorukij fishing-book. But absolutely true that a man who was Aznir did well to take a woman into his lap, if she was not herself also Dolgorukij.

"I've heard rumors of the sort." Her exclamation was so calm as to almost be no exclamation at all. "About Dolgorukij men. My girls all wanted to know, but I'm their mother, I take precedence."

Their figurative mother, needless to say. Or perhaps not. She was not a young woman; perhaps so old as he was, and that meant that it was not impossible that some of the girls— the younger ones especially—actually were children of her body.

Which in turn implied . . .

"I am honored." Andrej acknowledged it with all humility. "And can only trust to live up to what rumors you may have heard. If it can be done."

She supped her rhyti demurely. Her hair was falling out of its damp knot, slowly, slowly tumbling down her back. She was Nurail, to look at her; she might well have borne her children under wretchedly primitive conditions. If no lover's tuck had been taken after the birth of any one . . . there were those who found a woman more desirable, rather than less, for the evidence of motherhood, but the point was that it might yet be that he could pillow himself upon her bosom as though she had been Dolgorukij after all, without fear of causing her an injury in an excess of enthusiasm.

"Fishing, you say." Setting her cup aside; leaning over the look, leaning close beside him. Letting him feel the soft round of her shoulders, beneath her robe. "How is this 'fishing?' Explain yourself to me."

Yes, he had called it by a Dolgorukij name, used a Dolgorukij phrase. Andrej blushed without being able to quite decide why. "In the language of my childhood a fish is as to say that part of a man which shows he is not female, and yet is not his beard. If he has a beard. I mean to say a chin-beard." Because he did have that other kind of beard, though many Dolgorukij did not grow facial hair. He was getting fuddled. Had there been something in the bath-water?

Or was it simply that she smelled of the ocean, subtly so, faintly so, but sweetly and irresistibly so, so that his fish half-raised itself to listen for the glad sound of the surf?

"A fish." She stared at him very frankly, and made no secret of her amusement. "A codling, then. Or perhaps a brook-trout. Bring you to me a salmon-fish, young Andrej? No, a tunny, yes, perhaps."

He didn't know what she was talking about—except in the general sense, of course. Which it was better to ignore, or he would not complete his explanation.

He put the book aside.

"There is in the life of a man a fish, which is rude and inconstant, but which knows one great piece of true wisdom." Putting an arm around her Andrej helped her hair down, letting the tendrils curl around his fingers. Loving the smell of her. "And that is to seek the ocean, which is where all fish come from, to which therefore it is only natural for fish to wish to return."

If he stroked the far side of her face very gently there was the chance that she could be persuaded to turn her face toward his, so that he could provide proper punctuation for his explanation as he spoke on. Explaining himself with kisses. She had a pleasant if somewhat cool taste to her mouth, flavored with rhyti. "It is the ocean we were all rocked in as infants yet unborn. Madame, my fish desires thy ocean."

She wound her arms around his neck and considered his proposal for long moments as he kissed her mouth. It seemed to Andrej that there was the suspicion of a blush beginning to rise into her cheek, but it could just as well have been a shadow from the fireplace. There was no way to be sure.

Sighing—as if she were letting go of some anxiety—she let her hands fall away from his neck and shoulders.

Into his lap.

She slid one cool slim hand beneath the hem of his sleep-shirt and up his thigh with such an air of professional detachment that Andrej almost didn't notice the gesture until she seized upon his fish, which had caused no trouble yet this evening for which it should be reproached in such a manner, and tugged at him indelicately.

"Is this then the terrible weapon from which all off-world women must flee in fear? Surely it cannot be so."

That had been her point about codlings and tunny-fishes, then. In point of fact he was neither remarkable for size and girth or lack of either. At home it didn't matter. A fish was a fish, and a burden no matter its particular rudeness or strength in leaping.

Only when he had left home for the surgical college on Mayon had Andrej discovered that there was an entire world of insult and one-upsmanship that could be draped around the fins of a man's fish.

He had never had complaints from the ladies.

He would have nothing of the house-mistress's impertinence now.

"Oh, let us by all means discuss this issue." Her caress had not been sweet or tender, but it was still arousing in its utterly frank focus on what she could expect to concern her most immediately. Andrej didn't really mind. "And when morning comes you will do me the kindness of declaring whether it is an honest fish or whether you have been disappointed in its vigor. Let us seal a bargain on it."

"Well." She had released her grip, but rested still with her hands laid flat atop his thighs beneath the sleep-shirt. "Far be it from me to deny your fish a chance to show himself a, well, a fish. And perhaps he only needs encouragement, shall I give him a kiss for an apology?"

Andrej's fish stiffened and raised its head at the suggestion, greedy for affection as it always was. But Andrej would be stern. "We will have no apologies." His fish was eager for a kiss, but more than one sort of a caress would soothe a fish. Fish had so little true discrimination. Such favors as she proposed were available to him at any time, whether or not he had ever indulged himself. "Favor me with your name, Madame. May I not call thee something other than the lady of the house?"

She had one great mystery to offer him that he could only share at intervals. She was the ocean to his fish. He would make his way to the sea, and lose himself in the salt depths of her, and drown there.

If he slipped one hand beneath the neckline of her robe he could put the robe down from her shoulders, on one side. She had very adequate shoulders, and Andrej sat and admired her nakedness shamelessly, stroking that smooth round curve with his left hand. Foreign women did not know what bared shoulders did to Dolgorukij. And the best of it was that their ignorance did not diminish the impact of their beauty.

"Fallon, then." She'd put her head back, her eyes half-closed. Suffering herself to be caressed. But not pretending she did not enjoy it. "You may call me Fallon, since I've said Anders before this. Just for tonight. Give me your mouth when you do that, you make me as nervous as a cat."

Yes, willingly.

The sound of the surf was in his ears. He could smell the ocean.

There was nothing in his mind but where he was and what he was to do, no reality beyond the simple truth of the joy of his body and the kindness of her hands.

For this eternity of an evening he could even forget he was Inquisitor.

◇ Six

So this was what a Dohan Dolgorukij made of a Center House, Captain Lowden mused appreciatively, looking all around him. Normally standing in reception lines was not among his favorite occupations, but this time it was almost worth it—just to get an eyeful of the Danzilar prince's décor.

"Who did you say?" Captain Lowden prompted, turning the gift-flask in his hands with the expected expression of impressed respect and gratitude. "Bermeled's distillers? Of course. The pleasure is mine, I assure you."

Clearwall doors to the garden full two stories tall and more. Lighting fixtures made of spun glass and fractured crystal hanging in great glittering ice-blooms from long chains in the ceiling. Painted walls papered over with figured silk, and the pattern showing through from behind with jewellike intensity and unnerving depth. Dance floors, three of them, laid on raised squares of resilient wood, and as many different octets of musicians playing the same tunes in variation in perfect synchronization so that the combined effect—coming at one from several different directions at once—was almost overwhelming.

That was it right there, in summary, Lowden decided.

Almost overwhelming. And just that necessary touch of restraint sufficient to keep it all coherent and splendid at once.

"You're very kind. Permit me to introduce my First Officer, Mendez. Ralph, these are Sarif Pelar and her partner Chons, local representatives from Bermeled's distillery."

120

Center House was roaring with people, staff, servants, Security. Griers Verigson Lowden stood with the Danzilar prince at the front of the great foyer doing his duty, lending his presence and that of his officers to the reception line as Danzilar greeted his subject people and the hangers-on who hoped to make a profit under the new administration.

Lowden wished them luck of the attempt. Dolgorukij in trade were as ferociously efficient as his favorite little Aznir in torture, as if the thirst for mastery and the habit of dominion were a genetic determinant of the ethnicity. Maybe they were, Lowden mused, watching a senior businesswoman work her way up the long line to Danzilar's position, a wide-eyed youngster in tow. Maybe if you reached the age of discretion without having demonstrated an instinctive grasp of the profit equation you were sold off as Sarvaw, or some similarly disgraceful fate.

"Dame Ranzil Tavart," the majordomo whispered near Lowden's ear, at his back. Just in case Lowden had missed the Danzilar prince's cue. Lowden bowed, his mind half-distracted by the pleasingly substantial pile of booty that the majordomo was accumulating for him on a table against the wall. "Cordage and Textile" didn't sound very promising from that angle, though; what little treats could a textile manufactory offer?

"Oh, and I understand you've had great success with recovering seed-stocks. Weren't we told that those beautiful flowers in front of the House came from your greenhouses?" The polite phrases were automatic, and nobody really expected him to mean a bit of what he said. He didn't have to think, just smile and speak a word, and smile again. Sickening.

"Ralph Mendez—my First Officer, here—is Santone, not much by way of flowers of any sort where he comes from, I'm afraid. What do you say, Ralph?"

Not as if Lowden cared one way or the other; no, of course not. But a man was expected to demonstrate his skill at managing the flow of traffic in a reception line. He certainly wasn't going to be shown up by Danzilar, of all people.

Glancing around him at the crush, Lowden knew that he was genuinely impressed at what Danzilar had done with a few hours and a very great deal of money. There was no way in which Vogel would have overlooked the beautiful parquetry floor or the fine rich wood wainscoting in his final audit. Paval I'shenko had to have brought them. Bought them, brought them, laid the floor and hung the chandeliers, painted the walls and then papered over them, and all in the few hours between the final signatures on the formalization documents and the opening of the Center House for this reception.

"Well, no, I'm actually not. In fact I haven't any relatives in that Sector. An orphan, sorry." Two in a row with no presents. He could hear Chief Medical further down the line, talking with the textile people; and cocked an ear, curious.

"Very expertly done, Dame Tavart," Koscuisko was saying. "If I may say so, the young lady has done us proud. Perhaps I may be permitted to impose further and dance with the daughter of the house, later on in the evening."

In all, three of Lowden's officers stood in the reception line, beside Lowden himself. Mendez, Two, and Andrej, who ranked lowest out of the Ship's Primes on the scale of things. Lieutenant Wyrlann wasn't required, since Lowden was here to represent Command Branch. The Engineer was back on *Ragnarok* with the Ship's Second Lieutenant.

Lieutenant Wyrlann was in trouble, and Lowden meant to be sure that Wyrlann understood that.

This was going to be a spectacular party before it was finished; a real work-out. A reception, dinner, dancing, late supper, until finally the guests were dismissed to their homes over fastmeal. A man wanted for companionship to share such an event. Especially if a man was expected to uphold the Bench presence and be on his best behavior. Especially when a man was expected to make good the poor impression created by his miserable excuse for a First Lieutenant.

And it was going to cost Wyrlann at performance review time; but meanwhile—as a result of Wyrlann's little lapse— relaxing, truly enjoying himself at the service center was all but out of the question. He'd have to mind his manners. There was little amusement to be found in that.

"What an unusual decoration. Is it an heirloom? No? A personal award? Sir, my very sincere congratulations. It's also quite elegant, you know. And your respected companion as well, if I may say so."

Oh, he'd end up at the service house before the evening was over. There was no question about that. But he'd have to restrict himself to a boring menu of basic exchanges. No spice, no heat to speak of.

Lowden turned the next in line over to Mendez, a question fighting its way up into his consciousness through the layer upon layer of polite social inanities in which he was so thoroughly submerged.

Where was Wyrlann?

The Lieutenant had successfully avoided him since they'd arrived, not that Lowden had been the least bit interested in seeking him out. There had been too much to do between making one last review with an eye to concessions, executing the final security transfer, and calling Koscuisko back from amusing himself with Paval I'shenko's people—and Fleet's pharmaceuticals, a minor irritation but a real one—at the charity hospital.

"Lowden. Jurisdiction Fleet Ship *Ragnarok*, commanding. No, we're still on proving-cruise; it's quite an experimental craft. Black hull technology."

His joke on Koscuisko had gone flat before Koscuisko had even left the *Ragnarok*. So Wyrlann was going to have to fill the void left by the failure of Lowden's prank.

"That's the Intelligence Officer. We just call her Two because that's her staff section, and no one can pronounce her name. We just insult her, trying. No, really, she's almost perfectly harmless, it's Koscuisko you've got to watch out for. Oh? No, trying to make a joke, I do apologize if I've given any offense."

There were Security on display here, on loan as a symbol of Fleet's power. But he was going to leave the bond-involuntaries alone. He had an arrangement with Koscuisko, and as long as Koscuisko continued to conform there was no percentage in violating his agreement; it would only destabilize his relationship with Chief Medical. Who was unstable enough already.

Lowden had called out Koscuisko's bond-involuntaries particularly for duty at Danzilar's party, as a gesture of goodwill toward Koscuisko. Bond-involuntaries were exotic and interesting. Much more liable than the run-of-the-mill Security to be beckoned into a dark corner by some curious and experimentally minded young woman, and no violation committed either, the requirements for ceremonial event Security being as liberally defined as they were.

He wouldn't be surprised—Lowden told himself, cynically, picking out the straight and somber bodies posted around the far walls at precise intervals—if Security didn't get as much exercise at parties like this as he planned to have at the service house. And free, too.

"Not at all, I would be delighted. You're very kind." This was more like it. The best way to meet new masters was with a gift in one's hand, after all. It was Danzilar who was to be their new master; but Lowden appreciated tokens of respect for the Fleet and Bench every bit as much as the next man. It wasn't as though any actual advantage would accrue to the donors, after all. "I understand that the best quality cortac brandy isn't even available for purchase. It's a distinct privilege to have a bottle."

He was taller than most of Danzilar's people; he could see over the heads of most of the crowd. He thought he saw Wyrlann at the drinks table, tossing back a thimbleful of wodac, holding out his glass for a refill. Lowden frowned. It was an impropriety for junior officers to approach food, let alone drink, while their seniors were still on reception line.

On one level, though, Lowden could understand why Wyrlann might wish to be drinking. It could well be that Wyrlann was still trying to decide what excuse he could provide for having done just as he'd been warned not to do, and breaking something while the Bench still had to pay to have it fixed.

"Well, there are always opportunities, and service in Fleet only rarely sets a career back. On balance, though, you might advise the Combine fleet. There *is* the Free Government problem to be considered. No, of course not, I didn't mean to imply any such thing."

The line seemed of people still waiting to be introduced seemed to stretch on forever.

When this was over he was going to want to have a drink. And then he had a word or two to say to his First Lieutenant.

Skelern Hanner climbed the shallow white stone stairs from the now-dark garden lawn to the veranda that ran the length of the outside of the Danzilar prince's great dancing-hall. The lights that they'd placed at the lawn's perimeter were each of them worth the sum of eight years' pay, and it wouldn't do to embarrass the Danzilar prince by failing to use them to their best effect. Soft yellow glimmerers, glowing in the darkness, beautiful and welcoming in the night . . . it was full dark, but it wasn't cold yet. Not too cold. Not yet.

Scanning the arc of golden light with a critical eye Hanner tested the curve against the measure in his mind's eye and found no fault. It was beautifully done. It was beautiful.

Full clearwall behind him, and the party going on. White stone veranda extending five, seven paces between the clearwalls and the steps; a series of shallow white steps, like a beach, like the shore of the sea sloping down to the water, an ocean of lawn.

The light at the back of the cove of new grass shimmered like the lights that shone from the far shores of Carrick Sound. The delicate blooms frothed up like spume in waves against the lights, which not only showed their luxurious profusion but drew out the sweet scent of young marbat blossoms in the early dark.

The lamps would keep the garden warm, at least at their level. With luck the frost would not come hard tonight and the blossom would live to set fruit, and bloom again next year.

Three weeks of hard labor, well used, well fed, well housed—and well worked. Three weeks, all leading up to tonight, and all of the money and all of the labor just to show a pleasant vista from inside, looking out.

And they couldn't even see out, not clearly. Could they? It was light inside, brilliant, white light glittering from faceted hanging-lights and reflected in glassware and mirrors. Surely they would not even know that the garden was there, but by the same token Skelern Hanner could see into the room clearly from outside where he stood on the broad veranda.

He had to get to the back of the house. His tools lay ready, waiting, cleaned and assembled, on the path going back. There was to be a party for them as well tonight, a party for them as had broken their backs for the Danzilar's garden. Plenty to eat and drink, and a three days' paid holiday afterward on top of their bonuses. The Danzilar was generous, and labor was cheap, but a party was nice.

Still Skelern stood.

No one would see him from inside, standing there; they would see only their own reflections. It was too dark outside. Nobody would take offense at him watching the privileged folk, not just for a minute.

And then he saw Sylyphe.

Dancing with the torturer, with Black Andrej, a man with so much Nurail blood on his hands—and yet the same man who had helped to make it right for poor Megh, the only man who had been able to make it right with her. And had cried vengeance on behalf of murdered Nurail against the Domitt Prison, but dancing with the little daughter of the Tavart, his Sylyphe—

Mute with misery Skelern stood and stared. It was the black of the officer's uniform that had caught his eye at first, and now he couldn't take his eyes off the two of them, following them as the figures of the dance carried them into clear space and then concealed them behind the bodies of the lookers-on once again.

His Sylyphe?

Never his.

A man like Koscuisko could well mate with Sylyphe. Buy her from her mother in the manner of a great prince, pay the bride-price. Take her to his home and into his bed, and breed children of his body within her sweet little belly, sons and daughters with blond hair and pale eyes that had no color to them to suckle at her breast and call her "lady Mother."

A man like Koscuisko had a natural right to take such as Sylphe to be his bride. It was the way of things. People should keep to their own place. It made life much simpler and more bearable; so why did his flesh crawl at the sight of Koscuisko's hand around her narrow waist, why did the sight of Koscuisko's beautiful smile and Sylphe's rapt admiring gaze make his blood boil?

His Sylphe.

His.

Perhaps it was true after all, and he'd done what he ought not to have done, and lost his head over a woman that could never share in his life. But she was a gardener her own self. She could not consort with Anders Koscuisko. The mere sight of the torturer would turn milk in the breast of the nursing mother, and if he even spoke to a woman who carried a child in womb the babe yet unborn would wither and die, blasted, destroyed, derelict in the mere presence of a Ship's Inquisitor.

Andrej Koscuisko was not a proper man for Sylphe.

He was a blight, a smut, a rust, a mold, a canker of worms, a creeping plague of parasites boring into the honey-heartwood in Sylphe's breast to destroy her from the inside out. Andrej Koscuisko would kill Sylphe Tavart—not in body, but how could he but kill her in her heart?

She would be honored, she would be transported to be taken by the hand as his consort, but within weeks the life would start to ebb within her, she would fade, she would fail, her pretty little fingers would crumble into dust and the dimple in her sweet ruddy cheek would dry up and crack into a gaping gray-fleshed wound.

And he couldn't stop watching his Sylphe dance.

Fleet First Lieutenant G'herm Wyrlann was drunk, but for once liquor wasn't helping, didn't make him feel better. He obtained none of the sense of effortless power from Danzilar's wodac that he usually found in wine: For once he had too much on his mind. That was unfair. He was a Fleet First Lieutenant. That anything external should have attained so much weight and importance as to interfere with his enjoyment of life was an offense—but there he was.

Captain was going to want to talk to him.

Captain was not going to be cordial and friendly.

He'd put the problem aside for as long as possible; but it was not going to be possible to put it aside any longer.

Captain had told him after the last time that he was to exercise more restraint.

Go to an unlicensed house if you have to, Captain had told him. *You don't have the rank to do as you please in a service house without Bench Audit noticing. You have to wait. You have to wait your turn. There are claims against Fleet to reimburse the Bench for damages. Sooner or later it's going to start counting against your career potential unless you're careful.*

Wyrlann remembered every word; all too clearly, really.

What was he going to do?

What was he going to say?

There was no problem with the Port Authority, of course. They didn't dare look crosswise at a Command Branch officer. It wasn't that.

His mind was fuddled with alcohol. He had to think. He couldn't face the Captain in this condition.

Stumbling a little, Fleet Lieutenant G'herm Wyrlann made his way unsteadily across the crowded room toward the great clearwalls that let out to the side garden. It would be quieter outside. It would be cold, but the coolness would help him to clear his head. He could see the white steps, gleaming in the nightlights, falling away from the terrace in shallow tiers toward the dark lawn, and the necklace of warming-lights that seemed to float at the outermost edge of the lawn, illuminating the ghostly gaiety of flower-blossom in the night.

One of the doors was cracked halfway open, and the fragrance of the cool garden night was calming. Fumbling with the catch, almost tripping over the threshold, Fleet First Lieutenant G'herm Wyrlann stumbled out into the cold dark night air.

And then he saw that he was not alone.

From where he stood on post Robert St. Clare, keeping his eye out for officers, saw the dark mass of the Fleet Lieutenant's Command Branch uniform moving through the crowd. The intensity and hue of Command Branch uniform black could not be mistaken for anything else: That was precisely why the color had been chosen, with its peculiar intensity and particular hue. Regardless of how one's class of hominid perceived color or tone Command Branch black could be consistently identified for what it was.

Robert watched the Fleet Lieutenant go with mixed feelings, personal and conditioned instincts warring in his heart and mind.

This was the beast who had brutalized his sister. His poor sister, his sweet sister, his darling Megh. She'd been like a mother to him . . . and to see her like that. After all of these years of not even knowing. His sister.

But this was also a superior commissioned officer, and Wyrlann was going out into the garden. Command Branch officers were not expected to go anywhere without a Security escort.

No one else seemed to have noticed, and it was in Robert's area of responsibility, after all.

His sister. . . .

But Wyrlann was Command Branch. Robert St. Clare was a bond-involuntary. He was expected to behave like one. His governor knew what he was supposed to do. His governor wouldn't let him stand and permit the Fleet Lieutenant to go out into the garden alone, not when he knew quite well what was expected, not when he knew that to stand would comprise a violation.

It was a profound violation, an extreme violation, a violation of all that was right and decent and moral to let such a man walk free to enjoy a party, after what Wyrlann had done to his sister—

Robert could sense the conflict building within himself. Conflict was dangerous for bond-involuntaries. Conflict confused the governor. He had to control his own internal state, or fall prey to the punishment his governor would assess; not for doing something wrong—his governor didn't know what was right and what was wrong—but for doing something that Robert had been carefully taught Fleet meant him to take to be a violation.

And it was a violation to permit a senior Command Branch officer go out without an escort. The governor didn't have to know right from wrong. It only had to pay attention to the conflict created in Robert's heart that arose when he did something he'd been conditioned not to do, or failed in some task that he'd been taught he must always complete.

Robert stepped back from his post, back into the shadows, back into the service corridor that surrounded the great hall. There was a door out to the side of the house. They'd had their briefing. They were expected to know all of the ways to get into and out of the special event location.

Out through the service corridors to the side of the great hall. Down the leafy avenue of trees. They were still losing their foliage, but the turf had been swept free of debris not two eights gone and there were no dead leaves to make a sound as he passed over. Nothing to betray his foot.

There was a work-bundle sitting in the pathway, and Robert reached down for the nearest object without thinking. A trowel, that was what it was, but one with a good edge to it. Robert tried the edge against the side of his thumb, absent-mindedly, as he went deeper into the garden, down the long avenue of trees that bordered the lawn. It was careless to leave tools unattended.

Where was the Fleet Lieutenant?

Robert came around the side of the steps to the wide stone veranda, and saw the damned bastard. Standing as smug as anyone could please, free and easy and secure in his rank. If there was any justice—if there was any right—Wyrlann would die. He deserved to die.

His body knew what had to be done, if his mind dared not

think of it. Almost not noticing, Robert loosened the trowel-blade from its handle, staring at the Fleet Lieutenant from the shadows at the foot of the stairs.

She could have been anyone's sister, even that cheeky young Skelern Hanner's sister. She wasn't just anybody's sister. She was his sister. It was his to punish the man who had hurt her. It was his right. It was his duty. It was more right that he avenge his sister's near-murder than anything Robert had ever known.

He raised the blade.

He knew.

One step, two steps, and he stood on a level with the Fleet Lieutenant, who turned toward him even as he came.

Was there someone else there, with his back to the decorative support-pillar?

What did it matter if there was someone there?

He had no doubt; he was secure, serene, utterly certain at his task. He had to do this. It was right. He didn't have to think, and if he thought—

But no. He knew what he had to do.

Fleet Lieutenant Wyrlann raised his arm and pointed, started to shout, angrily. Robert didn't hear him shout. He saw that hateful face convulsed with angry spite and threw the trowel, absolutely sure of what he was to do. He threw the trowel, he engaged the crozer-hinge in his shoulder to add enough force to the flight of the weapon to separate a man's head from his shoulders.

He was out of practice.

He threw, and the weapon found its target, and it was finished. He'd done what he had been supposed to do.

That was all.

Now he should get back to his duty post.

Someone would see the movement of the Lieutenant's body as it fell, if nothing else. There would be an alarm. He had to be back before he was missed.

He went as quickly as he had come, as quietly, his mind utterly empty of triumph or concern. It had been necessary, and he had done it. He hadn't really thought about it; he was a little surprised at himself. Should he have been able to?

His governor had never been quite right. They'd told him. Even so, should he have been able to—

To what?

He couldn't afford to think about it. He wasn't even going to think about why he couldn't think about it. That was a trap.

Slipping back quietly into the crowded room, Robert returned to his post. No one seemed to have missed him; it had taken him only a short period of time. He smoothed his face into its mask of professional readiness and stood at his post.

What had he done?

He couldn't think about it.

But it was too immense, and too unimaginable, and he couldn't not think around the edges of it, no matter how desperately he tried.

The First Lieutenant was unhappy to begin with, and the sight of a Nurail workman staring greedily through the clear-wall at his masters and their women within was intrinsically offensive. "You!" Wyrlann shouted, meaning to call Security from within doors, raising his arm and pointing. "You, you scabby piece of Nurail trash, what do you think you're doing?"

The workman seemed to jump, as if startled, turning a pale anxious—guilty—face toward the Lieutenant, backing away. Opening his mouth to speak, but Wyrlann wasn't interested in anything any Nurail had to say to him.

"Lurking around out-of-doors, you've no business here. Free Government, is it?"

Advancing on the workman where the Nurail stood with his back to a tall while pillar. Security had better be here quickly, or they'd look foolish in front of the Danzilar's house-staff. There would be penalties assessed for embarrassing Captain Lowden in front of the Danzilar prince.

"I'll have Security on you before you can—"

Something hit him.

Something struck him in the throat, he couldn't breathe.

Cast down into a black unreasoning world of blind bewil-

derment Wyrlann tried to fix his mind on what had happened,
but could not.

And died.

A door in the clearwall of the great assembly room had
been left halfway open, because of all the people that were
inside, Hanner supposed. There was a man come out into the
night; and Hanner didn't see him, didn't so much as notice
he was there, until the harsh shout of confrontation shook him
from his anguished focus on Sylyphe and the Inquisitor at
last.

"You!"

The First Lieutenant, Wyrlann. It had to be. He had heard
the man described to him, and there was the uniform, Command Branch markings—this was the man who had hurt
Megh that way, the black beast, the obscene monster, it was
him.

"You, you scabby piece of Nurail trash, what do you think
you're doing?"

The dreadful image of his friend's abused body rose up
white and red in Hanner's mind's-eye to overlay the figure of
the Lieutenant as he stood like a chipped piece of semi-opaque
layer-rock stuck in a hole in his gardener's shed to let a little
bit of light in. Skelern could not focus on the man. He could
scarcely even stir, for the horror of it. To see the Lieutenant,
and not so much as spit on him, after what he had done—to
see him standing on his feet, in his fine uniform, and Megh
helpless and naked in the white light of the recovery room,
with just a hospital blanket to cover her over from the casual
gaze of any stranger—

The Lieutenant stalked toward him imperiously, and Hanner shrank back against the roof-pillar but could not seem to
move himself further than that to flee. There was too much
conflict in his heart between hatred and self-preservation.

"Lurking around out-of-doors, you've no business here.
Free Government, is it?"

In the extremity of his surprise and shock Skelern's senses
seemed preternaturally sharp. The Lieutenant's voice sounded

as if it was a very long away. He could hear himself breathing. He could hear his heart beat. He could hear the little sounds all around him, behind him, as if of something or someone with them on the veranda. An animal in the shrubbery, or a little breeze.

Except that there was no breeze, no little wind, no animal free to move about within the Danzilar's garden. This was too large an animal. What Skelern heard was footsteps.

A sudden and irrational panic paralyzed him, held him to his place without a single movement. There was another sound now, a sound like the swift passage of a diving-bird, or the drop of a heavy piece of ripe fruit from the highest branches of a tree. A knife, a thrown knife, passing swift and sure over Hanner's right shoulder to strike the First Lieutenant with such force that the blood shot upward like a fountain, clean and bright, and Wyrlann's head reeled sideways from his neck to hang at the tether-end of a narrow scrap of flesh as Wyrlann's body collapsed from the blow.

It was a frightful thing, gut-wrenching, and Hanner's face worked without any sound, trying to call out. Trying to shout. Trying to warn the Lieutenant by sheer reflex, but it wouldn't do the Lieutenant any good, because the Lieutenant lay crumpled across the wide white steps that led down to the garden, with the blood running down into the earth and his head hanging from his carcass by a thread.

Trembling, Hanner took step forward, desperate to give the alarm. But an entire ocean of people was coming toward him now, rushing out of the great hall onto the veranda steps like the water in a tidal bore. Security. And they had seized Skelern and bound him, carried him down into the garden toward the grisly thing and forced him to his knees on the blood-sodden lawn next to the still-twitching body on the stairs before he could so much as catch his breath.

Sylyphe Tavart was awake, and at the same time dreaming.

She had never seen so grand a dancing hall in all of her life. It outshone even the great ceremonial cathedral at Saldona, where her mother had been chief of accounts.

She was wearing the traditional colored scarf of a marriageable woman for the first time in her life, and before she had left the house her mother had examined the folds of fabric over Sylyphe's modest bosom and sighed—but declined to rearrange the folds, a habit of her mother's that Sylyphe had been dreading.

And then walking down the reception line Andrej Koscuisko had called her out, spoken to her, kissed her hand with flattering courtesy and released her fingers from his grasp with something that seemed very like reluctance to Sylyphe. Dance with the daughter of the house, he had said, and Sylyphe had loved him then and there for treating her like the grown girl that she was, if her mother only realized.

Had loved him for suggesting it, yes, and had not dared to put any more weight on it than that; so when Andrej Koscuisko—the reception line broken up, the dances about to begin—had sought them out and presented himself to her mother once more to "request the pleasure of your daughter's company" it was almost more than Sylyphe could believe.

It was a sallbrey, the first dance. She had studied the Dolgorukij folk-dances diligently in order to be able to be a credit to her mother and to Jaccary Cordage and Textile when the time came to demonstrate their desire to participate in all of the Danzilar prince's goals. She knew the steps in a sallbrey, they were among the easiest to learn and to perform, and she could concentrate all of her energies on fixing this moment in her mind forever and ever after this.

He was the inheriting son of the Koscuisko prince, and in the Dolgorukij Combine he outranked the Danzilar prince himself. The wealth of the Koscuisko familial corporation was staggering, but more than that, he was the Ship's Inquisitor, a man with the power of life and death—sweet easeful healing or atrocious torment—both under his authority.

Dancing with her.

A little taller than she was, but not too much so; she felt perfectly at ease with him—or at least she didn't feel awkward. Taller, and all in duty black, for everyone to see—the warmth of his body, the feel of the supple muscle of his fore-

arm, the elegance of his small white hands, the effortless grace
with which he danced, the strength held in reserve. . . .

The figure of the dance carried them across the dance floor
and back again. She could catch glimpses of their reflection
in the clearwalls at the side of the room, the bright lights
reflecting off the glass like a mirror. He was her lord, and she
was his princess—at least while they danced the sallbrey.

She was beautiful.

Partnered by the son of the Koscuisko prince, a grown girl
now even in her mother's conservative estimation, she was a
princess in his arms, and he smiled and chatted with her with
unaffected simplicity and candor while they danced.

*How does the daughter of the Tavart this evening? The
medication you prepared is very good indeed, it works quite
well. And kind of you to take thought for the leavings. I saw
a man for an arthritis of the joints who sat and wept as we
our interview conducted, and all to be back at his home for
so long as he could smell the flowers.*

He carried a faint perfume with him for his own part, a
musky-peppery scent that seemed to be a thing of soap and
skin rather than a grooming-fragrance. She could not analyze
it into its component parts, but she dizzied herself trying to
fix the exact taste of it within her heart and mind forever. Oh,
if she could only make it last, if she could fold the fabric of
time back upon itself and keep this instant of transcendent joy
forever she would not grudge the price. Whatever it might be.

The dance could not last forever.

But they were interrupted even before the last few measures
of the tune signaled an end to bliss and fantasy.

One of the Danzilar's house-men stood at the front of the
ranks of observers, and as Sylphe passed by in the arms of
the Koscuisko prince she noticed one of the *Ragnarok*'s Security was there as well—a very tall man, and ugly, with a
ruined face so flattened by nature or by accident it looked as
though his features had been razed flat from forehead to chin.
She saw them there, and knew that the Koscuisko prince could
see them too; maybe they had only come to watch?

She knew as soon as she caught sight of them that she was

not to be so lucky. Koscuisko turned his head away when they passed, but almost at once turned back and gave a nod. So it was over.

"Oh, this is—very unfortunate indeed," Koscuisko said. "Come, we must escape. Follow with me."

He danced her out of the figure of the dance, off of the dance floor, so gracefully it seemed part of the dance itself. The Security were waiting for them; how had Koscuisko brought them so precisely to the place? She could spare little of her mind to wonder at that. She was to be deprived of her lord, who had never been her lord, who had been hers only so long as she could dance with him. She was bereft. She was her mother's daughter all the same, and knew she could not show her disappointment.

No words passed between Koscuisko and his man, who only bowed. His fingers seemed to twitch, was it just nerves? Or was it a message? Because Koscuisko sighed, and spoke to the Danzilar's house-man.

"Escort the daughter of the house Tavart back to her mother, then, with my profound apologies. Sylyphe. Miss Ta-vart. I must beg that you excuse me. I am asked for."

He was not just asked for but desired. Profoundly. Passion-ately. Fiercely. Couldn't he tell how much she wanted him?

Or could he tell, and saved her face as best he could?

She cast about for some polite response, but Koscuisko didn't wait.

Koscuisko bowed and kissed her hand, and it seemed to Sylyphe that he almost touched her fingers to his cheek as he straightened from his bow.

She could not be sure.

And he was gone.

The house-man bowed in turn and gestured with his hand for her to precede him through the crowd. To go back to her mother. To sit alone for the rest of the evening, for how could she countenance another partner, who had danced with the Koscuisko prince?

◇ Seven

"**T**his piece of trash." Hanner knelt low on the ground beside the now-covered corpse with someone's boot planted firmly between his shoulderblades to ensure he wouldn't be tempted to try to run away. He couldn't see a thing except for blood, and the boots. What he could hear was hard for him to understand, stunned as he was by the shock of the event and Security's rough handling. "Andrej. Is there anything to be done? Anything at all?"

"No, nothing, Captain." He'd heard that voice before, not long before, cold and moderate in pitch, with an accent. Dolgorukij accent. "Traumatic amputation, there's complete severance for spinal, and the brain is more than six-eighths gone already. It would be a very slim chance even if we had the resources and had caught it sooner. And the resources are not here, and we did not catch it soon enough by half. There's nothing I can do."

He didn't know what a Dolgorukij accent might be, but Koscuisko was Dolgorukij, and he had heard Koscuisko in hospital. And in the Tavart's parlor, of course, later on.

"Were you able to actually see anything, Captain Lowden?" Maybe that voice was familiar, too. But Hanner was still too confused in his mind to put a name to it.

"Unfortunately not, Specialist Vogel." Captain Lowden, again? That would make sense. The dominant voice one way or the other, or so it seemed. Skelern felt sick to his stomach, and hoped he wasn't going to vomit. It would be such a mess.

And there was such a mess already. . . . "All I really saw was Wyrlann turn and point. And then his head jumped off his shoulders. Quite a sight."

The Captain's voice came closer; the foot moved off his back. "And this is the man poor Wyrlann was pointing at. Hadn't expected to be caught about his dirty business, obviously. I'm surprised he had the nerve to go through with the assassination, what with Wyrlann looking right at him."

What man was that? There'd been someone on the veranda, moving as quietly as a small breeze in the bushes?

"You're quite sure there was nothing else, sir," the second voice urged. Someone kicked Hanner in the stomach, suddenly and very hard, and laid him flat on the ground, gasping for breath. The lawn held the blood like a sponge, and yet somebody put his foot to the side of Hanner's face and pressed down hard.

"Vogel, I as good as saw him throw the knife. We need to move quickly on this."

Hanner couldn't breathe for tasting blood. The knowledge that it wasn't even his own blood sickened him, and the pressure of the foot against his face filled him with irrational fear. He tried to breathe as best he could through one nostril, shuddering at the stink of the fluid that he could not help but draw into his lungs.

Shuddering was a mistake.

The Captain stepped down harder on his face, and Hanner stilled himself as best he could in desperate horror. Captain Lowden was still talking; and though Hanner couldn't quite grasp the meaning of the words, he knew with sickening certainty they meant that something terrible was going to happen to him.

"I don't doubt but that there's Free Government behind this, in light of the recent intelligence reports. We can't leave the port to the Danzilar prince with a potential cell of insurrectionaries unaccounted for."

The horrid pressure of the booted foot shifted at last, and Hanner gulped his breath in great gasping sobs. There were people at him again, pulling him to his feet, straining his arms

painfully against the restraints that they latched around his
wrists behind his back. He was having a hard time keeping
his balance, but fortunately for him Security still held him
fast.

"I'll want you to get started right away, Andrej, bring me
confession before fastmeal and I won't ask First Officer where
Security were when all this happened. Though come to think
of it—"

Things began to come back into focus as he finally caught
his breath, now that he was no longer doubled over to the
ground. The body. Andrej Koscuisko, his rival in a contest
for Sylyphe's attention that could be no real contest at all.
Security, and some other people, important people he'd no
business even looking at. Why had they shackled him?

Captain Lowden was looking past Koscuisko at one of the
few Security troops here that Hanner had met before. "I don't
think I saw you on post, where were you? No. Never mind."
The Captain of the *Ragnarok*. Hanner stared up at him in awe.
"We have more important issues to address. I'll let it go for
now. Confession in due form, Koscuisko, and go as lightly as
you can, we wouldn't want to cheat the Bench of its lawful
revenge."

Koscuisko bowed; and Hanner could not see the expression
on his face, shadowed as it was by the light from the great
room within. There hadn't been an alarm. Had there been?
He could hear music, laughter, as if the party was continuing,
oblivious. Why hadn't there been an alarm? Shouldn't they
raise the hue and cry, to track the murderer?

"Instruction received is instruction implemented. Stildyne," Koscuisko said. "If you would go relieve the other
gentlemen. Specialist Vogel. There is a Record still at the Port
Authority, one presumes? And come to think of it, will the
courthouse have power?"

The Captain clearly had other ideas. "Take my Security
one-point-three rather, Andrej. Your people have been worked
too hard, too long. You told me so yourself, as I remember.
I'll see you in the morning."

Then Captain Lowden moved away back toward the lights,

back toward the warmth, back toward the music.

"What was that all about?" The voice was the one that had been identified as Specialist Vogel; the man wore a different uniform, one without rank-markings. "Captains interfering in the First Officer's business?"

"A game." Koscuisko's response was savage. Hanner wondered what Koscuisko was so angry about. "Captain Lowden likes to play games. In this one he reminds me that if I don't do as he has instructed me he has a complaint to cry against my Security. Just in case I had had any ideas about consulting my own judgment in how quickly a lawful confession was to be obtained."

"I'd say he made it pretty clear what he expected." Vogel's agreement was not an entirely approving one. "Makes a man a little uncomfortable, if you don't mind my saying so. He didn't actually see the murder."

Hanner had. Hanner had seen the murder. But no one had asked him about the murder. Why hadn't anyone asked him about it? Maybe they had, and he didn't remember. His head was spinning. He could hardly keep his balance, and his stomach was going to pitch at any moment. Just as well he hadn't had his supper.

"What does it matter?" Koscuisko asked. Hanner knew it mattered. Hanner knew it mattered critically —but Koscuisko was still speaking. "If he's guilty he will confess. If he is not guilty there will be no confession."

Only . . .

"As you say, sir." Even to Hanner Vogel sounded dubious enough to strike a spark from Koscuisko, who exploded in challenge quick and sharp almost before Vogel had finished.

"Do you suggest otherwise, Specialist?"

For a moment it seemed to Hanner that Vogel might do just that. But the moment passed. Was that a good thing? Vogel bowed. "Of course not, your Excellency. You'll excuse me, sir, getting back to the party, and all."

Koscuisko glared after the retreating man until Vogel reached the steps; then abruptly transferred his attention back to the grotesque gory scene in the garden.

"Very well." Koscuisko glanced at him now; met his eyes, and let his gaze travel down the length of Hanner's body, soiled from kneeling in the blood that pooled at the foot of the stairs. "Young Hanner. I am heartily sorry to see you here. The Bench makes no provision for family feeling where its officers are concerned."

There hadn't been an alarm, and there would be no alarm. Because they thought that they had found the murderer. That he was the murderer.

"I've done no murder!" Skelern protested, so horrified by his realization of what he was accused of that he nearly stuttered in his frantic need to speak out. "Only watching Sylyphe, for a little moment, there's no harm in watching Sylyphe dance, is there?"

But Koscuisko only snapped his fingers. Rough hands began to drag him away, across the lawn toward the maintenance-track beyond the screening trees. Maybe it was a killing offense to have desired the consort of an Inquisitor. But Uncle Andrej dealt honestly with a man, and Skelern had not realized until he'd seen them dance that Sylyphe was to be soul and flesh of Anders Koscuisko. Surely he could not be put to death for having offended in error.

"What does his Excellency think, a crozer-lance?"

He could hear the words behind him as Koscuisko followed after. Koscuisko. But it was all right then, after all. Wasn't it?

"No, it seems to have been a trowel-blade, Robert. Perhaps a hoe. We'll have the details soon enough."

"It—must have been—the crozer-hinge. The force, the height—"

He knew the voice. St. Clare. Robert St. Clare, a Nurail, but not one like himself. The reproach Koscuisko made grew fainter, in its volume, as Koscuisko stopped while Hanner was hurried off.

"Yes, of course, Robert. What is your point, exactly? You are to go back to your duty post. Captain Lowden will be watching for you. You are to go now. I do not want to be angry with you."

Anybody else, and he would only have been able to despair. But this was Andrej Koscuisko, the bloody butcher, Koscuisko, Black Andrej. And everybody knew that if you were guilty there was no hope, no chance to escape punishment.

But every Nurail also knew that Andrej Koscuisko had the truth-sense on him, the curse of the blood was upon him, and he knew when a man was telling the truth.

It didn't mean a great deal, since Koscuisko was required to test, and the test itself was terrible; but it meant enough. Koscuisko did not condemn the innocent for crimes that they had had no action in.

And Hanner was innocent in word or deed of the murder of the man who had tortured his poor friend. Koscuisko would know.

He would have to bear the testing of it, yes.

But Koscuisko would know.

Robert St. Clare stood in his place. He was safe and secure as long as he was in his place, and at attention-rest as he was expected to be.

Safe and secure, but far from serene. What had he done? And why hadn't he stopped to think that someone would be taken for it? He should have known. Someone had to be taken for it, and there were Nurail all over Port Burkhayden; it was a Nurail port. They had taken that gardener away, and he knew that Hanner hadn't done it. He knew that Hanner couldn't have done it, but did Koscuisko know?

He'd tried to tell Koscuisko, once he'd realized. He'd tried to tell him, and he hadn't been able to. Why had his governor let him do the deed and then prohibited him from speaking of it? He'd known that he was right to do it when he'd done it, and he could even guess that that was why he'd been able to do it at all. But he was wrong to keep silent and let Hanner go to torture. Why wouldn't his governor let him confess himself now?

Because—even though she was his sister, his beloved sister, his sweet sister that he hadn't seen for so many years— even though she was his sister, *his* sister, not that Skelern

Hanner's sister, he would not have done the thing if he had
been thinking and had realized that someone would have to
be taken for it.

He knew what a Tenth Level Command Termination
meant, and at his maister's hands particularly.

And if the gardener had not done the murder, as Robert
knew quite well that he had not, still Hanner might well prove
guilty of enough besides; and Captain Lowden forced such
compromises on a man. Trades. If Captain Lowden were to
tell Koscuisko to either execute the Tenth Level or keep after
other prisoners from Danzilar's people until someone confessed, would not his maister be forced to bend his neck and
do the horrible and unjust thing?

It had never been so blatant, so horrible, ever yet, but had
Koscuisko not agreed before to execute at a more advanced
Level in order to keep as many still-unaccused souls from the
torture as he could?

Why had his governor let him do the thing, the thing which
until it had been well done he had not known for certain that
he could do, and then not let him do the smaller task, confess
himself to keep an innocent man from coming beneath his
maister's hand?

If only, if only Koscuisko could have heard him, if only
Koscuisko could remember. But Robert was too confused now
in his mind between his private torment and the stress on his
governor to be sure of whether he'd even really managed to
say, about the crozer-hinge. If Koscuisko had heard him, Koscuisko would remember, but would his poor maister be too
deeply sunk into his passion to call the point to mind before
it was too late for Skelern Hanner?

Closing his eyes as tightly as he knew how, Robert tried
to set a governor on his mind, since the one the Fleet had
given him was not helping. He could do nothing now for
Skelern Hanner. He had not stopped to realize what would
have to happen, if he did it right, if he could do it at all.
Perhaps in another little while he would be able to speak to
Chief Stildyne, and Hanner not more than a few hours the
worse for it. Not that he cared about Hanner, he didn't know

Hanner; although the man seemed to be fond of his sister.

Oh, his sister, after so many years, and then to see her so unkindly served, knowing exactly what the Lieutenant had done. . . .

He blinked his eyes open hastily, feeling his balance beginning to erode.

He could not move from his place. He did not have permission. His governor was that much more strict with him now, it seemed, now that the damage was already done, now that he only wanted to surrender himself to punishment—because he could get away with it, he had gotten away with it, but an innocent man was to suffer if he could not confess.

He could not move from his place. His governor protected him from punishment, would not permit him to speak the word that would put himself in jeopardy. It was intended to help him censor his incautious tongue, to ensure that he would not challenge an officer or speak an actionable violation of some sort.

It protected him too well.

He trembled with the fearful frustration of it all, and stood at attention-rest in his place.

It wasn't far enough to the local Bench offices by half, and transport got there entirely too soon. Captain Lowden's Security handled the gardener with the exaggerated roughness typical of people who were not accustomed to the task, and overdoing things accordingly; but what difference could it make?

Andrej said nothing, absorbed in his own gloomy meditations. He knew Skelern Hanner, at least in a manner of speaking. He almost thought that if he knew Hanner any better he'd like the man. But Lowden had said the word. There was to be no help for it.

There was a night watchman. Andrej sent two Security with him to bring the auxiliary power on line. It was true that he didn't need the Record to obtain a lawful confession; he held the Writ, which was necessary and sufficient of itself for that function.

But he had to be able to see to do it.

He went through to the courtroom while he waited. It was empty, of course, but Miss Janisib—the senior Security on this team—had already found a chair for him from somewhere; and as Andrej was trying to decide whether she'd had rhyti leaf on her—or had simply borrowed some in a hurry from Center House—she came back into the room with one of her fellows, carrying a table sturdy enough to be used for his purpose if he elected it.

Janisib knew.

She wasn't bond-involuntary, but there weren't enough bond-involuntaries to go around, and she'd been on one of his Security teams when he'd got to *Ragnarok*. She'd transferred soon after, but the fact remained that she knew enough of what went on around an Inquiry to direct the other members of her team.

By the time the power came on to reveal the depressing extent to which the courtroom was stripped, Miss Janisib had things arranged quite creditably, all things considered.

A heavy armchair for him to sit down in when he got tired of standing or wanted to catch his breath.

A table, long enough to stretch a prisoner at length upon, sturdy enough to take the various stresses of weight and blows and the tensions to which it might be subjected. Rhyti in an open pan with a cracked flask to sup it from, but it was good rhyti. It was not to be imagined that Jan simply carried rhyti about on her person, for such an eventuality. "Thank you, Miss Janisib. If I could see my prisoner, now."

Hanner himself they had left under guard in a closet outside while Security did what could be done to make a workspace out of an abandoned courtroom. Andrej stared at his interrogations kit while he waited, brooding about things.

Confession for breakfast, the Captain had said. Lowden was sure to seek recreation at the service house; it was an unfailing habit. Andrej could only hope that his Captain wouldn't be so insensitive as to beat up another Service bond-involuntary.

Now Security was marching Hanner in through the double doors at the foot of the room; and it occurred to Andrej that there wasn't any place in particular he wanted them to put Hanner. Looking around for a secure chain from the ceiling or a post or hook in the wall Andrej thought hard and fast, aware all the while of how ridiculous this was.

If he took up his trefold shackles and used the interconnecting chain he could pass it beneath the surface of the table they'd brought him, and shackle Hanner's wrists one to a side. Hanner couldn't possibly work the chain down to one end of the table and under the table-legs to free himself; or if he could he wasn't going to be able to manage the trick without Andrej noticing. So that would do.

But there was something that Andrej needed before Hanner was chained. He could have Hanner stripped just as easily after as before; but the gardener was probably not well paid. His clothing was probably all he possessed that was worth handing on to someone who might want it to remember him by: his sister, perhaps, and how could Andrej hope to check on her recovery after this, knowing what he was about to do to her brother?

"You'll want to undress, Hanner," Andrej suggested, holding his hand up in a sudden sharp gesture of warning to Security to let Hanner alone. "Or your clothing will be damaged, as well as soiled. We'll see to it that Megh gets your things, at least."

It was hard for the gardener to strip himself naked with so many unfriendly eyes watching him. Yet Andrej knew better than to even think of dismissing Security to leave him alone with an unbound prisoner: Inquisitors died that way. It was a form of suicide, one that masqueraded as a lapse in judgment. Andrej Koscuisko had not come this far to die of an accident, however deliberately courted. Security would stay.

Had he survived so long for this to come to him, then?

Was it not better to die if to live meant to ruin a decent young man who had avenged his sister, and draw Hanner's death out for seven to ten days in vengeance for a man who tortured helpless women?

But *he* was a man who tortured helpless women.

And something inside of him was focused on a quite different issue. *Eight to eleven*, the voice of his appetite whispered to him, encouragingly. *Eight to eleven. You can do better than you did at the Domitt. This man is fit and strong, and inured to hard labor and to privation. He'll last much better. You could get twelve.*

Andrej shut the seductive meditation off with an effort. It was not time. All too soon he would yield to his own thirst for Hanner's pain because he would not be able to do his work without consenting to take pleasure in it. But he didn't have to start that this early. Captain Lowden wanted a clean confession. He could do it without succumbing to his own beast; there would be need enough—pain enough—grim red atrocity sufficient to slake Andrej's fiendish appetite, later. Tenth Level. Command Termination.

Eight to eleven, you could go twelve . . .

No, Andrej told himself firmly. He'd have none of it. Hanner unclothed himself to the skin and folded his garments into a stack; Miss Janisib carried the clothing away to wrap up in a bundle and stood by the door as the rest of Captain Lowden's Security followed instruction and chained Hanner over the table.

"Thank you, gentles. Now you are excused." Andrej lifted his field interrogations kit onto the table and opened it in front of Hanner, so that Hanner could see what he was doing. "I will call, if I want you. Yes? Go away."

They seemed a little startled at his blunt language, but Andrej didn't care. He was accustomed to being blunt in torture room.

The door at the far end of the room closed behind them; Andrej and Hanner remained alone in the center of the room. One of them clothed. One of them chained. Andrej found what he wanted, and loaded the osmo-stylus with the dose.

"This is the way of it, Skelern." No need at this point for the formal introduction, *My name is Andrej Koscuisko, and I hold the Writ to which you must answer.* So much was understood. "You are taken under accusation for the murder of Fleet First Lieutenant G'herm Wyrlann, Jurisdiction Fleet Ship *Ragnarok.* It is the Captain who cries you guilty, and has also laid it on me that you confess before sunrise tomorrow."

Hanner's face was dirty, stained with mud and dried blood. Dried filth: the blood of the man who had savaged his sister. And very pale, underneath it all, but resolute of spirit for all that. "Or else what, your Excellency?"

Which was a good sign; or a bad sign. And Andrej wasn't going to indulge himself even so far as to try to guess which. "Or else I will be hard pressed to protect my Security, but that's not your problem. Now. This is commonly called extract of allock, class-five speak-serum, from the Controlled List."

Setting the loaded stylus down on the table where Hanner could watch it for him, Andrej started to unpack his kit. Showing the instruments of torture was one of the oldest traditions of the craft. It was also one of the most useful and least hurtful of the persuasions Andrej had at his hand; if Hanner could be persuaded to speak freely, they would both be the better for it. For the time being.

"There is circumstantial evidence that places you at the murder site when it happened. The Captain's cry against you is very serious, because of his rank, but it is still hearsay of a sort and not direct evidence. Your confession is absolutely required to find you subject to the penalty for this shocking crime."

Why was he telling Hanner this? Why should he waste his time being honest or candid? Wouldn't it be the same in the end if he forced a confession and lied about how he'd obtained it? The Bench didn't care, not when it came down to it. As long as what could be made to pass for justice was done the Bench overlooked any number of merely procedural irregularities.

"You have two choices before you now. You can confess to me the murder, I will confirm it with an appropriate speak-serum, and we will be done until the time arrives for the penalty to be assessed." *Eight to eleven days*, the voice whispered, eagerly. *You could go twelve*. Andrej frowned, concentrating.

"Or I will administer this dose, which encourages but will not compel truthful utterance. It is still only circumstantial evidence. My authority is to test you with this drug and a degree of coercive persuasion until you say truth."

Hanner looked relieved. He had no cause to be, but Andrej knew what was on his mind even before Hanner spoke. "Then there's no need, your Excellency, and I'll get dressed, it's cold in here. Give me the speak-serum, your Excellency, I'll tell you the truth here and now, drug or no drug. It was only watching you dance with the little maistress. I had neither word nor deed in the murder of the Fleet Lieutenant, though I can't deny that I'm not sorry for it."

Watching him dance? Oh, watching Sylphe Tavart, rather. If only it was so easy as that. "I appreciate your willingness to cooperate. But I cannot take your word at face value, not with the charges that my Captain has cried. If you confessed to the murder—but since you do not you must be ready to ask yourself, very urgently indeed, whether you had better not do so."

Andrej picked up the dose and pressed it through the browned skin at Hanner's shoulder as he spoke. Hanner was right. It was cold in here. Hanner had goose-bumps; but the dose went through all the same.

"I can't say I've killed the Fleet Lieutenant." Hanner was frightened, and rightly so. But Hanner was firm. "Because I'd no hand in it. And you'll know it, soon enough I hope. I'm innocent. Even if you're to beat me for being so rude as to contradict such a man as the Fleet Captain, Lowden."

Andrej had no respect for Fleet Captain Lowden for his own part, but that didn't mean Andrej lacked respect and sound understanding of what Captain Lowden could do, with his rank. What things Captain Lowden was lawfully entitled to say, or plead, or demand by virtue of his rank.

"Thank you, but it is not good enough." Andrej didn't have the drugs that it would take to elicit a confession at the Fifth Level with speak-sera alone. Results were required. More direct forms of physical coercion were authorized for use in tandem with a speak-serum. Andrej picked up his favorite whip. "We have some hours ahead of us to test, then. Why should you deny the deed? You had the motive. You were there. What could be more natural than to have revenged your sister?"

Once he had laid the soles of Hanner's bare feet open with his whip he would not need to take quite so many precautions against Hanner running away. There were important psychological issues there as well. It would be very awkward for Hanner, chained to the table as he was, if he could not put his weight on his own two feet. It might help him toward an appropriately submissive state of mind.

"I had no weapon, sir, and had I done I'd still have no knowledge of how to use it—your Excellency—"

Hanner spoke on as Andrej moved around the table and behind him. But Hanner's nerves betrayed him to himself. He could not help looking back over his shoulder, his words trailing off as Andrej ran the length of the lash through his lightly clenched fist to straighten it of any stray kinks.

"Face front, if you please."

Oh, Andrej knew the hunger for it, now. Even though he thought that he liked Hanner. Even though Andrej felt sorry for him. Hanner was meat to the knife, nothing more. Andrej Koscuisko was come into his dominion, and rejoiced to recognize it for his own.

"Yes, sir, but I'm innocent, I didn't—"

Swinging the whip around in a long, almost lazy arc, Andrej made his first mark on living canvas. Skelern Hanner shouted with surprise and pain, and stumbled to regain his footing where he stood chained to the table. That wouldn't do. That wouldn't do at all. Andrej moved more quickly, this time, and brought the snapper-end of the stout whip down brutally hard against the bottom of Hanner's foot. The left foot. Just below the ball of the foot, nestled in to the tender place above one arch of muscle and beside another.

Hanner was not so much surprised, this time.

It was a good beginning.

Andrej knew he could have confession before morning. One way or another: and he no longer cared which.

*   *   *

Mendez liked the fancy pattern-dancing, the men and women of all ages in different traditional modes of dress representing different Dolgorukij ethnicities, each of them cheerful and energetic and all apparently having a good time. He tried to picture the Chief Medical Officer on the dance floor, unable to make sense of the projected image. Still, it looked like fun. Under other circumstances he might have been tempted to join in the demonstration, and see if he couldn't interest one or two of the ladies in a Santone sawelling.

"I had thought to tempt your Chief Medical Officer with the fanshaw." The Danzilar prince, beside him, sounded nothing short of gloomy; and Mendez didn't blame him. "I wonder if you know, First Officer. My cousin is a very pretty dancer, especially in fanshaw; because after all his family *is* Koscuisko."

Quite right, too. He wouldn't have guessed Koscuisko even could dance, which made him regret not having seen it all the more. Stildyne gave the Chief Medical Officer good marks for a sufficient degree of athleticism, true enough, but Stildyne was notoriously prejudiced, and combat drill was not an infallible index of how well a man could dance.

"If his Excellency would care to explain, about a 'fanshaw?' Can't say that there are many opportunities for such as this, on board ship."

The Danzilar prince was a little taller than Koscuisko, and his hair was brown. Blue eyes, though. There were people out there on the dance floor who looked so much like Koscuisko and Danzilar put together that it was easy to imagine a blood relationship.

Now Danzilar smiled a little sadly, gesturing politely with his cupped hand palm-uppermost at the demonstration dance. "Fanshaw is a challenge-piece, by nature. Here they are dancing mixed fanshaw, a courting dance, although the relationships that one dances to obtain are courtships of very short duration. Little permanence."

Or weeklong wedlock, Mendez guessed. "Is that why they're all tricked out so bright?" He'd never seen Andrej in a ruffled shirt, much less a brilliant blue embroidered vest. He'd never seen Koscuisko wearing bright green leggings or a painted leather skirt. In fact the only color he'd ever associated with Koscuisko was the little bit of crimson in the cording on his sleeves that identified his area of service. Oh, and the bar of matching crimson that lined through his rank-plaquet, in token of his custody of the Writ to Inquire.

"Well, one wishes to impress the ladies. He has unfair advantage there, because one need not wear one's land-holdings for everyone to be impressed by them."

Andrej was rich, was that what Danzilar was saying? Hard to tell, with Dolgorukij. He already knew that Andrej was rich. The comment gave him an idea, though. There were probably questions he could ask his host, with Koscuisko gone, about all the things he didn't know about the Chief Medical Officer; he might well learn something interesting. About Koscuisko's children, for instance, since Two dropped maddeningly vague hints about their number and situation from time to time.

If a man couldn't pry into the private lives of his fellow Primes then there was no reason to keep on living; gossip was the spice of life.

For Intelligence Officers and Ship's Executives gossip sometimes provided information that came in very handily at the most unexpected points. But the dance was breaking up, and he had already seen Lowden signaling for him; he could not see his way clear to pretending that he hadn't noticed, not since Danzilar had apparently seen it too.

"I hope we get a chance to watch some more of that. It's interesting. With your permission, your Excellency, Captain Lowden seems to need me, if you will excuse the interruption."

It probably wasn't strictly necessary to excuse himself formally. He didn't really need Danzilar's permission. But somebody should probably be at least polite to their host, especially after having soiled his clean white garden steps with blood and an ugly corpse. And if anybody was going to be polite it would have to be him, because Lowden wasn't even pretending very hard any longer.

Nodding, Danzilar frowned a little. "Naturally I do not dream of impeding. Come back to me when the music starts, I will have the dancing-master tell to you about the time when the son of the Koscuisko prince took out nine of his cousins in one set."

Which sounded ever so much more interesting than whatever Lowden could have on his mind. The Captain had been all but publicly gloating about getting a Tenth Level from Koscuisko ever since they'd taken the gardener away. Mendez bowed out of courtesy and retreated; Lowden was visibly impatient, and the sooner he got whatever it was out of the way the sooner Mendez would be free again to pump that dancing-master for juicy tidbits about Koscuisko's other life. His real life. Well, maybe he should just think of it as "other," after all.

Lowden had started for the front entrance, once he had apparently assured himself that Mendez was following. Ralph only just caught up with him on his way out.

"I've had enough of this," Lowden said firmly, his voice sufficiently emphatic to get the attention of everyone within wire range. "I'm going to the service house to take some healthful recreation. I'll need Security, of course, and you'll cover for me if Danzilar notices that I've gone."

Predictable. But very impolite. "Choice of Security, your Excellency? Double teams, perhaps." Apart from it being rude to leave their host's welcoming party without so much as telling Danzilar about it, there was a safety issue to consider. There were Free Government agents in Burkhayden, by Intelligence report—Two had said so. Well, she'd said that there were reports. And then of course a person might want to be a little prudent, when it was Lowden's Lieutenant whose assault had set things in such an uproar. Wyrlann was dead, and maybe that would turn out to be all there was to be to that. Still, Captain Griers Verigson Lowden was an unpopular man even in quiet ports, among people who'd had a chance to get to know him.

"Where's that bunch of Andrej's? The slaves. He'll be distracted; I might just have myself some fun with them. Not that I care. But it makes him so edgy when he doesn't know."

If Koscuisko was going to be distracted—and who would know better than Lowden, about that?—then what real difference could it make whether Lowden took Koscuisko's bond-involuntaries or not?

Mendez didn't feel like playing. "His Excellency has relieved the advance party, but Koscuisko's people have been on line for almost as long. And Koscuisko takes more energy out of a person. Take another of Koscuisko's teams, if you want to make a point of it."

At the rate Koscuisko was going one more worry, one more uncertainty, one more outrage was going to send him off on a hard oblique so sharp that they'd never find his mind to stuff back into his skull again.

"Forget Koscuisko's people, he's going to be giving them enough of a workout." Lowden seemed to have changed his mind anyway, but whether it was because he'd accepted Mendez's point was anybody's guess. "Give me, oh, who've you got? All right, one-point-four. I'll take one-point-four."

Mendez lifted an eyebrow at the senior man on one-point-four, Anji Ghaf; and, bowing, she went to collect the rest of her team. Security one-point-four it was. "Will the Captain be returning to Center House, or shall we send for you in the morning?"

"I'll let you know." And why not? Mendez asked himself rhetorically. Why shouldn't a ship of war with a crew of more than seven hundred souls hang impotent in neutral orbit while its Captain slept off an evening's sensual indulgence in the service house that no one else had been granted leave to visit? Command Branch had its prerogatives, after all. And that was one of them.

"Captain Lowden will be needing you for the rest of the shift. Carry on, Miss Ghaf."

And now that Lowden had reminded him about Koscuisko's Security, one of Andrej's bond-involuntaries had been looking a little less than eight in eighty. He was going

to have to ask Chief Stildyne to check on St. Clare, just in
case there was something more than usually wrong with that
damned defective governor of his.

Then maybe everybody would just leave him alone, and he
could go back to ferreting out the deep dark secrets of his
Chief Medical Officer's youthful days of cheerful frolic.

Eights passed.

The table had proved itself more useful than Andrej had
hoped. Hanner's chains had caught beneath its surface on a
rod or brace of some sort, and prevented Hanner's weight
from pulling him by the shackled arms painfully down to the
end of the table to the floor. No, Hanner was caught there, as
efficiently as though Andrej were at home in Secured Medical
and Hanner lying across the whipping-block.

Hanner wept, half-strapped onto the table, wept with pain
and with the fear of more pain. He could see the whip when
Andrej came from his left side, and he was quite properly
apprehensive of it. Andrej had worked him hard in the past
eights: and yet something wasn't right.

The dose he'd administered and refreshed was a solid per-
former even at the next Level, one Andrej could rely upon to
eat away at a man's will to keep his truth still to himself.
Hanner had had two doses of it, one even moderately increased in consideration of Hanner's wiry muscular frame—
it could well be that Hanner was heavier than he looked.

More than two doses in a space of four eights Andrej could
not see his way clear to administer, and still there was the
fact that the first dose should have been enough. It was not
to be expected that a man yield to confess himself of such a
crime on the persuasion of the whip alone, no matter how
thrilling the sound of its impact against helpless quivering
flesh, no matter how honestly Hanner reported the pain that
the whip granted him. But there had been the drug.

Andrej strolled forward to stand at the middle of the table.
Here was where Hanner lay face-down on the table's surface,
one cheek flat against the sweat-damp wood. Trembling. Trying to catch his breath. Andrej wiped tears of pain from Han-

ner's cheeks carefully with the gathered coils of his whip, and waited, caressing Hanner's cheek with bloodied leather while Hanner settled down.

"What is the matter with you, Skelern Hanner?"

Hanner winced, and closed his eyes tightly. Andrej tried to explain. "I am at a loss to explain your stubborn behavior. One would almost think you had no desire to confess. Is that the problem, Hanner? Have I failed to inspire the correct sense of urgency? Do you lack motivation to make your confession?"

Hanner was polite; it was one of the things that made his intransigence confusing. "No, thank you. Sir. I wish. Very heartily. That I could confess, and be done with this. Your Excellency."

That was all to the good. "Is it that you do not wish to confess to the murder of our Fleet Lieutenant? Because that is the only confession that is of interest, you know that."

Eights, and Hanner was marked from neck to foot, bleeding and bruised. Andrej knew. It had been hard work, if not without its satisfactions. Now he was becoming bored and a little anxious, and he had rather liked young Skelern Hanner; he wanted to make as clean a confession of it as possible. It would mean less to be suffered in the long run, if that could truly be considered when there was the Tenth Level—

"I. I would like. To confess." For a moment Andrej was hopeful, resting his hand against Hanner's back encouragingly. "But must not. To a crime. Which I have not committed."

"You must not want it hard enough." In truth that was the only conclusion to be drawn. Since Hanner had committed murder—and Andrej had no reason, no real reason, to doubt but that he had—the only thing Andrej could think of to explain Hanner's stubbornness was a failure of motivation. Not even the half-choked cry of desperation with which Hanner answered him was good enough.

"Your Excellency— "

"I am sorry to have to say it. But you are simply not adequately engaged in the process. I wonder how I am to be sure of your attention?''

Whether or not he liked Hanner had nothing to do with what he craved from him. And what Andrej knew he was working toward was a good confession; Lowden had required it. But in the mean time he could make Hanner cry; and Andrej's fish sought each whimper of anguish as eagerly as it might seek the blue ocean. His body ached with it. Hanner would pay him back for the aggravation.

Reaching beneath the table, Andrej unfastened the shackles that bound Hanner wrist to wrist at opposite ends of the table's width. Trefold shackles. Hanner didn't move, being freed; Andrej wrapped the chain around Hanner's throat and tightened it snugly. Then snugged it a little more tightly.

''Come, let us discuss this once more in detail.'' Hanner made a gesture as though he wanted to raise his hands to his throat, to catch at the cord. Hanner didn't dare. Andrej cinched it more sharply yet, just to enjoy the choking sounds Hanner made in his throat. ''Onto the floor with you, my young friend. Onto the floor—''

Andrej pulled, and Hanner fell, putting out his hands as he tumbled over the edge to try to break his fall. What a bore. Should he have Hanner back up to the table again, and fasten his wrists behind his back, watch to see how Hanner took the impact then?

He was getting drunk. But his fish would not rule him.

''Here is a thing that I learned long ago.'' Crouching down to the floor over Hanner's prone body Andrej knelt, with his left knee squarely planted in Hanner's back and his foot flattened sideways against weeping flesh. ''It is about Nurail and stubbornheadedness. That is perhaps redundant. And yet the trick was a useful one.''

He'd had Security to help him, that once long ago. He was much more practiced in atrocity now than he had been. He could do this himself. One hand flat to the shoulder to keep it in place. One hand at the elbow, to draw it around, to twist it up behind and pop the crozer-hinge—

Then, as before, his prisoner had screamed.

But now, shockingly, there was no slipping of a joint out of socket, but the ugly grinding snap of a bone fractured brutally. A compound fracture. Not a disjoint.

Andrej stared at the shoulder, the undeformed shoulder, the shoulder that showed no hint of the crozer-hinge; stared at the shoulder, and at Hanner's arm, still gripped firmly in hand.

Holy Mother.

In the name of all Saints.

Hanner had called the woman Megh his sister, and she was hill-country Nurail. Andrej realized with all-consuming horror that he had assumed—

But the evidence could be interpreted no other way.

Skelern Hanner was from Burkhayden. He was not hill-people. He had no crozer-hinge.

Hanner was Burkhayden Nurail, not hill-station, but there was no way in which a Nurail without a crozer-joint could have thrown something that hard and that fast. The Lieutenant's neck had been all but completely cut through. There was spinal bone, and the trachea was tough, and a good deal of muscle was always required to hold a man's head up upon his shoulders—

"Please, Uncle, please, I didn't mean harm by it, just watching. She's such a pretty thing. I can't confess a thing that isn't true—"

Andrej pushed himself away from Hanner's wracked body and backed away a pace, afraid. Two paces. Three. What could this mean, if Hanner had no crozer-hinge, if Hanner had no crozer-joint, if Hanner could no more throw a crozer-lance than he could?

"Please, Uncle, please Uncle . . . it was only Sylyphe, I couldn't stop watching. I can't bear longer, maybe it's better—oh, take me to death—"

Hanner was not thinking. To confess now would be to be relieved of pain, but only temporarily. And for Andrej to permit Hanner to confess at all would be a sin, as well as an error: because Hanner was innocent.

Andrej knew that now.

What had Captain Lowden said to him, about confession?

It had been important.

Crossing the room to the door at an unsteady jog Andrej shouldered it open to hail the Security who stood on watch outside. Or sat on watch, but he wasn't going to be difficult about it, it had to have been difficult enough to keep watch at all outside the courtroom, empty as it was. Sound would carry.

"His Excellency requires?"

It was Janisib, his Jan. All to the good. "A medical team, and immediately, Jan. Also to the Port Authority call for an escort, but to the hospital first. There is no brief. This prisoner is innocent."

He didn't wait for an answer. He wasn't interested in discussing the issue. Turning back into the wide cold room Andrej closed the door again with a decisive clicking of the latch; and made his way across the floor to where Skelern Hanner lay. Hanner cried out to himself when he saw Andrej coming; Andrej didn't know how much more of Hanner's anguished fear he could abide, not now, not now that he knew that Hanner was not for him.

His fish didn't know.

His fish thirsted for the caress of Hanner's cries.

And fish had the power to cloud men's minds with the thought of the ocean. How else was he to understand how he had spent these hours with Hanner, and never once asked himself the obvious question?

There were painkillers in his field interrogations kit, but hardly enough of them. Andrej approached Hanner with a dose, but Hanner was afraid of the dose, and the persuasiveness of Hanner's terror was almost more than Andrej could stand.

"Sh, there is nothing, not any more." Could Hanner hear him? Could Hanner understand? "It is an anodyne. We are well past the time of testing, Hanner, the drug has not failed. You will be released, and you will go to hospital, but for now you must try very hard for me. To be quiet."

The ocean was made of salt water, and to drink in the imagination only made a man more desperate for the draught.

His gentlemen understood. But his gentlemen were not here.

"Ex. Len. Sie," Hanner sobbed aloud, through obediently clenched teeth. "I. Don't under. Stand."

Loose the cord around Hanner's throat. Loose the manacles around Hanner's wrists. The medical team would take—how long? There were not very many mobile units. And there was a party going on in one form or another across the greater part of Port Burkhayden tonight. He needed a blanket to cover Hanner, to keep him safe from cold and shock until the medical team arrived.

"Hush. Rest yourself. It has been a mistake. You were right all along." There was no chance of an apology, no. But under the circumstances the fact that the error had been discovered in time would have to do. It had been a close thing. Hanner had been close to confessing a fault that he had not committed, and—Andrej asked himself—would he have understood the difference? As urgent as his fish was for its playground?

Hanner was naked, Hanner would get cold. Andrej fetched his overblouse from the back of the chair they'd set out for him and draped it carefully over the worst of the whipping. "I am only going to see about a cover for you, Hanner. I'll be back. Don't try to move. You will be safe now."

Once Andrej had but spoken to the Port Authority Hanner would be safe. And not before: but Hanner need not know that.

"I can't fault you for wanting her, but please." Hanner's voice arrested Andrej in mid-flight, halfway across the room. Hanner spoke in a lisping sing-song characteristic of the euphoria that pain-ease could create. "She'll pine if she's to go from her garden. Oh, please."

Whatever that meant.

He would have to carry the news to Captain Lowden—

But first.

There was something that Andrej had to do, first.

If only he could remember what it had been before it was too late.

◇ Eight

Ordinarily the staff gynecologist was not an emergency services physician, and wouldn't be found pulling duty past midnight. But the public-funded here at Port Burkhayden was still too grossly understaffed for such considerations to be honored, and Barit Howe had more of a general grounding in trauma than many in his specialty. It came from the years he'd spent assisting Inquisitors in Secured Medical, inflicting trauma at the direction of a superior officer.

Also since he had those years behind him Howe figured himself for the natural choice, if someone was to go speak to Andrej Koscuisko.

"All right," he said, low-voiced, to his transport team. "Safe to load. I'll just speak to the officer, carry on." Or carry out. Out of this room, Koscuisko's ad-hoc torture chamber, what had once been Judicial chambers. Away from Koscuisko.

The officer himself sat with his back to the wall, well apart, a bottle of overproof wodac in one hand and an unreadable expression on his face. Barit knew it was overproof wodac, which made him a little concerned about the fact that Koscuisko was nearly halfway into it already. Overproof wodac was poisonous. But Koscuisko was Dolgorukij.

"Your Excellency," Howe called out, firmly, and approached Koscuisko where he sat. "You're to come to hospital, sir? We're ready to transport."

He wasn't quite sure whether he was asking Koscuisko or

telling him. That would be funny in a little while. Right know he didn't yet know whether he had a problem.

Koscuisko started a bit, as if surprised to be spoken to. Koscuisko was drunk, or Koscuisko should be well on his way, with half a bottle of overproof wodac under his belt. Or waistband. Whatever. Koscuisko didn't sound particularly tipsy, for all that.

"I must to the Port Authority rather go," Koscuisko said. No slurring. No halting; no particular lack of control over the pitch or pacing of his speech. "How is Hanner? I fear for his future, if the shoulder has been too badly compromised."

From another Inquisitor this might have been a plea for reassurance, a petition for kind soothing words about how the prisoner really wasn't all that badly hurt, or had only gotten exactly what he deserved. Barit couldn't read anything of the sort, coming from Koscuisko. Koscuisko was talking to him plainly, man to man, without excuse or apology: one professional to another, and no pretense between them.

"Looks as though the officer meant to go for a fracture?" Barit asked, carefully. It would help if they knew how Koscuisko had approached the traumatic event. All in all Koscuisko had been remarkably careful with his prisoner, in light of the charges and the amount of time Koscuisko had been working on the man. Barit was impressed. Koscuisko knew what he was doing.

"No, I thought to put the crozer-hinge out of joint." Koscuisko's explanation sounded perfectly rational, but Barit was worried about it regardless. Hanner was Burkhayden Nurail. Hadn't Koscuisko known? "And splintered the bone rather. I am an idiot, Mister Howe. I should have realized hours ago."

All right, Koscuisko had made a mistake. Koscuisko was not perfect. The fathomless depths of self-disgust and loathing that seethed beneath the surface of Koscuisko's calm recitation were frightening to behold. Above all else Barit didn't want to fall in. And Koscuisko had done less to harm his prisoner, these hours past, than a lesser torturer might have done in half the time; Koscuisko could afford the error. He had ample margin.

"Better late than never, sir." Wait, that wasn't a particularly graceful thing to say, was it? Fortunately Koscuisko had lifted the wodac bottle to take a pull at its narrow mouth, and did not seem to have noticed the clumsiness of the attempted reassurance. "The Port Authority, you said, sir."

"Yes, absolutely." Koscuisko lowered the bottle, and frowned. "This is a defective flask. See, it is near empty. . . . Yes, I must to the Port Authority go, Mister Howe. The Captain has cried the offense against Skelern Hanner, I must be sure the gardener is protected under law before I tell Captain Lowden of the disappointment. He is to be very displeased with me, I'm afraid. I do not look forward to it."

Unfortunately, Koscuisko's nonsensical phrasing made sense. Barit Howe had heard rumors about Fleet Captain Lowden that made Andrej Koscuisko look like a paragon of ethical behavior. The officer wanted to go on Record about Hanner's innocence before Captain Lowden found out, and for that the officer had to go to the Port Authority. Barit wondered what it was that made Koscuisko so certain of Hanner's innocence.

"We're away, then, sir. If his Excellency will excuse me."

"Have I said extract of allock?" Koscuisko asked suddenly. "Nine units per body weight. Based on estimation I went eleven and three, with another ten and six to follow up after the first two eights had elapsed. It is a sizable dose, and you know how stubborn extract of allock is to metabolize. Have you sufficient sansanerie for his pain?"

Because with that much allock in his system the standard anodyne would be close to useless. Barit bowed. "We'll find enough, sir, I promise. Is there anything else?"

Koscuisko held the bottle up to the light, squinting suspiciously at the fluid in the bottom quarter of the flask. "Tell them to bring wodac." Barit couldn't decide whether Koscuisko was actually answering him or not. "I need to go to the Port Authority. And I want a bottle of wodac. This one is not working, someone has adulterated it."

They were lucky to have gotten the word on the speakserum. He wouldn't have guessed allock. Koscuisko had clearly been determined to give his prisoner a fighting chance of standing the test and living through it: He hadn't cheated with the speak-serum.

It had been well done of Koscuisko, in a sense, even if the pressure Koscuisko had brought to bear had more than made up for the relatively benign action of the speak-serum. Hanner would not be crippled. And Hanner would not be put to death, either, or at least not for the murder of the Fleet Lieutenant.

His emergency team had already cleared the room; Koscuisko's people were waiting a little uncertainly at the door. None of them were green-sleeves. Barit had wondered what they were doing there.

"He says he wants wodac," Barit advised the senior man, a tall Shikender woman whose fine clear features were set now in a grimace of concern. Barit could only suppose they knew how to handle Koscuisko on a drunk; they were his people, after all, whether or not they were bond-involuntaries. Weren't they?

What he didn't know was how aware they might be of what else seemed to be going on in Koscuisko's mind. "If you don't mind my saying so. I'd keep a careful eye out. Not as though I think I need to teach you your job, mind you."

He didn't want to insult anybody. He would have been much happier about leaving Koscuisko to get to the Port Authority had these Security been bond-involuntary. But he had a patient. And Koscuisko was not his officer, after all.

"Thanks." The senior Security troop was frowning through the open doorway at the dark slumped figure of Andrej Koscuisko in his chair, emptying a bottle of overproof wodac. Koscuisko had put his overblouse back on, but he hadn't fastened it. And his overblouse had been soaked with blood from Hanner's back. Koscuisko hadn't seemed to notice. "We'll keep it in mind."

With a patient waiting, and with a keen appreciation for the fact that these people knew Koscuisko as he could not pretend to, Barit Howe knew he had to be content with that. That was all he could do. The limit of his authority. The extent of his influence.

That, and to get a call in to the Port Authority, and let the people on staff there know that Koscuisko's people might need some assistance in dealing with their officer.

Assistance: and if it could be managed, a bottle or two of overproof wodac.

Stildyne worked his way through the shadows and the service corridors around the periphery of Danzilar's great glittering dancing-arena collecting people one by one, alerting others. If he was going to have a problem he needed for it to be well contained; and well concealed, of course. Robert would have seen him coming: Robert knew how to watch, and what to watch for.

Mendez had been right about the man. Even from across the room Stildyne had been able to tell that Robert wasn't in top form immediately, while Robert for his part had reacted to making eye contact with an expression that seemed almost one of fear.

Robert surely had no reason to be afraid of him, no serious reason, not as long as Andrej Koscuisko stood between them both; and in point of fact the only thing Stildyne had against Robert St. Clare was Andrej Koscuisko. There was no reason why the man should be so white in the face on his account.

As Stildyne came up quietly from the safe dim passageway behind Robert he could see that Robert was actually shaking as he stood. Robert's light gray duty blouse was black between his shoulders, stained with sweat. Worse than he had guessed. Not good at all.

"Robert. Would you come with me for just a moment, please."

He knew Robert had seen him coming, and had heard him approaching through the corridor behind his back. Yet Robert gave a start, as if surprised; and stamped one foot hard, flat upon the floor, as if he'd been a nervous yearling racer. Turning slowly, without speaking, Robert followed Stildyne's pointing hand into the small as-yet-unfurnished private room at the opposite side of the service corridor, and waited there— facing the wall—while Stildyne checked to ensure that the others were in place before he followed in his turn, closing the door. He had the corridor sealed as far as necessary. He wanted to be sure that there would be no interruptions.

The door-latch clicked, and Robert started again, his trembling more evident now than before. Robert was bond-involuntary, and his governor had never been quite right. There was a distinct possibility that it chosen this particular time and place to slip out of tolerance; which was a very unpleasant thing to happen to a man, even in return for the years of relative freedom Robert had enjoyed as a result of its diminished function.

"Turn around and talk to me, Robert; you don't look well. Are you all right?"

He had to be careful, because he didn't know for certain what was going on. He had to be compassionate, because sometimes Robert could not bear up under disapproval, and there was nothing to be gained from tormenting a man who was at the mercy of imposed constraint. But mostly he had to take good care of Robert because of Koscuisko. He took good care of all of them; Koscuisko did not play favorites. But Koscuisko had favorites. There was nothing anyone could do about that, and nothing in particular wrong with it, either.

Robert had not yet moved, had not yet spoken. Stildyne went up to him, to take his shoulders in what he hoped would be a reassuring gesture. "Can you tell me what is happening to you, Robert?"

But the moment Stildyne touched him, Robert cried out. Not loud, but high-pitched and hoarse and desolate, falling down heavily onto his hands and knees on the floor. Crouching swiftly down beside him Stildyne tried to see how bad it was; he wasn't going to be able to help unless he could get an idea of what was going on. "Talk to me, please, Robert, what's hurting you so much?"

Because that was the expression on Robert's face, his eyes closed tightly against the sight of something terrible, his teeth clenched behind drawn lips that were white with tension. He could not keep his balance even on all fours, apparently. Collapsing slowly, Robert rolled onto his back, half-leaning against the freshly covered wall.

And then he spoke.

"Give me a knife, oh, if you ever loved him. Please. I couldn't stand, for him—to have to—"

A knife? Robert went under arms; they all did, all of the Security who had come down here with Koscuisko days ago. What did Robert need a knife for that he couldn't do as well or better with his sidearm?

"Can you tell me what is happening to you? Do you need a doctor?"

Robert pulled his knees up to his belly, in an apparent spasm of ferocious pain. "It's not a thing that I'm allowed to say. But it's my only chance, you've got to see."

Physical pain, yes. But something more than that was going on, because if Robert could speak at all he should—all else being equal—be capable of making much more sense than he was making just at present. Asking for help, at the very least. That was the natural thing to do, the first thing most people did when they started to hurt as badly as Robert seemed to be.

"All right. We'd better get you to hospital, something's gone wrong with your governor. We'll get sedation there, hang on, for just a while longer—"

Speaking as soothingly as he could Stildyne started to move away. They needed to get a dose into Robert, first off. Then they could start to try to understand what he was on about. Robert surprised him, though, clutching at his sleeve in a clearly desperate attempt to call him back.

"No dose, no doctor. He's going to know. He's got to. And he'll realize. And then what comes next, it's not for myself that I'm asking, but him, what will it do. To him. You can guess—as well as I—"

"Who? His Excellency?"

Maybe he did need to try harder to understand.

Because what he was beginning to think that he almost imagined Robert might be interpreted as hinting indirectly at was too potentially terrible for him to be able to afford to take any chances.

"I tried to tell him, oh, I tried, I swear it. And the—damned thing—wouldn't let me. He'll remember. And after he's looked after me—for years.''

The phrases were beginning to break up, but not enough. Stildyne began to believe that he knew what Robert was saying.

''You. Are worrying about Koscuisko.''

Why?

What crime could Robert, of all people, possibly have committed, that he should go in fear of Andrej Koscuisko?

What crime had been committed recently—

Robert caught his breath, as if even thinking about it gave him pain. If Stildyne was right about what was on Robert's mind, then it should cause him pain to even think of it.

No, his governor wouldn't let him speak unless questioned, because he was supposed to be protected against self incriminating utterances to a limited extent.

But the governor would punish a violation as well. It had access to pain linkages.

A carefully moderated access, at least when the governor was working properly; but if Robert had managed what Stildyne thought Robert was trying to tell him that he'd done, the governor could hardly be said to be working at all. Except now, when it was too late to prevent a violation. Now it was being very thorough about punishment, from all indications.

''If I'd even tried to think . . . it would have stopped. Stopped me.''

Indeed. It should have stopped him anyway. Robert was right to beg for a knife, to kill himself. Stildyne realized that deep down at the innermost core of his constantly compromised moral self he really didn't care what happened to the man they'd taken for the murder, one way or the other. But if Koscuisko was to be required to execute the Protocols against Robert St. Clare it would destroy him. Completely. Irrevocably. Past any hope of self-forgiveness or recovery.

He was going to have to shut Robert up, because if he could grasp the problem there was the danger that someone else could do the same more quickly. First Officer, for one. He needed to keep Robert safely silent until he had a chance to find out how it was going with Koscuisko's interrogation. If there was going to be a problem then he would take Robert out before Koscuisko could begin, no matter what the consequences. Koscuisko would understand, Koscuisko would not blame him; not then.

But he couldn't risk preemptive action, dared not silence Robert forever—yet. It was too soon. There was a chance that it would be all right, if he could just keep Robert under wraps until he had more information.

"He loves you. You know that, don't you?" That meant that he was going to have to play a dirty trick on Robert. Stildyne regretted the necessity, because all else aside he did respect the man and hadn't ever actually disliked him.

It was the only way he could think of, on such short notice, to ensure that Robert would be still and not say anything potentially compromising on their way to the hospital. He chose his challenges with care accordingly, confident that at the least he knew what was going to hurt.

Robert folded himself into a compact and defensive huddle, lying on his side now on the carpeted floor. "I did not think. About." The anguish in his voice was deep and genuine, but Stildyne was jealous for Koscuisko's interest, and refused to let himself be deterred from his purpose.

"Loves you, and you know he has the dreams, you know how bad they are. Just think. If it hurts him the way we've seen it hurt him in a dream. Just think, Robert, imagine how much worse it's going to be when it's all real. Tenth Level—"

The sweat ran down Robert's colorless cheeks in little rivulets, his eyes gone wide and staring. "I saw my sister. And. I had to, like." But he could still speak. Stildyne could not afford to let him speak.

"It will kill him. Kill him. But not all at once. You've got to know he won't be able to live, with that in his dreams. Because of you. You've murdered him. How could you do that to him, after all these years?"

Brutal, but effective. Robert moved his lips as if he were trying for a word; but no sound came, just a strained wheezing noise of air passing through the constricted passageway of his windpipe. Crouched down beside Robert on the floor, Stildyne waited until he felt that it was safe to bring the others in on this—until he could be sure that Robert could no longer speak, because of pain.

And now he had to hurry, to get Robert to hospital. Where he could get painease for Robert, and as soon as possible.

Because the pain was clearly terrible.

But silence was of paramount importance.

Jils Ivers watched the Danzilar prince lift his dance partner down from the dance floor with perfect and chaste gallantry, and suppressed a grimace of rueful jealousy. Yes, she was very much the senior of that very young woman, and she didn't regret more than half of the years she'd spent attaining that status.

It was still true that a woman's knees stopped flexing quite so nimbly somewhere between knowledge and wisdom. She hadn't had the bounce that characterized that young woman's step since she'd been . . . since she'd been how old?

"Oh, fine," Garol snarled at her under his breath, standing beside her with his arms folded hermetically over his chest. "And it's little Sylyphe Tavart, none other, wouldn't you know. It's her gardener. At least it's her mother's gardener, and what do you suppose she's been talking to our host about? Four guesses, Jils, and the first three are tax due the Bench."

Garol had been in a filthy mood all evening, ever since prince Paval I'shenko's party had gotten off to such a hideously disastrous start. A completely contained and controlled disaster, she'd grant them that.

The news had started to trickle out, of course, but only in bits and threads, so that no five people heard it all at once, and no one would be able to quite credit it at all until some magical psychological mass was attained beyond which everyone would know but no one would be able to remember quite how they'd heard. It was delicately done. It was beautifully done. It was impressive.

It made her wonder whether Garol was right about the

threat he claimed the Dolgorukij Combine would ultimately pose to the rule of Law.

Their host paused halfway between the dance floor and where she and Garol were posted to kiss the young Tavart's hand with formal courtesy, and then slip his arm around her waist and kiss her again, very cordially indeed, upon the cheek, with every appearance of having been overcome by a spontaneous impulse.

Jils didn't believe it.

But she wasn't about to ruin the girl-child's dance by even thinking about her skepticism too loudly. The Danzilar's people came up around him; laughing and panting, fanning himself with a whitesquare and stumbling a bit in apparent tipsiness, prince Paval I'shenko made his way across the crowded room to rejoin them and continue the discussion he had interrupted to go dance. Danzilar had been working hard and steadily all evening. Jils was sure he'd danced with half the women there. He knew his business, did the Danzilar prince.

"Yes, now," Paval I'shenko greeted them, waving his whitesquare. Someone plucked it out of Danzilar's hand and replaced it with one delicately scented with jessamine and clovax. The Danzilar prince took no apparent notice, leaning up against two of his house Security and opening his collar; smiling all the while as though being out of breath was an enormous joke. "We were talking Garol Aphon, you are not drinking, how can this be so? Jils Tarocca, I upon your kind offices fling myself, as for mercy. Garol Aphon is not having a good time."

"It's against his religion, your Excellency." This brisk bantering came as second nature to her. She never felt she was particularly good at it, but she enjoyed it regardless. The genius of the Dolgorukij autocrat-entrepreneur lay in making a person feel as though they were masterful in repartee even as they stumbled. "Or if not, then perhaps our standard operating procedure. I haven't checked lately."

Paval I'shenko had gestured to someone over the heads of the house staff that surrounded them. Taking a break from his host duties, he stood alone in the middle of the bustle and to-do of a very brilliant evening; alone, with only herself and Garol for company. "As long as you are not in a mood which I am in danger of violence to gaiety doing, Garol Aphon, I would like to talk. There is a problem."

Security parted ranks to admit three servers. One with a huge platter of all sorts of sweetmeats and savories; it looked to Jils as though everything Danzilar had laid out for his guests was represented on that great wheel, in miniature, of course. One with a tray and a napkin. One to pour glasses of liquor or rhyti from the flasks on the tray, and sweeten it before it was presented.

"Problem, your Excellency?" Garol prompted, as Paval I'shenko accepted a tumbler full of clear liquid so cold that the glass frosted immediately. Jils fervently hoped it wasn't alcoholic, whatever it was. She couldn't imagine working as hard as the Danzilar prince was working tonight, and drinking at the same time.

Danzilar drained half the flask at one draught and handed the tumbler back to the server. "Indeed, and I wonder if, now that Captain Lowden has removed himself. First Officer. You are not drinking. I am offended, deeply, personally. I am a liar."

What was he saying? Garol wasn't First Officer of anything; but she was distracted by the sight of all the nibbles on the savory-tray.

The house staff had melted away to either side, opening up an avenue of approach that excluded everyone except for Mendez without seeming to exclude anyone. That was what Danzilar had meant. He'd seen the *Ragnarok*'s First Officer, who was approaching with a Security troop in tow and a very reserved expression on his face.

"Your Excellency." Mendez glanced from Danzilar to Garol to Jils herself, but whatever it was that he had to say it was either too important or not important enough to object to them sharing in the conversation. "Here we've already bled all over your nice white steps once tonight, sir, and I've got bad news. We don't have the murderer."

The Security troop was as tall as Mendez, with the golden complexion of a Shikender hominid. Her looks were distinctive, but Jils didn't think she'd seen the woman recently. Which could very well mean that this particular Security troop had left with Captain Lowden—or with Andrej Koscuisko.

"Indeed? Have a drink, First Officer, tell to me your news. I don't think this is bad. Please."

Mendez declined the offered refreshment with a reluctant bow. "Your Excellency, if I tried to swallow one. More. Bite. I'd explode, and that would be two of the *Ragnarok*'s officers in one night. Our Ship's Inquisitor sent word from the Port Authority. The man who was taken for the killing can't have done it."

And why did she have such a sharp suspicion that Paval I'shenko was not surprised? "One wondered, First Officer, from the very start. And did not like to challenge the Captain, but was it not odd? The gardener and I, we are of a height. And yet such a blow. It was very level."

If Paval I'shenko had had reservations why hadn't he voiced them before now? Jils reconsidered. The circumstances were very delicate. He was only just now come into possession of his Port, and Lowden was a senior Fleet officer—the most senior officer in Burkhayden. The murdered man had been Lowden's subordinate.

"Crozer-hinge, she says," Mendez agreed, betraying no sign of entertaining the confusion Jils felt. "Gardener hasn't got one, and Koscuisko says it can only have been done by a man with a crozer-hinge. Or an engine that mimics one. He's at the Port Authority clearing the documentation, and sent the gardener to hospital."

Paval I'shenko frowned, but so briefly that Jils wasn't sure she'd even seen it right. "They are busy, then. What is it that we can do, First Officer? It has been these hours. Is there hope of good finding, if we mounted a search?"

Shaking his head, Mendez declined the offer of bodies to perform a function that Mendez wasn't expected to direct any more. It was Danzilar's Port. "As you think best, sir, absent strong feelings on the Captain's part. And speaking of whom.

I'll need to be notifying my commanding officer.''

And Captain Lowden was not going to be pleased. That was the unspoken subtext of this conversation, whether or not Paval I'shenko was in on it. She and Garol both knew what was on the First Officer's mind. And Garol was fidgeting, absentmindedly, drumming the fingers of his left hand against the fabric of his overblouse, arms still folded across his chest. Left hand, right portion of his overblouse, and as Garol tapped his fingers in sequence against the fabric Jils thought she heard something.

''Let me suggest this, First Officer,'' Garol said, suddenly. Paval I'shenko looked moderately startled to hear Garol's voice. ''You've had experience with your Ship's Surgeon. Maybe you'd better go to the Port Authority and see how he's doing. Can't have a senior officer off alone at the Port Authority, and I can tell Lowden just as well as you. If you don't mind my saying so.''

''Garol Aphon offers himself as the person who bears the bad news,'' Paval I'shenko announced, to the ceiling. ''In this way he demonstrates his charity and accumulates merit, for will the Captain not vent his frustration on a man he does not know, saving the First Officer the unpleasantness? I am impressed, Garol Aphon. Have a drink.''

What was Garol tapping at there?

Mendez seemed skeptical. ''Thanks all the same, Vogel, but I'd better—''

''Excuse me, First Officer,'' Garol interrupted, but so cheerfully that there was no offense in it. ''But you'd better go police up Koscuisko. Pardon the blunt language, Paval I'shenko. I know you're related, but Jils and I came from the Fleet to here with him. It was a small craft. I think someone who knows that there could be a problem should go and make sure things are settled. And I was just about to excuse myself for the service house anyway,'' Garol admitted, unfolding his arms finally to give his overblouse a sharp tug at the hem to straighten the lines. ''Hadn't mentioned it, didn't want to be obvious about leaving the party. Apologies all around.''

Paval I'shenko shrugged. ''It seems efficient, First Officer, what do you say? Bring my cousin back to Center House if he is fatigued, or wishes privacy in which to drink. After all, a guest suite has already been prepared for him, as for the rest of Captain Lowden's party.''

All of the *Ragnarok*'s officers were to have been the Danzilar prince's guests for the night. Danzilar had a point. And there was something about the way the fabric pulled at the seams of the inner lining when Garol pulled the hem of his overblouse level at the bottom. . . .

''Better you than me,'' Mendez admitted candidly, giving Garol the nod. ''I'm beholden to you, Specialist Vogel.''

Garol shook it off. ''Not a bit. But I should go soon, if I want to brief Captain Lowden while he's still available. If you'll excuse me, your Excellency, First Officer. Night, Jils.''

In his pocket.

Garol bowed to take leave, and as if unconsciously he raised his left hand and pressed it to his chest. Right side. A courtly gesture: but Jils understood, now.

Garol had a warrant.

He was carrying it in the inner pocket of his overblouse, and whatever it was for, it distracted his subconscious mind when he wasn't thinking about it. So that he kept checking, absentmindedly, to make sure it was there.

''I will give you an escort,'' Paval I'shenko started to say; but Garol was already almost out of range, moving quickly to the door. Whether or not Danzilar believed Garol had heard him, Garol's intent was clear enough. What did he need an escort for? Port Burkhayden was on holiday; nobody knew who he was. And he was a Bench intelligence specialist. Bench intelligence specialists didn't take escorts from anybody.

Garol had a warrant?

For what?

Or on whom?

Why hadn't he said anything to her about it?

Wasn't it obvious?

Fleet Captain Lowden.

The man was notorious for his corruption, and yet the Fleet

refused to give him up to the Bench for trial and punishment. Lowden's corruption was echoed throughout the Fleet at too many levels. He had protection.

Now, having failed to remove an unfit officer through normal channels, someone on the Bench had decided to effect removal in a more direct, if covert, manner.

A Bench warrant.

For the death of the Fleet Captain.

"I'll go check in with the Port Authority, then, your Excellency." Now that it was out of his hands Mendez was clearly not unwilling to accept Garol's offer. "Specialist Ivers, I owe your partner. Later. Your Excellency."

Paval I'shenko waved his whitesquare; and Mendez excused himself, taking the Security troop with him.

On reflection Jils didn't think that the troop was one of Koscuisko's, though.

Was that a problem?

Did the idea of Andrej Koscuisko in company with Security other than people who really knew him make her uneasy? And if it did, why did it?

"The bandmaster is playing choice-of-partner," Paval I'shenko said suddenly. He'd left off leaning against his Security some time earlier. His collar was fastened, again. "Specialist Ivers. Do you perhaps in a meuner wish to join me; it is a much quieter dance, I assure you."

She'd sort it out later.

Paval I'shenko wouldn't ask her to dance a second time unless he felt that his guests might have noted their conversation, and the departure of two senior people; and might be wondering. There was nothing to wonder about; everything was under control.

And she'd dance with the Danzilar prince to prove it.

Andrej Koscuisko stood in near-darkness in an empty room on the fifth level of the Port Authority's main administrative building drinking the last of a bottle of wodac and gazing out of the unshaded window toward where the lights from the

service house shone brightly amid a Port that was blacked
out.

The power had failed, of course, again. The Judicial offices
he had come from an eight ago were doubtless dark once
more, and here at the Port Authority power was dear enough
that the portalume was all that was granted him to light the
room.

It didn't matter.

The less light in the room the less obvious its depressing
bareness. The less light in the room the more easily he could
see the differences in the dark outside the window where the
buildings stood back from a street that cut through ranks of
warehouses, or whatever stood between the Port Authority
and the service house.

Something bothered him, had been bothering him since his
experiment with Skelern Hanner had broken Hanner's arm.
Now that the formalities were all completed—now that the
Port Authority had opened its Record, and transmitted Andrej's findings, and closed its Record once more—he was at
leisure again to ponder on what it was.

Captain Lowden had said something. And it had to do with
a crozer-hinge, or why else would he have thought he caught
the tail end of the thought just at the moment he'd realized
that Hanner hadn't got one?

Captain Lowden wouldn't know about a crozer-hinge one
way or the other. He was going to be in trouble with Captain
Lowden. He'd had his instructions. And Lowden was going
to be almost equally happy with losing his victim as with
being exposed in front of the people who'd been there as a
bit too quick to condemn a man as guilty of a crime which it
was physically impossible for him to have committed. Captain
Lowden's self-love would smart at the idea.

The Bench specialist, Garol Vogel, he was no great problem; because they would probably never see him again. But
there had been Security.

Bond-involuntary Security.

Lowden was exposed in front of Security, and Lowden
would want to soothe his frustrated peevishness by giving

Security good reason to forget all about the garden. By reminding Security to live in fear of him. Hadn't Lowden threatened as much already? If Andrej thought of it—

The bottle was empty. There was another. Andrej stripped the seals and checked the first mouthful for quality and consistency. Yes, it was wodac all right, and if his judgment did not fail him it was overproof as well. Wodac warmed the blood, and Andrej was hot, even though he still wore his overblouse open.

The room was too stuffy, close and confined—that was it. It was the portalume's fault, undoubtedly, the generator was clearly throwing off too much heat. He could go and tell Security just outside the room, though he wasn't quite sure if they were there to guard or to prison him. Security were hard to fathom sometimes. It was just the way things were.

If he tried to go to the door he would know, and he didn't want to. Andrej opened the window instead, forcing the pane up through rusty tracks to the uttermost reach of his outstretched arms. There. Cool air. Cold air. It was better. There was a very great deal of it, all of a sudden, and Andrej shuddered in the cold, taking a drink of wodac. Wodac would warm him up. What had he been thinking?

About the garden. Captain Lowden's humiliation, to have ordered an innocent man to the torture. Lowden's certain displeasure when he learned how Andrej had put Hanner out of his reach; his probable instinct to punish the Security who had been there to witness the embarrassing lapse.—

Who had been there?

Vogel, yes, but Vogel was nothing to do with Andrej. Paval I'shenko's house Security. Some of his Bonds, no, one of his Bonds, and Mister Stildyne?

One of his Bonds.

Robert St. Clare.

The man on whom he had first tried his trick with the crozer-hinge, all those years ago, when Robert had played prisoner-surrogate at Fleet Orientation Station Medical, and Andrej had thought he was a true prisoner.

Robert St. Clare, and Captain Lowden had made his point

very clearly—that Robert had not been at his post when Captain Lowden went out into the garden. Robert, who was hill-country Nurail, who could engage his crozer-hinge to hurl objects with surprising speed and astonishing force. Andrej had seen him. Robert, and the woman was named Megh. Robert had a sister.

The enormity of the conclusion that presented itself stunned Andrej into half-staggered immobility for a long moment. He almost fell against the sill of the open window; but he caught himself, looking out over the sill to the ground far below. It was a long way. A man wouldn't like to lose his balance. If he should go through by accident he would have very little chance of catching at the grid of the fire-track to break his fall, and there would be no telling whether a man would even survive.

Andrej took a drink, shaken at the narrowness of his escape. Robert.

Did the Captain know?

Was that what the Captain had been saying to him?

Had Lowden known all along that Skelern Hanner had no part in the crime, and expected that Andrej would take a false confession to protect Robert from the penalty for such a murder?

Such a thing was horrible. It was unthinkable.

But it was Fleet Captain Lowden, to the life.

Time and again Captain Lowden had pressed him to go back to prisoners who had confessed. Time and again Captain Lowden had pretended to find cause for suspicion where no real cause lay, in order to generate another few eights' worth of entertainment for himself. Time and again Andrej had bent his neck to the falsehood, and done the deed, and sworn to himself that each was the last time that he would torment some poor creature who should have been allowed to go quickly to death. Time and again. And he whored for Captain Lowden again, every time, and here was where his self-compromise had led him.

Captain Lowden believed that Andrej would condemn an innocent man to a Tenth Level to spare the life of the guilty man, when the guilty man was one of his people.

Could he be sure Captain Lowden was wrong, to have made that assumption?

How could he hope to protect his gentlemen once Captain Lowden heard that Hanner was cleared of all suspicion?

He would cut Robert's throat with his own hand, rather than let Robert face such a death. He would murder his man, even though Andrej loved him, or perhaps because Andrej loved him. He could see St. Clare safe from such sanctions, now and forever after, and take such consequences to himself as might be assessed. He could make Robert free.

But Robert was not the only bond-involuntary on the *Ragnarok*.

How could he protect them all?

Was he to be forced to murder each of them, all of them, every one of them, to put them out of Captain Lowden's power? Did they all have to die?

A knock on the door, someone calling out to him. He could make no sense of what they were saying; he called something back by way of reply, and he had no idea what he'd just said, but whatever it was seemed to work for an answer. There was no further inquiry from the other side of the door, one way or the other. Andrej took a drink. This flask was much lighter than the other had been. It was nearly half-empty.

Trying to murder nine bond-involuntaries would be inefficient.

All he really needed was one death.

One murder would do it. One murder—and one particular murder alone—would ensure that Captain Lowden presented no further threat to either Security or to hapless prisoners unlucky enough to be imprisoned pending Charges when the *Ragnarok* arrived in local space. Only one murder. Obvious.

And if he did the only-one-murder they could have him for it, and that would be only what he deserved, and not enough of it. He should have known. He had had no right to trade the prolongation of suffering of guilty parties for the security of his gentlemen. It hadn't been his bargain to make, because the people who paid the price were not even asked for their thoughts in the matter.

Only one murder.

Setting the wodac-flask down on the floor Andrej leaned carefully out of the window, trying to decide if the fire-track went all the way down to the alley below.

Only one murder.

He had killed so many, and this would be one of the few he had a real right to, even if it would be much more clean and quick than his victim deserved. That didn't matter.

All that mattered was to get the man dead, and for that Andrej had to go to the service house. That was where to find his prey. Andrej knew his habits.

Fortunately—he told himself, with utmost gravity—he was much too drunk to remember that he didn't like climbing down from high places.

Carefully Andrej swung his weight over the windowsill. Carefully Andrej found his foothold on the fire-track to climb down out of the building.

He couldn't possibly take Security with him.

They were supposed to see that murder didn't happen, and that meant that they could only be in his way.

The fire-track was old, but it held his weight.

Only one murder.

It was past time.

He should have killed Fleet Captain Lowden four years ago, when he'd first realized what Lowden meant to the world.

◇ Nine

Stildyne had meant to shut Robert up, and he had, well and truly. The closer they got to the hospital the more anxious Stildyne was to arrive. Robert wasn't just suffering. He wasn't only in agony. Robert was wrapped six atmospheres deep in frightful torment, unable to move. Unable to speak.

Stildyne didn't dare simply cuff him across the back of the head hard enough to deprive him of consciousness. Governors were delicate at times, and making so abrupt a transition from fathomless anguish to the painease of oblivion could do Robert damage. Stildyne dare not risk it.

He'd seen a bond-involuntary die in overload, once, only once, before Andrej Koscuisko had come to *Ragnarok*. Captain Lowden had forced Lipkie Bederico into overload. It had been three days before Medical convinced the Captain that there would be no sound or speech from the man ever again.

Only then had Lowden authorized termination. Only once Captain Lowden had realized that he would have no sport out of pain that extreme.

Why hadn't he just knifed the man?

What had he been thinking?

No, he knew what he'd been thinking. He'd been thinking that he needed to keep Robert quiet until he could determine whether or not the gardener confessed. If the gardener confessed Robert was safe, except from his governor. If the gardener didn't, then Koscuisko would want to kill Robert himself.

Emergency admitting was surprisingly busy. The man who brought the tech team out onto the loading apron to greet them was someone Stildyne had seen before, when he'd come to the hospital looking for Koscuisko and his people. Barit Howe. A man reborn. Garrity and Pyotr got Robert loaded on his back on the mover; and Howe took one look deep into the pupil of Robert's staring eye and said something surprising.

"Should have just pulled it way back when," Doctor Howe swore to the world. "And us not so well equipped. All right, you lot. Through there. Emergency, gross cranial. Damn the officer for being drunk."

Whatever this meant to Barit Howe it meant nothing to Stildyne, who followed the mover into emergency and through to the treatment room with Security trailing. "Hey. Wait. Come on." Doctor Howe had to talk to him, let him know what was happening. Didn't he? Shouldn't he?

The tech snapped the neural cradle into place, and Robert's body began to relax. But the registers on the diagnostics fluctuated so wildly that they looked random and meaningless. Stildyne tried again. Robert had friends who had a right to know. "Doctor Howe. What's going on? What's the matter? Talk to me."

Doctor Howe ignored him for long moments, watching diagnostics. Registers rising, and slowly stabilizing. An orderly came in with a fistful of styli, and Doctor Howe put them through one by one. At the throat. At the groin. At the back of Robert's neck, lifting Robert's head from the neural cradle.

Some of the registers started to fall.

Stildyne could hear Robert breathing now, or half-sobbing, and Robert had been so quiet that Stildyne was glad to hear even the sound of Robert suffering. But Robert shouldn't be permitted to suffer. Koscuisko wouldn't like it.

"Primary failure on governor," Doctor Howe said, finally, staring out through the open door of the room at Pyotr and the rest of Robert's team. "Going to terminal. We're going to have to try for a disconnect. It's all we can do."

The Devil Howe said. "This place rated a neurosurgeon

with the specs?'' Stildyne demanded. It was up to him to
defend Robert's interest. "I don't think so, Doctor. You'll
stabilize. And wait for the officer. We'll pull him out of Inquiry if we have to. He wouldn't tolerate anyone messing with
Robert's governor but him, if it has to be done.''

The cold stare Stildyne got from Doctor Howe in response
was more than adequate reminder that Howe was a man reborn, and had little use for Chief Warrant Officers. Little
cause to consider their words or advice. "Your officer's out
of Inquiry already," Doctor Howe claimed. Stated flatly.
"And under the influence of overproof wodac. I've just left
the team that's repairing the man who was being questioned.
Koscuisko's gone to the Port Authority to make things
straight, but he's drinking. He's unfit. And if we botch it he
can blame us."

Instead of himself?

What did Howe mean, out of Inquiry?

"We can't let him bide like this; Koscuisko wouldn't want
us to.'' Doctor Howe was speaking almost gently, now.
"There isn't a Safe in Burkhayden. We've no choice.''

Stildyne stepped up to the head of the level on which Robert lay, stunned by the magnitude of this disaster. Of his
crime. He'd known Robert would suffer. He'd meant to overload Robert's governor and put him out of the range of coherent communication. He'd never imagined that it would go
terminal. What was he to do?

"And we can't let Koscuisko try to operate, even if Koscuisko wanted to. Because if the man dies Koscuisko would
blame himself, and there's history between them, in case you
didn't know.''

Drugs or no drugs Robert's suffering was terrible to look
upon. Stildyne didn't want to hear about history. He didn't
care about Robert's history. He'd wanted to save Robert's life
if he could, if he could keep Robert safe. But it wasn't going
to work. He'd made a mistake. He'd killed Robert, wanting
to preserve his life. That was what Barit Howe was telling
him.

"You've got to make it stop." Stildyne had no choice but

to submit, after all. Doctor Howe had made that clear enough. "I don't know about history. I only know that Koscuisko loves him." In Koscuisko's fashion. And Andrej Koscuisko was a passionate man who loved passionately, even while the affection Koscuisko bore his bond-involuntary troops never seemed to connect with Koscuisko's sexuality.

But Stildyne had known all along that Koscuisko loved Robert, and would never love *him*, so that was nothing new. "And he's a good troop. And nothing he could ever have done would deserve this. When will we know?"

If Robert would live.

Doctor Howe put his hand to Stildyne's shoulder and pushed him gently out of the room.

"See to this one," Doctor Howe advised Pyotr, giving Stildyne a little push—to move him out into the center of the room, Stildyne supposed. "We'll get started. We'll know in two eights. Think positive."

Koscuisko at the Port Authority, Doctor Howe had said. Stildyne didn't dare go to the Port Authority now. And he didn't have the heart to send Security; these were Robert's team. If the Day dawned for Robert St. Clare in the middle of the night in Port Burkhayden, they should be here when it happened.

He was to blame for this, and it was a heavier burden than he'd expected. The fact that he'd only meant to hurt Robert, and not to kill him, and for his own good and Koscuisko's comfort, meant less than nothing.

Stildyne's courage failed, and he lacked the strength to send Robert's teammates away while Robert lay dying, waiting for the knife.

They would wait together.

What was he going to tell Andrej Koscuisko?

By the time Andrej Koscuisko got to the service house he was almost sober, which he took to be a bad sign. He had completed an Inquiry, he remembered that very clearly; and the only safe thing to be under such circumstances was as drunk as possible, for as long as possible. Mister Stildyne was nowhere to be seen. It could even be that he would find enough wodac to end it all, finally.

The doors to the service house had been forced open by crowds of revelers in the street, intent on alcohol and fearless of the Port Authority. If the Port Authority had any sense they would stay well clear of the service house, and Andrej certainly saw no Security he could recognize as such.

The lights from the service house were brilliant compared to the greater blackout in Port Burkhayden, but not all so very bright except in relative terms; auxiliary power was limited by definition. Andrej made his way through the streets that were increasingly crowded as he neared his goal, pausing only when invited to take a swallow from someone's flask. Polite people, the Burkhayden Nurail. Hospitable. Generous. He wondered if they would be as inclined to share their liquor with him had they recognized him for who—and what—he was.

Nobody did. It was unnerving, being out under sky, let alone without Security; but in the dark obscurity of the streets his uniform, blouse undone and collar loosened, went unremarked upon, and Andrej felt truly anonymous. It was tremendously liberating. But he *was* still drunk.

Struggling up the shallow flight of stairs he shouldered his way into the service house, his mind fixed on his goal. Ignoring the indignant shoves of people he displaced. Not hearing jeers from men more drunk than he, about young gentlemen who were in too much hurry to match threads in a weave to take a neighborly sup with honest men. It was less crowded inside the service house, but hardly less chaotic, and Andrej wandered toward the back of the house for some moments, looking for the housemaster.

Nowhere to be seen.

There was a floor manager within reach, though, hurrying from the kitchen out toward one main salon with a box of panlin tucked under one arm and a crisp white linen towel flung over his shoulder. A floor manager would do in the absence of the house-master. Andrej didn't need to keep him for very long.

Reaching out for the floor manager's arm as he hurried past, Andrej caught him at the crook of the elbow. The floor manager spun round to face Andrej, coming near full circle of his own momentum, stopping himself from knocking headlong into Andrej just barely in time. "Ah—"

A muted cry of frustration and surprise. Andrej wasn't interested in making conversation with the man. It was dark in the main hall with only the auxiliary lights to go by, and in the uncertain shadows the expression on the floor manager's face was unpleasantly haughty.

So Andrej spoke first.

He was the senior officer.

People were expected to listen for his word and perform his will without sneering at him, no matter how disarranged his clothing might have become in shimmying down a firetrack five stories to the alley, no matter if his face had got dirty when he'd taken a fall. No matter if his underblouse was soiled with dried blood. Hanner's dried blood. Andrej didn't want to think about Hanner; he'd probably brutalized the man. No. Where was to drink?

"I need to see Captain Lowden," he said, and loosened his grip on the floor manager's elbow as he read a change in attention in the man's body-language. Because there was no reading the expression on the man's face. It was too dim, and too deeply shadowed. "I have important information which must be set before him. Immediately."

And so much was only true. The floor manager passed the box of panlin and the towel to a woman as she went by.

"Clarie. Take these in, I'll be right there. Sir. Captain Lowden. It's got to be the back lift, sir, the viglift's, I mean to say the reserved lift's out of order, sir. Power out and all."

Viglift. That tickled Andrej. Very important guest lift. Had he ever heard it called a viglift before? But to get to the viglift one transferred at a nexus in which a senior officer customarily left his Security to recreate themselves and secure access to privileged suites at the same time. So it was just as well. If he'd gone up the normal way Security would have wanted to accompany him to the next floor to see Captain Lowden.

And Security would likely have tried to prevent him from doing what he'd come for. He hadn't even thought.

He was thinking too much now. "Quite all right, floor manager, but let's go now. If you please." Further toward the back of the house, through to the kitchen. Very lucky for him. There were liquor bottles stacked in careful pyramids along the wall. Andrej plucked the nearest bottle off the top of one stack as he passed. It wasn't wodac. But it would do.

The floor manager keyed the security admit on the service lift, and it opened before them. Andrej was reluctant to step into the darkness.

With a half-swallowed curse of distressed frustration the floor manager reached into the lift, and there were lights there. They'd just been turned off. Not very bright, but enough, enough to prove that there was a lift there, and not just an empty lift-shaft waiting to swallow him up.

"You'll excuse me, sir," the floor manager said, "if I don't accompany. Trying to maintain some control. Sir."

It occurred to Andrej that he was as deep into the lift as he could get; he'd run into the back wall. He hadn't noticed. It was a surprise. "Quite all right," he repeated. "Carry on." As long as the service lift would get him to where he was going he didn't need the floor manager any longer.

By the time Andrej turned around the lift doors were all but completely closed, and the lift started moving before he could take half a pace forward to see if he could understand the floor codings in the near-dark.

Oh.

Good.

The floor-manager must have done that for him, already.

The lift moved slowly, under auxiliary power; Andrej had plenty of time to sample the bottle of drink he had borrowed from the kitchen. Very ordinary sort of liquor, distilled from rotten grain rather than honest tubers, of a sort a Nurail would call "drinkable" but barely even that to a Dolgorukij. It was far from optimal. But it would do. Andrej leaned up against the back wall of the service lift and drank as the lift labored up to the floor where the *Ragnarok*'s Captain would be waiting for supper.

The lift stopped, and for a panic-stricken moment Andrej was certain he was trapped between floors.

But then the doors opened, and he realized that he was only arrived. That was all.

It was much brighter, on the luxury floor. So that was where all the auxiliary power went, Andrej mused—to the luxury floor. It was a moment before he was comfortable standing in the little service area on the landing, it was so bright. Then his eyes adjusted. He knew where he was. The floor-plans for luxury floors in service houses did not vary much across Bench installations.

He needed privacy.

It was a shame to waste the liquor, but he could rely on the bar in the guest quarters to be well stocked. So—much as it grieved him to spill the drink—Andrej smashed the flask into the control-panel, to open a port into which he could poke with drink-clumsy fingers till he found the communications module that the lift used to talk with its motivator.

And pulled it through the holes in the wall that he'd broken with the bottle, displacing baseboards and chipframes and nodes as he did so.

Not neatly done.

But it would do the trick.

Now he would go and see if he could talk Captain Lowden into giving him a drink.

Port Burkhayden was full of Nurail, natives and non-natives, and it was very poor. These things together combined to very satisfying effect for Captain Lowden. There was a certain degree of commonality between one run of Nurail and some Dolgorukij: and this service house had an employee on staff who could almost pass for Aznir. In the dark. If he kept his mouth shut, and why would he speak, if not spoken to?

Two housemen to assist, and the one to comprise Captain Lowden's entertainment—he could play out some favorite fantasies, to while away the hours before he would hear from

Koscuisko himself. Had the gardener done it? Lowden didn't care. It didn't matter. Koscuisko would bring him the confession, or Koscuisko knew who would suffer for it, and it would be an additional point of interest—Lowden decided—if he were to keep the blond houseman with him, all through the night and into the morning, and take Koscuisko's report even as Lowden performed certain select of his morning ablutions with the assistance—no, with the enforced assistance—of someone who looked at least enough like Koscuisko for Koscuisko to get the idea.

There was no knock, but the door to the suite opened anyway. So unexpected was the appearance of the man who stood in the open doorway that Lowden almost thought for a moment he'd made his choice known to the housemaster already, and the houseman had come dressed up in costume to play his role.

Surprise lasted a moment, but no more than that. It was Andrej Koscuisko. And Koscuisko was drunk: So much was clear by the stumbling of his feet as he crossed the threshold.

"Andrej. A surprise. Had I asked for you?"

Because Koscuisko was uninvited, unexpected, and would be unwelcome unless he had very good reason to have come this soon. Koscuisko turned his back on his Captain, back toward the door, locking it and throwing the privacy-bolt with sudden single-mindedness. Drunk. Yes, absolutely.

"I need a drink, Captain, one moment. What have they got for us? Oh, good. Here's wodac."

Drunk, and no keepers. All of Koscuisko's Security were back at Center House. The Security that Koscuisko had to have brought here with him, and left downstairs with the others, were Lowden's Security. They didn't know. In all of these years Chief Stildyne had never once let Koscuisko be seen out of quarters when he was drunk.

What was Stildyne afraid of?

"Excuse me, here, Andrej, you're forgetting. I'm the Captain. You're the Chief Medical officer. You answer my questions. What are you doing here? I thought you had work to do."

The suite had a dining table as the central feature of its outer room, with the bedroom and an exercise room through chastely half-opened doors at either end. Pulling a chair clear from the table, Koscuisko sat down. "Oh, we are finished. Yes. I need to talk to you about that. A disappointment."

Took the lipseal off the bottle of liquor with a casual gesture and drank, slumped in his chair at the table. Leaning well back. Koscuisko's blouse wasn't fastened properly. The neckband of his underblouse was undone, and all in all the effect was unprofessional in the extreme.

All right. Captain Lowden had never seen Koscuisko drunk. So he'd never had this experience before, of being ignored by Koscuisko, of having to work to extract meaning from what Koscuisko said. Lowden sat down at the table facing his inebriated Ship's Inquisitor. The houseman he would order up could be made to sit there, later on—an agreeable juxtaposition. Not too much later on, though, or the administration would hear about it. Lowden already knew that the port was busy. That was no excuse for keeping Command Branch waiting.

"Explain yourself, Andrej," Lowden suggested, in a carefully genial tone of voice. Koscuisko didn't seem to have remembered that an explanation was owing. "Why aren't you at Bench offices?"

Shaking his head, Koscuisko all but interrupted, gesturing with the bottle. Which had already lost a noticeable amount of weight. "A mistake, Captain Lowden, and that is the charitable explanation. Were I a suspicious man I could think much worse of you. But out of charity I must insist that you actually believed that the gardener might have done it."

What did that have to do with anything?

"Charges are preferred, Andrej," Lowden warned. Had he made too quick an assumption? How else could the situation have been interpreted? "And that means Inquiry and Confirmation. You're good, but you're not that good, no one is. It's only been—how long?"

Charges were charges. And Koscuisko would answer to

him for any failure to obey his master's instructions. That man of Koscuisko's, that Nurail, St. Clare . . .

Koscuisko shuddered, and took a drink. "Oh, eights and eights, Captain. And he was very obedient to me. And I wanted him, Captain, I wanted him a very great deal. It was difficult."

Had Koscuisko made a mistake, and killed the man?

Why else would he be speaking of the Inquiry in the past tense?

If Koscuisko had—Koscuisko knew better than to stage any "accidents"—

"Frank language, Andrej." Much more frank, or even coarse, than Lowden was accustomed to hearing from Chief Medical. Lowden began to wonder whether his longstanding suspicions—about what Koscuisko got up to in quarters with his Bonds when he was drunk—were true after all. There would be a good joke in there if so; Lowden could pretend to misunderstand the precise nature of Koscuisko's mission. "You don't want him any longer, I take it? Why is that? Is it—"

Captain Lowden rose to his feet and leaned well over the table, bringing his face closer to Koscuisko's. He could smell the alcohol on Koscuisko's breath. If the joke came off it would be worth enduring the stink of wodac, for the leverage it would give him with Koscuisko ever after. "Is it something I can help with? Perhaps?"

Had this been the key to managing Koscuisko all along, and him in ignorance for all of these years?

Koscuisko just stared.

Then Koscuisko started to laugh.

"Holy Saints, Saints and sinners. Holy Mother. Captain. I would say that I am flattered. But already I am a sinner, without adding so obvious a lie to the list of faults for which I must answer."

Koscuisko's reaction was too pure and immediate to be feigned. But that didn't mean Captain Lowden had to let go of the joke. In fact it only made the joke better. Lowden moved around the table to insinuate himself between it and

Koscuisko, who pushed his chair back, frowning. The chair-legs snagged on a fold in the too-worn carpet. Koscuisko couldn't push it back any further than it was.

"Andrej. After all these years. Why didn't you just tell me? There was no need for you to have suffered. Come to bed. You can tell me all about your gardener, in the morning."

"Suppose I tell you all about the gardener now."

No reaction to the invitation. That was rude. He could make Koscuisko regret having rejected him. It wasn't that he had any particular overwhelming interest. It was a matter of principle, now.

"The gardener is innocent. The Lieutenant was killed by a sharp-edged object thrown with more force than most hominids can muster. It takes a crozer-hinge. And Hanner hasn't got one. I checked, Captain."

The more obvious it was that Koscuisko didn't want to play the more Lowden was enjoying pretending he believed Koscuisko did. "Well. If you say so, Andrej. It's all right. You can have another. You look tired, Andrej, you're half-dressed. Why don't you just get out of these dirty clothes—"

Koscuisko's clothing was soiled, now that Lowden got a closer look at it. Reaching out one hand for the front of Koscuisko's blouse Lowden began to play with one of the fastenings in the most obviously seductive manner he knew how—"and we can talk. If it's not Hanner. Who else? What about—"

Koscuisko simply knocked Lowden's hand away, but with the bottle, so Lowden couldn't be sure Koscuisko had meant to make an overt gesture or had merely been raising the bottle for a drink. Lowden was getting a little tired of Koscuisko's studied obtuseness. Time to get Koscuisko's attention. And one thing never failed.

"—what about Robert St. Clare?"

Koscuisko stopped his drinking in mid-draw, and lowered the bottle slowly. Lowden couldn't decide whether Koscuisko looked more startled than sick. Afraid, perhaps; now to press his advantage. Lowden reached out for the open front of Koscuisko's blouse once more, hooking two fingers between the underblouse and skin this time. Koscuisko stood up.

"What difference does it make? It could have been my Robert, I suppose."

This surpassed all expectation. Koscuisko's stubborn resistance to suggestion was shading fast into out-and-out insubordination. Providing sexual services was not among the duties of any ordinary Ship's Prime, true enough. But Koscuisko had a weak spot. And that weak spot was his Bonds.

"A very great difference to St. Clare, I think, Andrej. There's a death owing. I wouldn't have thought you wanted it to be St. Clare's." He kept his grip on Koscuisko's underblouse. Lowden could be as stubborn as Koscuisko when it came to that. Koscuisko seemed to have forgotten that Lowden had a hold on him: in more than one way.

"Quite right," Koscuisko agreed. Too readily. "I should very much regret having to kill Robert, though it may come to that. If he has done murder, and there is no other way around it."

Crazy.

That was it.

Koscuisko had gone out of his mind.

There could be no other explanation for the matter-of-fact way in which Koscuisko seemed to have swallowed the suggestion that had kept him to heel all of these years. Captain Lowden wondered where the emergency call was, in this part of the suite. Under the table?

"If he has done murder? Tenth Level," Captain Lowden reminded Koscuisko. Thinking fast. "Command Termination. Are you sure about the gardener? It's a very unpleasant way to die."

Koscuisko stared again, stupidly. At least he wasn't violent, just a bore. "Nothing like that, Captain, for either of you. If Robert has to die I will kill him. But that isn't what I came about."

What had Koscuisko come about?

Koscuisko hit him so suddenly that Lowden almost didn't even see it coming, a swift powerful punch to the middle of his torso just beneath his ribcage. The breath went out of

Lowden in a huge violent exhalation, propelled by the force behind Koscuisko's fist. Lowden fell back across the table, gasping impotently for breath. Not finding any.

"I came to deal with you."

Koscuisko moved on him, leaning over Lowden where he lay with his head and shoulders on the table. It was a very awkward position. But Lowden couldn't move. He recognized the experience of paralysis from report: but this had never happened to him before, ever in his life. Nobody had ever hit him in the stomach. He couldn't catch his breath. His chest wouldn't move to draw breath.

"I am as much at fault as you, Captain, I grant you that freely. I should have known from the beginning that a man could not shield one at such expense to another. And yet I have a duty to protect them; they are my people, they belong to me. It is a solution so obvious now that I have finally realized, and after so long."

Koscuisko put his hands around Lowden's throat, wrapped his hands around Lowden's neck as Lowden struggled for air. Thumbs overlapping. Pressing to either side of the trachea. Panic combined with paralysis now; Koscuisko was trying to kill him. Koscuisko had lost his senses. If he couldn't throw Koscuisko off Koscuisko was going to do him serious injury.

He had to throw Koscuisko off.

He couldn't move.

"You have helped me clarify my choices, Captain." Koscuisko was leaning very close to him. The pressure from Koscuisko's grip was increasing steadily, and through the rushing sound in Lowden's ears that threatened to drown out Koscuisko's voice Lowden could hear whispers and promises. Cries, and gleeful laughter; they were waiting for him. But who were they?

"It is either murder them or murder you. And there are fewer of you. And you deserve to die, Captain, perhaps as much as I do, perhaps—more."

The room had gone black, Koscuisko's face disappearing behind a firestorm of ebon sparks. Captain Lowden struggled frantically to flee from the spirits he sensed gathering around him, but though he could finally move his arms and his legs he could get nowhere with them. Flailing wildly at the table, Captain Lowden fought to take a breath.

"And I'll not whore for you or anybody else. Again. Ever."

Koscuisko said something; but Lowden couldn't tell what it was.

Hands reached out of the dark and seized him, hands like claws. Spirits and shadows, they tore him from his body. He could look down from above the table, down on Koscuisko's bent head, and see his own face discolored crimson and white, his eyes staring up at himself as he floated in the air above his body. He reached out for his body, if he could touch his body he could get back to his body, and if he could only get back to his body he would not die. He couldn't die, not here, not now, not with the room full of harpies bent on revenge. He reached out, but he could not touch. His hand would not reach to his body. He could not make contact.

Then the spirits bound him with chains and drove him on before him with whips and blows.

His body stilled where it lay, and moved no more.

Well.

Andrej loosened his grip, finally, surprised at how much hatred he had had for Captain Lowden, surprised at how hard he had had to grip to kill him. Of course Lowden was vermin. And vermin were resilient by nature.

It wasn't any good just killing an insect; one had to make sure it stayed dead. If you put evil into the earth it bred more evil and rose up again, stronger than before—like twining-weed. That was one of the holy Mother's mysteries. Putting evil into the earth was sacrilege, and would be punished.

Only after it was purified in flame could evil be truly laid to rest and confidently expected to stay there.

Only once it was burned. . . .

He couldn't risk the chance that Lowden wasn't dead, that Lowden would rise and walk. He needed fire to cleanse the hatred from his body. Hatred was poison. Andrej wanted to be as whole as he could be; because he was going to die for the murder of his commanding officer. The cleaner he could go to death the better fit he would be to plead his case before the Canopy, and hope to obtain some small measure of mercy.

Fire.

The body lay on the table. It would move in a fire; he had seen the furnaces at the Domitt Prison. He needed to tie the body down, and the toweling wouldn't do, it was too short. The bedlinen tore in strips, though, and the surplus linen piled very nicely beneath the table. He broke up the chairs and laid them on the linen, and soaked the lot with overproof liquor from the stores. Once the fire was well lit it would feed itself. The problem was getting it well lit.

Andrej found a firepoint laid ready in the washroom, in case a patron desired to smoke. The toweling draped over the body quite well. That was dampened with alcohol, as well, though of lesser proof; Andrej had a few anxious moments, when he touched the pyre off, but after a moment or two of uncertainty the sheeting caught fire with an explosive rush of flame that reached the ceiling and set fire to the lacquered plaster there.

Very satisfying.

The fire ran across the ceiling and down the wall, igniting the wallpaper, setting off the wainscoting very cleverly. And in the middle of the room the fire grew and gained in confidence, reaching up to embrace the body, consuming the sin-offering with grateful greed.

Fire.

There was a sudden shuddering sound from outside in the corridor; the firewalls, Andrej supposed. Why hadn't the fire-suppression systems gone off? Was it because they were on auxiliary power? Or was the sudden additional drain simply too much for even the auxiliary power to handle?

It was just as well, one way or the other. This way the body would burn. It needed to burn. Captain Lowden himself would burn as well, in a manner of speaking; but that was none of Andrej's business, any more.

He'd done his business.

He'd finished what he'd come for.

Now he should probably leave the room.

It was very hot, and the thick black smoke from the body as it began to roast was stifling. It would be best to leave quickly. The fire alarms had gone off. Everyone was to evacuate the building, when that happened.

There was a fire on the wall, fire around him, but the fire-door itself did not burn. It was cool to the touch. Andrej knew there was no fire outside the room. Nothing to worry about.

The door closed behind him, flames reaching through the door as he left to snatch at his clothing and try to play. It was a young fire, and very earnest—but easily distracted by the carpet in the hall and the furnishings. Andrej left it all behind him.

The service lift would be out of order.

There was a fire-path toward the emergency exit, the only thing still lit in the rapidly dimming hall as the service house lost all of its power. Andrej opened the emergency exit and got out onto the fire-track, climbing down carefully, hearing people all around him doing the same thing. Joining a steady stream of people struggling down the fire-tracks in the dark.

Hadn't he climbed down a fire-track once already this evening?

He couldn't remember.

Andrej reached the street level, and went to see if he could find some Security. The Captain was dead. He had killed the Captain. Security should be told.

Whatever happened after that, at least Lowden was dead, and would never demand that Andrej exchange one prisoner's pain for a bond-involuntary's safety again.

Ever.

By the time Garol Vogel drew near to the service house the alarm had gone up, and the streets were filled with people and with smoke. It was a clear cold night, with a steady breeze that blew from the bay through the city; so the smoke didn't linger—but there was a lot of it.

The service house grumbled furiously in the night and held

its great gouts of black smoke to itself as jealously as it could, so that when a cloud of smoke escaped it was pursued by a shriek of rushing air and the house's utmost ill-will.

The Port Authority was there in force, what there was of one. The fire-machines were there, but the pressure in the fire-fighting web was low and there were only manual pumps to draw the water through long lengths of pipes from the bay into the city to the sprayers.

Hopeless.

The firefighters weren't giving up, and they had enough willing help with manual pumps to keep the nearby buildings dampened down. But the service house itself was going to burn. The firefighters could either struggle with the fire in the service house and hope to slow it down, or they could keep the fire from spreading; and they knew their business, and their responsibility to the city.

The fire would not spread.

But it would burn out in the service house. It could not be put out.

There was no hope of making sense of the chaos without plunging into it. No hope of crowd control; that could work in his favor, Garol told himself. He was already familiar with the area. That would help too. Locking off the little two-man transfer he'd borrowed from Center House to get here, Garol left the vehicle ten blocks out from the service house and jogged the rest of the way. To see what was going on. To find Captain Lowden.

The nearer he got to the service house the more crowded the streets, but they were all onlookers, curious people, everyone pointing and staring and nobody badly hurt. The service house had clearly been packed to capacity when the alarm had gone off—at its lower levels, at least, and a good crowd making a party in the streets as well from what Garol gathered. Nearer Garol went, closer he came, and still there were no burn injuries; still it was a party, and the burning of the service house—while not a cause for celebration in and of itself—was a spectacle worthy of attention.

No one crying in panic for a friend, though there were some

concerns voiced about finding people here and there. Garol wondered if the fire alarms went off more frequently in ports with problems with a power supply. He wouldn't have thought it, but it seemed some of these people at least had had practice with fire alarms, practice that had stood them in good stead.

He hadn't found any officials yet.

Garol pressed on to the front lines, within two blocks of the burning building. The night seemed to glow: the firewalls within the building kept the blaze contained, and it was only by accident that a tongue of flame escaped to illuminate the black smoke that boiled furiously now out of every seam and aperture in the building.

He found some officials.

Port Authority.

Joining a huddled group of senior officers Garol introduced himself, to establish his credentials.

"Evening, gentles. Bench intelligence specialist Garol Aphon Vogel, here. If there's anything I can do to help."

The senior man was too occupied with a schematic to more than nod in Garol's direction; but Garol could wait. He was in no hurry. There were people in this gather from the Port Authority, from the service house, from Center House; but Garol saw no Security. No representative from the *Ragnarok*.

One of the people bowed to him formally, as though the man recognized him; Garol couldn't quite place the man himself, but cheerfully responded in like kind. There was a fire on. No sense in standing on formalities. He was informal enough in his dress and demeanor; but jogging was warm work. Garol intended to apologize to no man for his unbuttoned overblouse and open collar. Where was the sense in rank distinctions with everyone's face equally smudged by flying soot?

"All right. Everybody. Hear me and heed me," the senior firefighter said. Garol waited for the noise to die down: the noise from the crowd, not so far distant; the noise from the fire. Which was not going to die down. "We're asking you to establish a cordon on a three-block perimeter. You'll be spread thin, but at least we can channel people. Find out if anyone's missing. We haven't heard any confirmed reports of people trapped inside yet; we could be lucky.''

Or they could just not have heard any confirmed reports yet. And Garol hadn't seen either Captain Lowden or Lowden's Security. If Lowden were in the area at all he'd be here, with the senior people at this command post. Or he'd have given the whole thing up as a bore and returned to Center House. Which was it?

''With only the auxiliary power we can keep the triage pumps on line. But that's it. Seven eights till sunrise. This place'll smoke for three days.''

Maybe next time he was in a port being transferred like this, and the fire suppression systems in the service house were stripped out as they had been in this service house, he would close the service house for the duration. It wouldn't be a popular move. But so few people were hurt so far in this fire that to count on it happening so gently ever again would be irresponsible.

Garol stepped back into the shadows and melted away, wondering where Captain Lowden's Security were.

In a few blocks he found them.

They'd married up with the Port Authority, and were providing assistance with relay communications. But Captain Lowden was nowhere to be seen. Garol considered just asking one of them, but they were busy. And he was beginning to make up his mind that if he hadn't found Captain Lowden yet, Captain Lowden was simply not going to be found. For three days yet. If ever.

Within the circuit of two or three blocks Garol encountered the first of the Port Authority's triage stations, comprised of two people. One to write. One to talk. Interviewing the man who had bowed to Garol earlier; while a small crowd of people waited patiently for their turn, as though it was part of the game.

''—Fleet Captain,'' the man was saying. ''I showed him to the service lift, since the other one was out. I saw the officer around here not too long ago. Name of Vogel, I believe.''

This was a surprise. And clearly a mistake. Garol kept to the crowd, anonymous and invisible. Listening hard. It wasn't difficult to get close and still stay hidden, not in the dark, with the smoke and the chaos.

"Bench intelligence specialist, he said. Just now, that is. But I haven't seen the Fleet Captain. I haven't seen anyone who has. And the alarm went off on the preferred suite level, so I'm pretty concerned."

Had it indeed?

The preferred suites, where Captain Lowden would have been quartered.

But Garol knew he hadn't been shown to any service lift. It made a man wonder. Who had?

Who had the service house employee mistaken him for, who had obviously gone up to see Captain Lowden not long before the fire alarm had gone off on the floor where Lowden was staying?

It made no sense. But that was what Bench intelligence specialists were for. Problems that made no sense.

Methodically now Garol worked his way out from the innermost line of defense against the fire through the crowds of gawkers and the people working out to the far edge of the excitement, where people coming in to see the sight traded places with others who'd had enough and were ready to go home.

Looking for Captain Lowden.

Listening for anyone who had seen Captain Lowden.

Not finding anybody.

But there, out on the periphery of the fire's excitement, weaving a bit and strolling quite casually toward an alley, Garol Vogel saw a man he recognized.

About his size.

With a dark uniform, and no real telling the crucial differences, not in the dark.

The overblouse hanging open all down the front.

The collar of the underblouse loosened, bare skin showing through.

And the blond hair smudged and darkened with soot, with

smoke, with whatever else Garol did not care to guess.

Andrej Koscuisko.

Drunk: Not disorderly, no, but clearly six measures into a five-measure flagon, and where would a man have picked up a bottle of cortac brandy of that vintage if not in the bar of a luxury suite in the preferred quarters of a service house?

Koscuisko hadn't gotten it from Center House.

Because Koscuisko hadn't had it with him when he'd left. Garol had watched him go. And Koscuisko hadn't been back to Center House since. Garol had come straight from Center House. Koscuisko had been reported at the Port Authority.

It all came together; and when it did it all added up.

Breaking into a quick jog Garol pulled away from the loosely grouped crowd he'd been hiding among to chase after Koscuisko. Garol caught up to him within the sixth block from the service house fire, and greeted him politely.

"Good-greeting, your Excellency. I trust the evening finds you well?"

Koscuisko close up was much more clearly drunk than Koscuisko from a distance had been. There was no response. As far as Garol could tell Koscuisko didn't so much as hear him. Garol tried again.

"Nice night for a walk, sir. Taking any particular route? May I join you?"

This seemed to give Koscuisko pause; but no, he was only steadying himself against a warehouse wall for as long as it took him to take a drink. There was still no way to tell if Koscuisko had heard him.

Where was Koscuisko going?

Where had he been?

"Well, in that case." Andrej Koscuisko was the son of one of the oldest, most influential, trading-houses in the Dolgorukij Combine. The inheriting son. Men with rank and influence couldn't be allowed to wander around strange ports in the middle of the night. It wasn't done.

"In that case I'll show you to the door, your Excellency. If you'll permit. It's this way, sir, I've got a mover."

Particularly when men who by virtue of their birth or position had political importance were also Ship's Inquisitors, and unpopular as a class, and there was already at least one unsolved murder in Port Burkhayden. Garol had no desire to go for two.

Where were Koscuisko's Security?

Had Koscuisko left them at the service house? At the Port Authority? Where had Koscuisko been? What had Koscuisko done?

Garol knew better than to discount his gut conviction that he already knew.

First things first.

He'd get Koscuisko back to Center House, where the Danzilar prince's staff would put him to bed and watch over him.

And then, and then, and then—

And then he needed some more information.

"Yes, sir, this way. Careful. You'll break the bottle, and it's not empty yet."

If Koscuisko had done what Garol thought he'd done the potential political consequences were staggering.

It was best for them all—and for the Judicial order—to keep this anomalous encounter with Koscuisko as quiet as could be, while they found out whether what Garol suspected could be proved.

◇ Ten

Andrej Koscuisko rose slowly into consciousness from the depths of his alcoholic stupor.

There were people in the room: and they were arguing.

Dare lay a hand on him. He's a guest under this roof. The Danzilar prince's hospitality. It's a blood crime.

And arguing back, *not going to hurt a hair on his precious head, relax. Beauty. Come on.*

Nurail voices, by the accent. But why speaking Standard? Because Andrej didn't have any Nurail vocabulary, beyond a few words here and there that he'd learned from Robert over the years. It was odd. He could think of no reason why two Nurail would speak Standard with each other when they were alone.

Someone was coming, and for some reason it was only on hearing someone approach that Andrej realized his eyes were closed. And he was in bed. Divorced from his body, strangely clearheaded, he took stock of his surroundings untroubled by the panic that usually accompanied such midnight wakings.

His body felt sore, but there was no pain. The smell of clean linen: and another fragrance, a perfume. A flower. Danzilar poppies. Beneath that, a stale taint, a sour hint, the smell of soot and street-dirt; and a taste in his mouth. Drugs prescribed Dolgorukij for a surfeit of alcohol, mixed with the peculiar tang of a Nurail remedy for body-wrack.

"Uncle," someone said, very close, very near, as if crouching down by the side of the bed. "Come on, Uncle, don't sleep, we've waited for so long. Open your eyes. Speak to me.''

What was the matter of such urgency? Andrej did as he was so forcefully bid; he opened his eyes to look around. Where was his Security?

''Yes. Uncle. Now. Look at me, do you remember, we've met before.''

Some Nurail or another, sitting on his heels at the side of the bed. A young man by the looks of him, beardless, his forehead furrowed with concentration in the dim light. It was a very furrowy forehead. Andrej's stomach threatened to pitch, and he raised his head, looking for the flask of medication that was sure to be nearby. Trying to sit up. Failing miserably.

''Beauty, give us a hand—''

Two of them now, helping him sit up, handling him as carefully as if he were made of glass. Spun angel's-hair glass, as brittle as the ice from a single night's freezing. One of them held him, and one fed him a drink of medicine from a flask, and after a moment or two Andrej leaned back. Gazing with mild curiosity at the man called Beauty as he did so. Closing his eyes with an involuntary spasm of horror to see a man so disfigured, the terrible scar that ran the full diagonal of the man's face pulling eye and mouth and chin into grotesque misalignment.

''Remembers me, doesn't you, Uncle.'' Beauty seemed amused, if bitterly so. ''Dressed me as daintily as never-you-mind. And all the while there was our Chonniskot.''

Once awakened not even this odd conversation could stop Andrej's mind from returning to its troubles, and he began to wonder about how he'd come to be here. He was at Center House, that seemed clear enough. Someone had brought him, because he certainly didn't remember coming on his own. But if he was at Center House, washed and undressed and put to bed, where were his Security?

Where were any Security?

Were these Nurail here to serve as Security?

''No, open your eyes, please, Uncle. Don't pass out on me,

I've been waiting for years for a chance like this, don't ruin it now.''

He had no intention of opening his eyes. His eyes were burning. He couldn't keep them open. But the young Nurail sounded desperate, so Andrej blinked twice, squinting in the dim lights at the man at the doorway. Who were these people?

"You're Andrej Koscuisko. You were at Rudistal. At the Domitt Prison. Surely you remember.''

He was not interested. "I cannot forget.'' His voice sounded rusty; he waved for another swallow from the flask, just to moisten his mouth this time. "I am dreaming, yes? Mostly I cannot forget when I dream. Do not speak of it.'' The Domitt Prison. He would never be free of the Domitt Prison.

"Just this small bit, Uncle. You can give me just this small bit.'' Wheedling. Persuasive. Andrej turned his head, and met the young man's keen concentrated gaze in the dim light from the nightglims and what made its away around the man in the doorway from the room beyond. Something about the Nurail was familiar. Something about the eyes.

The young man's voice was low and soothing, but even so vibrant with some unexpressed tension. "And I'll never ask you more, but Uncle, I've heard stories. You're the only one alive who knows the truth.''

There had been no truth at the Domitt Prison. It had all been a lie, from start to finish.

"You are giving me a headache. Go away.'' He had more than enough to think about without being distracted by a dream. And he was dreaming. Andrej had no question in his mind about that.

"Only the weave, Uncle, and we'll go. I swear you'll never even see us again, but Uncle, please Uncle, try to remember. My father's weave. The Shallow Draft.''

It meant something. Things in a man's dream almost always did. "You've no business with your father's weave. How dare you? Have you no shame? Insolent puppy.'' And yet if this young Nurail's father was dead. . . .

"I beg your sweet forgiveness.'' And the Nurail sounded

sincere. "But it's lawful if there are none other. And I'm the only one survived. The Shallow Draft, surely you remember. He was my father, and you killed him in the Domitt Prison. The war-leader of Darmon."

Now Andrej was there, again, imprisoned in the stinking cell of his dreams, and a tortured man before him. Trying to tell him something before it was too late.

"Have you no charity in your heart." He heard the dread in his own voice, but knew that it would do no good to beg. He was dreaming. This young Nurail was only his own self, it was a dream. He could never get away from the Domitt Prison at night. "It has been so long. Holy Mother. To be away from there."

"There was no charity for my father, why should I have a care for you?" But the Nurail sounded only reasonable, not accusing. "And I have followed you as closely as we dared forever since. Hoping for this chance. Do you remember?"

Oh, he remembered. It had something to do with a clinker-built hull, a warship with so shallow a draft that it could skim over the chains that zig-zagged the mouth of the harbor and tied into a net of mines to destroy any ship that tried to escape. There was a very great deal more to it than that, of course. There always was.

"No, please, you're fading out on me, give it to me again. You must remember."

Well, he didn't.

Not any more than that.

"You expect too much." Always he demanded so much more of himself than anyone else. Why couldn't he just forget about it, and forgive himself?

There was certainly no sense in looking for forgiveness from a Nurail—

But the young man was weeping. "Oh. Is there no more? Is there no more that you remember, Uncle? Please."

The Nurail was in pain, whoever he was, whatever he was doing in Andrej's dream. And Andrej felt sorry for him. He could do nothing. "No. No more. How could you expect me to remember? Why else do you think I had to write them down?''

The arms of the man who was holding him—''Beauty''— tightened around him suddenly, as if in shock. Surprise. Whatever for? Beauty knew perfectly well about the books. Because Beauty was just Andrej, a splintered piece of Andrej, a dream-piece of Andrej Koscuisko with a scarred face.

''Wrote them down,'' the young Nurail choked. ''What did you say, wrote them down?''

This was becoming tedious. Andrej was beginning to feel exasperated with this dream. ''There were too many of them. I couldn't be expected to learn one, let alone so many, and in so short a time. Of course I wrote them down. Five. Six. Maybe eight pocket-manuscript's worth, I lost count, I've never so much as looked at them since.''

In fact he'd all but forgotten that they were even there, tucked at the back of a records-box. The Bench had not taken them into evidence, because all he'd written in those books was the weaves. It was illegal for any Nurail to possess such material. He'd had a vague thought about transcribing them for posterity. The Nurail would not be the Jurisdiction's whipping-people forever, after all.

Transcribing them, when he went home.

He wasn't going home.

Eight years—

But when he stood within the Domitt Prison in his dreams he knew, he'd known all along, that he was never to be permitted to go home.

And he was dreaming.

It was entirely up to him if he wished to wallow in self-pity for a while.

''Holy God,'' the young Nurail said. ''Beauty. Beauty. We have to get on board of *Ragnarok*. Did you hear him? He's written them down.''

Yes, that was what he'd said—

Andrej turned his head and closed his eyes.

And wept.

Never to go home.

Never again.

And as he wept he fell back through the layers of this perplexing dream experience and deep into profound un-dreaming sleep once more.

Stildyne sat and stared at the wall for two thousand years, trying to understand what had happened. Why it had happened. He'd meant well. He'd meant to hurt Robert, but not to kill him, and he'd done it without malice or pleasure in what he did. To save Robert's life.

Robert had asked to die.

It made no difference, or not enough.

What was he going to tell Koscuisko?

Someone jostled him from behind; people were moving around him. Startled. Concerned. Stildyne looked up. Pyotr was staring across the room, at the door to the place where Robert lay. Pyotr was black, and when he paled the deep color of his skin grayed to sooty ashes. Pyotr was pale now.

"No, it's all right," Doctor Howe called. "Had some trouble with that thick Nurail skull. Doctor Orklen's a genius."

People were leaving the room. Looking tired. But only that. Not looking disgusted, or angry, depressed or accusing.

So it was all right?

"Send in your chief, I want a word with him."

Maybe not.

Maybe they were just putting a good face on it for the troops' sake.

Stildyne rose unsteadily to his feet and stumbled across the floor toward the treatment room, cursing his body for not being as resilient as it used to be. He was getting old. He'd never been beautiful. Life was unjust.

How was Robert?

It was dark in the treatment room, and the ventilators' hushed vibration generated so much white noise that it almost drowned out the sound of Robert's breathing. But Robert snored. It had tripped him up more than once. He was still learning how to sleep on his feet and not give himself away by snoring while he was about it.

"Wanted to show you," Doctor Howe confided. "Didn't like to show the others, not this. They've seen one already. They show it to you before they implant it." The last of the techs left. Nobody had drawn a sheet up over Robert's face. And he was snoring. Stildyne wanted to weep; but he didn't know how. "Have you ever actually seen a governor?"

Having no practice in weeping Stildyne merely held out his hand, numb and silent, to receive the object that Doctor Howe presented to him. It was almost too light to register in the palm of his hand as being there at all.

A governor.

A tiny bit of dull gray metal, with a glittering eye like that of a malevolent spider.

Whisper-thin filaments like gossamer legs, too thin to bear the weight of so much as an idle thought, and yet capable of invoking such ferocious pain that a man could be governed with absolute rigor by fear of it.

This was the thing that had dealt Robert such horror. This was the thing that had put Lipkie Bederico to death by torture, that ruled the lives of bond-involuntaries, that had the power to make a man execute atrocity rather than disobey a lawful order.

If Stildyne had had any religion he would have wanted to exorcise the thing. But he had no religion. So he decided that he simply wanted to crush it underfoot, instead.

"Interesting." Words seemed inadequate. "Take it back. I don't want anyone seeing it. Save it for the officer. How's Robert?"

Doctor Howe sobered. And he hadn't been particularly giddy to start out with. "We were lucky. The governor was half-dead already, or it would have done some damage coming out—it's got a self-defense mechanism, naturally. Can't have people doing surgery to pull governors. Might contribute to the loss of bond-involuntary troops before the completion of their terms."

Doctor Howe was reborn. There was language behind his words that Stildyne did not want to hear. And fortunately for him Doctor Howe continued smoothly.

"One thing, though, and your officer will expect this. He's not going to remember coming to hospital. He's not going to remember much about the few hours immediately preceding arrival, especially any incident that might have been stressful. Extreme stress condition, traumatic amnesia, you know. Now, usually traumatic amnesia will recover over time."

Doctor Howe was wrapping the governor in a bit of bandaging as he talked. And Stildyne was even halfway familiar with what Doctor Howe was talking about. "But in most cases a person will never recover some portion of his life immediately preceding. And with a governor gone terminal— I'll be surprised if he can remember anything after his midmeal, when he wakes up. Fastmeal for sure, yes. Thirdmeal for certain no. If he had one."

Was Doctor Howe actually giving him absolution, all unawares?

Was Doctor Howe telling him that what he'd done to Robert had actually protected Robert so well that not only was Robert safe from immediate horror, but Robert would not remember anything that might put his life at risk in the future?

"So tell me." Stildyne struggled for words, overwhelmed with gratitude. "When does he wake up? The others. They'll be anxious." Not him, of course. No. He cared only so much for Robert as for any troop, and not so much as for the next troop either, because Robert annoyed him. For himself he would just as soon Robert St. Clare had never come into his life. Complicated.

"You could wake him up now." Doctor Howe sounded a little thoughtful. "Or you could let him rest. The scans are all good. That kind of pain, he'll be exhausted, even with good drugs in him. Send the rest in. You can all sleep in here, if you'd like. But he's snoring. We could put you all on ward with the diagnostics; they'll move. I expect he'll wake up before midday, sometime."

Or sooner.

Robert liked his fastmeal.

It would be all right.

He could face Koscuisko with a clear mind, secure that he'd

done what he could to protect Robert, knowing that Robert was safe from himself.

And he'd tackle everything else there was to deal with, in the morning.

Someone came into the room with fresh rhyti and hot bread, setting the tray down beside the head of the bed before leaning over to kiss the back of Andrej's hand where it lay on the coverlet. Andrej woke so easily and naturally as to be unable to make the distinction between waking and sleeping; the habit of the first twenty-odd years of his life still ran strong in him. At least when he was asleep.

Opening his eyes he looked up at a ceiling gaily decorated with a motif called beard-of-grain. Very pleasant. Traditional. The man who had waked him was standing quiet and patient at his left, waiting to be noticed. One of Paval I'shenko's house staff; one of the Danzilar Dolgorukij house staff, that was to say. He'd been on active duty for more than eight years now. He'd never met a Security troop who waked a man in so old-fashioned a manner.

"Holy Mother, bless this child to your work," Andrej said. Half-unthinking. The houseman smiled and bowed in apparent appreciation.

"And prosper all Saints under Canopy this day. Good-greeting, your Excellency, you are anxiously awaited, if you would care to rise and take bread."

Anxiously awaited was probably an understatement. He had several missions he needed to accomplish himself, but first things first. Sitting up in the bed Andrej took note of the fact that he was wearing someone else's nightshirt; not his, anyway. Reedstalk-work. Very respectable. But all of his linen was worked in lapped-duckwings.

"Thank you. I will wish to dress. There are Security waiting for me?"

He was a little surprised none were here, in the room with him. He just hadn't decided exactly which Security he'd expected to see, or for what precise purpose.

"The prince's majordomo waits upon your will, sir. I'll send someone to see to the towels."

That meant that Security was not waiting outside. He would have to get past the house-master before he got more information, perhaps. Nodding without bothering to probe further Andrej lifted the covers aside and stood up. He was a little shaky. Shouldn't he be sick? Shouldn't he be crawling to the basin, after the drinking that he'd done last night?

Maybe whomever had brought him here had drugged him as well. There stood a glass of water at the bedside with a stack of appropriate dose-powders beside it, right enough. And the dregs of a dose in the glass as well. All right. That explained that. He couldn't remember having been fed medicine, but that didn't surprise him. He was lucky—he supposed—to remember as much as he did, about what he had accomplished during the past sixteen eights.

By the time he was washed and combed and had changed back into his own linen—freshly laundered, of course, and laid out waiting—there was fastmeal laid out, and the house-master waiting. That could be a good sign, Andrej told himself; to be waited on by so exalted a personage as the majordomo was a mark of significant respect. So he probably wasn't under arrest. Yet.

"His Excellency may wish for a brief summary of what has taken place in Port· Burkhayden since yestreen," the house-master suggested, nodding to the houseman to pour Andrej's rhyti. This was different rhyti than that he had taken with him into the washroom. A guest could not be permitted to drink rhyti from a flask that had stood for so long. Certainly not. Shocking idea. "As his Excellency was, with respect, very drunk last night. When the Bench specialist Vogel brought him to Center House."

All right, so that was how he'd got here. He wasn't certain he remembered. Andrej had a quick sip of rhyti, and gestured for the morning-meat tray. He was hungry. Whatever doses whomever had used on him last night had been good meds; but the body still knew that it had been worked beyond the limits of its tolerance, and demanded he make it up in extra sustenance. Morning-meat. And hotbread. And quite possibly several slices of ripe melon.

"Captain Lowden had cried Charges against a gardener. Skelern Hanner. He and I had gone to Bench offices." Andrej insisted on buttering his own brodtoast; anyone else used either too much or too little. There was a precise ratio to be preserved between melted butter and marmalade. "But the gardener was quite guiltless. I sent him to hospital. And went to the Port Authority to make him clear with the Record."

Updates went more quickly when they could start from a mutually understood jumping-off place. The majordomo smiled. "Yes, your Excellency." The majordomo was Nurail, one of the tall broad-shouldered run of Nurail. Fair skin, light-colored eyes, brown hair. Not the sort of Nurail that Andrej Koscuisko would ever be mistaken for.

"As for his Excellency's personal movements nothing is known, sir, after that. You were reported missing from the Port Authority when First Officer Mendez arrived there. And located some time later near the Port Authority by the Bench specialist, if his Excellency will excuse, seven points before the gale, with all sheets flying. Several additional elements should be placed before you, though. It was a busy night."

Had he been somewhere near the Port Authority? Had he got that far once he'd left the service house? It was possible. The other alternative would seem to be that Vogel was glossing the actual location a bit. And why would he do that?

"One wonders in particular where one's Security have got to," Andrej agreed, Reaching for a dish of egg-pie. He wondered whether the majordomo was Nurail enough to flout tradition and sit down with him; or majordomo enough to stand on his dignity and decline absolutely to sit down with a guest of the house.

On the other hand since the house-master was Nurail, there was no reason to expect him to be willing to sit down with a Judicial officer of whatever sort, guest or no guest. Andrej abandoned the whole idea as a bad lead.

"His Excellency's Security troop St. Clare experienced a medical emergency last night."

This startled Andrej; he stopped where he was in mid-bite, and set his fork down. Carefully. The house-master was still talking. Never before had Andrej been quite so sensitive to the number of extra words that politeness was held to demand, when a house-master was speaking to a guest.

"The warrant officer, Chief Stildyne, went to the hospital with the man and the rest of the team. Security five point three? Thank you, sir, Security five point three. An emergency surgery was successfully performed. They're all still at hospital, sir."

Emergency surgery. Did he have to ask what kind? He'd forgotten what he'd decided about who had killed Wyrlann. He'd been distracted by problems of his own. Now Andrej was as sure as though he'd been told that he knew that the medical emergency had been a governor on overload, a governor which should have prevented the murder from ever taking place. Which would have prevented it, had it not been defective from the very beginning. He knew that Robert's governor had gone critical. He believed he knew why.

"I'll want to go to hospital first thing. Soon, too."

"Yes, sir. So much was in fact anticipated. The Bench specialist requests a few eighths of his Excellency's time be made available this afternoon or after third-meal, with specific provision that you were to feel no need to send excuses for seeing to other business first if you slept later in the day."

He might be Nurail. But he was damnably good at the language of a majordomo. At the same time his conversation was redeemed from the very purest form of mind-numbingly indirect discourse by his persistent tendency to use a second person singular pronoun rather than a noun phrase in the third person. Someone would probably take him gently aside and speak to him about that, before too long.

"For the rest of it the port is under quarantine, and all movement is under escort. There was a fire at the service house last night that may or may not have claimed the life of Fleet Captain Lowden. There are apparently some indications that the fire was set to conceal a crime, but the officer is either dead or missing and presumed dead. The Bench specialists are conducting the investigation, with the Danzilar prince's permission.''

Well, of course Lowden was dead. Or at least Andrej hoped and expected that Lowden was dead. He had very carefully killed Lowden himself, with his own two hands. Which were fortunately free from embarrassing scratches. But he hadn't set the fire to cover the crime. He'd set the fire to be sure that Lowden went to Hell and stayed there.

''Other casualties?''

There was a problem with having set a fire at all, now that he was sober enough to consider the potential consequences of such an act. But service houses had fire suppression systems to protect their patrons. Didn't they?

The sprinklers hadn't gone off in the suite where he'd burned the body, had they?

''Surprisingly few,'' the housemaster assured him. ''All in all there seems to have been an orderly evacuation. There are injuries, but none of them very severe. Sprains and bruises mostly, from people being in too much of a hurry. But portions of the service house are apparently still burning.''

Fire suppression systems had been as completely stripped out as the hospital had been, then. He should have stopped to think. Andrej stared at the sweet rolls, stricken with horror. Oh, what he had almost done. What he *had* done. That it had not become a disaster was clearly better luck than he deserved, and certainly no reflection on any merit of his.

Or was it?

Couldn't he say that to have killed Captain Lowden and set the whole service house on fire, and nobody else killed, meant a species of approval for the act, from the Canopy of Heaven?

It had been fairly early yet in the night.

People had been drunk, but not too drunk to find their way out of a burning building.

He was a sinner, but perhaps—just perhaps—the holy Mother had put out her hand to shelter and protect him, whether or not he was unreconciled still to her Church.

''House-master. I am astonished. Almost I would say that I was sorry to have missed it. But my First Officer has probably been up all night, and would know this for a lie.''

Wait. Should he say such a flippant thing about the event that was presumed to have taken the life of his commanding officer?

Certainly he should.

Nobody in Port Burkhayden, nobody on the *Ragnarok*, nobody in Fleet, nobody on the Bench would be the least bit astonished at an indication that the death of Fleet Captain Lowden did not afflict him with an excess of grief.

''His Excellency's First Officer has in fact just gone to bed two eights ago. And leaves expressed concern for your health and well being, sir. I'm directed to advise you that he's been to hospital and everyone's asleep. And that he will expect to see you at some time, but that you're to satisfy the Bench specialists first on any issue.''

Probably not quite as Mendez had said it, but Andrej took the meaning. It had been four years. He could speak Mendez.

''Very well, then. I will go to the hospital, and then to see Vogel. But in the meantime I will have some more rhyti.''

There was no telling what he was to confront, today.

It only made sense to be sure he was well-fortified to face whatever might come.

Security Chief Stildyne lay on a thin padded mat on the floor with a rolled-up wad of sterile wrapping under his head and a doubled thickness of toweling over his face to shut out the bright light from the unshaded window. He'd had a long night. He'd slept through fastmeal, and he had every intention of sleeping through midmeal as well. Why not? There was nothing to do, and nowhere to go. He'd spoken to First Officer. He didn't want to see Koscuisko.

He heard voices, coming down the hallway toward the front room of the ward his troops occupied. Robert in the inside room with the diagnostics, sleeping off the exhaustion of having experienced the extreme pain that he'd endured. Despite Stildyne's expectations to the contrary, Robert had slept through fastmeal and midmeal as well. If he didn't wake in time for thirdmeal they would have to call in a resurrectionist, Stildyne supposed.

"Through here." Stildyne recognized the voice. "Couldn't leave them cluttering up the emergency treatment areas. Security being on the large side."

Who would Doctor Howe be speaking to like that? Respectful and restrained, to an extent. Quite unlike the way Howe talked to Stildyne himself. Someone come to see about Robert, obviously, and that meant—

"Indeed I have always noticed that for large people they are capable of dealing with surprisingly confined spaces." The officer. Andrej Koscuisko. Stildyne rolled off his floormat and staggered to his feet in one swift if ungraceful motion. Koscuisko. He wasn't ready for this.

"One of the tricks of the trade, sir, disappearing in place. So your Chief doesn't notice you. Good-greeting, Chief, slept at all, did you?"

Yes, coming into the room. Doctor Barit Howe and Andrej Koscuisko. Stildyne bowed, still clutching the towel that he'd been using as an eyeshade in the fist of one hand. "Tolerably, Doctor Howe. Your Excellency."

Doctor Howe wasn't more than slowing down on his way through. Stildyne stood aside to follow behind Koscuisko, but Koscuisko paused, putting one hand to Stildyne's arm and looking up into his face with a very measuring sort of an expression in his eyes—which looked almost white to Stildyne in the bright room, but he was used to that.

"Have you had a bad night of it, Chief?" Oh, Koscuisko didn't know the half of it. "I should apologize for being drunk, and not here to help out. Tell me what happened."

Damned if he would. Not here. Not now. There was no telling whether they were on monitor, somewhere. "Robert may have been upset that the murder had happened while he was nearby. I don't know, your Excellency. All I really know is that he was suffering, and we assumed his governor was cooking off. We nearly lost him."

Sir, I'm sorry. I'm sorry I did it. I didn't realize how much it was going to hurt him. I'm sorry you weren't here. But

Stildyne knew that those were words he'd never say.

"We'd met the gardener," Koscuisko said, as if he was agreeing with Stildyne on something. "Before, I mean. I knew Robert was unhappy about the Captain's accusation. I cannot say I was pleased myself. It may have been enough to push things over."

Yes, that made sense. And it didn't have to. All it really needed was for Koscuisko to say that it made sense. That was what senior officers were for.

"Let us go in," Koscuisko suggested, and started forward. *Let us go in* was not a suggestion from a senior officer. Not really. So there were drawbacks in having senior officers available to one, as well as advantages.

Doctor Howe was standing by the cot where Robert had been sleeping. Robert was sitting up on the edge of the cot in his hipwrap, with his naked feet splayed firm on the floor and his knees every which way. It was a low cot.

"Name of the Mother," Koscuisko said, as Robert started to stand up. "Sit as you are, Robert. For the love of all Saints."

It couldn't be that Robert was undressed, because he did have some clothing on. Koscuisko was just responding to how white in the face and generally unhealthy Robert still looked. Joining Doctor Howe at the bedside Koscuisko leaned forward to peer into one of Robert's eyes, pulling against the lower lid of the eye with a touch of his thumb; Robert suffered the examination in stoic silence, apparently resigned to letting Koscuisko express his anxiety that way. "How do you go?"

For his own part Stildyne hung back, unwilling to present himself where Robert could see him. Afraid, after all, that Robert would remember at least enough to blame Stildyne for what he'd done.

"Well, thank you. Sir. Your Excellency." Robert's voice was strong, but hesitant. Stildyne realized he'd half-expected Robert to sound different. "Confused, though, with respect. I don't know what's happened. Except—something's missing— I think—your Excellency."

"Indeed, something is missing," Koscuisko agreed, and

put his hand to the back of Robert's neck in an affectionate gesture that Stildyne had envied Koscuisko's Bonds on more than one occasion. "There is a soreness, here? It is as it should be."

Robert bent his head in apparent response to some gentle pressure from Koscuisko's hand; Koscuisko examined the back of Robert's neck, carefully, in the light from the unshaded overhead fixture. "I wish someone would tell me what's going on," Robert grumbled. And then seemed to hear himself talking, and find himself startled by what he had said. "I mean. With respect. Sir. I'm confused."

"A beautiful mark, here," Koscuisko said to Doctor Howe. And it was Doctor Howe who came to Robert's rescue, as Koscuisko continued to consider the site where the surgeon had gone in with whatever he'd used.

"Your governor went critical on us, Mister St. Clare. We had to go for emergency disconnect. I have to remind you, now, don't get used to it. Fleet will see to it that you're Bonded again in double-quick time."

That was a point, Stildyne realized, though he wouldn't have thought of it. Not right away. Koscuisko stepped back from Robert, lifting his hand, apparently happy with his examination; Robert reached out and snagged Koscuisko's hand on its way past.

"Sir. I've got to tell you. If I could have a word. Please."

Stildyne shot Doctor Howe an angry glance, betrayed. Oh, this was bad. Doctor Howe had promised. Hadn't he? "Now, Robert, it's nothing that won't wait, I'm sure—" Stildyne started to say. In the best, most convincing, *shut up now or I'll shut you up myself* tone of voice that he could muster. But it never did him any good with Andrej Koscuisko around.

"Chief. Be still."

And Stildyne shut up. Seething in internal torment: but Koscuisko was the senior man here. And nobody argued with Andrej Koscuisko. It wasn't done.

"Robert, be easy. What is it? Of course."

Robert looked up past Koscuisko to Stildyne where he

stood, to Doctor Howe on Koscuisko's left. As if he was trying to decide on something.

"Sir. You might not remember. But Megh. It's my own sister, sir. *My* Megh."

Koscuisko raised his free hand in an abrupt gesture of warning. "Be careful of what you say, Robert. Someone has murdered the Fleet Lieutenant. Do you not remember? Last night? At the party, at Center House?"

This was the meat of the problem, just so. Yes. Stildyne hadn't thought to be hitting it so soon: but maybe it would work out better this way. Get it all over with. Finished. Complete.

Robert looked confused. "Murdered. The Lieutenant? No, sir. Don't remember. I'm sure it'll come to me, though. If you say so."

Too clear and too open, too honest. Too real. Stildyne was convinced, but he wasn't the expert. Nor was he the person whose judgment mattered in things of this nature.

"Doctor Howe?" Koscuisko looked back over his shoulder; and Doctor Howe stepped up to the bedside.

"Going by what the Chief could tell us the governor was probably dying all day, your Excellency. It was already out of maximum tolerance when they reached the hospital last night."

A long moment, as Koscuisko considered this. And during that moment Stildyne imagined that he could see Robert realize what the issue was; but Robert didn't flinch from it. Why should he?

Everyone knew that a bond-involuntary was ruled both by conditioning and by the governor.

The last thing a bond-involuntary was supposed to be able to do was to assault a superior commanding officer. They knew it was wrong, by the rules they'd been taught. And knowing that it was a violation rendered them incapable of executing it without invoking sanctions from their governor well before any actual act of violence.

In a manner of speaking Robert was protected by the fact that he was a bond-involuntary . . . except in the eyes of people who knew that his governor was faulty. And who could guess that what Robert had done had been overwhelmingly right, in his own mind: right enough to overpower even his conditioning.

"The authorities will want a statement, Robert. You were on duty at the time of the murder. As part of the rest of the special event security. It will have to be a speak-serum, I suppose." Koscuisko was thinking out loud. Not revealing, but seemingly unable to quite accept what Doctor Howe had told him, nonetheless. "Robert, it would be better, I think, if you did not tell anyone else, unless of course the Bench specialists ask, and there is no reason for them to . . . that she is your sister."

And as much sense as this made to Stildyne at least, Robert seemed incapable of accepting it. The pain in Robert's voice was too much like the pain that had been there yesterday evening. Stildyne didn't like hearing it.

"But to know that she's here, sir, and not see her. So many years. Please. Stildyne, speak for me. Couldn't I be allowed to just sit with her?"

If Robert could appeal to him, of all people, then Robert truly did not remember. Stildyne thought fast.

"Sir, if there's evidence, speak-sera will bring it out." Unless the searing agony of a governor gone critical had well and truly erased the slate. "So it'll clear him. Why not, sir? No harm done."

And Robert might never see her again. That was the unspoken subtext, here. Either because he would not live to see the Day, and come back to Burkhayden—Security troops suffered a much diminished life expectancy, by definition. Or else because the Bench would decide that sufficient circumstantial evidence existed to take Robert for the crime, and he would be executed. Which wouldn't happen. Robert would be killed first. Stildyne was sure of that.

Was Koscuisko trying to read some special meaning from his words, trying to fathom some looked-for secret message in his face?

It seemed to Stildyne that the moment stretched.

But neither Doctor Howe nor Robert apparently noticed any such thing.

"It would be very difficult to deny the justice of your claim. Very well. Doctor Howe, there is the orderly's duty, the salve for her bruises. Perhaps Robert could be put to work on ward."

Robert turned his head away, and rubbed at his forehead with one hand. Covering his eyes.

"Settled, then," Doctor Howe agreed.

"Mister Stildyne. I must to the Bench specialist Vogel go and speak. Do you care to come with me?"

So Stildyne would know if there was to be a problem, perhaps?

Or so Koscuisko could pump him in transit for any additional details?

He could leave Pyotr in charge. Pyotr had been in charge, right enough. Stildyne hadn't been doing much chiefing over the last few hours. "Very good, sir. Robert. Get rested. Your orderly, Doctor Howe."

Maybe Robert had done the crime, and maybe Robert would be put to death for it—one way or another.

At least he could see his sister once or twice before he died.

Andrej meant to take Chief Stildyne out of doors and walk the secret out with him, as soon as he had satisfied Bench intelligence specialist Vogel. There was a secret, he could tell. He and Stildyne had known each other for too long, and while their intimacy had not approached the sort that would satisfy his Chief, it had developed over time into a true relationship of sorts.

Stildyne would confess himself, Andrej was certain of it. Stildyne always did. Because as painful as it was to him to suffer diminishment in Andrej's eyes, it was more painful yet to enjoy a false regard founded on concealment.

Andrej meant to have it out of Stildyne, and he had to speak to Specialist Vogel.

But he wanted to see how last night's victim fared, before he did a thing else.

He knew the hospital well enough after his brief tenure here; he didn't need a guide to get from here to there, and no one seemed to think twice to see him in the halls. Well, perhaps they did think twice—they would all have heard of his disgraceful behavior last night.

Though they had known him to be Inquisitor before, the near reminder could not but create some consternation. He only appreciated their courtesy in simply greeting him and going on their way all the more deeply for that.

On his way in to the intensive care wards Andrej heard a commotion of a sort in corridors ahead, and quickened his pace. Commotion was not allowed in hospital. There were too many unavoidable emergencies to countenance the raising of voices for any other reason than great grief or agony, and since he thought he recognized the voice Andrej felt sure it was not so dire a cause as that.

Great grief, yes, perhaps, but not for a loved one's death. Great agony, but of spirit and heart alone. A woman was expected to rule her temper better than that, especially in hospital. If Sylyphe Tavart was not a woman yet, it was still time that she learned better how to be reticent.

"You must let me at least see him. He's our own gardener—I have a right—"

Sylyphe Tavart. As pale as she could be in the unkind light of the bright day, her face scrubbed clean of cosmetics and her eyes ringed with deep bruise-purple shadows born of sleeplessness. Very unbecoming. Arguing with the orderly at the record-station, she had not heard him approach.

"That will do, Miss Tavart, you are making a scene on ward, and that is not seemly of you. Come with me."

The orderly was grateful to be rescued from her insistent pleading, but Andrej kept a straight face. He knew something about Sylyphe Tavart he hadn't known at this hour yesterday. Since she was here there were some things that he could tell her, if she could but be made to hear.

"Indeed I will not, take your hand away—"

But she was too young to make her indignant protest stick, and to her credit she didn't raise her voice. Andrej escorted her firmly to the duty physician's station and nodded at Stildyne to shut the door that separated the small room from the rest of the ward.

The admissions report was in the scroller; it took him a moment to find what he was after. He searched the record with grim concentration, conscious of Sylyphe standing in the middle of the room staring at him. She could not break away and flee from him. Stildyne was at the door, and Stildyne could do one of the best impressions of an immovable object that it had ever been Andrej's pleasure to behold.

Here was the admissions report, Doctor Howe's notes as to the status of his patient Skelern Hanner. Very precise. And very detailed too; it was not for nothing that Howe had survived his years under Bond, and lived to be reborn.

Sylyphe spoke at last, unbidden and unasked but not unexpectedly. Her voice was quiet and calm in the hush of the small room; very cool and formal. "You know, I thought that it was wonderful that Andrej Koscuisko should come to Burkhayden. Such a man, with such a reputation. And now I wish you had never come at all."

She was to be a formidable woman, when she came into her majority. There was no scorn in her words, and that only made the implicit rebuke more telling.

"Oh, don't be tedious. You cannot imagine I have never heard that before."

As seductive as her interest had been, as tempting as he had found her innocent desire for him, it was time to make a proper separation. She was not for him, nor he for her. Andrej meant to leave no traitorous hint of wistful longing in her heart, and if that meant that he would be a brute—so would he be.

"No, I am sure it is all old to you." Very plain she spoke, and wrung her hands. "I didn't know. How you must have laughed at me. . . . How is . . . ? What did you . . . ? Skelern."

She offered up her self-pride with a contrite humility that nearly staggered Andrej where he stood. It only made him the more sure of his purpose.

"It's not for me to say, Miss Tavart. That would entail a

violation of his privacy, and that would not be lawful. Now. Not since.''

Hanner had suffered horribly. Andrej knew his craft, he knew his own skill. Captain Lowden had insisted Hanner be harmed as little as possible, and Andrej had obeyed that order too. It would still be days before Hanner could walk, days longer yet before he could be released to light labor. It wasn't Sylyphe's business unless Hanner himself acknowledged it to her.

"They will not let me see him. May I see him? I only want to tell him. There's a message. From the Danzilar prince.''

The strain was too much for her; she began to fail beneath the enormity of her self-appointed task. The tears were all too clearly audible in her now-trembling voice. She wrung her whitesquare with shaking hands, and as much as Andrej wanted to take her into his arms to comfort her he knew that it would not be welcomed if he tried.

"You may not see him now. Nor would you be able to deliver any sort of message; he's asleep.'' Asleep or still unconscious, under the influence of pain-relief drugs. It didn't matter. "You must trust the doctors to act in Hanner's best interest, Sylyphe. I do not ask you to trust me. Only to believe that I am telling you the truth.''

Wait, wasn't that the same?

She untwisted her whitesquare with deliberate determination. Folding it flat, she creased its folds against the soft curve of her young stomach with an unselfconscious childlike gesture and put the thing away. "You won't let me see him. I can't know what you did to him. I will go home, now. Only. Please.''

That you had never come to Burkhayden. Yes. Andrej knew. Another woman might have cursed him, struck out at him, spat in his face. Sylyphe merely announced that he was unwelcome, now, as unwelcome as if he had only come to Burkhayden to torture her friend and break her heart.

"You have asked me nothing of what I may in fairness tell you.'' Andrej shut the scroller off at last and leaned his back against the wall, folding his arms across his chest, facing her.

"Such things as what excuse he had to make for being where he was. And yet it may well be that you should know."

In an odd and indirect way it was his own fault Hanner had been put to torture for the crime. Andrej's fault. He had not put Sylphe in her place, beguiled by her sweet innocence. Because he had indulged himself in her adoration Hanner had seen them and assumed the worst. It was his fault. He had to make it up somehow, or part of it, at least.

"Very well." Rolling her underlip between her teeth she took a deep breath. Waiting for the blow. "I am listening, your Excellency."

Torturer. Your Excellency, which was to say *criminal*. And so he was. Straightening up, Andrej pushed himself away from the wall; Stildyne caught the gesture Andrej made and moved to one side of the door. Ready to leave. Because Andrej had no intention of staying here for a moment longer once he'd had his say.

"Watching us dance. You and I." He had to select his words carefully. He knew it was his fault: he did not meant for her to conclude that she was the one who was to blame. "He imagined that you   Well. I hardly know how to say it. Did you know that he is in love with you, Miss Tavart?"

There was a moment, there, an instant of pure vibrant energy, a shimmering in the air as the sound of Andrej's voice fell away. The space between one breath and the next. Forever. Forever, an eternity of time in which to realize not only that what Andrej had said was true but that she had herself somehow become in love with Skelern Hanner while she'd not been looking.

She only looked at Andrej now, her eyes like great luminous gems. Glittering with tears. He could not stay a moment longer, because if he did he would kiss her quivering mouth, and that was for Hanner to do. Not for him.

So Andrej took her trembling hand and kissed the air above her fingertips, instead. And left the room with her still in it, pure and chaste and suddenly aware. A word or two with the physician's assistant made it right, and they would let her in to see her mother's gardener after all; and now Andrej could leave the area entirely. Not only could, but had to, or risk setting a blight on an uncertain romance by some awkward gesture.

Had he ever been so young as that?

Could he remember how it had felt, when he had first known that he loved Marana?

And now he was in a filthy mood, tired and hung over, and sorry for himself.

There was no time like the present to visit Specialist Vogel.

◇ Eleven

Bench intelligence specialist Garol Aphon Vogel sat over a shuffle of documentation laid out on a lab table, the lab stool drawn well up to the work surface, his feet tucked behind the lowest forward rung. Not so much puzzling over his conclusions as weighing their implications. Andrej Koscuisko stopped in the corridor, declining to step into the doorway, taking a deep draw at the smoldering lefrol he carried and releasing the greater part of its thick gray-white smoke into the hall. Rather than into the room. Garol wondered why Koscuisko was smoking at all, in a hospital—deserted wards or no. Koscuisko knew better than that. Surely.

"Your Excellency." Tired and depressed and unsure of the best route to take out of the mess that murder had made of Port Burkhayden, Garol didn't bother to straighten up. "Good of you to stop in. Doing rounds?"

The person who thought he'd seen Garol himself go up to Lowden's suite had turned out to be the floor manager at the service house. Once the floor manager had gotten it into his head that it was Garol he'd shown through, his tentative identification had hardened into rock-solid certainty. Memory was like that. Played tricks on a man.

A Bench intelligence specialist was clearly an appropriate person for a harried floor manager to have shown straight through. If the man to whom the floor manager had given access to luxury quarters was an assassin, though, then the floor manager was potentially to blame for a murder—if that

was what it would turn out to be. So it was much safer for
the floor manager to be convinced that he'd seen Garol Vogel,
and as long as Garol didn't contradict him they could all be
happy.

"I came to see my man, and also to check on the gardener.
You left word, Specialist Vogel. You wanted to see me."

Reaching into the frontplaquet of his overblouse, Koscuisko
drew out a smooth silvery tube, matte-dull with age and use
as only an antique of rhinsillery alloy weathered: A lefrol-
keeper. Tucking his lefrol into the container Koscuisko put it
away and then stepped across the threshold, but stopped just
inside the open doorway.

"How's the gardener doing?" Garol asked, mildly curious.
What was the etiquette observed between a man who had been
unjustly tortured, and the very much senior-ranking man who
had tortured him? "Does he remember anything about the
event that might help to identify an assassin?"

Koscuisko frowned, as if as much annoyed at Garol for
asking embarrassing questions as out of shame or diffidence.
"Hanner is unconscious. Sleeping. Well drugged. Surely you
do not imagine that I would have the face to confront him.
After what I did."

What Koscuisko had done was only what Koscuisko had
been ordered to do. But Garol thought he understood. Koscuisko believed that he should have caught the anomaly with
the crozer-hinge right away. Koscuisko was probably right,
on one level at least.

"You don't have to make any excuses for doing your lawful duty, not even with the gardener. We all heard the Captain." And though Koscuisko's private passion was fearful
sadism, it wasn't Koscuisko who used and indulged it. It had
been Captain Lowden who had been responsible for Koscuisko's extravagances.

Koscuisko swore. "Holy Mother. As if there was any excuse to be made for the time that it took to discover. I will
not be patronized, Garol Vogel."

Only two names. Did Koscuisko know all three? Koscuisko's point was unarguable. If Koscuisko would not accept

rationalization to cover the gardener's ordeal then Koscuisko would not—and was a better man for it than otherwise.

Garol set it all aside as a bent pin and took up the threads of his problem. "All right. The gardener. I'll need a statement. He may have heard something. Seen something. From your man St. Clare, as well."

Koscuisko hadn't stirred to come near or sit down. Koscuisko stood still now. "On a speak-serum, in the presence of a Judicial officer—of course, Specialist Vogel. But Hanner will not remember. Still less will my Robert remember anything. I have just come from having a word with him, and he has lost most of yesterday. Amnesia can be transient when its cause is trauma to the brain itself, but in this instance it is the processing which has been disrupted. I am convinced that any information Robert might have had will be unrecoverable."

Calm; not the least concerned. Garol Vogel was not a Ship's Inquisitor; but his survival depended upon his ability to read people and situations, which was as a consequence fairly well developed. Koscuisko was not worried. So neither man would be able to incriminate anybody. If Koscuisko was that sure that Garol would get no evidence, even under a speak-serum, then there was really no point in even trying; though it would have to be done, of course.

"I'll schedule the interviews for once the gardener's awake and strong enough for it. For the Record. Two or three days?"

He had to complete the investigation, or risk leaving a hole that might arouse suspicion simply by virtue of the fact that he had discarded suspicion without comment. Koscuisko merely nodded. Garol spoke on.

"That's about all I had, sir. Except to ask if you happened to remember what you were doing in the streets last night, when I found you."

"And took me to bed," Koscuisko agreed, with a little smile. "Excuse me, the phrase is not what it was to have said. Conveyed me to Center House. I was drunk, I think."

And wasn't about to tell Garol if he did remember anything. Why should he? Because if Koscuisko wouldn't talk the whole matter would either go forward on a supposition or be allowed to lapse for lack of evidence. Risking the chance that Koscuisko would let slip something incriminating some year; while he slept, for instance.

"We won't know how many are dead in the fire until the Port Authority can get people in to what's left at the site of the service house." Garol had no real doubt in his own mind about it. He knew he wasn't the one who had asked for the Captain at the service house. He hadn't gotten there till the place was already on fire.

But he could see where an overstressed floor manager might mistake Andrej Koscuisko in the dark of a house on auxiliary power, and convince himself later that the man he had seen was Garol and none other. Koscuisko had been there. Koscuisko had gone up. And shortly thereafter the fire alarms had gone off, and the service house had been evacuated; all except Captain Lowden.

As nearly as the Port Authority had been able to determine so far, only one person who had been in the service house had failed to get clear with his life. That was powerful evidence for the supposition that Lowden had been dead when the fire had started.

Koscuisko was waiting for him to finish his thought. Garol took a deep breath. "But we know that Lowden was in there. So he's dead. Can't say I'm sorry."

"As long as no innocent man must be taken," Koscuisko agreed. "I'm not sorry myself."

No, Koscuisko knew. Koscuisko remembered. Koscuisko would say something if he had to. But if he didn't have to, why should he say anything?

Captain Lowden had needed to die.

They both understood that.

Garol rubbed at the front of his overblouse idly, feeling the crackling of the folded document in the inner pocket. Bench warrant. He'd got Jils thinking it was on Lowden. Why shouldn't it have been?

"Yeah, well. Once we find the body maybe we'll know more." But probably not. Probably no more than that it was Lowden's body, or at least verifiable as such from a genescan on whatever was left of it. The chances that the body was undamaged enough to prove so much as that a murder had even happened were almost nonexistent. Circumstantial evidence was all they would ever have, in the absence of a confession.

Who had killed the Fleet Lieutenant?

Had it been St. Clare?

How could a bond-involuntary have done such a thing?

And what did Garol care, one way or the other?

Wyrlann was dead. The gardener hadn't killed him. Wyrlann had been a bully with a developing reputation as a man who needed killing. He was better dead. The Judicial order was better served by Wyrlann dead than alive, and Captain Lowden as well.

"Call for me when you wish the Record to complete, Specialist Vogel," Koscuisko said, bringing an end to the interview. As if it had been his interview. As if it were Koscuisko who had sent for Garol, and not the other way around. That was the way of it, with people who held rank.

Garol had dealt with people like Koscuisko for all of his adult life.

He still couldn't quite manage the absolute self-assurance.

"And I will for you the speak-sera administer. To the upholding of the Judicial order in completion of the Record. Though neither man will have any words for you."

That wasn't the point.

Both of them knew that.

The point was that all avenues had to be laid out on Record, drawn out, described, then decisively cancelled. Or someone might follow one of the avenues back to a problem, someday in the future.

"Very good, sir."

And get out.

Why should Koscuisko get away with murder?

What difference did one more murder make, whether the Bench had ordained it or not?

Koscuisko went away with a nod; and left Garol to brood

over life and injustice, alone by himself in the deserted lab, with a shuffle of depositions for company.

Megh heard them coming down the hallway toward the half-closed door to her room, and grimaced in irritation. She didn't mind the hospital very bitterly; she hadn't had so much time to herself since she could remember. But that the orderlies came to her to touch her was an irritation. She had to bear it; it was her life to be handled at the will of another, not at her will.

And still she was in hospital, not in the service house.

Which had burned down.

Somehow it seemed more distasteful to her that she should be outside the service house and yet still be subject to someone else's judgment as to where and how she was to suffer being touched.

She closed her eyes and turned her head away from the door, toward the window. It was Doctor Barit Howe. She recognized his voice. And to listen to him he was bringing yet another unfamiliar face, a new orderly, to lift the bedding carefully away from her legs to salve the bruises or to take the bed-wrap down from her shoulders to daub an ointment on the still-healing skin of her arms and shoulders.

"—your fifth-week," Doctor Howe was saying. "You know how to treat a patient. Only take a little more care, we're not a ship of war. This is a civilian hospital. My patients aren't to be told what to do, not like your shipmates. Clear?"

Yes, someone new. Megh looked across the room, out of the window, at the clear light beyond. There was nothing to see, of course; the window let out onto a courtyard. Sometimes looking out the window helped her to take herself away until she was alone again.

She didn't like being handled by anybody, let alone unfamiliar hands. She wasn't supposed to like it. It was the punishment that the Bench had put her to; and still she resented the treatment she got as a patient. Why wouldn't they just let her alone?

But then the orderly spoke.

"Clear, Doctor Howe. You'll not have cause to complain of me to my maister, nor to my Chief either. I can promise you that."

The small hairs at the nape of Megh's neck rose in a swift rush of prickly apprehension. Apprehension that was not fear.

Where had she heard that voice, before?

"Good-greeting, Maistress Megh." Doctor Howe stood at a pace's remove from her bedside, in respect for her privacy. He knew she didn't like being confined to bed in such a public place as a hospital. "Here's company for you. His Excellency has loaned him out for the duration, since the *Ragnarok* will be on site until the investigations are all closed. You can throw him out when you like, but please permit him to apply the ointment before you do."

Oh, she had no call to be rude to Doctor Howe. But no one was making her speak peace to him either. It was only that she had conditioning. She would be lowly and submissive. It was her role. "Thank you, Doctor Howe. I'll bear whomever, as best I can."

Turning her head, she spoke to the doctor.

Turning her head, she saw the other man, who stood beside the doctor staring at her as though his heart could travel through his eyes into her bosom.

She knew that man.

She had never seen him before—and she knew him.

"Thank you for your gentle courtesy. I'll be on my way."

Doctor Howe nodded to her and to the orderly, and left. And shut the door.

Megh stared; and the orderly stared back.

Who was this man?

He had grown tall.

His uniform said that he was a bond involuntary, like her, only different.

It was their uncle's ghost, risen from the dead and wearing boots.

It was their father's brother Fipps, the one who lived nine days' walk down the coast and fished in a boat for his living.

"Oh, say a word, Megh, darling," the ghost said. "Else I'll explode. It would make such a mess."

It was Robin.

It was her own brother.

"You are grown." He knew that, probably, but she could not but marvel it out loud. "And gotten handsome. Robin. It is you. But can it be?"

He stepped forward to her bedside, falling to his knees. Taking her outstretched hand to numb it with kisses that spoke of the years of loneliness. "Wondered myself, I have, Megh. To have seen you, when my maister came here. I thought that I would die."

His maister, and Doctor Howe had said Excellency. She had heard. The orderlies had told her.

"Robin, you belong to Koscuisko?"

It was beyond belief. It could not be true. She was dreaming this.

But as long as she was dreaming it she would make as much of it as she could. She would stare at him until her eyes turned solid stone and dropped from their sockets, and not see enough to fill the void within. She would hold to him until her hands dried into willow-twigs and turned to dust, and still not get enough of his existence.

Robin.

And alive.

And grown, grown to a man, and such a man, tall and so good to look upon. They had always warned her family that Robin was sure to be a beauty, and was to be carefully nurtured that he not bring some too-trusting soul to grief before he knew the meaning of his actions.

"Anders Koscuisko. Yes. His Excellency. I wouldn't have known it was you, Megh, the Lieutenant used you so foully. But Skelern Hanner said the weaves. I knew."

So it was Anders from the Domitt Prison who tortured Nurail for Jurisdiction, but had brought her Robin safe to her side. *Ragnarok* that had sent the Fleet Lieutenant who had beaten her, but *Ragnarok* that had sent healing to her as well, and had brought her brother to be with her here besides. Jurisdiction had taught Nurail how to lament, but Jurisdiction was teaching Nurail how to believe in miracles of coincidence. It was her brother. It was Robin. He was here.

If only for a while.

But he was here.

"Now." Robin wiped the salt tears of his face with the back of his hand, and it nearly broke her heart to see him do it, it was their daddy to the life. She could endure it. She could live. Her fate had brought her brother living to her. She could brew beer out of spring water and three grains of last year's wild-grass. She could make cheese out of ram's-milk. She could do anything.

"Now. Megh. Oh, darling. There's an ointment to be laid on bruises, my maister went particularly to beg jellericia blooms from a garden here in town, your Hanner's garden. Because he knew the fragrance of it would be a comfort to a woman from the hill-stations, and never even guessed until I said to him."

She'd wondered about the ointment. She'd even wondered whether the materials had come from Skelern's garden. "I haven't seen Skelern, Robin, and I would have thought that he might come see me. Do you know if all is well with him? He's been kind to me, cousin-like."

Something was wrong. Robin ducked his head. "All's right now, Megh, but there's been trouble on the path from then till now. For him to tell you, really. But everything is all right now. Everything's well."

He wasn't only talking about Skelern, but about himself. About her. About them.

For as long as Fleet would grant them time to speak in each other's company, all unwittingly, by accident—for so long, everything was well with the world. Everything was all right.

Robin opened up his jar of salve and commenced to daub it at her bruised shoulder, working it up gradually into a gentle massaging sort of a caress.

She'd never hoped to see Robin alive.

She would happily forgive the Bench another six such beatings, in return for the joy she had now in seeing her brother.

*   *   *

Five days. Hanner was not to be permitted to leave the
hospital, not yet, but he had leave to move around a bit. It
hurt to walk, although his feet were healing; if he was careful
he could take three steps at a time before he had to sit. It ate
upon him more to be idle, and to lie in a bed all day when
the sun was out and there was work to be done.

Of course he wasn't to even think about worrying that the
gardening would go to ruin. Sylyphe had told him so; and so
sternly that he could have wept at her solemn dignity, poor
thing. The Danzilar prince had sent word to the Tavart to
excuse him, and the Tavart had been sent gardeners in the
Danzilar prince's pay to keep things up in his absence. He
was not to lose his place, though he was to feel free to accept
a better offer should one come—as the Tavart apparently felt
was likely. It was all but too much for a man.

It wasn't as though he'd never been beaten before in his
life, and more than once badly, and had mended bones and
scars to show for it. There was no comparing to his most
recent experience, there was that, but still for all his life he'd
been expected to suffer a beating and lose his day's pay until
he could work again, and all for the crime of having been
born Nurail. Nothing like this.

Sylyphe had come to see him on an embassy from her
mother, carrying her errand as tenderly as if it had been a
newborn infant. She'd done well. But then when she'd done
with her errand Sylyphe wept to look at him, tender-hearted
as she was. And how was he to comfort her? Him in bed, and
in bandages, and hating that she should look at his uncovered
skin.

Though he had done the best he could Hanner still felt the
lack of it. He could never dream to comfort Sylyphe properly,
with kisses and love-words. She was too far above him. And
she deserved so much better than an underfed gardener who
trimmed her mother's turves for his wages.

Five days, and he had leave to dress himself and walk
around the hospital with crutches and a mover. Someone had
cleaned his clothing, and he remembered that Koscuisko had

let him strip himself at his own pace, and stayed the security from handling him too roughly. That had been kindly intentioned, in its way. He'd been wearing the best shirt that he owned, in token of respect for the Danzilar prince—or for the Danzilar prince's gardens, at any rate.

The hospital staff said that he might go and see Megh. There was to be someone with her, but Hanner could deal with that; it wasn't like there was intimacy between them. He came to the place and signaled at the door, and the door opened, and the tall broad-shouldered person whose body blocked the doorway gave him pause and made him fearful. One of Koscuisko's people. Hanner recognized the troop.

The troop recognized him as well, luckily, and stepped aside; and having petitioned for entry Hanner felt that he could hardly not go in. Even if there was one of Koscuisko's people here. Even if the last person in the world that Skelern Hanner was interested in seeing was anyone with anything to do with Andrej Koscuisko. His Uncle had dealt fairly with him, in the end, but it was too terrible in Hanner's mind for him to find any charity in his heart to spare for Black Andrej.

"Here to look in on Megh," Hanner explained. Surely unnecessarily—wasn't so much obvious by the fact that he was here? "How does she go? Is she awake to greet me?"

The troop closed the door behind them, and Hanner crossed the room to look. Megh, in the bed, the covers drawn up very prettily over her shoulders, and someone had done her hair into a braid. The troop? Surely not. But it wasn't the kind of braid a woman did on her own, not easily.

And if Skelern thought about it that one troop was Nurail. He knew the man.

He'd met him before.

Hanner had thought he looked familiar, from the start.

"Asleep, the poor darling," the Security troop said; and it was unlike anything that Hanner would have expected to hear from a bond-involuntary troop, surprising him into a fresh stare at the man. And then once he started staring there was something he could not stop staring at.

The last time he'd seen Megh she'd been marked in the face, blue and black, bruised and swollen. But her face was more familiar to him, now, and there was no mistaking the similarity when the Security troop glanced over at her with transparent fondness.

Hanner checked the sleeves of the troop's uniform with a quick sidewise glance. Just to make sure of it. Green piping, bright green, like wet-moss or the bloom-canker on the sweetstarchie flowers that ruined the crop.

Bond-involuntary.

And had spoken so to Koscuisko in the garden till Koscuisko, not understanding the point, had sent him sternly away—the thing he did not have, not him, not Hanner, but Megh's brother had to be from Marleborne—

He didn't know what to say. He had no right to be here with her brother, no right to be between them for the short time they would have before the *Ragnarok* left Burkhayden space.

"She, does she know you're here?" he asked, his voice hushed in the surprise of it all.

Robert St. Clare, that was his name. Megh's Robin. He grinned, and rubbed a spot at the back of his neck behind his ear in a gesture that was familiar to Hanner. "We talk when she's awake, but the pain-meds make her drowsy will-she nill-she. She's mostly sleeping. They let me look after her, to see that she gets her meals and lacks for nothing."

Hanner could understand the love, the longing in those words. He was so glad, for Megh; but her brother pulled himself away from staring at her, as if he was distracted.

"How did it go with you, man, and my maister?"

Koscuisko. Hanner shook his head. "Oh, let's not speak of it. I was so feared of him."

St. Clare nodded, as if he understood. Well, of course he'd know, from observation; but no, it didn't seem to be that he was talking about something that he'd only just watched. "I came under his hand, once, at the beginning. Before he knew that I was to be bound to him. Before it was decided."

There was nothing Hanner could say about that surprising

idea. Perhaps Megh's brother had just wanted to offer comfort to him? Because he was still talking.

"And I was feared of him. I still am when the mood is on him, even though he's my good maister. I mean to tell him so, if I can catch him right before they put my governor back in. He'd not believe me, otherwise."

Hanner could only look at Megh's brother with wonder, not understanding why the man should say these things to him. But Megh's brother nodded yet again, and as if it had been a question asked, this time.

"It's malfunctioned, you see, and the doctor had to pull it. So I can speak to Anders Koscuisko like a man, and he'll know there isn't any constraint to the telling of it. So I can tell you what you need to know, young Hanner."

Young Hanner? Oh, no younger than St. Clare's own self, from what Megh had told him. What did he mean, tell what was needful to know?

"The doctor's to come in an eight, there's not much time. You'll want to concentrate. The first thing that you need to know is the traveling. From the corn-field stock. To the brook foot-path. To the post at the edge, with the shelf and the dipper-cup."

Quite suddenly Hanner was chilled to the bone with an icy shock of unimaginable power that stunned him. He could hardly think, but he had to think, he had to hang on, and he reached for the words like an anchor to steady himself with.

"From the edge-post shelf to the left of the break, to the ridge of the roof."

To the Ice Traverse.

He'd claimed the name to claim the right to see her, never dreaming. Never meaning to lay his hand on what was not of his, ready to steal the name of the weave to get his way and nothing further meant by it. Not to pretend that he had a right to it. Not to pretend he knew.

"Talk it to me, cousin, state you your claim, and call my Megh your sister like an honest man."

There was no more profound a gift in all the Nurail tongues than to give a weave. And him a gardener, not from the hill-people, but to stand from now on with the proud folk, and equal with any—

Hanner closed his eyes, thinking hard, steadying himself with one hand against the wall. "The Ice Traverse stems from the ridge of the mountain-roof. To the right from the break, where the valley parts. To the pitch of the roof of the way-shed rest, to the post at the edge and the brook foot-path. To the corn-field stack, in the field, with the reapers."

St. Clare was smiling at him approvingly when he opened his eyes from his concentration. "And the next things that are needful to know are the callings of it, see, these kinds—"

He had the Nurail right, then, if St. Clare approved his Standard of it. He could not stop to congratulate himself; St. Clare was telling out the pattern with his fingers, and Hanner recognized the first part of a lullaby, the mid part of a drinking song, the fifth part of a workingman's chant, all recombined, all reunited to form the background that upheld the weave.

That held the power.

A unity too perfect to be challenged or forgotten, once it was but recognized in whole—

And the power frightened him, but it had to be borne, because the gift of a weave was beyond any fear, and this could be the only chance that Megh's enslaved brother would have to recite it for years. Or forever.

"The first part of the second thing is conny-towing, seabird-tumbling, sense and pease and coin. Right?"

The pattern was there. And, oh, but it moved him. "So, the second part of the second thing must be dark tan leaf and water blowing, blue clouds in the half-sun sky, and barge turned over on the shore-sand." He hoped, he thought, it was so strong within him. It was so right. St. Clare alarmed him, grasping him at the back of his neck suddenly, and kissing his mouth in the fashion of the hill-folk with tears in his eyes. But smiling.

"Thou art a man, and a very clever man, to have caught this—caught this—caught this, thing. And the third thing, third thing, what would be the third thing, can you tell me the third thing, cleverness, my cousin?"

The Ice-Traverse, a gift, a weave. It still could not be sung, but it was passed, and it would not be lost. He was its keeper. His to see the pattern would survive, to hold a piece of the great heart of his scattered nation.

"Oh, I. Could hardly say. If it were not. To say the fourth."

The pattern led to the tune, and the tune led to the telling, and the telling and the tune and the pattern all together held power that even the Jurisdiction's Bench had feared.

Would fear again?

No, he was a gardener. He never would have dared to claim the weave, not even to see Megh, if he had known that there might be a man who knew the weave, with him having no right to it.

"Then there would be such mockery that kites could not collect the air, if salmon ran in podge-meal, while the sisters pondered."

He had to mind the gift, to take it perfect from the only man who lived who had preserved it.

And he had to concentrate.

Governor or no governor Megh's brother was taking a significant risk, speaking his weave. Hanner had to learn it as quickly as he could, and give it back whole and entire, complete and correct.

Before Megh chanced to wake.

A woman was not to hear her mother's weave. It was indecent.

He had to hold it carefully, for Megh's children.

◇ Twelve

The Danzilar prince's business meeting room was in a library at Center House, middling in size, luxuriously appointed to the tastes of a Danzilar Dolgorukij with rugs and printed texts. The Record stood out as an anomaly in this place, and somehow Jils felt out of place as well, although the number of people in the room who were in uniform outnumbered the single man in civilian dress by four to one.

The Record was under Andrej Koscuisko's Writ, and had been removed from Secured Medical on the *Ragnarok* and ferried here by the custodial officer himself under careful escort. Now it stood on the table, nothing more than a flat square frame only as large as a printed text in quarto with a holographic projector in its base. Square, but shallow. Koscuisko had carried it on his person, in his overblouse.

The murdered officers had been assigned to the *Ragnarok*. It was appropriate that the Writ under Andrej Koscuisko record and report their findings. And although a Record was a Record, the one from the *Ragnarok* had more transmit authority than the one the Bench had left here in Port Burkhayden, the one that she and Vogel would remove as the final step in ceding the port to the Danzilar prince.

Once the Record was removed the Bench would have no further claim on Port Burkhayden absent a request for intervention from the Danzilar prince. Or absent Fleet intervention at the Bench's direction if collection of fees began to lag or collusion with Free Government agencies was suspected.

"I've never seen one," Paval I'shenko was confiding to Koscuisko, who sat at the Danzilar prince's left. "Andrej Ulexeievitch. This is the Record of which we speak?"

Seeing the two of them so close together was instructive. The secondary subracial characteristics of the Dolgorukij contributed to a substantial degree of likeness between them; but more than that, they were related to one another, if a little distantly. The resemblance was unmistakable.

Nurail subspecies ethnicity could be invoked to explain why Robert St. Clare and the woman from the service house that Wyrlann had abused looked like they were related, as well. In a pinch.

"This is the piece of the Record that belongs to *Ragnarok*, Paval I'shenko. Yes." Like many things that could be abstract and concrete at once a person had to know context before understanding what was meant by the word "record." "To this Record I make my case and through this Record I record my findings. Secure encodes and access to the validation matrices at Camberlin Judiciary, and so forth, but this Record need only know me, it saves in transmit time."

The Record at Port Burkhayden was a more restricted instrument, that had to transmit for verification and then return with evidence. It had taken two days for the Record at Port Burkhayden to return acceptance validation for Koscuisko's clearing the gardener of the murder. Koscuisko's own Record would transmit direct to Bench offices once Koscuisko declared the Record complete. Quicker. More efficient. And they could all go home.

"Gentles, shall we begin," Jils suggested. Garol was getting impatient, sitting beside her, worrying at the cuticle of his thumb. He had something on his mind, and Jils thought she knew what it was. "Your Excellency. If you would, sir."

There were three Excellencies here, Koscuisko, the Danzilar prince, the First Officer; but only one of them could open the Record. Koscuisko nodded, rising to his feet. "Very well. For the Record. Andrej Ulexeievitch Koscuisko, Jurisdiction Fleet Ship *Ragnarok*, the following parties also present. Please state your names—"

And the crimes of which you have been accused. It was formula. Koscuisko stopped himself just in time, and grinned a little sheepishly at the near-misstep. One by one the people at the table named themselves, starting with the Danzilar prince, and going around the table. Ralph Mendez, the *Ragnarok*'s First Officer, as the representative of his Command. Garol Vogel and Jils Ivers, Bench intelligence specialists, investigating office.

Andrej Ulexeievitch Koscuisko held the Writ, and attended in his capacity as a Bench officer. Once the circuit of identification was complete he spoke once more. "And no others are here present. Presentation and discussion of findings follows for adjudication and decision by parties here present. Suspend Record until further notice."

No recording of discussion, because there was no sense in taking up valuable storage space on recapitulation or controversy. Once they decided what the evidence meant their decision would go on Record. Once that happened it was final.

"Specialist Ivers, Specialist Vogel. Your meeting, gentles."

Koscuisko sat down. Jils rose to her feet. "Thank you, your Excellency. Prince Danzilar. We have two issues here before us."

Two murders. The Danzilar prince had a report already of the actual findings, transcripts of interviews, all of the evidence that she and Garol had taken over the course of the last ten days. Well, not all of it. But all of it that belonged on Record. It saved time. She could get right to the point.

"As to the first, the assassination of Fleet First Lieutenant G'herm Wyrlann. If it wasn't the gardener, who was it? Several considerations, here. The Captain identified Skelern Hanner as guilty, so detail search for physical evidence in the garden itself was delayed until much later that evening."

Because there was no call to search for physical evidence with an accused in custody. With an accused in custody the presumption was that any physical evidence would stay put until whenever, as along as the garden was quarantined—as it had been. To have initiated a search at that point could have been taken as accusing Captain Lowden of bearing false witness, by implication.

"By which time there was none to be found," the Danzilar prince agreed. "Whoever did the murder had a chance to get away. And remove any evidence with him, or her."

Or else third parties, sympathetic to the murderer's cause for whatever reason, had tidied up the garden well before then. No use in suggesting that, though they all knew the possibility existed. The Danzilar prince's house staff was full of Nurail. The Nurail community of Port Burkhayden—by far the majority of the people here—had been quite reasonably outraged at the abuse the bondswoman had suffered at the hands of the Fleet Lieutenant. It was only natural that they might endorse any measures taken in retaliation by shielding the murderer. By destroying evidence.

Jils continued. "There's no weapon, and the accused has been cleared. We have two choices. One is an anonymous Free Government assassin. The other has to do with the fact that the woman is the sister of the bond-involuntary, Robert St. Clare."

Nobody was surprised. That didn't surprise her. It was only reasonable for Koscuisko to have told his First Officer, since Koscuisko knew quite well that St. Clare was protected from accusation by the evidence he'd given.

And as for the Danzilar prince, well, the Danzilar prince knew a great deal more about what was happening at his port than he shared with them. He had good people. Jils suspected some of them were Malcontents, under cover, and the slaves of Saint Andrej Malcontent were intelligence agents that even—or especially—a Bench intelligence specialist had to respect.

"Your report's got the talk you two had with St. Clare. Here," the *Ragnarok*'s First Officer pointed out, tapping the document in front of him. "Speak-serum trial, proved for truthful utterance at the Execution levels. Did you have anything to do with the murder, you asked. St. Clare said he had no knowledge of it. He couldn't have lied. He's clear."

Actually Garol had asked, but Mendez was right. Koscuisko had used the most powerful such drug on the Controlled List, one usually reserved for confirming confession to a capital crime. Absolutely sure of himself, absolutely sure that St. Clare remembered nothing, one way or the other.

"The issue is one of memory, First Officer." Koscuisko's polite qualification rather startled Jils. It was clear to her now—if it had not been before—that Koscuisko was willing to go to great lengths to protect his troops. She hadn't anticipated his participation in this, but she had to admit that it was more convincing coming from the medical professional than from her. "He can state absolutely that he does not remember, because it is true. He cannot say that he had no hand in it, because he doesn't remember."

"So—" Mendez's voice was thoughtful. "If he starts to remember, some year, and turns out to have had something to do with it . . . ?"

Such as committing the crime, to avenge his sister. Koscuisko looked unruffled, serene. Confident. "He will be under governor, and will have to report the recovered information or suffer the consequences. There will be confession at that time. But without evidence, and with a legally supported claim to have no knowledge, he cannot be pressed further."

And he had been under governor in the first place, technically incapable of the act as far as the Bench knew. No sense in belaboring that point any further.

"All we're left with is that Hanner heard something behind him on the veranda. There's no evidence." She was only saying what they all knew. And they needed a way to close the case and move on. "The rule of Law is not well served by unsolved murders. If it was a Free Government agent the explanation satisfies our responsibility to uphold the rule of Law, even though the criminal goes undetected and unpunished."

Free Government agents could be anybody, but the point was that no one would be put at risk. Everybody knew about Free Government political terrorism. A Free Government assassin could be safely supposed to be far away from Burkhayden, and nothing to do with anyone who lived here. If it was a Free Government assassin the Bench had no brief to continue to search for a murderer amongst the Danzilar prince's people, Dolgorukij and Nurail alike.

"A Free Government 'assassin." The Danzilar prince sounded a little dubious. "If you say so. It could well be."

"We so recommend." Garol spoke up for the first time. He'd been abstracted lately. No, he'd been abstracted since the beginning of this whole enterprise, from the moment they'd started to Meghilder space with the Danzilar prince's fleet. He just kept getting moodier by the day, was all. "There's absolutely nothing to be gained by leaving it open."

Once Jils had realized that Garol was carrying a Bench warrant, of course, she'd understood. Garol was opposed to Bench warrants on principle. The system should be able to take care of its problems through normal channels, Garol said, and when the Bench had to resort to secret execution it was a failure in the system. But he did his job. He always did his job. And he was good at it.

"Do you know, my Security felt that we were being stalked, when I first to Burkhayden came," Koscuisko said suddenly. "Someone came into quarters when they were unoccupied, and rearranged the doses in a drugs-pouch. Nothing more than that. And yet Pyotr insisted on shifting to more secure quarters, and I had not thought of it to mention this, before."

No reason for Koscuisko to have made it up to convince his cousin Danzilar. Jils was glad he'd said it. The Danzilar prince looked much more comfortable than he had before, and said as much.

"So there has been activity. Very well. We do not cover up for the crime, we merely select the most likely of several unprovable possibilities. I am content. Let us go on."

Not as if it rested with the Danzilar prince, but as the planetary governor he did have a great deal to say about the disposition of the case. It was under his jurisdiction, not that of the Bench—or very nearly so. Jils picked up the thread.

"All right. Next. Captain Lowden. Positive identification of the body." Lying across the table, what was left of one. The floor had held but everything within the room had burned.

The fact that Lowden's body lay amid the ashes of the table and traces of napery told them less than nothing, except that he hadn't been in bed.

From all the evidence showed he might have just collapsed over his meal, and died of heart failure—except of course that there was no trace of a meal, which hadn't been sent up yet by report, and that the body lay face up and not face down. Captain Lowden had been murdered. Jils was sure of it.

"The floor-manager's given evidence that Specialist Vogel came to see the Captain shortly before the fire. This evidence is on record, but may plausibly be discounted."

Koscuisko raised an eyebrow at that. Garol hadn't told Koscuisko, then. Odd. She would have expected Garol to level with the Judicial officer. On the other hand she and Garol were a species of judicial officer, themselves.

Garol made a face that Jils recognized, lips pursed together and rolled toward his teeth, raised eyebrows drawn together in the middle of his forehead. Embarrassment. Disclosure of some mildly shocking secret.

"Go ahead, Jils, blow my cover. Prince Danzilar. This is very awkward. I'd owe you an apology, if it wasn't Bench business."

The Danzilar prince looked confused, so Garol had to continue. Had Koscuisko guessed, Jils wondered? Something about the phrase "Bench business" seemed to mean something to him.

"It feels like a violation of your hospitality. Which has been very gracious. Here's what we mean. Someone's given evidence that I went up to see Captain Lowden. Now, this is a Bench warrant."

Drawing the document out of the inside pocket of his overblouse, Garol gazed at it thoughtfully for a long moment. Giving the implications of the statement a chance to sink in. Giving them time to consider what it meant.

"A Bench warrant, or, specifically, a termination order. It's not very good guest behavior to murder VIPs during Port accession celebrations, your Excellency. But it is my job. At least from time to time."

Garol's Bench warrant meant that though there was evidence connecting him with the murder on record, there would be no challenge from the Bench to a finding of Free Government assassination. Why he'd set fire to the service house to cover the job she didn't understand, but maybe he hadn't. Maybe that had been an accident. Or unrelated. There was no reason to cover up the crime, after all. All he was expected to do was to make it look good enough that the Free Government could be blamed.

"And personally. I'll say this in light of what we all know. Lowden deserved to die. I believe he gave false witness. I was there. I don't think he believed the gardener did it. The gardener was just a convenient victim."

Koscuisko turned his face down and away from her; the Danzilar prince—half-rising—put his hand out to Koscuisko's shoulder, his concern clearly evident.

"You could not know, Drusha," Danzilar said. "Please. You must forgive yourself. You had orders."

The *Ragnarok*'s First Officer, Ralph Mendez, had been quiet for the duration, obviously content to sit and absorb. Now Mendez turned his attention to his hands, clasped before him on the table's surface. It was awkward to be witness to this. Jils could sympathize.

"Orders can never justify." Koscuisko's voice sounded choked. "Oh, Shiki. There is always someone who must do the thing, and that man has a choice, Shiki, truly. I am ashamed."

That it took him so long to realized that Hanner hadn't done it, could not have done it. Garol had told her about Koscuisko's conflict. She honored it; but Koscuisko was wrong. Lawful orders upheld the rule of Law. Obedience to lawful orders was the duty of every responsible citizen under Jurisdiction. Only unlawful orders brought shame on the head of the one who executed them. And as soon as Koscuisko had realized that the gardener was innocent Koscuisko had taken appropriate measures.

"One way or the other," Garol said, in a voice that struck Jils as being curiously soft. "Captain Lowden's death was required by the Bench under warrant. That's all there is to it. We recommend a finding of Free Government activity, targeting officers of the Jurisdiction Fleet Ship *Ragnarok*. Unless there are any questions.''

Koscuisko covered his face with his hands. But after a moment Koscuisko straightened up. The Danzilar prince, still watching Koscuisko with concern clearly written on his face, shook his head.

''No. I am content. As long as the Bench will have no expectation of launching a hunt for any such assassins here. I will not have a Fleet interrogations group at Port Burkhayden.''

Quite right of him, too. Fleet interrogations groups were very efficient at identifying and locating Free Government operatives. The problem was that a Fleet interrogations group was perfectly capable of finding such activity where there wasn't any. It made no difference to a Fleet interrogations group. Someone could always be brought to confess to the crime, and from there things escalated.

''We'll sign up to that, sir, and go so far as to promise that no further action will be taken.'' Jils could make that claim honestly, with confidence. Garol would declare his Bench warrant. That would be that. ''I think we can go on Record, your Excellency.''

Koscuisko stood up, and looked around the table at each of them. Mendez nodded. ''Go for it, Andrej.''

Koscuisko decided.

''Terminate suspension of Record, conclusion of discussion of evidence and findings. Let the Record show that the death of Fleet First Lieutenant G'herm Wyrlann was accomplished by a person or persons unknown, but presumed to be associated with Free Government terrorists. Let the Record further show a similar finding in the matter of the death of Fleet Captain Griers Verigson Lowden, presumed murdered in the absence of evidence. Let all here now state their concurrence with these findings.''

Koscuisko recited the legal formula without inflection, dispassionately. It took a moment for the Danzilar prince to take his cue. Once he did, however, the Danzilar prince spoke his piece clearly and calmly as well.

"Paval I'shenko Danzilar, Bench-proxy governor of Burkhayden in Meghilder space. In the matter of the death of Fleet First Lieutenant G'herm Wyrlann by an assassin of unknown identity, I concur. In the matter of the death of Fleet Captain Lowden by an assassin of unknown identity, I also concur."

Formula. But they all had to say it. Mendez made his statement, and when it came to Garol—next, going around the table—he put the crucial piece of information on Record.

"In the matter of the death of Fleet Captain Lowden by an assassin of unknown identity, I concur. I report the cancellation of an outstanding Bench warrant received."

Because he had exercised it. Port Burkhayden was safe from Fleet interrogations groups. Nobody who reviewed the Record could entertain any doubt about what had really happened. That was one of the reasons that access to the Record was so strictly controlled. Not even Koscuisko—who held the Writ—could invoke the Record to recall information; he could only supply it.

"Bench intelligence specialist Jils Ivers, on assignment. In the matter of the death of Fleet First Lieutenant G'herm Wyrlann."

Done.

Finished.

"The decision is unanimous," Koscuisko said. "It is so found. No further action. The Record is complete. Close the Record."

Now they could get on with their lives, to the extent that Bench intelligence specialists had lives.

Whether or not the bond-involuntary would ever remember the murder Jils didn't know, and she didn't really care. What was important was the rule of Law. Nothing more. Sometimes that meant that the innocent were sacrificed to the public order; that had almost happened with Skelern Hanner. It was well worth one man getting away—for now—with the murder, which he might not have committed, of a bully who disgraced his Fleet rank, rather than risk a mistake in the other direction.

"Thank you, gentles." The Danzilar prince rose to his feet, and spoke their dismissal. "Shall we go to midmeal. There is Nurail meat-pudding. We do not have to eat any of it."

The Danzilar prince would be much happier when they were all out of Port Burkhayden.

And now there was no longer anything to keep them.

Andrej Koscuisko got out of the transport half-a-block from the wreck of the service house. "Wait for me," he warned Security, to forestall Chief Stildyne. "I will go alone. There is something that is between just the two of us."

Himself, and Specialist Vogel, who stood with his back turned in the middle of the street at the end of the block. By himself. All alone. Andrej had been told that Vogel could be found here.

He had a word or two to say to Vogel before they all went their separate ways.

The burning of the service house had left a gap in the long row of buildings in this part of the port; the walls still stood, and several of the floors had not collapsed, but there was sunlight shining through blackened window-openings from within empty rooms. There was soot everywhere. Vogel heard him coming, but Vogel didn't move, and Andrej stood for a moment and looked at the destroyed hull before he found anything to say.

"They will have to rebuild." Well, obviously. He was just making conversation. "But that no lives were lost, it is a cheap price to pay for such a blessing. Perhaps I am not the man who can say that. Because I am not the man who must pay for the rebuilding."

The Danzilar prince would rebuild the service house. The woman Megh would have to go back, but only in an administrative capacity. She would not be called upon to provide any services more personal than balancing a tally-sheet in the laundry. He could feel good about that. It would be a great comfort to Robert to know that his sister was safe, even if not free.

"Yeah. Well." Vogel squinted up at the top surviving level of the building, the floor where the fire had started. "Shouldn't have left it open, with so little by way of fire suppression. What do you want. Your Excellency."

Because Andrej hadn't tracked Vogel down to the scene of someone's crime in order to talk about casualties. They both knew it. Andrej was convinced they both knew what the crime had been: and who had committed it.

"I wondered, Specialist. I do hold the Writ. And I am a Bench officer accordingly, as well as a Fleet officer on board the *Ragnarok*. Why didn't you tell me."

He had a right to know, in his capacity as a Bench officer. In a sense. But more than that. If the murder was under Bench warrant, and Vogel intended to declare it as such, why had Vogel kept it a secret for so long?

Vogel sighed. As if only now making up his mind to an irreversible step of some kind. "Fair enough. I'll tell you. There's something wrong with the warrant. I don't like it. I hadn't decided whether I was going to execute it or not."

Something wrong?

With a Bench warrant?

What did that mean?

"But once it was done." Vogel hadn't executed the Bench warrant, but Lowden was dead. "There have been these ten days past."

Vogel shook his head. "No, not really. Here. You may as well have this."

May as well have what?

Vogel reached into the inside pocket of his overblouse, and plucked the Bench warrant out of its place there. Handing it to Andrej, who took it eagerly. He'd never seen a termination order. He was interested. Bench codings. Counter-secures. Marks and sigils he'd never seen, at whose meaning Andrej could only guess. Formal Judicial language, *as regards the person of the following named soul the bearer is to exercise the solemn ruling of the Bench in support of the Judicial order*. The name.

Which was not Lowden.

The document trembled in Andrej's hand. Was it only the breeze?

This was his life, that he was looking at.

An order for his own execution.

What could this mean?

"I've declared it exercised," Vogel said, as if that could explain. "Somebody knows. Somebody knows it was issued for you, and not for Lowden. You know what I think? I think it's bogus. And whoever made it up isn't going to stop at a faked warrant, Koscuisko, so be advised."

The words meant nothing. "Why do you tell me this?" Andrej asked, in a horrified whisper. "When we both know . . ." That he'd killed the Captain, and was vulnerable to the most extreme penalty under Jurisdiction. That Vogel had just covered up. Andrej couldn't stop staring at his own name on the warrant. Someone wanted him dead.

But who?

And why?

Was Chilleau Judiciary so intent on revenge on him that it was willing that he should die rather than go free?

Vogel shrugged. "It's academic now. The only people who even care are you and me and whoever wants you dead. And I don't care that Lowden's dead. I meant what I said. I think he gave false witness. I think he knew."

"You're a Bench specialist. You cannot stand by and let murder go unpunished." Andrej held the Bench warrant out for Vogel to take back; but Vogel didn't move. "Where does this come from?"

"I am a Bench specialist," Vogel agreed. "That means I decide what best serves the Judicial order, and I consult my own good reason when I do so. On site. No revisits. No reversals. And I think it's best that they both died by Free Government assassination. I don't have to explain myself to you."

Nor was Vogel doing any explaining, not really. So at least he was consistent.

"And where does it come from, well, that's the big question. Bench warrants are issued by the First Judge or a delegated authority. In reality they can come from any Bench under Jurisdiction. And they do."

Andrej had an abstract sort of knowledge that Vogel was talking to him. And talking sense. He must be in shock, he told himself. All he could think about was his name on the warrant.

"What am I to make of this? What am I to do?"

He hadn't felt so helplessly at a loss since—since he wanted to remember. There were no real answers to questions like that, Andrej knew. Yet Vogel answered him.

"You've got enemies. You know that. But the rule of Law is not to be subverted for anyone's personal vendetta, Koscuisko. If I were you I'd put the Malcontent on it. As for the rest nobody knows which eight's their last, so deal with it accordingly."

Vogel had had enough of Andrej's shocked incomprehension; that seemed clear enough. Vogel turned his back, and walked away; Andrej stood where he was with the Bench warrant in hand, staring at the blackened vaults of the once-service house.

Enemies.

And no man knew which eight would be his last. That was true.

The thought was somehow calming. Andrej folded the warrant up into the frontplaquet of his own overblouse, conscious of Chief Stildyne coming up behind him.

"I need home leave, Chief." He'd have to tell Stildyne; it was in Stildyne's professional interest to know. "Let us go home. Well, to my home. Let us take Security five point three." It would be fun to take his people home to the Matredonat, and spoil them thoroughly. They could meet his child. He could meet his child, for that matter.

He had not wanted to go home with the taint of torture contaminating everything he touched. But if he was to die there were things he needed to do first; and whether or not

Specialist Vogel was right about the Bench warrant it was a useful reminder.

No man knew the hour of his death.

It was prudent to leave no crucial thing undone to be accomplished in a future that might never be granted one.

"Yes, sir. The shuttle's waiting, your Excellency."

To go on home leave it was necessary to first return to the ship. That was all right. There were probably not assassins on board *Ragnarok*. He would go home. Perhaps he would seek out the Malcontent.

Had he not suspected for some time that Saint Andrej Malcontent, rather than Filial Piety, was his true name-saint?

"Let us by all means go." Andrej turned his back on the service house and everything it stood for. "We have had altogether too much excitement, Chief. We need a rest."

Ten days of wondering what Vogel would do, whether there was evidence to link him to the murder, whether he would have to speak up and accuse himself in order to prevent some other—innocent—man from the penalty. Ten days of considering a Tenth Level Command Termination and finding himself unable to regret what he had done, even if he should have to pay so high a price. Ten days of holding his breath. He was exhausted.

"To the contrary. With respect." Security was waiting for him, and Robert in his place. It would be hard on Robert to leave his sister. At least they'd had ten days together. "His Excellency has not participated in combat drill for upwards of twenty days now. We have some serious catching up to do. Sir."

Well, Andrej decided.

He was going to be demanding quite a bit out of Stildyne, if what Vogel had said was true.

He could afford to let Stildyne have the last word. This once.

Therefore he merely nodded; and stepped into the transport, to go back to the *Ragnarok*.

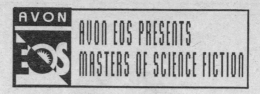

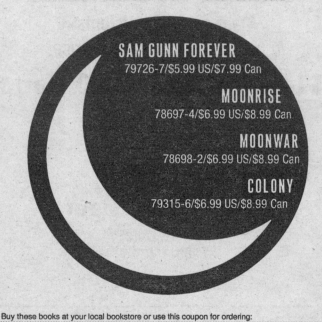